FATE & FREEDOM

KTKnight

1619-2019

FATE & FREEDOM

BOOK III: ON TROUBLED SHORES

K. I. Knight

First Freedom Publishing

First Freedom Publishing, LLC

Fate & Freedom
Book III: On Troubled Shores

ISBN 978-1-7338077-2-2

Library of Congress Control Number 2019904003

www.firstfreedompublishing.com

Book Design by Pro Production Graphic Services
Jacket Design by SJulien.com

Printed in the United States of America

First Edition

FOR MY HUSBAND

CONTENTS

Acknowledgments   ix

Part One Tidewater Ripples

 1   Margaret: Sheppard's Plantation—Early Spring 1630   3

 2   The *White Lion*: Virginia—Spring 1630   13

 3   Departures: The James River—Spring 1630   25

 4   Warwick: London—Spring 1630   33

 5   John: Virginia—Spring 1630   41

 6   Sea Changes: Virginia—Summer–Fall 1630   51

 7   John: Virginia—Fall–Winter 1630   61

 8   Hatching Plans: England—December 1630   71

 9   Hog-Killing Time: Virginia—January 1631   81

10   Requests: February 1631   95

11   Surprise: Virginia—March 1631   103

12   Union: Early April 1631   113

13   Trickery: Early May 1631   121

Contents

14 Repercussions: Winter 1631–Late Fall 1632   131

15 Jope: The Miskito Coast—1633   139

Part Two Endings and Beginnings

16 New Arrivals: Virginia—1633   147

17 Priscilla: Virginia—1633   155

18 John: Virginia—1633   165

19 Two Named Frances: Virginia—Summer–Fall 1633   173

20 Another Arrival: Virginia—1634   179

21 Maryland: Virginia—Summer 1634   187

22 New Life: Virginia—Fall 1634   197

23 Ousted! Virginia—Spring 1635   207

24 Mihill: Virginia—Summer–Winter 1635   217

25 Frances: Virginia—1635–1636   227

26 Another Wedding: Virginia—Summer–Fall 1636   237

27 Settling In: Virginia—1637   247

Part Three Expansion and Growth

28 Agnes and Dorothy: Virginia—Spring 1638   259

29 Initial Tensions: Virginia—Spring 1638   269

30 A Walk in the Woods: Virginia—Spring–Fall 1638   279

31 Trouble and Woe: Virginia—Spring 1639   289

32 Disagreements: Virginia—Spring–Summer 1639   299

33 Robert Swett: Virginia—Summer 1639   309

Contents

34 Wyatt: Virginia—Fall–Winter 1639–1640   317

35 Rupture: Virginia—Spring–Summer 1640   329

36 Departures and Arrivals: Virginia—Early 1640   337

37 Discovered: Virginia—Fall 1640   347

38 Judgment: Virginia—October 1640   355

39 Punished: Virginia—October 1640   363

40 Aftermath: Virginia—Fall–Winter 1640   371

41 Another Court Case: Virginia—Winter–Spring 1641   381

Part Four Children of the Future

42 Changes on Both Sides of the Ocean:
England and Virginia—1641–1642   391

43 Three Weddings: Virginia—1642–1643   401

44 Life and Death: Virginia—1643–1644   411

45 Swett's Legacy: Virginia—Summer 1644   421

46 Emmanuel: Virginia—Summer–Late Fall 1644   429

47 Jane: Virginia—Spring 1645   439

48 Leave-Taking: Virginia—1645–1648   447

49 Margaret: Virginia—1648–1671   457

50 The Eastern Shore: Virginia—1676   469

Epilogue   477

ACKNOWLEDGMENTS

This book would not have been possible without the unwavering love and support of my husband, Thomas Knight, who over the last thirteen years allowed me to dedicate thousands of hours to research—at times a muse, but ultimately, a catalyst in the quest for the truth about the first Africans who arrived in 1619 and 1620, one of them his ancestor.

I am grateful for those who have guided me along the way: whether a fellow descendant, author, historian, genealogist, librarian, community organizer, or truth seeker, your appearance during this journey was pertinent. From sparking the smallest of clues to triggering the largest of realizations, all of you were necessary to put the pieces of the puzzle back together. The truth is a story buried deep, veiled under turmoil and deceit with the many variable parts assembled four hundred years ago to hoodwink the councils and courts and allow a powerful earl to retain his head.

On my production team, I want to thank:

Chris Angermann (*www.bardolfandcompany.com*) for his guidance, advice, and numerous other contributions.

To my editor extraordinaire, Bob Land (www.boblandedits .blogspot.com); my superb graphic designer, Rosanne Schloss (www .proproductiongs.com); and Sharon Julien (www.sjulien.com), my

Acknowledgments

national award–winning cover artist—a huge thank-you. Without you all, this very important history wouldn't be seen with such bright light.

Richard C. Moore (*www.ship-paintings.com*), whose beautiful works of maritime art and other paintings grace the collections of many museums, for the lovely cover images for both volumes of the book.

I also want to express my appreciation to Victoria Lee and Daniel Y. Cooper for lending their likeness to Margaret's and John's images on the cover, photographed by Michelle Brown Photography (*www.michellebrownphotography.com*).

And last, but certainly not least, to the descendants of the "twenty and odd"—I hope and pray a new light of truth will shine down upon us all, allowing the first Africans of 1619–1620 to take their true place in history.

THE SAGA CONTINUES...

FATE &
FREEDOM

BOOK III: ON TROUBLED SHORES

MONHEGAN
7/95

PART ONE

TIDEWATER RIPPLES

R. C. MOORE

1
MARGARET
Sheppard's Plantation—Early Spring 1630

The unexpected early-morning thundershowers have passed and the rain has turned into a gray drizzle. Inside Lieutenant Robert Sheppard's house, a fire keeps the living room warm and comfortable. Margaret Cornish, sitting on a wooden bench near one of the windows, is darning her wool stockings. She casts an occasional glance outside, unhappy that there is little likelihood that John will visit today.

Under normal circumstances, she welcomes these rare spring showers. At this time of year, the rainfall is no longer icy cold, and the ground, parched from the long, dry winter months, soaks up the water quickly. When the sun returns, the leaves and blossoms on the trees and bushes grow with vigor. The herbs and flowers she planted in her kitchen garden benefit, too.

Because of the inclement weather, no one in the household attended the Sunday service at Lawne's Creek Church on Hogg Island. Margaret doubts anyone else made it either. She doesn't mind having to skip church once in a while, although she misses singing the hymns and chatting with people from other plantations before and after worship. Life along the southern shore of the James River is anything but predictable, and everyone understands that there are times when allowances must be made. Going to church at least once a month is considered discharging one's Christian duty, so long as people also honor God in the privacy of their own home.

Earlier this morning, Lieutenant Sheppard gathered everyone in the living room around the makeshift breakfast table—Jason, the overseer, who had served under him as a soldier; Paul and Thomas, the two white indentured servants; and Margaret. He found a verse in his Bible he deemed fitting and read it out loud:

> And you shall again obey the Lord, and observe all His commandments which I command you today. Then the Lord your God will prosper you abundantly in all the work of your hand, in the offspring of your body, and in the offspring of your cattle, and in the produce of your ground.

Then they all joined in a prayer of thanks, said "Amen," and fell hungrily upon the corn hash Margaret prepared earlier.

Now they are enjoying their sabbath indoors as best they can. Jason, Paul, and Thomas sit at the table playing All Fours, their favorite card game. Lieutenant Sheppard occupies his usual chair near the windows and cleans his muskets. When not called upon to use his military skills on behalf of the Virginia Colony against troublesome Indians, he hunts deer, rabbits, squirrels, turkeys, and possums, keeping the household supplied with fresh venison and meat. As a result, their little community has weathered its second winter better than the first, when they exhausted their salted pork supplies and had to go to James City to buy extra provisions.

Margaret looks out the window again at the new fields cleared for growing corn and tobacco. The girdled trees, with blackened bands around their trunks where the bark has been cut away to stop them from sprouting leaves and blossoms, remain standing there like abandoned watchmen at their posts. In contrast, the distant forest looks like a colorful tapestry of budding trees with tender green leaves, dark pine needles, and mint-green blossoms ready to burst.

Typically, John would emerge from there for his Sunday afternoon visit. Margaret would recognize him right away by his distinct, rolling sailor's gait, a vestige from his years at sea on swaying decks, and her heart would stir with pleasure. Sometimes, as he'd come closer, the flintlock of the pistol stuck in his belt would gleam in the sunlight.

She sighs and returns to her sewing.

Sheppard glances at her, knowing full well why she is feeling melancholy. "He won't come today," he says kindly.

"No," Margaret replies, downcast.

She looks down at the socks in her hands, embarrassed that her emotions are so apparent. The lieutenant's observation makes her realize how much she looks forward to seeing John, watching his eyes light up when he catches sight of her, feeling cherished by him. Usually she walks along the creek with him, or they saunter to a quiet clearing in the forest, where they talk about the things that happened to them during the week and share the latest gossip. But not today.

It has been nearly two years since John disembarked at Ewens's plantation and became a landlubber, giving up the life of a privateer raiding Spanish ships. Margaret had just left the household of John Chew and his shrewish wife in James City to come to work for Lieutenant Sheppard. Thus, they were both newcomers to the area, although Margaret had some experience of plantation life on the south side of the James River from her time as a cook's helper at Warrosquoake before and after the great Indian uprising. Now she is in charge of the whole household.

When John first arrived, Thomas Goodman, the manager of Ewens's plantation, and the other workers and servants looked at him askance because he had been given special privileges. His contract of indenture, signed in London by the plantation owner, William Ewens, himself, allowed John to make use of the extensive library at the main house, and he took advantage of the opportunity whenever he had free time, often reading by candlelight late into the night. But he was also a hard worker and he won their respect and acceptance. Everyone appreciated his polite manner, genial bearing, and thoughtful approach to any task—a rare combination of qualities in anyone, least of all in a young man. Many believed him to be in his twenties and would have been surprised to learn that he was only sixteen years old at the time.

When Goodman found out that John could not only read and write but could wield a quill better than him, Goodman started to rely on John for all correspondence and had him file legal documents with the colony clerk in James City on his behalf. As a result, John frequently travels across the river. He has made a point of getting to know government officials and spends time with many of the laborers in town, especially the handful of African servants. Working in the houses of wealthy planters and merchants, and the mansion of the acting governor, Dr. John Pott, they keep each other informed of mischief and intrigues, and they know all the latest news, rumors, and scandalmongering, often long before their employers. It always amuses Margaret when she overhears the wives of planters at church proudly sharing the latest tidbit of gossip, which she has known for a week already.

From John, she first heard that King Charles appointed a new royal governor for Virginia. Sir John Harvey is still in London settling his affairs prior to assuming the office. How long it will take before he arrives in Virginia remains uncertain. A few years back he headed the Royal Commission investigating conditions in the colony when it was still owned by the Virginia Company. He liked James City and stayed on long enough to build a house there for himself. Margaret remembers him from the dinners he attended at the Chew residence when she was a house servant there: an arrogant, opinionated man with sharp eyes and a high-pitched, nasal voice.

John also told her about the arrival of Lord Baltimore in James City the previous September. It was a great honor to have such an exalted peer visit the colony, and she thought that the burgesses would compete with one another for his presence at their dinner table. But everyone gave him the cold shoulder. Although a charming, cultivated man, he was an avowed Catholic, and Virginia's leaders didn't trust him. They rightly worried that he wanted to take a part of their territory to found a colony of his own. After Lord Baltimore left a few weeks later, Governor Pott expressed publicly at a church service in James City what was on everyone's mind when he uttered loud enough for everyone to hear, "Good riddance."

Worse news came in December in the form of a royal proclamation announcing that King Charles had granted Sir Robert Heath, his minister of justice, lands that reached from south of the Chesapeake Bay all the way to Florida. The territory was to be called "Carolana." Many people responded with outrage, as Virginia had laid claim to that land since its inception. Even Lieutenant Sheppard, who usually kept a cool head, slammed his fist on the table at supper one night when the subject came up. Governor Pott hastily convened a special assembly of the burgesses, but despite much venting of indignation, the attendees concluded that they could do nothing against the King's wishes.

Margaret didn't understand why everyone was so upset. As far as she could tell, there is plenty of land for anyone who wants it, although most of it is occupied by Indian tribes.

She was much more interested when John told her that Richard Stephens and Elizabeth Piersey had returned to James City from England as newlyweds. Elizabeth's stepmother, Frances West Piersey, had not looked kindly upon Richard and had warned that she would withhold Elizabeth's share of her father's inheritance if they married without her permission. But the young couple had ignored her threats and eloped to England, where Richard's family supported their union. It helped that Richard, as a well-to-do merchant, doesn't need his young wife's money. The newlyweds have taken up residence in his house in James City in the style Elizabeth was accustomed to when her father was still alive. Margaret is happy for them. She had watched their budding affair blossom from the Chew residence next door and knows how much they care about each other.

Soon after their return, Frances West Piersey married again herself, this time to Samuel Matthews, a wealthy planter with large landholdings on the north side of the James River close to where it flows into the Chesapeake Bay. The wedding took place in early June there at Denbigh Plantation near a bluff called Blunt's Point. Many settlers raised their eyebrows when neither of the bride's stepchildren attended. Both Elizabeth and Mary declared that they were still in mourning for their father, who had died less than a year earlier, although you couldn't tell from the bright clothes they wore around town. Margaret would have liked to go to spend time with her oldest friend in Virginia, also named Frances. She and her son Peter became servants at Matthews's plantation when their mistress moved there just prior to her wedding.

Margaret hasn't seen Frances for some years and misses her. There is no one else with whom she can be free to share her innermost doubts and feelings. The closest other person is Katherine, the wife of Michael, both Africans who work at Ewens's plantation with John. Like Frances, Katherine is older and more experienced, but Margaret has come to know her only since arriving at Sheppard's plantation. Their friendship is still at an early stage.

The crackle from a log shifting in the fireplace rouses Margaret from her reveries. She rises to put more wood on the fire when there are footsteps on the front porch, followed by a loud knock on the door. The men look up, instantly alert. Sheppard glances at the wall where his sword is leaning against the wattle and gestures for Jason to see who it is.

The young overseer gets up warily and opens the door a crack. As he peers outside, his shoulders relax, and he calls out, "It's John!"

As the others return to their activities, Margaret feels a jolt of elation. John has come after all! She straightens her dress and hurries to the door. How did he manage to sneak up on the house without being seen? And why?

When she steps outside, she realizes that the rain has stopped. Moist air sweeps over her, saturated with the fresh, earthy smells of the spring soil.

John is standing on the side of the porch, sheltered from the breeze. When he sees her, he starts to grin from ear to ear and his eyes dance with delight. He seems ready to burst. Margaret can't remember ever seeing him so excited.

"Hello, Margaret," he says. "I brought someone to see you."

A tall, bearded man steps around the corner of the house. He is clad in dark boots and a leather coat. A sword hangs by his side from a broad leather belt. His eyes are bright blue, his ash-blond hair curls from beneath a wide-brimmed hat, and a large pearl dangles from his ear. It is Captain Jope—her Captain Jope!

"Hello, Margaret. It has been awhile," he says, his voice husky with emotion.

A cry escapes her before she can clap a hand over her mouth. Her body shivers with emotion, and tears of joy well up in her eyes. Her feet carry her down the steps as if of their own free will and into his arms, where she buries her face against his chest like a child seeking shelter in her father's embrace. She hardly feels against her cheek the rough leather coat he's wearing as she breathes in his familiar smell, pungent and salty.

When he disengages himself and holds her at arm's length, his hands resting lightly on her shoulders, he inspects her from head to toe. He takes in the outlines of her narrow waist, rounded hips, and shapely bosom beneath her work gown. "My, my, Margaret, you've become a fetching young woman!" he says with admiration.

"It's been more than four years," she burst out.

"Aye. Too long."

"But what are you doing here? How did you find me?"

"All in good time," he says, squinting up at the porch where the men have come from inside, curious who else is with Margaret and John. Lieutenant Sheppard walks down the wooden steps, nodding to John in greeting, while the others linger by the door.

Jope strides up to him and offers his hand. "I am Captain John Colyn Jope, an old friend of Margaret . . . and John's. You must be Lieutenant Sheppard. I believe we met some years back when you were building a fort near Warrosquoake Plantation."

"I'm not sure, it's been so long," Sheppard replies. "But any friend of Margaret's is welcome here."

The two men take each other's measure with a firm handshake.

Smiling, Jope says, "My ship is anchored in the river. We rowed up the creek and brought along some provisions and sundries— sugar, seeds, candles, nails, and a barrel of salted fish."

He puts his fingers between his lips and whistles. Immediately, four sailors emerge from where the sloping meadow descends to the creek below. They are carrying two small wooden boxes and rolling a heavy barrel. Jope watches them with arms at his hips as if he were standing on his quarterdeck.

Sheppard turns to him, a calculating expression on his face. "I'm much obliged, Captain, but we weren't planning on making any purchases this spring. We don't have we anything to offer in trade."

"These are gifts, Lieutenant," Jope says affably. "May they be a boon to you and your household. I have plenty more aboard to trade at James City and other plantations." Scratching his beard, he adds, "But I would ask a favor of you."

Sheppard gestures to Jason, Paul, and Thomas. As the three men lumber down the slope to lend a hand to the sailors, he gives Jope a crafty glance and says, "I'm not one to look a gift horse in the mouth, Captain, but do enlighten me: what can I do for you?"

Jope answers lightly, "You've done a great deal already. I can't tell you how pleased I am that Margaret is no longer at the Chew residence but here with you." Then he takes Sheppard by the arm and leads him to the far side of the porch, out of earshot of the others.

Margaret wishes she could hear what they're saying. They seem casual yet intent, two men with military bearing who are comfortable in each other's presence, despite their difference in age, because they share a common bond: commanding others. They remind her of the wealthy burgesses she's seen in James City engaged in discussions outside the assembly hall, confident of their elevated place in the world.

When Sheppard glances briefly in her direction, Margaret gives John a questioning look.

His face full of promise, he whispers, "It's actually a present for you."

The sailors and the lieutenant's men return from stashing the barrel and boxes behind the house near the kitchen and stand around, eyeing each other awkwardly.

Jope and Sheppard shake hands again, sealing a deal. As they walk back toward their men, Jope gives a slight nod to John and winks at Margaret.

Sheppard calls her over and says amiably, "Margaret, Captain Jope has asked that you join him and John on his ship for this afternoon and tomorrow morning. I am happy to give my consent. You are free to go, if you wish."

For the second time this day, Margaret feels tears of joy come to her eyes and her body tingle with excitement.

"Oh yes," she says. "Thank you, Robert. Yes!"

2
THE *WHITE LION*
Virginia—Spring 1630

Heading down the creek in Jope's skiff, they make good time negotiating the winding bends between narrow banks overgrown with birch trees, live oaks, and button willows on the verge of blossoming. The spring air is fresh and redolent with sweet, musty smells.

John knows two of the sailors who are guiding the boat as much as rowing it, taking advantage of the downstream current. The other two are unfamiliar, new hires who must have signed up for this year's privateering voyage. Except for an occasional glance, they all ignore their passengers and concentrate on their task.

Jope doesn't say much except to explain that he'd expected to find Margaret in the Chew household in James City, but when he made landfall at Ewens's plantation, John told him she was now working for Lieutenant Sheppard. John mentions that the captain brought letters from William Ewens for Thomas Goodman, including one that gave approval for John to take this brief furlough. The plan was to bring John to the *White Lion* first and take the pinnace to James City to see Margaret, but when Jope heard that she lived nearby, he decided to pick her up right away at her new place of residence.

"I like it much better over here," Margaret says, but does not elaborate.

A shadow crosses Jope's face. John has told him the story of how Margaret had to challenge Mr. Chew about her contract of indenture when he tried to cheat her regarding the time of her service left, figuring she didn't know how to count the years. Jope almost wishes Margaret still worked there. He would have wrung the merchant's neck. He is glad John told him because Margaret, never one to complain, would not be as forthcoming about her experiences.

As they reach the wetlands close to the shore, the trees give way to reeds, rushes, sedge, and other marsh plants, and the air is noticeably cooler. Margaret feels goose bumps in anticipation, knowing that all they have left to cross is a narrow glade of trees and a tongue of sand before the creek flows into the James River where the *White Lion* is lying at anchor.

She thinks back on the last time she saw Jope's ship six years earlier, and another image comes up in her mind, unbidden—looking out over the bay of Luanda in Angola as a young girl and seeing the ships bobbing up and down on the ocean waves. Suddenly she is back in the fetid hold of the slave galleon, chained next to John, hungry, lying in her own filth, and praying for release, before Jope came and rescued them. She hasn't thought of that time in many years. Shuddering, she squeezes her eyes shut, seeking to banish the memory from her mind.

When she opens them again, she sees the *White Lion* straight ahead, floating untroubled in the tranquil river water. With sails struck and lashed to the spars of the three masts, the ship seems almost asleep.

As they get closer, Margaret can make out a few deckhands and sailors on the ratlines leading up to the spars. Someone on lookout must have noticed the boat coming because a high-pitched whistle trills from above and suddenly the main deck turns into a beehive of activity, tars scurrying everywhere. The four rowers renew their efforts, straining at the oars, their knotted muscles bulging. When they reach the side of the ship, several sailors are waiting, perched on a narrow ledge, holding on to ropes. They reach out to grab hold of the rowboat, pull it close, and lash it fast against the hull.

Jope climbs the rope ladder first, as befits the captain of the ship, but he takes awhile, moving with care and deliberation, his limbs not as supple as they used to be. Then John clambers up swift as a squirrel. Margaret is next, at first tentative, gaining confidence with each rung. When she nears the top, Jope and John reach down, grab her by the arms, and hoist her up onto the main deck.

Straightening, Margaret feels the eyes of many crewmen upon her. Most are curious, but a few greet her with sullen expressions. One tar who has pockmarks all over his face scowls at her. Perhaps he and the other hostile onlookers are superstitious that having a woman aboard brings bad luck.

One young man looks familiar. He has reddish hair, a russet beard, and brown, intelligent eyes. Margaret searches her memory but can't recall his name or where she has seen him before.

He approaches her and says, "Welcome aboard, Margaret. I don't know if you remember me. I am Gareth. It has been six summers since I last laid eyes on you." He grins. "We once rode in a stagecoach together in England from Bristol to Cornwall."

Margaret has a vague recollection of that time, fragments of memory—desolate rocks, brown heather, patches of snow, a lightning bolt illuminating a rain-swept inn—traveling across the Cornish countryside from which she took her last name. It takes her a moment to match the brawny young man before her with the image of a scrawnier, less seasoned sailor, but she recognizes something about his smile and she nods.

Pleased, Gareth says, "I am quartermaster now, and this is our navigator, Samuel Teague."

The dark-haired man next to him bows. He has pudgy cheeks and looks quite different from the navigator during Margaret's trips on the *White Lion*. She remembers that man's name—Marmaduke—because it sounded so odd to her ears.

This is not the last time during her visit she experiences the odd feeling of discord between something strange yet familiar. Mostly, it is mundane things—gear and rigging, smells and sounds—that spark memories, pictures in her mind of seagulls circling the ship, sailors hauling up the anchor, the first sight of land after weeks on the boundless water. After all, she traveled twice on this ship across the Atlantic Ocean.

Looking at the spiderweb of ratlines and shrouds running from the railing to the masts, she barely hears Jope say, "You two must be hungry. Let's go to my cabin. I have some food prepared."

It is only when John says, "You go ahead, Margaret. I'm going to look around a bit first," that she realizes they have been talking to her.

Jope ushers her inside the door to the area below the quarterdeck, down a dark, narrow hallway. When they enter his cabin, it takes a moment for her eyes to adjust. Nothing has changed. Everything is just as she remembers it—the slightly sour, moldy smell; the low ceiling; the table and chairs in the middle of the room; the small desk by the door heaped with books, papers, and maps; the simple bed; the altar on the other side of the bed with candles and a small cross. The afternoon sun shines into the rear windows above the wooden seat, and she remembers sitting there, looking at the undulating waves and clouds reaching to the distant horizon. For the first time since stepping aboard, Margaret feels at home.

There are bread and cheese on the table.

"We stopped at Denbigh Plantation and Martin's Hundred yesterday and traded for food," Jope explains, gesturing for her to sit.

He joins her at the table, breaks off two chunks of bread—one for her, the other for himself—and hands her a knife to cut herself a wedge from the white cheese. Then he leans back and says, "Now tell me everything that's been happening with you."

Meanwhile, John, touring the *White Lion* for the first time since he left it more than two years ago, experiences none of Margaret's sense of dislocation. Instead, he feels melancholy, almost homesick. Everything about the ship is familiar and oddly comforting, from the notches on the railing to the capstan, tiller, and crew cabins. With the sails struck, he has a clear view of the crow's nest high up, just below the topgallant mast, where he used to perch as a lookout during the raids on Spanish galleons. When he visits lower decks, the row of cannons at the gun ports brings back the barking voice of the old master gunner, which used to make his ears ring. The man is no longer aboard, having retired some years back.

John recognizes a number of his former shipmates. They tip their caps in greeting as he walks past or they engage him in brief, somewhat awkward conversations, which end with good-luck wishes and an affectionate slap on the back.

Most of the new crewmen give him a brief glance and get on with their work. Only a handful take more of an interest. A ferret-faced youngster polishing a cannon gapes after him, as does a bearded ruffian with a scar on his cheek. A bald deckhand with skin like worn leather glowers at him with obsidian eyes as John walks to the ornate beakhead at the bow of the ship. Coming back, John stares at him until he looks away and goes back to mending a torn sail. John wonders what, if anything, Jope told the new hires about him and Margaret that they would display such open hostility.

As he approaches the quarterdeck, he hears a familiar voice hailing him from above. Looking up, John sees Gareth leaning over the railing, gesturing for him to come join him. As he climbs the curved wooden stairs, John suddenly feels shy. He has known the young quartermaster almost as long as Jope. Gareth taught him the ropes and always looked out for him. Will he still treat him as a friend? When John gets to the top, there is no one else, as if Gareth cleared the deck so that they can talk alone.

"You look well fed, John. I didn't think being on land would become you, but I may have been wrong about that," he says, smirking. "Of course, it's not too late to change your mind and come back." He points up to the crow's nest. "We'll always have a spot for you there." When he sees John's flustered expression, he quickly continues, "I'm jesting."

As John relaxes, they stand side by side at the railing and trade stories about the ships the *White Lion* raided in John's absence and life on Ewens's tobacco plantation. As the setting sun bathes the houses of James City across the river in deep orange, John realizes that he can't convey to Gareth what makes his new existence interesting and exciting—learning about the history of the Virginia Colony, reading up on legal cases, and spending time with Margaret.

When he asks about Jope's eyesight, Gareth hesitates a moment, then shrugs and says, "He's fine, except for reading and writing, but you know that." He adds, "I take care of that for him, just as you did."

John is not reassured but decides not to pursue it. As darkness descends, he says, "Time for me to see what the captain and Margaret are up to."

"I'll see you in the morning then," Gareth says.

On his way down the stairs, John feels another twinge of regret about leaving the *White Lion*. Life at Ewens's plantation offers different friendships than he experienced onboard ship. The bond is similar attitudes toward work and the future. John is close to Michael and James, a white field hand, because they both have ambitions beyond their indenture at the plantation. Michel raises hogs on the side and sells their meat in James City. James wants to start a tobacco plantation of his own. Those attachments are not as strong, however, as the camaraderie forged at sea in battling storms and plundering Spanish galleons together. But when John enters the captain's cabin and sees Margaret earnestly talking to Jope, her face lively and radiant in the candlelight, any remorse he feels flies out the window.

He joins them at the table and listens to her telling Jope about her new contract of indenture with Lieutenant Sheppard. "It will be another seven years before I'll be free," she says.

"I think it's a good thing, so long as you're all right with it," Jope says. "You'll both have your freedom at the same time."

"At least a copy of the contract is now safely filed with the clerk in James City," John chimes in. "Many of the Africans you brought here lost their contracts when the Indians burned the houses during the massacre, and those Africans haven't asked for them to be renewed. Margaret is one of the few who did." He leaves unspoken what is likely to happen to them, that they will remain servants with little say about their future.

"Then it's a blessing that you are boon companions again and can look out for one another," Jope says affectionately. He squints from Margaret to John and back again before continuing. "Now that you're both here, I have a bit of news myself." He sits up and bursts out with pride, "Mary had another baby. We have a son!"

Margaret claps her hands together in delight. "That is most wonderful news. I am so happy for you and Mary. You named him John, of course?"

Jope nods, flushing with pleasure.

John is pleased, too, but then furrows his brow. "Three Johns— that could get confusing," he says, a bit self-consciously.

It seems to Margaret that he is trying to act older in the captain's presence as if to show him how much he has grown.

Jope gets up and goes to his desk. He comes back holding a parchment letter with "John Gower" written on the front in black ink. John recognizes the neat, delicate handwriting.

"Yes," Jope says, handing him the letter, "it is from Mary to you. She asked that you read it out loud when we're all together." He turns to Margaret. "That is one thing I miss—John being my scribe. Gareth does well enough in his stead, but John was always more facile with the quill."

Margaret wonders what has happened to his eyesight as John breaks the dark brown seal, unfolds the pale-yellow sheet of parchment, and reads,

Dear John,

There is still snow on the ground here in Tavistock, but we are so very happy with the new addition to our family, little John. Our daughter Joane is well, too. We all miss you.

I trust that you are settled into your new life, confident that you made the right decision. I hope you will be able to fulfill your dream of being with Margaret and starting a family of your own. Give her my love when you see her. I often think of you both and pray for you.

May the Lord be with you.

Mary Jope

By the time he finishes, tears are brimming in his eyes, and he wipes his face with his sleeve.

Margaret is moved, too, taken aback by what Mary has written, something that John has never put into words: that he came to Virginia for her! She takes John's hand and squeezes it. Grateful, he presses back. For a while, they sit quietly, lost in their separate thoughts.

Margaret has an image in her mind of a pretty, blond woman with a melancholy expression, waving good-bye from the front door of a house in England. Then the rest of the evening is imbued with her presence.

The three talk until the tallow candles burn down to a nub, their acrid smell filling the cabin air.

At some point, Margaret raises a question that has been on her mind for some time. She looks at Jope with a serious expression and starts softly, "You have said on many occasions that John and I are special, that we are fulfilling a God-given purpose. Lady Isabel told us the same thing at Aldwarke." Blushing, almost bashful, she continues, "I can see that you have a purpose and John has his, but I can't for the life of me figure out mine. Sometimes I wonder if you and Lady Isabel made a mistake."

Jope, who has been listening intently, responds with unexpected vehemence, almost shouting, "Don't you ever say that!"

His reaction is so fierce that Margaret recoils as if he had slapped her. John flinches, too, and draws back in dismay.

Seeing that he has frightened her, Jope continues less passionately, speaking like the Calvinist minister he once was: "We don't ultimately know if we are among God's chosen, Margaret, but we must continue to act in the belief that we are." He takes both her hands in his and looks at her with his penetrating blue eyes, trying to infuse her with his conviction and faith. "Ever since I first laid eyes on you, I've known in my heart that you and John are God's chosen." His stern expression softens. "You are young yet, Margaret. God willing, you have a long life ahead. Trust that your purpose will reveal itself in time."

Margaret nods earnestly, wanting to believe him. For the first time, she notices that his eyes, though still robin-egg blue, have small, milky patches.

Jope thinks for a moment, then gets up and goes to his desk. He brings back two pouches, one leather, the other made from green silk with gold trim. "I had planned to give these to you tomorrow morning, but it seems more appropriate that I do so now."

He hands the leather purse to John. "This is your share of the profit we made during your time on the *White Lion*, as promised. Go ahead, open it."

John loosens the leather thong and pours some of the contents onto the table. The silver and gold coins clink as they hit the wooden surface. Startled, he cries out, "It is too much."

"You've earned every farthing," Jope assures him.

It is a bittersweet moment for John. Although pleased to receive what is his due, he also feels that a door is closing on his former life.

Jope seems to understand what he is going through and gently says, "The coins are well deserved, John." Then he grows serious. "As a man of means, you must do two things now. One is to hide the coins in a safe place where no one will stumble upon them by accident. The other is to take up a trade or work in addition to your duties at the plantation so that when you decide to spend your money, people won't wonder where it came from and accuse you of stealing it."

John looks at him in admiration. Although he hasn't thought that far ahead, he immediately grasps the importance of Jope's advice and nods gratefully.

When Jope hands the embroidered pouch to Margaret, he says, "You'll have to do the same—hide this from the eager eyes of others."

Margaret fingers the smooth material to determine what is inside. Unable to figure it out, she undoes the string, reaches inside, and slowly pulls out a gold chain. At the bottom of the necklace hangs a blue pearl. It glints in the flickering candlelight.

"A pearl for a pearl," says Jope.

For a moment Margaret is speechless, touched that her captain remembered that her name means "pearl." Then she says, "It is very beautiful."

"I have always wanted to replace the one you lost during the massacre," he says. "Mary picked it out."

John, eyes aglow with love, encourages her, "Put it on."

"Yes," says Jope. "You won't find many other opportunities."

Margaret unclasps the gold chain and, reaching behind her neck, threads the small hook into the tiny ring. When she adjusts the necklace, the pearl settles on her gown in the swell of her breasts.

"It is beautiful, like you," Jope says in admiration, voicing what John can't bring himself to say.

"Thank you," Margaret says shyly. "And thank Mary for me."

It is a moment she will remember for the rest of her life.

* * *

They spend the night in the cabin, just like old times. John and Margaret share the bed, lying next to each other in their clothes, chaste, but feeling the warmth of each other's bodies. It has been a long day for both of them and they are dead-tired. By the time Jope returns after checking with the night watch to make sure everything is fine, they are both sound asleep, Margaret turned onto her side and John with his body molded to her back, his arm resting on her hip.

Jope peers at them in the dim candlelight and for a moment sees the children he first rescued from the Spanish slave ship. Then his eyes adjust, and he perceives them as they are now—older, taller, more mature, yet unworldly—safe for the moment. He wishes he could protect them at all times but knows that it is a foolish fantasy.

Yawning, he spreads out a woolen blanket on the floor to cushion the wooden planks and lies down, thinking of Mary, his son, and his daughter. He wishes he could protect them, too, but knows he cannot determine whatever fate may have in store for them.

3

DEPARTURES

The James River—Spring 1630

When Margaret and John awake the next morning, they are alone in the cabin. There is no sign of Jope having slept there during the night. Yawning, they stretch their limbs and walk out onto the main deck. The still air is fresh and clean. The ship is quiet. Only a few crewmen are up and about.

Past dawn, the sky is pale blue and cloudless. On the port side of the *White Lion*, they can make out James City's waterfront houses. On the starboard side, a fog bank lies low on the river between the ship and the shore, hiding the sandy strand of Hogg Island. The upper portions of the oak and pine trees hover above the opaque, white mist as if they're floating in midair.

"That will burn off by the time we take you back. It's going to be a splendid day," Gareth says, joining them at the railing. "I trust you found our humble accommodations to your liking."

Margaret can see why John is fond of him. Playing along, she lifts the hem of her skirt slightly and curtseys. "Yes, kind sir, we did."

Gareth grins appreciatively and says to John, "You didn't tell me that Margaret has a sense of humor." He turns to her. "He always said you were a very serious-minded person."

When Margaret doesn't respond, John realizes that Gareth's teasing, although good-natured, has missed the mark and embarrassed her. Gareth doesn't know the half of what she has endured and how it shaped her temperament. The silence among them grows awkward.

They are rescued by Jope's arrival. Although he spent the night on the hard floor, he looks none the worse for wear and seems to be in high spirits.

"I'm glad you two slept late," he says cheerfully. "I thought of waking you but figured you could use the rest."

Gareth takes the opportunity to bow out. "The captain wants me to get the ship ready to sail as soon as he gets back from taking you to your homes, so I'll say my farewells now. It has been short and sweet."

He shakes Margaret's hand. "Godspeed." Then he hugs John and whispers, "Take good care."

Before they can react, he gives Jope a half-salute and leaves.

As they look after him, Jope asks, "Hungry?"

When they nod in unison, he steers them back inside to his cabin. The table is set with a plate of scones and three bowls of steaming porridge.

They sit down and Jope says a prayer of thanks. Then he offers a small pewter bowl filled with brown sugar to his guests. John declines, but Margaret accepts and sprinkles some on her oatmeal. The porridge tastes as good as hers and is just as filling. The apple cider in the drinking cups is a surprise, a rare treat. Although they've planted fruit trees in back of Lieutenant Sheppard's kitchen, it will take grafting and at least another year or two before they can harvest any apples or peaches.

As they make small talk, Margaret realizes that Jope, and Gareth earlier, are doing their best to make the parting easy for them and keep the inevitable sadness at bay. They dealt with all crucial matters the night before.

She notices Jope gazing at her and John from time to time as if trying to fix them in his memory. She is doing the same, aware of how he has aged, that the crow's feet at his eyes have deepened, and that his beard is beginning to gray at the edges of his mouth.

There is a moment when they catch each other at the same time and break out in mutual smiles of recognition, which lift the melancholy mood of parting for a little while.

"I will miss you," Jope says.

"Yes," Margaret replies.

John looks down at his empty bowl.

After a moment, Jope gets up. "Time to go."

"Wait," John stops him. "I want to write a letter to Mary."

Jope's eyes turn lambent with emotion. "She will like that very much."

He brings a quill, a brass inkwell, and a blank sheet of parchment from the desk to the table and places them in front of John. Then he stands back, looking over his shoulder.

John tests the tip of the feathered quill against his finger to make sure it is sharp enough and takes a moment to decide what to say. Then he dips it in the inkwell. Margaret watches him worry his lip as he starts to write carefully, yet with ease, the nib making soft scratching sounds.

For a moment Margaret is enchanted. Although she learned to write at Aldwarke, she no longer can do more than sign her name. While Jope and John are preoccupied, she steps away, raises her skirt, and ties the satin pouch around her waist to hide it from view. She straightens her dress and continues watching.

When it looks like John is finishing up, she says, "Give her my best wishes, too."

John writes another line and adds his signature. Jope brings a pounce pot and sprinkles powder on the paper to dry the ink, squinting at the writing. Dusting it off and folding the letter, he says, "It will be my pleasure to deliver this to her."

Meanwhile, John retrieves his pistol from the side table and sticks it in his belt. He picks up the leather pouch and attaches it to his belt. When Jope gives him a questioning look, he says, "I will hide it before I get back to Ewens's plantation."

When they step out on deck this time, the *White Lion* has become abuzz with activity. Crewmen haul sails up the masts with ropes and lower others from the spars, letting the canvas sheets flap loose. Deckhands are feeding cables through tackles to be used for rigging. John looks around at the efficient hurly-burly: Gareth has the crew shipshape. When John nods to him appreciatively, Gareth acknowledges the compliment and moves away, barking an order to a sailor hanging on one of the ratlines.

It is difficult for John to tear himself away. The bustle of everyone getting ready in anticipation of casting off is spellbinding, but when Margaret tugs at his sleeve, he comes out of his trance and follows her to the railing.

Jope climbs down into the waiting rowboat first so that he can help Margaret when she reaches the bottom of the rope ladder. John deftly descends after her. When they're settled on the wooden benches, Jope gestures to the oarsmen to push off.

As they head for the inlet, Margaret decides not to look back, adhering to the superstition that if she doesn't, she will see the *White Lion* again. Jope, sitting next to her, stares straight ahead, too. But John can't help himself. Twisting awkwardly, he keeps looking over his shoulder to watch the ship for as long as possible.

The sun has burned off the fog, just as Gareth predicted, and they have no trouble locating the mouth of the creek. The weather is balmy, and the four rowers soon work up a sweat. Other than an occasional bird chirping and the oars splashing and grinding in the oarlocks, it is a quiet morning, and they travel up the creek as if entering into a magical, green land. Margaret finds Jope's hand on the wooden bench next to her and holds it for the duration of the trip.

Too soon for her liking, they arrive at the dock of Sheppard's home. Jope and John jump out and help Margaret on land. Jope folds her into his arms, and they stay entwined for a long time.

When they finally part, Margaret looks into his eyes and says, "Thank you . . . for everything. Give my best to Mary."

Jope holds her gaze and says with confidence. "I will be back . . . sooner. I promise."

He turns to climb back in the boat, expecting John to follow him.

But John remains ashore. "I'll stay with Margaret awhile and walk to Ewens's plantation from here," he says, trying to keep the tremor out of his voice.

At first Jope is taken aback, but then he notices John's clenched fists. He understands how hard it is for the boy who would be a man to assert his independence and declare where his loyalty lies. He approaches him and squeezes him tight in a bear hug until John's quivering body settles down.

"I am so very proud of you," Jope whispers in his ear.

He lets him go and walks to the dock where his oarsmen have turned the boat around to face toward the river. He waves to Margaret and John and, to their surprise, takes off his wide-brimmed hat and performs an elaborate bow that has them laughing with mirth. Then he gets in the boat and has the crewmen push off. He does not look back as they head down the creek.

Holding hands, Margaret and John wave after him until the boat rounds a bend and is gone. Then they start to walk along the bank in the other direction, following the contours of the creek to where John can cross and walk to Ewens's plantation. They tread on in silence for some time, with too many thoughts and emotions tugging at them.

Finally, Margaret says, "I am certain that we will see him again. I feel it in my heart."

John, knowing the dangers Jope is about to undertake at sea, is less sure, but he nods vigorously.

When they get to the spot where an uprooted oak tree leans precariously toward the water, its lower branch forming a natural bridge, they stop and look at each other. Margaret opens her arms and John embraces her. For a while, they stand together, eyes closed. When they part they gaze into each other's eyes.

Margaret is ready, holding her breath. John would like to kiss her but is too bashful, and the moment passes.

"I'll see you next Sunday," he says in a breathy voice.

Margaret watches him climb up the trunk and walk quickly across the limb, using his outstretched arms for balance. He jumps down on the other side, landing nimbly on the soft ground. Grinning boyishly, he waves to her and disappears in the forest.

A small smile appears at the corners of Margaret's mouth. As she heads back to Lieutenant Sheppard's house, she mulls over what Jope told her.

* * *

On the way back to the *White Lion*, Captain Jope sits in the boat deep in thought, too. With head lowered, he pays no attention to the surrounding greenery and wildlife. He hopes he has convinced Margaret, cured her of doubts about her destiny, and restored her belief in herself and in God's purpose. Still, he has to admit that he responded so severely to her because he was trying to convince himself as much as her.

Lately, he has been plagued by self-doubt about being one of God's elect. Although he took up privateering well over a decade ago, he has not come close to realizing his dreams. The recent hauls have been substantial, especially since he adopted the ploy of sailing in consort with other raiding ships, mostly belonging to the Earl of Warwick, and making off with all of the treasure. The booty has satisfied his crew as well as his brother Joseph, who loaned him the money to restore and outfit the *White Lion*.

But the hold of his ship has never bulged with enough gold and silver to make him a wealthy man. The big haul—a Spanish treasure galleon filled with bullion from the mines of Mexico—has eluded him. He and Mary are living well, but he can't afford to retire yet, and a growing household means more mouths to feed.

Jope feels age creeping upon him. His joints and back get sore after standing on deck all day. Cold weather seeps into his bones. His reflexes are not as quick as they used to be. Worst of all, his eyesight is failing. Although he denies it to others, he can no longer make out the letters printed in a book. He doesn't know how much longer he can live the life of a privateer.

Sometimes he wonders if he made the right decision when he rejected the Earl of Warwick's offer to join his fleet. It would have curtailed his freedom, but a steady income at this stage of his life would be welcome. Instead, he made the earl, Robert Rich, a mortal enemy—Jope is sure of it—and the earl is a powerful and vindictive man.

At least Margaret and John seem to be getting on in the New World as well as can be expected. If they become closer and grow to love each other, so much the better. He would like nothing more than to bless their union.

A change in the boat's movement, gliding along faster and bouncier, makes him look up. They are entering the cove where the creek is emptying into the James River, and he can feel a steady breeze on his cheeks. The *White Lion* is up ahead, all of her sails unfurled, some already billowing in the wind, others fluttering limply waiting to be lashed to the spars.

The sight of his ship, her sleek hull built for speed, always makes Jope's heart leap with pride. Marveling at her beauty, he forgets his worries. He can't wait to take her into the fray. Since King Charles recently entered into a peace with Spain and France again, his and other English ships can safely visit Spanish harbors in Havana, Santo Domingo, and other Caribbean islands, making it easier to replenish provisions. At the same time, the captains of British vessels on privateering missions will want to join up with him and sail in consort.

Since they're engaging in illegal activity and, if caught, could suffer the death penalty for piracy, they welcome his ability to fly the Dutch flag and give them some legal cover for their raids on Spanish ships.

He offers a silent prayer to God that this year's voyage will bring him his long-awaited triumph.

4

WARWICK

London—Spring 1630

More than thirty-five hundred miles away, Robert Rich, the Earl of Warwick, contemplates a different kind of venture. He is meeting with a number of important men in his study at Warwick House in Holborn, London. They include his younger brother, Henry, recently made Earl of Holland; Nathaniel Rich, Warwick's cousin and financial adviser on all private and business matters; and John Pym, the treasurer of the newly founded Providence Island Company.

The other two, wearing leather doublets and boots, commandeer ships in Warwick's fleet. Both have the deeply tanned faces of men who spend most of their time on deck under the burning Caribbean sun. John Elfrith, the corpulent captain whose girth exceeds twice the size of a regular mortal, set all this activity in motion when he discovered Providence Island the previous summer. Samuel Axe, an expert in fortifications, made his name during the Dutch War of Independence, fighting with the British forces against the Spanish Army.

They are looking at several maps of the Caribbean spread out on the large mahogany table. The one garnering the most attention shows the outline of two islands, Providence and the smaller St.

Catalina to the north. Connected by a narrow tongue of land, they create a sheltered harbor. Although the map does not indicate them, the earl knows that coral barrier reefs all around the islands provide further protection.

Axe points to a small cape on the southern portion of the Catalina peninsula. "This area would be the best spot for a fort to defend the harbor from attack," he says.

Elfrith weighs in. "Yes, by God's nails, it would be a fine spot, but this one is even better." He places his finger an inch farther east on the yellow patch of land. As the discoverer of the islands and the first Englishman to set foot on them, he knows the area better than anyone else in the room.

He and Axe are scheduled to travel with their ships to Providence to bring supplies and armaments to the thirty men he left there under Captain Sussex Chamock's command. Their objective is to secure the island and identify the best places to build villages, plantations, and defenses in anticipation of the arrival of the first wave of settlers.

When Elfrith first apprised Warwick of his discovery, Warwick convened a meeting at the house of his younger brother, Henry, inviting the most important and wealthy men who champion the Puritan cause to help launch the Providence Island Company. Nearly twenty showed up, including such luminaries as the Baron of Brooke, the Viscount Say and Seles, and Lord Mandeville. They all share Warwick's concern that England is in decline and that King Charles is doing nothing to prevent it. The monarch dissolved Parliament a year earlier, made peace with France and Spain to reduce his military costs, and announced he would rule on his own with a gaggle of Catholic advisers who wish to return the nation to the fold of the pope in Italy.

While this development poses a great danger to Puritan beliefs—Warwick doesn't want England to fall under the yoke of Roman Catholicism again—it also provides a great opportunity for the spread of the True Religion. Seeking to restore England's maritime power, the earl and his friends have been looking for undiscovered land to colonize to limit Spain's influence in the New World.

So, when Warwick told them about Providence Island, a hundred miles off the coast of Central America, blessed with fertile soil and a temperate climate, they became excited. The tropical island is an ideal place to found another Puritan colony in the New World and establish a God-fearing commonwealth that combines religious freedom and commercial success. Warm weather year-round would provide a more hospitable environment than the Massachusetts Colony, whose bitter, cold winters and poor earth did not bode well for its long-term survival.

Warwick did not mention his plans to establish a privateering base there as well, from which to hound the Spanish treasure ships. He did not want to worry investors about the possibility of military reprisals.

Seventeen of the attendees signed up on the spot, agreeing to pay two hundred pounds to found the Providence Island Company. Warwick is confident that they will not repeat the mistakes of the Virginia Company, where warring factions and the ill will of his old nemesis, Edwin Sandys, sidelined him with the result that Virginia became a royal colony again. It had given the earl no end of pleasure that Sandys died just a month before. Warwick celebrated Sandys's demise with a glass of his best port, however unchristian that may have been.

Besides the four other peers of the realm, a majority of the shareholders have been involved with Warwick for more than a decade in the Somers Island Company, his Bermuda venture. Several are directly or indirectly related to him, and the rest are wealthy Puritan squires who share his views on religion and the need to resist a haughty and disdainful king who believes in absolute monarchy. Little does Warwick know how important many of them will become a little more than a decade later during the English civil wars and Puritan revolution.

He was pleased when they elected Henry Rich governor of the enterprise, William Jessup secretary, and John Pym treasurer, the latter two members of the disbanded Parliament. Pym, although pudgy and innocuous in appearance, can be a firebrand. He frequently railed against King Charles's abuses and tax policies on the floor of the House of Commons. Though gruff of speech, having retained his Cornwall brogue, he is sharp and ruthless as a usurer when it comes to dealing with money.

The thought of the West Country reminds Warwick of Captain Jope, and it stirs his bile. It has been more than a year and a half since he asked Elfrith and his sullen disciple, Captain Bullard, to take care of him. But the "Flying Dutchman" has continued to sail in consort with his ships to raid Spanish galleons and make off with all the booty scot-free, depriving him, the Earl of Warwick, of his rightful share.

While the others are poring over the map, Rich gestures to Elfrith. When the obese captain comes over to him, Rich mutters, "A word in private, Captain."

Elfrith follows him into the hallway. They amble down the high-ceilinged passageway as if strolling in a park, past wall tapestries and paintings of Rich's parents. The heels of their leather boots echo faintly on the marble floor.

Seeing Elfrith's more than passing interest in the portrait of his mother, Penelope Deveraux, Rich remarks, "It does not come close to doing her justice."

"She must have been a great beauty in her time, my lord," Elfrith ventures.

"Yes, she was. Quick-witted, too, and unafraid to speak her mind."

Elfrith catches up to him. "I wanted to thank you, my lord, for proposing my son-in-law to be governor of Providence Island."

Rich waves him off. "Captain Bell has been doing a good job in Bermuda. We need able men to ensure the new colony's success."

The next painting is of Warwick himself, posing with a walking stick, his other arm akimbo. With his dark, piercing eyes and imperious stance, he looks like a man confident of his place in the world. Behind him, a drawn red velvet curtain reveals a balustrade overlooking a protected bay and a ship leaving the harbor.

"It was painted by Daniel Mijtens, the Dutchman," Rich drawls.

"A remarkable likeness, my lord."

"I'm thinking of hiring Anthony van Dyck to do another." He glances at the rotund figure next to him. "Don't you find it odd that the best painters are all Dutchmen?"

Having a good idea where Warwick is going with this, Elfrith remains silent.

Confirming his suspicion, Rich continues, "I'm surprised your scowling companion isn't with you. I can only hope that Captain Bullard is on the verge of taking care of our little problem."

Elfrith replies, "He is doing his best to track the Flying Dutchman, but the ocean is vast." When Rich starts to frown, he quickly adds, "I don't mean to make excuses, my lord, but Captain Jope is a crafty sailor. He can make port flying the Dutch flag in more places than we can."

Warwick's eyes narrow. It is the first time that Elfrith has uttered more than one sentence without lacing his words with blasphemy and cursing. Letting his displeasure seep into his voice, the earl says, "Which is why I sent my best men after him. Or was I mistaken?"

"Oh no. Bullard has been busy, by Charles's knotty stump! He's been in Plymouth and managed to get two of our men hired on as sailors aboard the *White Lion*. When they return from their voyage this fall, we will know all about Captain Jope's movements and can figure out how to set a trap for him. I'll be back in England by then."

Warwick gives Elfrith a speculative glance. If he is telling the truth, this is better news than expected. He moves to the banister overlooking the vestibule below, running his quicksilver mind over all the possibilities. What the rotund sailor proposes makes sense. He will have to be patient for another year before he can get his revenge. "All right," he declares. "It is a good plan."

Joining him, Elfrith growls, "By my gammer's withered leg, we will not let you down, my lord!"

"I will hold you to that. When are you shipping out?"

Relieved, Elfrith scratches his gut luxuriously. "Bugger all, what with all the supplies we're taking on, we'll be ready to weigh anchor in a fortnight."

Warwick leans toward him and speaks intently, "I have a special mission for you, Captain. While you're on Providence Island, I want you to look for a good place to create a privateering base from which to raid the Spanish ships."

Elfrith breaks out in a beatific smile, his eyes almost disappearing in the fat folds surrounding them. He slaps his hand on the stone rail and roars, "By Charles's prickly knob, I knew you had something on your mind, my lord. Providence is the perfect place for it. The Spanish sea lanes from Cartagena and Portobelo on the mainland pass by the island on their way to Veracruz and Havana."

Looking around to make sure no one is spying on them, Warwick warns, "Keep it to yourself. While Charles has declared a truce with Spain, we must proceed in secret."

Leaning toward him, Elfrith mutters, "You can count on me, my lord. By God's blood, I'll be as quiet as the grave." When Warwick draws back, he adds, "Will there be anything else?"

"Yes. I want you to explore the coast and befriend the Indians there. Native support has helped the Massachusetts Colony survive and can only benefit Providence."

"Aye, my lord."

"Good. Let us return to the others."

As they walk in silence down the hallway, Warwick contemplates what lies ahead. He must obtain a patent for the island from the King. With his brother Henry's connections at court, that should not be difficult. Charles needs money and will be only too happy to support a private venture for a stake in the profits. In the meantime, Warwick needs to increase the number of investors, preferably to an even twenty, an easy task as well. The challenge will be to get every shareholder to find as many people as possible to become settlers in the new colony.

5

JOHN

Virginia—Spring 1630

As John makes his way back to Ewens's plantation, the signs of spring are everywhere—budding cedars and oaks, squirrels chasing each other from branch to branch across the canopy overhead, birds chirping and singing. But he hardly notices, preoccupied with all the things that happened during the visit on the *White Lion* and afterward. His mind is bubbling with ideas and plans, triggered by conversations with Captain Jope.

Uppermost in his thoughts is what to do about his newly acquired wealth. Next, he wants to better understand the indenture system and what it means for him, Margaret, and the other Africans he knows. He tries to avoid thinking about what happened and didn't happen with Margaret, but his mind keeps returning to their near kiss, and it takes considerable effort to focus on the other issues. Being a thorough person, he runs through all the options he can think of, and by the time John sees the first fences of the plantation with the afternoon sun casting shadows from the wooden rails on the ground, he has figured out what to do about the money.

He will talk to Michael about raising hogs and selling for his own profit the meat the plantation doesn't use. Michael has an arrangement with Thomas Goodman in which he renders a portion of his earnings to William Ewens and keeps the rest for himself. It has made it possible for Michael to build a small cottage for himself and Katherine. John figures Michael will be happy to teach him what he knows. There seems to be an insatiable appetite for hog meat in James City, and having two people look after the pigs that run wild on the property and in the surrounding forests will increase the proceeds for both of them.

John has vague, yet pleasant memories of helping out in the pigpen at Aldwarke Manor in England—feeding the hogs, watching them birth new litters, and later on, seeing them butchered for meat. He is certain that he can master in no time what it takes to succeed at the trade in Virginia. After a few years, he will be able to justify spending his hidden money as legitimate earnings.

With that matter settled in his mind, John feels confident about the future. What he hasn't counted on is how much curiosity the visit of Captain Jope and the *White Lion* has caused on the plantation.

When he checks in with Thomas Goodman to let him know he is back to resume his duties, the plantation manager looks at him with an expression of wonder and doubt. "I thought you were from Holland," Goodman finally says.

John realizes that the explanation he gave when he first arrived, that he was a Dutch servant from the Netherlands, does not square with spending time aboard an English ship, and that he needs a better, more credible reason. Thinking quickly, he volunteers, "I served on the *White Lion* as a cabin boy after my parents died, and the captain was kind to me and taught me the Christian faith. He is a good man."

Goodman wrinkles his brow but seems to accept the story. Although it leaves unanswered questions, it does account for the letter from William Ewens granting John special leave, and the manager is not an inquisitive sort. In a surge of generosity, he says, "Don't bother with your chores. They can wait 'til tomorrow. Why don't you take the rest of the day for yourself as well?"

Surprised, John thanks him and heads to the library.

When he gets to the room with its smell of mildew and must, he looks around. Wooden shelves line the walls. Scrolls and other papers are stored in bins and recesses. The books sit above them. To reach the volumes at the top requires standing on a box. John steps up to look at the leather-bound quartos crammed into a corner between two larger tomes. The thick layer of dust that has settled on them indicates that no one has looked at them in years.

He carefully pulls two volumes from the shelf. Since all the books, quartos, and folios are lined up flush at the front, there is a hollow space behind them, just as he expected. The likelihood of anyone looking there is minuscule, as he is the only one who has used the library in the time he has been here. After looking over his shoulder at the door to make sure no one is watching, John carefully deposits his purse in the empty corner and slides the books back in place. Although the layer of dust on top has been disturbed, no one can see that from below.

John considers looking at the folder with the contracts of indenture, but a glance at the windows tells him that it is getting late. He wants to visit with Michael and his wife, Katherine, to discuss his proposal concerning hogs.

When he gets to their cottage, Katherine is preparing supper in a cast-iron pot hanging over a small fire. The flames lick at the black exterior, and John can smell the pungent odor of the stew, left over from the afternoon dinner. He sniffs, flaring his nostrils with pleasure—corn, beans, and smoked ham, spiced with thyme.

"Oh, you're back already," Katherine says as if she expected him to be gone longer. "Come and join us. There is plenty."

John accepts gladly. Katherine is a good cook who makes sure no morsel of food goes to waste. He likes spending time with her and Michael. They took him under their wing when he first arrived at the plantation and have treated him like a younger brother ever since.

"How was your visit?" Katherine asks, ladling the stew into wooden bowls.

"Very nice," John replies, accepting his.

They sit on the stoop, watching the sun turn orange-red as it dips toward the banks on the other side of the James River. They eat slowly without talking, savoring every bite.

As he wipes his bowl with his last piece of bread, John says to Michael, "You know, I've been thinking. I would like to earn some money on the side. Would you teach me how to raise hogs? I know there are plenty of them in the woods. We could work together and split the proceeds. While I'm learning, you would take a bigger share, of course."

If John's request surprises Michael, he doesn't let it show. "That is a great idea! Don't you think so, Katherine?"

His wife nods, pleased.

"We can go into the forest on Sunday afternoon, and I'll show you my hogs," Michael continues. "There is not a lot to do in the summer and early fall, except for marking the ears of the newborns. The hogs pretty much take care of themselves on their own until killing time. That's where all the work is, hunting and butchering them. You were here for that this past January, but you probably didn't pay a lot of attention. If you follow what I do next time, you'll learn just about all you need to know."

Gratified, John says, "I'll be watching you like a hawk."

"Then it's settled," Michael says.

Katherine gets up and collects the bowls and spoons. In passing, she says, "I recognized the captain who came for you. He's the one who rescued us from that slave ship and brought us here. How is it that you know him?"

John feels a prickling sensation on his neck. But before he can come up with a suitable reply, Katherine goes on, "You get along with Margaret well, too, like you've known her from before. Michael and I have been wondering who you really are."

John thinks quickly. Over the last two years, Katherine and Michael have become friends. Can he trust them to keep his secret? How many others on the plantation are wondering about him and the special privileges he has at the main house? He decides to try the explanation he gave Goodman.

"I served as a cabin boy on the captain's ship for several years," he says.

But it doesn't work this time. Michael looks at him searchingly. "I remember when they brought us here on that ship. Katherine does, too," he says carefully. "Margaret and a younger boy stayed in the captain's cabin and didn't get off the ship with the rest of us."

Katherine registers John's sharp intake of breath and says, "Don't worry. Your secret is safe with us. We're *malungu*. We look out for one another."

The part about being *malungu*, survivors of the Spanish slaver and the first Angolans to come to Virginia, is like a refrain. John has heard it before from African servants in James City, but he doesn't quite know whether to trust it.

Assessing the impact of her words on John, Katherine realizes how much their young friend is struggling with himself. "Would you like some more milk?" she says, trying to divert his attention.

John shakes his head no and reaches a decision. "You are right," he volunteers. "Margaret and I lived for two years in England. Then she came here, and I sailed with Captain Jope, raiding Spanish ships. That's why I don't want anyone to know. I would appreciate it if this doesn't go beyond us three, not even Mathew. It is important for Margaret's and my safety."

Michael's expression turns from gratified surprise to apprehension. "Of course, John, but why would you be in danger? Who would wish to do you harm?"

A look from Katherine silences him. She senses that John has said more than he wanted to already. "I'm going to have to rinse these in the creek now," she says.

Grateful for the opening she has given him, John rubs his eyes. "It is getting late. Tomorrow will be another long day in the fields. Thank you for the meal." He shakes Michael's hand. "Thank you for taking me on as a partner. It means a lot to me."

"We'll go the whole hog together," Michael says, grinning.

John laughs louder than the joke deserves. He says goodnight and walks back to the house elated and relieved. Sharing his secret with people he can trust feels like a load off his shoulders, and joining Michael in the hog trade is a big step toward becoming independent. He realizes he has a lot to think about and much to tell Margaret.

* * *

But the following Sunday at Lawne's Creek Church, John and Margaret don't get an opportunity to talk because there is only one subject on everyone's tongue: John Harvey's return from England. The new governor wasted no time upon his arrival to make his presence felt. He had barely debarked when he called for a meeting of the General Assembly, requiring burgesses from all over Virginia to come to James City. By the time he settled back into his redbrick house, east of Stephens's and Chew's residences, he'd also convened the Governor's Council, a smaller group of advisers made up of local leaders.

Everyone is eager to find out what ideas Harvey has for the colony's future. The only one unhappy with the change is Dr. Pott, who used his office as acting governor to enrich himself in the cattle trade. Everyone knows about his shady dealings and tolerated them because his position gave him considerable power and no one wanted to cross him and run afoul of his nasty temper.

"Pott is worried that people will tell on him and get him in trouble with the new governor," John whispers to Margaret. "Chloe, who works in his kitchen, told me."

"Did you catch sight of the new governor?" Margaret asks, wondering if Harvey still looks and acts as overbearing as she remembers him.

"No, but there are plenty of rumors flying about."

They are standing on the outer edge of the large crowd surrounding John Uty and Lieutenant Sheppard, who both attended the Governor's Council meeting. The other plantation owners and their wives have gathered close to the two men, while the servants and field-workers flock in back, craning their necks to hear, eager for any morsel of news.

John would rather spend time with Margaret alone, but it would seem odd not to join the group. He watches her wave to Anthony and Mary, two Africans who came with John Upton, and receive an acknowledging smile in return. Margaret has known Anthony almost as long as she has been in Virginia. He and his wife are the only other Africans in the colony, besides himself and Margaret, who actually met the Earl of Warwick in England and were subjected to his spiteful anger. John likes Anthony. He is skilled and ambitious and has plans for the future beyond the plantation where he works now.

The deep voice of Lieutenant Sheppard catches John's attention. Although not a burgess, he participates in all government meetings and assemblies because his military expertise commands everyone's respect. There are still occasional skirmishes with Indians that end in bloodshed and remind the colonists how vulnerable they are to attacks and how important it is to protect themselves, so when the lieutenant speaks, people pay attention.

"Harvey thinks that our defenses are in a poor state," Sheppard says. "Even though King Charles made a truce with Spain, he thinks we must be prepared for any attacks. 'I don't trust those Catholic bastards,' he told us."

Murmurs echoing that sentiment come from the crowd.

"He made a request to the King to send fifty soldiers for the next three years to be stationed at Point Comfort for our protection," Sheppard continues.

Margaret already knows all this from when the lieutenant returned from the meeting, impressed by Harvey's grasp of the colony's affairs.

"Our new governor also means to limit the production of tobacco so that we can grow other crops for food," says John Uty.

Immediately, the crowd's approval turns to scorn.

"Every governor we've had, from George Yeardley on, has preached planting more corn, wheat, barley, and rice, but their appeals have fallen on deaf ears," John Upton complains. "Tobacco is just too precious a crop to give up arable land for. I doubt Harvey will succeed where so many others have failed."

There are knowing chuckles from the other plantation owners.

"Well, Harvey said he will issue an order," Uty comments. "He has other big plans but didn't want to go into detail before the General Assembly meets." He glances at the sun and raises his voice over the disparaging mutterings, "It is time for us to start the service!"

No one really wants to heed his call, and it takes awhile for everyone to file into the church. Margaret takes a seat next to Jason, Paul, and Thomas while John joins Michael, Katherine, Thomas Goodman, and others from Ewens's plantation. Everyone seems restless, their minds elsewhere. Fortunately, John Uty picks a short passage to read from the Bible and keeps his sermon brief.

As soon as the service is finished, the members of the congregation head outside to resume their conversations. Uty and Sheppard no longer draw everyone's attention, however. As Margaret and John walk together to find a private spot, they pass small clusters of rumormongers and overhear various tidbits of gossip.

"I gather he is Sir John Harvey now, recently knighted by the King, and he insists on the title."

"But is he still as impatient and quick-tempered as before?"

"He's not married, not even betrothed. He'll make a fine catch for a young woman if she can tolerate his peevish disposition."

"As if that has ever prevented anyone from tying the knot."

Hurrying on, Margaret and John can't help but grin. When they reach the edge of the forest, John stops under an oak tree and looks around to make sure they are alone. A gentle breeze rustles the leaves overhead.

He takes a deep breath and says, "I hid my purse in the corner of the top bookshelf in the library opposite the fireplace. I want you to have it if something unforeseen happens to me."

Alarmed, Margaret asks, "Is something wrong?"

Seeing her worried face, he quickly adds, "No, everything is fine. I meant, just in case."

Margaret feels relieved. "I'm glad you told me. There is a gap between the stones of the fireplace and the wall in the kitchen. That's where I've put my pearl necklace. No one would ever think to look there."

John nods. "I've been thinking about what the captain said about me needing another job to justify my having extra money. I am going to learn to raise pigs. Michael will teach me. When we get back, he's going to take me into the forest to show me his hogs and tell me how to get started."

Seeing him so excited, Margaret feels a surge of happiness for him when she realizes what it means—he will not come to see her this afternoon. She was looking forward to spending time with him. They had so much to talk about. She sighs inwardly and smiles at him. "It is a good decision, John," she says. "You'll do well. I just hope it won't take up all of your time."

John quickly reassures her, "You don't have to worry about that, Margaret. I wouldn't miss our time together for the world."

6

SEA CHANGES

Virginia—Summer–Fall 1630

The new governor has arrived in Virginia like a hurricane, resolved to uproot the entrenched customs and traditions of the wealthy planters and merchants. John Harvey considers their leadership and understanding of the world too limited and self-serving to advance the fortunes of the colony. As far as he determines, little has improved since he left it in 1624, and he intends to do everything in his power to change that.

When the special General Assembly convenes in James City's church, Harvey sets forth an ambitious agenda for the future. Some of his ideas have been tried before and failed, others are controversial, and still others are new and arouse considerable interest among the attendees.

The plantation owners welcome Harvey's desire to bring more workers to the colony, male and female, to help with the shortage of field laborers for tobacco cultivation. They also like his promise to appeal to King Charles to send soldiers and much-needed goods and tools. His proposal to bring new trades meets with general favor as well. Introducing new craftsmen in Virginia, such as a potter, an apothecary to produce perfumes and medicines, and a brewer to make ale, will allow the colony to become more self-sufficient. The few Puritan burgesses, eschewing the consumption of alcohol, are not pleased with the last suggestion. Some of the older burgesses who remember the failed tannery and ironworks warn against wasting time and resources. But Harvey's counter, "Those were different times. The soil may be more fertile for such experiments now," carries the day.

Everyone supports Harvey's intention to make a truce with the Powhatan Indians and build a wall across the Virginia peninsula. The wooden barricade will open up some three hundred thousand acres for the colonists to use and settle, effectively separating native villages from new plantations and farms. Above all, it promises to reduce the all-too-frequent and often bloody encounters between the "red-skinned heathens" and God-fearing English.

But when Harvey demands that tobacco production be limited in order to use the land to grow more food, the burgesses revolt. It doesn't matter that the corn reserves from the previous year are depleted, requiring Harvey to send ships to purchase seeds and provisions from other parts of the world. No one wants to reduce the income from their most profitable crop.

But Harvey dismisses all complaints. Without calling for a vote, he announces his decree to curtail tobacco production by a third and plant the available lands with rapeseed, potatoes, wheat, barley, and corn instead. His pronouncement shocks the burgesses into momentary silence. Then the wooden benches start to creak, indicating everyone's discomfort, and Samuel Matthews, one of the wealthiest planters in Virginia, rises and asks, "Do you mean to govern by fiat without the consent of this assembly?"

Harvey draws himself up to his full height and in his high, snarling voice pronounces, "I have been installed as governor by the grace of King Charles, who rules by the Divine Right, and as his substitute, I will do so in his stead. I welcome members of the General Assembly to bring matters to my attention, present arguments for and against, and offer advice, but in the end, I will make the decisions, and my word is law!"

The burgesses have no immediate answer to such a blunt assertion of royal power. Although there are indignant rumblings, no one else stands up to question or contradict Harvey.

But after the meeting dissolves, the assembly members congregate in small groups and express their outrage. William Claiborne, one of the youngest burgesses, is the most vocal. "Who does he think he is, coming here after being away for six years, and tell us what to do?" he fumes. Richard Stephens, who has an incendiary temper as well, joins in: "We left England to escape an autocratic ruler and his tyrant son. The last thing we need is another one of his ilk on our soil." Francis Pott is a bit more measured: "Let's see how things develop. If need be, we have powerful connections in England, too, and we can call on them to persuade the Privy Council and the King that the governor is exceeding his authority."

* * *

When Lieutenant Sheppard returns to Hogg Island the next day, he relates over dinner what happened at the General Assembly and afterward. Since he stayed overnight at Richard Stephens's house, Margaret would like to know how his wife is faring. She has heard from John that Elizabeth is pregnant with her first child. But Sheppard is only interested in the political situation and its consequences.

"What does Harvey's new decree mean for the plantation?" asks Thomas.

"It won't affect us," Sheppard says. "We're already planting most of the land we've cleared with corn, beans, and squash, and using only a small area to figure out how to grow tobacco. When we are ready to go into full production, we will need a lot more property and help."

He looks around the table and catches the eye of Jason. "What does matter is that Harvey aims to make sure our defenses are secure. We'll be building a fort at Point Blunt. The bluff overlooking the water is a better position than the old fort at Point Comfort at the mouth of the river. To get ready for constructing the big fence,

Harvey also wants our militia in better fighting condition, which means I'll be away more often and you'll have to take care of things here on your own."

Jason says, "You can count on me."

Afterward, on the way to the creek to wash the plates and bowls, Margaret thinks about what Sheppard told them. What captured her imagination most of all was the possibility of an apothecary coming to James City. With the weather turning summery, she has been collecting herbs and bark from various trees to dry or turn into powder, and use for healing potions and poultices when needed. Word about her special skills has gotten out, and people from nearby plantations call upon her to help when cuts and bruises have become inflamed, and to cure indigestion, persistent headaches, and other ailments. There hasn't been any occasion for her to act as a midwife yet on this side of the river, but she feels prepared for when that situation occurs, too. In the meantime, she would like learn more from an expert and add to her stock of knowledge.

That Sunday at Lawne's Creek Church, once again everyone gathers around John Uty and Lieutenant Sheppard, before and after the service, for a firsthand account of what happened in James City. When John visits Margaret that afternoon, he provides a more scurrilous version of the aftermath of the General Assembly, much to the delight of Thomas, Jason, and Paul. He went to James City two days later to file some documents and managed to speak with a number of servants working in the houses where some of the wealthiest burgesses from other parts of Virginia stayed overnight. They were only too happy to share what they overheard at supper.

Richard Bennett, the Puritan planter, apparently referred to Harvey as "scurvy bumfodder." When his host, George Menefie, commented ironically, "Careful, that might hurt Sir John's feelings," Bennett said, "I don't give a fart for his feelings!"

Francis West describing the governor as having a voice that "curdles milk and sour beer" provoked a round of laughter all around the table, including from the lieutenant, as did Samuel Matthews calling Harvey "a mosquito-buggering pillock."

Margaret has heard worse, but the image of these fine gentlemen cursing like the fishmongers at the James City docks amuses her. She is glad that everyone at Sheppard's accepts John. Ever since Captain Jope's visit, her fellow workers have accorded him added respect, as if associating with a rugged, seafaring trader has raised him in their estimation. She has benefitted, too. Jason and Paul go out of their way to help her with some of her chores and often glance at her with admiration when they don't think she's looking. Even Lieutenant Sheppard eyed her with wonder when she returned from the *White Lion.*

* * *

As the summer progresses, Margaret and John see each other a good deal. They walk together along the creek; explore the woods to forage for mushrooms, raspberries, and medicinal flowers; or enjoy the afternoon sunshine in their favorite forest clearing.

The brief time spent on the ship that had been his home for five years seems to have resolved matters for John. He looks more thoughtful. He becomes more willing to talk about his experiences at sea as if sharing them with Margaret allows him to make his peace with them. In the past, he didn't say much about that time, except to relate one or two funny stories, but now he divulges more of his travels—visits to rough Caribbean port towns like Havana, San Juan, and Port Royal; the harsh life aboard ship and on land; and the demands of being the youngest among coarse and violent sailors.

He describes to her in detail how the *White Lion* would sail with another English privateering ship to pursue a Spanish galleon, how their superior speed and force usually compelled the captain of their quarry to hoist the white flag of surrender without a shot being fired, and how they interposed the *White Lion* between their consort and the captured vessel. John would climb up into the crow's nest high up on the mainmast to watch their pinnace board the Spanish ship and collect all the plunder. He would signal Captain Jope when they had finished so that he could give the order to move forward, pick up the crew and treasure in the smaller boat, and sail off, leaving the English consort ship in their wake with nothing, and an empty hold for their efforts.

Margaret can't envision the actual scene, but she understands the outcome. The idea of raiding Spanish enemy ships doesn't bother her, but to trick and swindle a partner out of his rightful share seems wrong. "That's stealing," she says, surprised that Captain Jope, a good Calvinist Christian, would go against one of the Ten Commandments.

"Aye," John says, with a serious expression. "I don't know all of our captain's reasons, but it has something to do with his quarrel with the Earl of Warwick. The captain is always pleased when he can cheat one of the vessels belonging to the earl."

The image of the angry face of Robert Rich threatening her and John at Aldwarke enters Margaret's mind, and it grips her heart with fear for Captain Jope.

For the most part, John relates his adventures easily, pausing only when an unexpected memory invades his thoughts. Margaret wonders if that means he is keeping things from her, but her questions usually bring him back quickly to resume his tale.

On only one occasion does his mood turn melancholy. One Sunday afternoon, they walk far afield, all the way to the sandy shore of the James River. Sitting on a fallen tree trunk, they watch the billowing clouds, bronzed by the afternoon sunlight. They point at the different shapes, which look like animals, people's faces, and familiar objects.

When Margaret sees one that resembles the bow of a sailing ship, with a buxom mermaid galleon figure trailing white wisps like sails in the wind, she indicates it to John and asks, "What do you miss most about being on the *White Lion*?"

He stares into the sky with a faraway look. Finally, he begins softly, "Sitting up in the crow's nest when we were just sailing along. I'd be alone and could see for many leagues into the distance. Even on a windy day when the waves were choppy, the horizon was a straight line. I would gaze at the blood-red sun setting or the moon rise like a silver sliver and think of you, wondering what you were doing right then. At night, I could see the stars and the constellations. I sometimes look at them now, but it's nothing like when you're high up on the ship with darkness all around, feeling the slight breeze and staring at the Big Dipper or Orion's Belt to see which way is west." He glances at her and says softly, "Sometime I'd like to sit with you under the stars and show you."

But Margaret doesn't hear the last part. His hushed account and tone of voice have woken memories of her own—all the way back to Africa when she climbed up a mountain with her friends. An image of looking at her Angolan village below flashes through her mind. Then she recalls sitting on the flat top of the mountain and gazing at the flickering horizon in the late afternoon sun. She remembers thinking that's the edge of the world. Only later did her father tell her about *Kalunga*, the Atlantic Ocean beyond, the gateway to the Other World where she is living now.

She reaches for John's hand and clasps it. It feels warm and reassuring. For a while they sit in silence.

When he finally says, "It's time to head back," Margaret holds on a little longer before getting up. He looks at her with shining eyes, hesitating, but then says, "Let's go." They walk back to Sheppard's house. In places, the trail through the thick green bushes and trees narrows so that they have to walk behind one another, John taking the lead.

That afternoon lingers long in Margaret's mind. John looking so boyish heightened the contrast for her of what he was and what he has become. For so many years, his behavior and appearance matched hers despite their difference in age, but now he has matured and become a handsome young man. His knowledge and experience of the world are greater than hers, and it shows in his attitude and the way he conducts himself.

Margaret notices that when he visits, the others at the farm, including Lieutenant Sheppard, like him and respect him. One afternoon he and the lieutenant get into a conversation about military strategy. Now that John can be more open about his seafaring experiences, they confer almost like equals. When Sheppard asks him about where a ship is most vulnerable to attack, John tells him that downing one of the masts with cannon fire all but cripples a vessel's ability to maneuver.

Similarly, when John engages Anthony in conversations at church, the older man gives him his full attention. Anthony knows all about breeding cattle and horses. Used to uproot dead tree trunks to clear fields and to pull carts in military undertakings, cattle and horses are second in value only to tobacco. But when he considers growing the latter for the money, John, who has seen how labor-intensive the crop is at Ewens's plantation, counsels against it—too much land and too many workers required. Margaret is surprised how highly Anthony regards John's opinion.

She wishes she better understood her feelings for him, feelings she has never had for anyone. John looks at her the way she remembers Captain Jope and his wife, Mary, gazing at each other, and she sometimes catches Anthony and Mary exchanging similar glances, but she doesn't know if she is doing the same. She always looks forward to John's Sunday visits and feels downcast when he doesn't arrive. Her heart beats faster when she sees him again or hears his voice from afar.

Frances, her best friend, would know. That look came into her eyes whenever she talked about Emmanuel Driggers, who lived far away then on another plantation, miles downstream on the James River. But around here, there is no one she can ask, not even Katherine, who has made an effort to become more of a friend, ever since Michael agreed to teach John the hog trade. But while Margaret likes Katherine, she doesn't feel close enough to share her most intimate thoughts and feelings.

Sometimes when Margaret is shucking corn, harvesting squash or beans, or walking alone in the woods collecting berries, she thinks dispassionately about her situation. She is getting older—in fact, she is the same age as Elizabeth Piersey, who has been married for two years already—and no other suitable candidate has expressed an interest in her. Quite separate from how she feels about John, he would make a good husband. He is thoughtful, hardworking, industrious, and caring, and he has ambitions. He thinks about the future concretely and more comprehensively than she ever has on her own.

Margaret cannot deny that she is attracted to John and would be happy to be married to him, and she is certain he feels the same about her. So, it puzzles her that, although there are moments when they come close to acting on their desires, John always backs away and holds himself in check.

7
JOHN
Virginia—Fall–Winter 1630

With the coming of fall, the corn and tobacco harvest demands everyone's attention. Managers, field-workers, and servants on all plantations around Hogg Island put in long hours, sometimes toiling seven days a week.

Determining the correct time when the tobacco plants, some as high as a house, are ready to be cut and stripped of their leaves requires considerable experience and expertise. That is where Thomas Goodman comes into his own, and John realizes why William Ewens has employed him. The plantation manager can tell by the look and feel of the leaves when a plant should be cut. During the weeks when the leaves are hanging from sticks in the tobacco barn to cure, turning in color from greenish yellow to light tan, he inspects them every day to make sure they haven't developed mold. When they are struck from the sticks and laid out on the floor of the barn to sweat for a week or two, he determines when the leaves have absorbed the right amount of moisture, not too little or too much, and can be stretched like leather. At that point, he divides the harvest according to quality and has the workers pack the leaves in hogshead barrels for shipping.

Although John is not involved in the day-to-day work of the tobacco harvest, there are times when he has to lend a hand. Because of the carpentry skills he developed at sea, he assists in mending old hogsheads that have been in storage, replacing rotted stays and tightening the wooden hoops, and constructing new barrels.

From time to time, Michael and John continue to venture into the woods with their dogs to locate female hogs that have given birth and not yet weaned their litter. They cut identifying marks into the ears of the piglets to indicate that they belong to Ewens's plantation. Later in autumn, Michael shows John what to prepare in anticipation of hog-killing days after the weather turns suitably cold. They repair the small pen near the kitchen and smokehouse, making sure the fence posts are solidly lodged in the ground and replacing broken rails. They also construct tall wooden frames from which to hang the carcasses and build simple, sturdy tables with wooden planks on top, where the hogs can be dismembered.

Margaret keeps busy, too. She has her regular daily chores—cooking and serving breakfast, dinner, and supper; baking bread; brewing beer; cleaning utensils and dishes; and feeding the chickens. In addition, she helps with the corn harvest, gathers vegetables from her garden to store them in the root cellar, dries herbs and medicinal plants, and washes and mends bedlinens and clothes. When it is time to clean out the soot from the tall kitchen chimney, she climbs to the top and drops a couple of chickens down the flue. Their frenzied flapping does a good job.

As the weather gets cooler, Margaret also starts to prepare for the coming season. One weekend she makes candles to provide extra light for the long winter evenings. She slowly dips wicks attached to wooden rods into a large kettle filled with melted tallow—leftover fat from the butchered meat of deer, hogs, and other animals they'd eaten. Then she lays the rods across a pair of poles suspended from two chairs for the dangling candles to harden. It is a tedious, unpleasant process because she must be careful not to dip the wicks too quickly or the candles will be too brittle and crack. Also, the tallow has a foul smell.

Making soap is even more laborious and takes all weekend. Throughout the summer Margaret has been collecting the ashes from the kitchen fireplace. Now she puts them in a hopper and pours water over them to leach out the lye. Then she boils the liquid down until it is the proper strength, indicated by an egg floating in it, half above and half below the surface. Next, she renders cooking grease and animal fat by boiling them in a kettle with water over an open fire far away from the house because the stench is horrendous. While tending to the flames, Margaret has a cloth tied around her neck that covers her nose and mouth. When all the fat has melted, she lets the mixture cool overnight. By the next morning, all the impurities have sunk to the bottom, and a layer of solidified, clean fat floats on the water.

At that point, Margaret combines the lye solution and fat in another kettle and boils them over an open fire. By the late afternoon, the mixture has turned into a thick, frothy mass. From time to time, she dips a spoon in it and places a small amount on her tongue. When it no longer stings, she calls to Paul and Thomas for help.

Holding their noses, they come over.

"How can you stand that stench?" Paul asks.

Margaret shrugs and directs them to pour the brown liquid into a wooden mold. As soon as they're done, they hurry away. Looking after them, she shakes her head and smiles, as she knows they don't mind using the finished soap. She waits until the gooey concoction congeals and cuts it into bars. When they have fully hardened, she stores them on a shelf in the kitchen.

With so many activities requiring attention, there is no time for Margaret and John to spend Sunday afternoons together. Seeing each other only briefly at church, they hide their disappointment and promise to make up for it in the winter months when there is less work to do.

* * *

John

In early November, word reaches Virginia that the Massachusetts Bay Colony has enacted a law that protects fugitive slaves who have fled from their owners because of ill treatment. John hears about it while in James City to purchase large quantities of salt in anticipation of the hog killing. He quickly grasps the implications, which disturb him deeply. Although created to provide a remedy against wanton physical abuse, the statute sets a legal precedent, officially acknowledging the existence of slavery in the northern colonies.

John knows what it means to be treated as a slave from his time fettered next to Margaret in the nauseating bowels of the Spanish galleon. Whenever he accidentally touches the cross that was burned into his flesh in Angola, he flinches and recalls the searing pain and humiliation he felt being marked by his captors. Visiting Havana, San Juan, and other Spanish port cities with the *White Lion*, he saw slaves being whipped and on the auction block—chained, yoked together, their mouths being forced open so that buyers could see their teeth—and he felt sick. Jope was just as dismayed. Back on the ship, he spoke with passion about why enslavement of any human being was abhorrent, an offense against God's will, and John took his words to heart.

He isn't worried that a version of the Massachusetts law might soon be enacted in Virginia. Besides, it would not affect his and Margaret's status—their contracts of indenture assure their future freedom—but he is concerned about others. He has read enough about cases in which laws were not clearly worded and justices almost always sided with litigants who had wealth and power. Thinking back on his most recent conversation with Jope on the *White Lion*, John resolves to study contracts of indenture to better understand how they work.

The next evening after work, he goes to the library in the main house and finds the shelf where the contracts are stored in a vellum folder. He knows the exact place because he has written additions to some of them at Goodman's request.

He sits down at the table in the middle of the room and lights several tallow candles, ignoring the acrid odor, and starts to look through the documents. Each is a single sheet of parchment describing the terms of service, with stamps and signatures at the bottom.

It surprises him to discover that, while more than forty people toil on Ewens's plantation as servants and field-workers, not everyone has a contract. Although he finds his own without difficulty, he cannot locate any for the three other Africans: Michael, Katherine, and Mathew. In fact, when John does a count, there are contracts for only three-quarters of the workers.

Puzzled, he goes back to the shelf and looks around. By now it is so dark that he needs to take a candle with him to see. In the flickering light, he spots another folder he didn't notice earlier. It contains the contracts of the workers who have finished their terms of indenture and have decided to remain with Ewens. Comparing their names to what he knows about them, John realizes that they all have greater privileges. Many live in their own cottages on the plantation instead of sharing communal quarters like the rest. He imagines they get paid wages, too, although that isn't noted on the documents. It surprises John that Michael and Katherine seem to have the same status, even though they never had contracts.

Over the following evenings, he starts reading each contract in its entirety. He becomes so fascinated that he often loses all sense of time and doesn't stop until one of the candles starts to sputter and extinguishes. He doesn't even notice their foul smell anymore, although he keeps trimming their wicks so that they burn brighter and give him better light. He learns that the period of indenture varies anywhere from three to seven years. When he discovers that his term of indenture is among the longest, he feels a surge of anger. Then he realizes that Jope would have argued with William Ewens if Jope thought that John was being treated unfairly. It occurs to him that, as a young African servant, everyone would assume that he had no money for transportation to Virginia and would expect him to serve that long to repay his debt.

The documents with attachments that add several years to existing indentures for women and their husbands, who have had children while under contract, make sense, too. Bearing children and caring for them while they're young takes away from the time spent working on the plantation, and the owner has the right to demand compensation accordingly. John wrote such an attachment for Agnes and Caleb Wilson six months earlier, and he understands the purpose and thinking behind it.

He is surprised, however, to find two separate contracts for the children of Ruth and Phillip Jackson. Joel and Heather, now six and eight years old, are indentured to William Ewens until the age of eighteen. When he checks the parents' documents, he finds that they were indentured for a full seven years and had four more each added after each child. At first, it seems that they were taken advantage of, but then John realizes they came to Virginia with nothing but the clothes on their backs. The contracts for the children ensure that they will be cared for, no matter what happens to their parents, and that their freedom is guaranteed.

That Sunday after church, he mentions his discoveries to Margaret. She listens carefully, not following all the details, but stirred by John's passion. She gives a quick nod in the direction of John Upton, one of the younger planters on Hogg Island. "I met him when he was an indentured servant working as the manager at Floridew Plantation upriver," she says quietly. "Three years later, he bought out the rest of his contract early. I don't know how he did it, but look at him now. He is a man of means and property."

John likes John Upton, who always treats Margaret and him with courtesy. Now John sees Upton in a new light. What he has achieved gives John hope for what he and other Africans can accomplish.

The following Sunday, when John takes the opportunity to engage Anthony and Mary in conversation, he finds out that they don't have a contract of indenture working at Upton's plantation. Like Margaret, Anthony lost the original document during the 1622 Indian uprising. Mary came to Virginia a year later, and in the aftermath—surviving food shortages and the deadly disease that spread throughout the colony—writing a contract never came up. They went to the new plantation on a handshake agreement when Richard Bennett transferred them as part of a property sale, and they haven't thought about it since, figuring that John Upton would be as good as his word. Knowing what Margaret went through at the Chews', John understands that Anthony's ambitions to be free to have his own farm might encounter serious obstacles.

John explains that, without contracts, Anthony, Mary, and their family could very well be stuck as John Upton's servants for life. As the implications sink in, Anthony's eyes narrow and his lips tighten. Although he has found the plantation owner to be a fair man so far, he also remembers the time the Earl of Warwick brought him to England to testify in a legal case. Warwick gave Anthony and Mary his word that he would take good care of them, but tossed his promises to the wind when the deposition didn't go well. Warwick had Anthony deported to James City and kept Mary on as a servant in England for another year out of spite.

Anthony looks out over the James River sparkling in the autumn sunlight. He much prefers Virginia to England and Africa. He'd like it even better if he could live here on his own terms. Turning to John, he asks, "Is there anything I can do about this?"

John mulls it over and replies, "Probably. You may have to serve another full period of indenture—you, Mary, and your children—just like Margaret. But if we get you signed contracts, you can be sure that you will get your freedom at some point. Let me look into it."

Anthony grasps his arm and says with emotion, "Thank you, John, we appreciate this."

"It is the least I can do," John replies in earnest. "At some point, we will need to speak with John Upton."

John

"I will do that," says Anthony.

When he and Mary go off, John looks around. Satisfied that no one has paid attention to their exchange, he returns to Margaret. Seeing her eyes glisten with admiration, he feels elated. For the first time, he has an inkling of how Captain Jope must have felt after rescuing him and Margaret. He hopes he can help Anthony and his family and wants to do more for others in similar circumstances.

Over supper that evening, he talks to Michael, Katherine, and Mathew about their situation. But when he explains to them what he has discovered about their legal status—that they are the only workers on the plantation without a contract of indenture—they don't seem surprised or concerned. None of them has given any thought to the future or the possibility of life beyond Ewens's plantation.

"We like it here," Michael says, wiping his bowl of fish stew clean with a hunk of bread. "Thomas Goodman treats us well. Why would we want to go anywhere else?"

"We would like to have children," Katherine adds. "I don't know if we could afford to if we were on our own."

"I'm not saying you should leave," John asserts. "But you should be free to make that decision yourself, not have it made for you. I'll be happy to pursue it on your behalf."

Michael and Katherine look at each other uncertainly, then nod their agreement.

Mathew, who is a few years older than John, remains silent. A simple, kind man, he works hard in the tobacco fields but has no special skills of his own. In his free time, he likes to go fishing in the nearby creek and the James River and shares what he catches with others. The catfish, which Katherine cooked in the stew they ate, came from him.

Finally, Mathew says in a low voice, "I don't want to make any trouble."

"Don't worry," John assures him. "I'll be careful."

Mathew considers for a while longer. Then he mumbles, "Okay."

That settled, the conversation turns to other matters.

Later, as John walks to the main house to do more reading, he thinks about the responses of his friends. He can understand them being cautious at first, but that they remained so reluctant, even after they learned what having contracts would mean to them, leaves him perplexed. Still, he is pleased that they trust him to have their best interests at heart and vows to himself that he will not let them down.

Little does he know how much the work he does here will impact Margaret and him in the future.

8
HATCHING PLANS
England—December 1630

It is early in December when Captain Jope takes a hired coach from Plymouth to his home in Tavistock. Returning later than usual from his privateering voyage, he is impatient to get there. He would urge the driver to go faster, but the rutted road is treacherous because of muddy depressions from the late autumn rains. They obstruct the path not only near the riverbanks but higher up in forested areas, too. The last thing Jope needs is for the carriage to get stuck in the mire or break a wheel or axle. He desperately wants to see his wife, hold her in his arms, kiss her, and feel the warm comfort of her embrace. So, he abides the snail's pace as best he can—at least the carriage doesn't bounce as much—and gazes at the stubble fields and the gray skies.

How to tell Mary about his less-than-rewarding voyage is another matter.

A month after the *White Lion* left James City, they met a captain in Port Royal looking to sail in consort with another privateering ship. Two weeks later, they came upon a promising Spanish galleon. They chased it together and quickly caught up to their prey. When the hapless captain hoisted the white flag, Jope executed the usual maneuver of interposing his ship between the other two vessels.

Everything went smoothly. But boarding the galleon, they found only some bolts of fancy fabrics, a few trinkets, and a small stash of silver coins. If the Spaniard carried any more treasure, he had hidden it well. With the captain on the other side of the *White Lion* getting impatient, there was no time to scour the galleon, and Jope gave the order to leave even though they got away with a pittance, hardly worth the effort.

The rest of the trip didn't go any better. They did not find any other captains willing to sail in consort in Port Royal, San Juan, or Santo Domingo—nor any good prospects for raiding, even though they trawled the Spanish Main south of Hispaniola for months. If they hadn't come upon a Spanish merchant in October just as they were about to give up and head home, the voyage would have been a disaster. Boarding the cargo ship without a fight, Jope discovered that the merchant was carrying tobacco in large barrels—hogsheads. He had his men take as many as the *White Lion* could carry and leave the rest behind. They also took pistols and muskets, gunpowder, and bullets. Then they headed to Vlissingen in Holland. Their haul was respectable as during the years when Jope used his ship to carry merchandise. His contacts were still doing business, and he made a decent profit selling the booty, but not the kind of prize money everyone signed up for.

There was plenty of grumbling among the crew, especially the new hires. Some even blamed Jope for bringing bad luck to the ship by having "that black wench" aboard in Virginia. Gareth and other crewmen who had been sailing with Jope for years quickly put a stop to that kind of talk, but they couldn't quell all the discontent. A number of sailors muttered that they might sign on to another privateering ship next time when they received their meager share of the profits in Portsmouth.

Jostled when the coach hits a stone in the road, Jope realizes that the situation still bothers him. If he were a younger man, he would take it all in stride, but at this stage of his life, such a setback is harder to bear. He feels that his time is running short.

Much of his worrying is dispelled upon his arrival when Mary greets him by rushing into his arms and smothering him with kisses.

"Welcome home, husband," she says with her mellifluous voice. "I have missed you."

As they part and stand and look at each other, holding hands, Jope no longer sees the young girl he married, but a mature woman. He observes her ash-blond tresses surrounding a pale white face, her gray eyes, her nose still pert, and her lips thin but full of promise. To him, Mary is more beautiful than ever, and he realizes how fortunate he is.

Someone tugs at his breeches, and he looks down. The blond girl with arms extended toward him looks just like her mother. Jope picks her up. "Hello, Joane, I am so happy to see you," he says and kisses her on her forehead.

"Did you bring me a present?" she asks.

Jope bursts out laughing. "Of course! Did you think I would forget?"

"What is it?"

"A seashell."

As Joane frowns, trying to figure out what that might be, Jope looks toward the front door where Agnes is swaying gently back and forth holding a swaddled baby, his son, John Jr. The captain feels a wave of relief wash over him. All's well with his world, at least for now.

He pays the coachman and indicates to his servants to bring inside his travel trunk, cape, and sword. Carrying Joane on one arm, grasping Mary around the waist with his other, he heads into the house.

Everything looks familiar, just as he remembers it, although he knows it will take him a few days to adjust to his life as a squire again. Mary, sensitive to his need to settle in, keeps conversation light while they eat dinner. After the monotonous fare at sea aboard ship, Jope savors the variety of foods and dishes—artichokes, radishes and turnips, cheeses, roast lamb, chicken, and an apple tart! He tells amusing stories to Joane and the servants, tall tales about fish jumping so high in the warm Caribbean waters that his crew could reach out from the quarterdeck and grab them in midair.

Before bedtime, he holds his baby son and speaks to him in soft, soothing tones to further reacquaint him with his voice. When John Jr. starts to cry, John hands him to Mary, who rocks the baby gently before passing him on to the wet nurse.

When the children are asleep, Jope and Mary sit together on the sofa in the living room. By then it is dark outside, and the crackling fire and candles illuminate the smoky room. Jope stares into the flickering flames in the fireplace, unsure how to begin.

Realizing that her husband seems preoccupied, Mary says, "You don't have to tell me everything tonight. Just tell me about John and Margaret. You did visit them, didn't you?"

Jope nods gratefully and starts to speak, at first choosing his words carefully, then with greater ease, sharing everything about his time with them, including Margaret's questions about her destiny. He pulls John's letter from inside his doublet and hands it to Mary. She unfolds the parchment and gets up to see better by the candlelight of the candelabra on the mantle. Jope watches her as she reads it carefully, sounding out and mouthing the words quietly.

When she is finished, she turns to him, holding the letter in front of her. "I am glad John is well; Margaret, too," she says. Then her composure falters. "I miss him terribly," she sniffles, tears glistening in her eyes.

Jope goes to her and puts his arms around her. She buries her head in his shoulder, crying quietly. When she calms somewhat, he leads her back to the sofa, and they sit quietly with their arms around each other.

At some point, Mary asks, "Do you think they'll get married and have a family?"

"I suppose so," Jope replies. He shifts his weight uncomfortably. "I sometimes wonder if I did the right thing, taking them to Virginia. Perhaps we should have kept them here with us."

"Oh no, John," Mary says, disengaging herself. "They would never have felt like they belong here."

"They're outsiders in Virginia, too."

"Are they happy? Well fed? Pleased about where they live?"

Jope nods. "I believe so. John likes having the library at the plantation. Margaret is responsible for a whole household now, and she feels valued by Lieutenant Sheppard, who owns the farm. I rather liked him. They tell me that there are a few other Africans in the vicinity—some of the ones I brought to James City—and they have befriended them."

"You see! They are better off there!" Mary exclaims. "They can make a good life for themselves."

But Jope remains silent, staring straight ahead.

She contemplates him, his handsome face looking troubled. "Margaret's question is weighing on you, isn't it?"

He nods yes, slowly.

Taking his hands, Mary says with gentle urgency in her voice, "You have done your duty, John—everything in your power to give them what they need to prosper. Now you must let them go so they can follow their destiny on their own."

Squeezing her hands, Jope says, "I know that, and I told Margaret as much. I am worried about her destiny because I am troubled about my own."

* * *

In London, the Earl of Warwick has no such concern at the moment. He is riding in his coach with his cousin Nathaniel, returning from the first official meeting of the Providence Island Company. Although it is only a short distance from his brother Henry's house in Holborn to his own domicile, they are both bundled up against the winter cold seeping into the carriage. Looking out through the window at the snow drifting down, Rich is nonetheless pleased. By the time King

Charles granted the patent to the Providence Island Company in early December, Captain Elfrith had returned from reporting sunny skies, balmy temperatures, lush tropical vegetation, and friendly Indians in the mainland jungles—he called them the Miskito Tribe—eager to engage in trade with the settlers. As a result, the ranks of shareholders swelled to twenty in no time, even after two dropped out.

Everyone at the meeting was excited at the prospect of establishing an ideal commonwealth based on Puritan principles and beliefs. If they were to succeed, it would be only a matter of time before many of the pilgrims in the Massachusetts Colony would tire of the harsh winters and head for warmer, more welcoming climes, even though John Winthrop just sailed late last spring to take four hundred new settlers there. Once they joined the exodus from New England, it would take but little time to colonize the whole Caribbean—all the islands—and from there invade the mainland and become the pre-eminent power in that part of the New World.

To advance the enterprise, the company has agreed to engage Captain William Rudyard, a seasoned mariner, and his ship, the *Seaflower*, to transport a hundred settlers to Providence Island in February. There they would join up with Captain Axe's and Captain Hammock's men, as well as the contingent of colonists from Bermuda who arrived over the summer led by Captain Philip Bell, the newly appointed governor. His small group of planters wished to trade their depleted fields, exhausted from years of tobacco cultivation, for more fertile soil.

"Nathaniel!" Warwick alerts his cousin as if struck by a sudden idea. "We must make sure the new settlers don't repeat the mistakes of Bermuda and Virginia!"

"Grow tobacco to the exclusion of food and other cash crops?" Nathaniel asks to make sure Rich wants to talk about a subject they have discussed many times.

"Yes, I am concerned that some of our investors don't share my concern that Providence Island attain economic independence as quickly as possible. They seem to be primarily interested in turning a fast profit."

"They don't have your knowledge and experience of what happened in earlier ventures."

"Having to pay for large food imports will cripple the colonists' ability to mount a vigorous defense against the Spanish and create a flourishing community," Warwick complains. "Some of our shareholders don't realize what that means—that they will have to invest more in the long run."

"Give them time and they will come around," Nathaniel counsels. "In the meantime, we're sending along a variety of plants and seeds with the *Seaflower*—sugar, flax, indigo, silk, wheat, rye, and barley—so they can experiment and find out what will grow best."

Warwick nods but doesn't feel reassured. He has little patience for utopian visionaries who don't have their feet firmly planted on the ground. It irks him that some of the most ardent Puritans in the company insisted on regulations that forbid card playing and gambling, whoring, drunkenness, and profanity. He engaged in all of those pursuits at Cambridge University, even if he rejected some as he grew older and exercises moderation for the rest. The earl well knows how human needs and desires can overwhelm even the most God-fearing of religious men. His mind turns to Daniel Elfrith, and he can't help but grin at the thought of anyone trying to curtail the corpulent seafarer's blasphemous cursing.

Nathaniel notices and asks, "What amuses you, my lord?"

"I'm thinking of Captain Elfrith," Rich replies. "I hope he has good news for us."

By the time they get to Warwick House, a fine layer of snow covers the ground. The earl steps down from the carriage first and walks toward the front entrance as quickly as he can, taking care not to slip on the white-fleeced cobblestones. The large wooden door opens, and his butler, Alfred, stands there as if he's been waiting there for him all along.

Stripping off his gloves, Warwick enters and asks eagerly, "Is he here?"

"Captain Elfrith and Captain Bullard are waiting in the antechamber of your study, my lord," Alfred replies, taking off his master's overcoat.

"Excellent!" Rich exclaims and rushes ahead, his heart racing with excitement.

Eager to hear what they have to say, he barges into the antechamber, well ahead of his servant. Surprised, the two men sitting on a bench spring to their feet and execute hasty bows. Sweeping past, Warwick gestures for them to follow him into his study, where he heads to the fireplace and warms his hands. Then he goes to his chair, the largest in the room, and settles in it.

"I hope I haven't kept you waiting for too long," he says languidly, arranging the pillows around him for comfort.

Bullard in tow, Elfrith bows again and says, "We are at your service, my lord."

"And . . . ?" Warwick eyes him sternly.

But Elfrith refuses to be intimidated or hurried. He scratches his enormous belly and says, "We have most excellent intelligence, by God's nails! Captain Bullard's men on the *White Lion* have told us a great deal."

Warwick cranes his neck and leans forward.

Elfrith gestures to Bullard, encouraging him to speak. The younger captain scowls and shuffles forward, his eyes darting around the room. Warwick can't tell whether he is looking for a familiar sight or something to smash. He sees Nathaniel and Alfred stepping quietly into the room and feels relieved. He would not want to confront this brutish beast of a man on his own.

When Bullard finally speaks, his voice is a low growl. "If it please my lord, we know the route Dutchman takes and how he goes about his raids. He's a canny operator, that one."

Rich waits, but nothing else seems to be forthcoming. He looks around and beckons to Alfred.

Elfrith, knowing that Warwick is easily frustrated, steps forward. "'Tis most peculiar, my lord. The Dutchman—a pox upon him!—started out visiting James City and brought two Africans aboard the ship overnight."

"What?"

"Aye, by God's blood, a young black cove and wench spent the night in his cabin."

Warwick ignores the wine goblet Alfred offers him. His mind is awhirl with thoughts and images of the meeting with Jope when he made a bargain with him regarding two blackamoor children, who were the captain's wards. He vaguely recollects meeting them at his aunt Isabel's estate in Aldwarke. He steals a glance toward Nathaniel, who, having moved to his side, gives a small nod. He drew up the contracts.

"This is most astonishing news, Captain," Warwick says. "By all means, sit down, both of you. Would you like some port?"

"Don't mind if I do, by Charles's pygmy prick," Elfrith says and settles comfortably on the sofa.

Bullard sits next to him, awkward and tense, unfamiliar with such luxurious cushions. Nathaniel takes a chair to the right of Rich, away from the fire, while Alfred serves everyone.

For the next minutes, Warwick listens carefully as Elfrith outlines Jope's travels, from James City to Havana to Port Royal to Vlissingen to sell his cargo of tobacco. Rich does not interrupt, not even when the outsized captain describes in detail how Jope tricked the captain from his very own fleet, making off with all the loot.

When he finishes, Warwick says, "So that is how he does it—clever bugger! But can we assume that he will follow the same route next year?"

"Gadsbudlikins, we can wait for him in Havana. He's sure to show up there at some point," Elfrith says.

Bullard leans forward. "I think he'll go to James City again. I'd wager a year's bounty on it." He sneers in revulsion. "My man rowed him upstream to the farm where the black strumpet lives and saw them embrace in front of everybody."

Warwick nods to himself. He doesn't know what Bullard thinks his man saw, but it tells him enough to know that the Africans are still Jope's Achilles heel.

"What would you have us do with him and his ship when we catch them, my lord?" Elfrith asks.

The earl's face hardens. He is about to say, "Show him no mercy," when he sees a feral bloodlust well up in Bullard's eyes. He beckons Nathaniel to come over, and they confer in whispers. Meanwhile, Elfrith takes a deep gulp of wine, wipes his mouth on the sleeve of his leather coat, and barely contains a belch. Bullard keeps staring at the wine goblet in his hands.

Warwick clears his throat to get their attention. "I want it fixed so that he never commandeers another ship, but I don't want him killed. The man is a Calvinist, after all, a member of the True Faith," he says regally. "As for his ship, strip her of what you will, but let her go. If she shows up in my fleet, it will raise too many questions. His wife's father is an important man and could stir up trouble."

Not happy where the conversation is headed, Bullard blurts out, "We should sink her!"

Nathaniel Rich speaks up for the first time, his voice quiet yet firm. "We are not Spanish heathens. We do not sink English ships."

Bullard is about to erupt, but Elfrith holds his arm next to him in a vice grip. "Aye, my lord, we can do that, by God's blood," he says casually. A crafty look appears on his plump face. "Did you have something particular in mind?"

Warwick's expression darkens. "Use the Africans as a threat. Their safety means more to him than the world."

9

HOG-KILLING TIME

Virginia—January 1631

It is just after dawn when John and Michael advance quietly through the woods beyond the tobacco fields, past the snake fences, careful not to step on twigs that would make cracking sounds. Their breaths fog in the crisp morning air. The dogs sniff around tree roots and bushes whose withered brown leaves curl on their twigs, seeking the scent of wild hogs hiding in the shrubs. Lieutenant Sheppard is not far behind, cradling one of his muskets in readiness. Jason follows him, carrying two more. Bringing up the rear are several workers from Ewens's plantation. Some of them are carrying wooden sticks with sharp points for protection. Not having spent much time in the forest, they tread gingerly, casting anxious looks about, for fear of rousing some wild animal.

With the arrival of the first real cold spell in January, Michael had sniffed the brisk morning air and said to John, "It is time to kill us some hogs!"

After they made the announcement to the rest of the plantation, John suggested to Thomas Goodman that they invite Lieutenant Sheppard and his household to join them. They could use as many extra hands as possible. Goodman agreed and discussed it with the lieutenant that Sunday at church. John watched them from afar, pleased to see them come to terms quickly and shake hands on it.

Of course, John had ulterior motives. It would be an opportunity to see Margaret for several days in a row, although they would both be busy. He wants to impress her, show off how well he is learning the hog trade, even though he is still acquiring the rudiments. Michael isn't as good a teacher as Gareth was. He doesn't know how to explain a task unless he's actually performing it, so John follows him and tries to copy whatever he does.

For the past days, everyone has pitched in—checking that the brine barrels for salt pork won't leak, plugging cracks and holes in the smoke shed near the kitchen with wadding so that no air can escape, and collecting plenty of brushwood for the open fires to heat water and render lard. John and Michael made sure they had enough salt on hand, repaired the old saltboxes, and constructed new ones from pine boards to hold all the meat they would be curing. They honed knives and the blades of axes and sharpened the saws used to cut through bones.

The night before the start of the hunt, John was so excited he hardly slept.

As they pass fresh furrows on the ground, signs of hogs rooting, the three Mastiff hounds pick up the scent and strain at their leashes, eager to pursue their prey. Michael gives a nod to John with excitement flickering in his eyes, holds up a hand for the others, and points forward. When he releases the dogs, they tear from their leashes and race ahead, disappearing between two hickory trees. Within seconds, there is a chorus of howls, enthusiastic barks, squeals, and ferocious growls.

By the time Michael and John catch up, the hounds have cornered a large female hog with dark brown and black fur. They snarl and nip at her legs until she stumbles and falls to the ground. One of the dogs seizes an ear with his teeth. The sow squeals and writhes, desperately trying to get away. But when the second dog grabs hold of the other ear, she stops struggling. Instantly, Michael puts a foot on the hog's shoulder, bends down, and cuts her throat. As blood spurts from the severed jugular, he jumps back to avoid the thrashing body. Gradually the death throes diminish to quivers, and finally the sow lies still. Blood puddles by the nearly severed head, seeping into the ground.

"You want to cut as deep as you can without forcing it," Michael explains, as he checks the ears of the pig for markings. When he finds the sharp three angular cuts that indicate the hog belongs to Ewens's plantation, he nods with satisfaction.

Meanwhile, the dogs have caught up to two smaller pigs, which probably belong to the litter the sow had earlier in the fall. They take one to the ground, and Michael quickly dispatches it in the same manner.

When the dogs knock down the other one, he looks at John and says, "Your turn."

John feels his heart pounding in his chest but doesn't hesitate. He approaches the hog with the knife drawn, puts his foot on the shoulder the way Michael did, slashes its throat, and steps back quickly.

"Well done!" Michael exclaims.

As they watch the pig bleed out, John feels the exhilaration of his first kill. It takes awhile before his panting returns to more measured breathing.

Suddenly, there is a musket shot, followed by Lieutenant Sheppard yelling, "I got one."

"Let's hurry," Michael shouts to John. "If we don't cut it soon, the blood won't flow, and we'll have to work to drain it later."

When they catch up to the lieutenant, he is standing near a large boar with tough bristles and dangerous-looking tusks, lying on the ground, gasping, its breath issuing from its nostrils like puffs of smoke in the cold morning air. The wounded hog tries to get up, but its legs keep collapsing under him.

"I got him in the side," the lieutenant says.

Michael nods and moves toward the boar. As he gets closer, the hurt animal starts to rear up in terror. Michael gestures to John to help hold him down. Carefully approaching from the rear, John kneels on the shoulder. As the beast tries to fight back, he can feel the muscles knotting beneath the skin, but it is no longer at full strength. Michael moves in from the other side and cuts its throat. He and John jump back quickly to avoid the sharp tusks flailing about as the boar takes its last gasps. True to Michael's prediction, just a trickle of blood seeps from the gash.

When Michael checks the ears, they have no markings at all. Grinning, he says, "Well then, it's ours for sure."

By then, the other men have caught up. It takes four of them to pick up the boar and carry it back to the farm.

Michael whistles to the dogs and puts them back on their leashes. He continues on, heading deeper into the forest, with John, the lieutenant, and others following. It has taken them less than an hour to kill four hogs. It will take them the rest of the morning to find and bag ten more.

* * *

Margaret, Katherine, and other women servants and field-workers sit around at a makeshift table covered with white-yellowish intestines from two gutted hogs. Oswald, a farmhand who knows how to butcher animals, has gotten started while the hunt is still going on. The women are cleaning the innards with knives: scraping off the fat, grit, corn, and bits of forest tubers and roots so that the remains can be used to make sausages and cook chitterlings. It is an odious chore because of the excremental stench.

Of the forty or so people living and working at Ewens's plantation, a quarter are women, and most of them are here. Only Hester, the wife of Thomas Goodman, who runs the kitchen, and two of her female helpers, Marcia and Phoebe, are otherwise engaged for now. But they will soon get their share of the noxious smell when they start to cook the cleaned hogs' entrails.

Margaret enjoys the company despite the vile stench. A special kind of intimacy develops among women sitting around a table cleaning out the innards of hogs. The wife of one of the tobacco field-workers tells bawdy stories about her time in England where she was a young maid in the household of a merchant and had to fend off his amorous advances. Her tales evoke much laughter, and others contribute their accounts of encounters with lecherous men. Margaret has never heard such a frank, ribald discussion of sexual matters. From time to time she catches Katherine's eyes and receives an amused, indulgent grin from her.

Margaret has been up since before dawn, traveling by boat with Jason and Paul to Ewens's plantation, bringing with them extra kettles and pots, as well as their bedrolls. Thomas stayed behind to watch the homestead after they drew lots and he lost. Ever since John invited their household to participate in the hog killing, Margaret has been looking forward to the three-day event. Not since her arrival in Virginia with a large contingent of Puritans led by members of the Bennett family, to establish a plantation at Warrosquoake, has she been part of such a big venture or spent as much time among such a large group of people. Everyone at Ewens's plantation contributes, even the handful of young children. Margaret is eager for the opportunity to socialize with others and to learn all she can about the curing process to preserve and keep bacon, smoked ham, and other cuts of pork.

Although the sun is high in the sky by now, it is still seasonably cold, and the women take staggered breaks to warm their icy fingers at the open fire nearby, where a large pot of water is kept hot. When it is Margaret's turn to go, she sees John, Michael, Lieutenant Sheppard, and two other young men coming out of the woods. Michael has the hounds on a tight leash. The lieutenant carries his rifle in his arms, and the two helpers are lugging a large boar. John has a smaller hog slung over his shoulders. He waves to Margaret, his eyes shining with the elation of participating in a successful hunt. She smiles and waves back, happy to see him swagger with pride. Katherine, nodding to her husband, watches the exchange with interest but doesn't say anything.

By the time the men deposit their hogs with the other carcasses, Oswald has finished sharpening his knives again and is ready to start on his third pig. A beefy fellow with a dark beard and booming voice, he directs his helpers to hang the lifeless body by its hind legs from a wooden gambrel and hoist it up on the poles so that it dangles off the ground. The two pigs he's gutted already, with their dark fur shaved and scraped off, and their chest and belly cavities empty, hang nearby. The rest of the killed animals lie side by side on the ground awaiting their turn.

A group of jabbering children follows a young woman who is hauling a bucket. It contains the hearts, lungs, and stomachs of the butchered hogs to be buried in the woods. The spleens, kidneys, and livers that will be used for sausages soak in another wooden bucket filled with a salt-and-vinegar brine.

While Michael feeds the dogs scraps of meat, John heads to the kitchen in back. He walks past an open fire where Marcia, one of the cook's assistants, turns a small hog on a spit, fat dripping off the browning body. The savory aroma of roast pork makes his mouth water. He gets three pewter cups of cider and some biscuits from Hester and brings them back to share with Michael and the lieutenant.

While devouring their snack and drinking, they watch as Oswald cuts his hog open from throat to bung, deftly catching the viscera spilling out in a bucket.

"He knows what he's doing," Michael tells John, appreciatively. "See how he keeps the knife shallow as he peels away the skin and fat, so he doesn't pierce the chest cavity or belly."

John nods that he understands.

When they have finished their cider, the lieutenant heads into the main house to clean his muskets. Michael waits until the helpers have hoisted another carcass next to Oswald's and proceeds to gut it, explaining what he is doing to John as best he can.

Then it is John's turn. He proceeds tentatively at first, making his incision too shallow.

"Better that than too deep," Michael says, encouraging him.

Gradually John gains confidence as he feels the resistance of the hog's skin and the softer layer of flesh underneath. But when he peels the belly layer too quickly, the guts spill out all at once. Some go in the bucket, but most end up on the ground.

"I am such a jolthead!" he yells in frustration.

Oswald roars with laughter. "Happens to just about everyone their first time," he says. "It is a trifling matter."

"Indeed!" Michael adds.

John accepts their remarks good-naturedly, even though he would have liked to be perfect from the start. He waits until a helper picks up the viscera before continuing.

When he is done, Michael uses a saw and ax to cut through the sternum, separating the ribs. He places a small board between them to keep them apart. Other farmhands wash the body again, then move it to where the rest of the gutted carcasses hang to cool overnight.

It takes the three men the rest of the afternoon to finish gutting the balance of the hogs.

Toward the end of the day, Katherine and Margaret leave off cleaning the innards, wash their arms and hands several times with soap in the creek, and help Hester, Marcia, and Phoebe get ready to serve supper to everyone. The chitterlings have been simmering for hours with bay leaves, carrots, peppers, onions, and garlic, but the pungent smell has not diminished. Meanwhile, Hester has made a corn stew and baked enough bread to last several days.

When it comes time to eat, everyone gathers around the front porch of the main house and finds a spot to sit—on the steps, on stools, and on tree trunks. Marcia and Phoebe bring the roasted pig to one of the tables, and Michael carves it up. Everyone gets a decent portion, a real treat! It's rare to have fresh meat so savory and tasty because it goes bad very quickly in the warm Virginia climate. Only during the winter does it keep for a while. It is the first time Margaret has eaten chitterlings, and she is surprised how chewy and tasty they are, considering how horrible they smell.

Everyone is pleased that the day has gone without any major mishaps. A few kitchen helpers scalded themselves while moving pots with boiling water, and Marcia burned her forearm when a smoldering hickory branch she carried exploded in flaming sparks, but none of the events required serious attention.

Soon, people huddle in smaller groups around the fires to keep warm. Working in teams has brought everyone closer. People lace their conversations with jokes, banter, chitchat, and gossip about the most recent events in James City. Margaret and John sit on a bench next to each other, their shoulders touching, and mostly listen.

Governor Harvey remains a favorite subject. His appeal to settle the land along the southern banks of the Pamunkey and York Rivers, offering the incentive of an extra five acres the first year and fifty-five acres the second, has been a great success. A number of adventurous settlers have heeded the call, despite the ongoing danger from the nearby Indian tribes. Harvey's talks with the Powhatan chief, Opechancanough, seem to be making progress as well.

But despite such accomplishments, Harvey's standing has not improved. Despite opening his mansion to James City's social elite, holding frequent and well-attended gatherings and dances, he continues to alienate many of the burgesses, planters, and merchants. His volatile temper, his habit of issuing orders without consulting the General Assembly or Governor's Council, and his ignorance in certain colony matters do not sit well with Virginia's high-ranking citizens. Nearly everyone smirked when Harvey made a land grant to his friend Richard Kemp near the Back River on the Chesapeake Bay, only to discover that Richard Stephens already held the patent for the property. Stephens was not amused.

By the time everyone has finished and cleaned up, it is pitch-black. Clouds mask the stars, and the silver moon that occasionally peeks through does not provide much light. Goodman invites Lieutenant Sheppard to sleep in William Ewens's room at the main house. Margaret joins Katherine and Michael at their small domicile. As she follows them in the darkness, trusting that they know the way, she hears Michael mentions how well John did today and feels gratified.

John heads for the two large bunkhouses. It has been a long day, and another one lies ahead, yet his mind is reeling with images, impressions, and more information than he can absorb all at once. But when his head touches the pillow of his cot, he falls asleep immediately.

* * *

In the morning, the weather remains chilly, with a brisk breeze blowing off the James River. All the people assembling by the kitchen behind the main house for a breakfast of biscuits, oat porridge, and beer beat their arms around their bodies to get warm.

Michael, John, and Oswald have already checked on the hog carcasses to make sure the cold has hardened but not frozen the meat, which will make it easy to cut straight through the fibers. After they finish eating, they select two hogs and have helpers carry them to the narrow wooden tables. John watches attentively as they start to cut up the carcasses.

They first remove the leaf lard—the soft fat that surrounds the kidneys and loins—from the stomach cavity. Its mild flavor and the fact that it doesn't start smoking until heated to a high temperature makes it great for cooking, frying, and baking, especially pie crusts. Then they cut off the heads—saving the brains, which some people like to eat fried—and saw and hack the carcasses into halves. As they carve out the shoulders, hams, loins, and bacon from the belly for smoking, they also separate the lard from the meat underneath. The fat makes the knife slippery and hard to hold onto, and John winces when Michael loses his grip several times and the blade hits the ground with a thud. Fortunately, he doesn't cut himself. The last step is slicing the rib sections into pork chops and showing their helpers how to put them into barrels and cover them with brine.

It takes Michael and Oswald close to an hour to finish up both halves of each hog carcass.

By then Katherine, Margaret, and several men have started the curing process, rubbing the meat with salt to dry it out. It is demanding work, but after enduring the stench of the intestines, it feels like a reprieve.

"You have to get the salt into all the crevices, or the meat will turn rotten when the weather gets warm," Katherine tells Margaret.

They place the finished pieces into wooden boxes and cover them with a layer of salt.

"It'll take a month or so before they're ready for smoking," Katherine explains. "John will let you know when it's time to come back for the start of that."

When the boxes are full, it is time to take them to the smokehouse to be stored. They are heavy and require two people to carry them. When Margaret trips on an exposed root in the path, her hand slips and a sliver from the pinewood punctures her middle finger. She cries out in pain but doesn't let go. As she sets the box down, the splinter digs in deeper and breaks off. It smarts and Margaret pulls it out carefully, leaving a flap of dead skin and blood seeping from the wound. She sucks her finger for a while before hiking up her gown and pressing it to the underside of the fabric until the wound is staunched.

On her way back to work, Margaret stops and watches the men and women who have begun making sausages. They've cut up the livers, kidneys, and spleens into tiny morsels and blended them with diced pieces of lard and pork meat. They knead the mixture until it is almost a paste and stuff it into the intestines, which have been tied off at one end.

She also sees men take large quantities of lard for rendering in big cooking vats to get ready for soap and candle making the following day. They are working a reasonable distance away and downwind. Margaret is glad she doesn't have to perform that task, where the stench is almost as stomach-turning as the hogs' innards. In fact, she is secretly delighted that Paul and Jason have been assigned that chore.

Looking about, she is amazed at how smoothly everything is proceeding.

During the brief dinner break in the early afternoon, she and John manage to spend a few moments together. He knows that, after observing Michael and Oswald, it will be his turn to butcher a hog on his own.

"I had no idea how much there is to learn," he says. "I don't know if I'll ever be ready to do this on my own."

"You won't have to," Margaret assures him. "Michael will continue to help you. He is very impressed with you."

"Do you really think so?"

"He said so last night."

Margaret can tell how pleased John is. His look of gratitude quickly turns to admiration. She notices others casting knowing glances in their direction as if everyone has decided that she and John belong together. Usually, a few men gaze and sometimes even leer at her with undisguised desire, but no one at the plantation has done so.

Returning to the salting tables, Margaret wishes she and John could have been alone longer, but they have too much work to do.

Perhaps tomorrow, when all that's left to do is soap and candle making and cleaning up, they can catch more time together.

The afternoon passes quickly, and the sun is low in the sky when everyone is finished.

With supper happening earlier, the meal turns into a celebration of a successful hog killing. Afterward, a few of the men bring out musical instruments—fifes, a fiddle, and a drum—and strike up a hornpipe. At first, everybody just listens and claps along. But then, a recent arrival from England gets up and starts to dance, stomping and kicking up his legs. The others encourage him, cheering and clapping louder, and when the music ends, they reward him with a round of applause. Then the musicians start to play reels and jigs, and others get up to dance as well. Other than holding hands, there is no physical contact among them, but plenty of lively jumping and strutting.

Margaret would like to participate, but she doesn't know any of the steps. Then she sees Hester with the children off to one side. She is showing them the rudiments of a reel. As Margaret lines up with them, she waves to John to join her, but he declines, a quizzical expression on his face. Shrugging her shoulders, she follows the children's movements and quickly catches on. When Hester points to the circle around the fire, encouraging her to dance with the adults, Margaret doesn't hesitate.

As she enters the fray, there are cheers of, "Go, Margaret!" and "Well, I'll be. . . ."

Before she knows it, she is jumping, kicking, and stomping with the others, letting the music reverberate inside her body. Time seems to slow down, and she feels a sense of joy and freedom she has not experienced in a long time. When the reel is over, she feels disappointed, but only for a moment. She returns to John, who looks up at her in wordless wonderment.

Suddenly, Margaret feels shy, just as baffled by what she has done, but when she looks around, no one is paying attention to her.

Surprised, she realizes that they all accepted her as someone who was having a good time.

As the evening draws to a close and it is time to say goodnight, Margaret and John get up and stand close to one another. She would like him to put his arms around her, but he remains still. Then Michael comes by and takes him aside to talk about tomorrow. Margaret feels disappointed.

Suddenly, Katherine is at her side and links arms with her.

"I want to talk to you alone, Margaret," she says in a soft voice.

Puzzled, Margaret lets Katherine lead her down the path to the little cottage. In the past two days, they have spent a great deal of time together, and Margaret has come to like her almost as much as Frances, her old friend from Floridew. Katherine has a no-nonsense approach. She seems worldlier, having experienced life on a larger, more populous plantation, yet she is also a caring person. When Margaret arrived the day before, Katherine showed her around and introduced her to everyone. She wonders what her new friend has in mind now.

It is as dark outside as the night before and just as cold. When they get to the cottage, Katherine brings knitted shawls from inside, and they sit together on the small front porch.

She comes straight to the point. "I want to talk about you and John," she says.

Margaret is taken aback. This is not what she had expected.

"I have seen you two making eyes at each other for quite some time," Katherine continues. "What are you waiting for?"

"What do you mean?"

"Why haven't you done anything?"

"I . . . I . . . I am waiting for him."

"Then you'll be waiting for a long time."

"What do you mean?" Margaret asks again.

"John would make a fine husband for you," Katherine explains. "But he won't do the asking. You will have to take the first step, just like at the dance tonight."

Despite the chill, Margaret feels her face flush with heat. She is glad it is too dark for Katherine to see her expression. "What do you mean?" she asks for the third time.

"When you first came here with your captain and then lived in England, you were like his older sister, protecting him. Now that you been some years apart, things are different. You're both older. But John will continue to defer to you."

"But he is so confident and competent," Margaret protests.

"Yes," Katherine says, with a little laugh. "But with you, he's a tongue-tied youngster. If you want him, you'll need to take the first step and let him know what you want. He will never presume on his own."

"Has he said so to you?"

"Let's just say that I understand him well enough by now, and I see what I see." She gives Margaret's hand a squeeze. "I know what I'm talking about. And so do you."

Margaret rises as if impelled and walks a few steps to the edge of the porch. She draws the shawl tighter around her as if trying to hug herself. Peering into the darkness, she feels her heart beating faster. Slowly, a sensation of excitement and anticipation spreads throughout her body and she feels a pleasurable tingling all over.

10
REQUESTS
February 1631

Riding on horseback to visit his brother Joseph, Captain Jope trots past barren fields covered with patches of snow. Although bundled in a heavy overcoat with a shawl covering his mouth, he feels the chill of the cold air but chooses to let it invigorate him, and to help him keep a clear head.

The time to leave on his next privateering voyage to the Caribbean is drawing near, but he has had difficulty tearing himself away, loath to leave Mary and the children. When he mentioned that his departure is but a fortnight away, her face dropped.

"It feels like you've just arrived," she said plaintively.

Although she made no efforts to dissuade him, there have been other times during his stay, usually late at night, when she has urged him to make this his last voyage. Although he has tried, Jope has been unable to hide how poor his eyesight has become and how stiff his joints are when he gets out of bed in the morning. Still, much as he would like to make her happy by granting her wish, he has insisted on postponing his retirement once again, joking, as in previous springs, that he will go on for "just another couple of years."

The real trouble is that he can't see himself as a country squire, blithely installed on his estate, collecting fees from his tenants. He'd miss the adventure and excitement of privateering too much. After a month or two at home, he feels restive, even though he knows that his days at sea are numbered.

What worries him most is his ability to continue to lead his crew. They are rough men used to being ruled with an iron fist. Considering what he demands of them, plundering Spanish vessels in consort with other raiders, he cannot show any weakness. If they sense any vulnerability on his part when responding to a threat or challenge, either physically or mentally, he may have a mutiny on his hands. No matter how much he trusts Gareth, Samuel Teague, and the long-standing members of his crew, he has to earn the loyalty of his younger sailors every day.

When Jope sees the turrets of his brother's lavish mansion up ahead, he admits to himself the real reason for his restlessness. He hasn't accomplished what he set out to do: amass a treasure large enough to match Joseph's wealth. They have never been close, and even though Joseph, after inheriting their father's estate, loaned him the money to repair and outfit the *White Lion* for privateering, Jope resents him. His brother has always counted his ducats first, and he has recovered his investment plus substantial interest from Jope's exertions.

By the time Jope gets to the mansion, he is trembling from the cold and grateful for the fire burning in the hearth of the drawing room. As he warms his hands behind his back, he examines Joseph, who lounges in a soft upholstered chair, chewing on a macaroon. His dark blue doublet is of the finest satin and matches the extravagant surroundings—wall tapestries and portraits of himself and his family. He has gained weight, no doubt because of his sedentary way of life and fondness for sweets.

Taking another confection, Joseph gives Jope a speculating glance and says, "Why are you here, John? If this is about the lean haul from last summer, don't worry about it. I'm happy to cover any temporary deficiencies."

Jope takes the chair close to the fireplace and leans forward. "We need to talk about what happens when I can no longer commandeer the *White Lion*."

Joseph stops in mid-bite. "Are you all right?"

"Yes, yes, I'm fine," Jope replies impatiently. "But I'm not getting any younger."

Joseph looks at him for some time. He has never known his younger brother to be impetuous or complain. There must be a reason that he is raising the subject now, although what that is may be difficult to fathom. "What is on your mind?" he says carefully.

Jope gets up and starts to pace, brushing his hand through his ash-blond hair, bleached by years of sailing under the unforgiving tropical sun. "There are three options," he enumerates using his fingers. "We could sell the ship and turn a profit. She would need some repairs, but she's in good shape. We could hire another captain in my place. Or we could take on other investors to cover the expense of overhauling and outfitting the ship without any cost to us and use her as a merchant vessel. That way we'd have ongoing proceeds, albeit smaller ones." He stops moving and looks at his brother expectantly.

Joseph considers the choices. He would prefer to know more before committing himself. "I would be inclined to keep going with a new captain," he drawls. "Do you have anyone in mind?"

"Aye. As a matter of fact, I do. My first mate, Gareth, has been with me for a decade now and knows the ship almost better than me. He'd make a fine captain."

Joseph gives him a shrewd look. "I see you've given this some thought, John. Why don't I come to Portsmouth before you set sail and meet your man? He'd have to accept a lesser share than you and I, of course."

"I'm confident he will," Jope replies, smiling. He is glad Joseph doesn't pry any further but still feels irked. "It's always about the money with you, isn't it?"

If he thought he'd annoy Joseph with his comment, he's mistaken. His brother replies languidly, "Of course. What's wrong with that?" Then he stuffs the macaroon in his mouth and licks his fingers luxuriously.

Jope thinks that it would be lovely if Joseph choked on it and feels not an ounce of remorse for his nasty wish. After discussing arrangements to meet at the harbor, he excuses himself. He means to make another stop before joining Mary for the main meal of the day.

On his way home, Jope visits the estate of her uncle. A leading member of the House of Commons, Sir John Glanville would normally be in London, but since King Charles dissolved Parliament to rule on his own, Sir Glanville has been pursuing his business interests. Because Sir Glanville is a wealthy man who loves his niece with all his heart, Jope has never worried about Mary becoming destitute if something happened to him. What he wants to discuss is a different, more delicate matter.

Sir Glanville welcomes him with his usual ebullient manner. "Why, John, this is a fine surprise. What brings you here? Don't tell me you got lost without your trusty navigator by your side."

Jope grins. "What better place to alight than in your home then?" But he gets straight to the point. "I have come to ask a favor."

Glanville drops all pretense at decorum and invites him into his study, just as Jope expected. It's one of the things he's always liked about Glanville. He made no bones about the fact that he wasn't keen on a privateer marrying his favorite niece, even if she loved him, but when he realized that Jope was honorable and trustworthy, he accepted him as if he were a member of his clan. He helped out without batting an eyelid when Jope brought Margaret and John to England.

Sitting across from Glanville at his desk, Jope takes a different approach than with Joseph. He mentions that privateering is a risky undertaking, and that he has had several close scrapes. Mary would like him to give it all up, but he wants to continue to seek Spanish treasure without worrying about her and concludes, "I am confident if something were to happen to me, you would come to her aid."

Glanville strokes his dark brown beard. He is only a few years older than Jope and understands both the lure of ambition and the need to take care of one's family. "That goes without saying, as you well know," he comments.

Jope hesitates slightly before going on. "What I am asking of you is your promise that you will make sure she remarries as quickly as possible," he says. "I can't bear the thought that she would pine for me and languish."

Glanville leans forward and searches his guest's face, realizing how hard it is for Jope to contain his emotions. "Are you all right, John?" he asks with concern.

"Of course. Quite."

Looking straight into Jope's eyes, Glanville notices the whitish flecks in his irises and comprehends that the captain is going blind. Knowing him to be a proud man, he makes no comment but says with passion, "I know you love Mary with all your heart and soul, John. I am honored that you would make this request of me, and you have my word that I will do as you ask." He adds, "I pray it will never come to that."

"Me too," Jope whispers, feeling a sense of relief come over him. He glances at his lap and realizes his hands are clenched into white-knuckled fists. Slowly opening them and working his fingers, he looks up and says, "Thank you, Sir John. It means a great deal to me."

* * *

The Earl of Warwick climbs stiffly down from his coach, relieved to be on firm ground again. For the past hour and a half, he has endured a bumpy ride from his Holborn home across London Bridge to the Deptford shipping docks on the south side of the Thames River.

Neither the ample cushioning nor down pillows inside the carriage managed to relieve the constant jolts due to dips and uneven cobblestones. It is a sunny day, although the temperatures are still cold and the breeze coming off the river is bracing. The earl draws his dark-green woolen coat closer around him.

Behind him, his eight-year-old son, Charles, and his cousin Nathaniel Rich emerge from the carriage, stretching and flexing their own stiff joints. Charles has never been to a shipyard before and stares in amazement at the *Seaflower* swaying gently in the water. The sister ship of the *Mayflower*, which took the first Puritans to Massachusetts a decade earlier, has three masts and a bulky hull, secured to the stone pier by thick, heavy ropes tied to iron fenders.

To Warwick's surprise, a good number of fellow shareholders of the Providence Island Company have already assembled—among them Lord Brooke, Lord Saye and Sele, Oliver St. John, Sir Gerard, and Sir Moundeford—all members of Parliament—and newly joined Sir Thomas Barrington, a cousin of Oliver Cromwell. Rarely have so many powerful and prosperous worthies convened to see off a contingent of lowborn travelers on a sea voyage. Of course, this is a special case. They have all been involved in recruiting the hundred passengers on board, mostly young men, who represent the first wave of new settlers for Providence Island.

Nathaniel has been providing Warwick with daily reports about the outfitting of the *Seaflower*, including the purchasing and laying in of supplies for the two-and-a-half-month-long voyage—barrels of salt beef and pork; caskets of butter and hard cheese; and boxes filled with biscuits, dried peas, currants, rice, and oatmeal. Captain John Tanner, an experienced mariner, and his crew have been making everything aboard shipshape, ensuring also that, despite Puritan edicts against liquor, the cargo includes demijohns of rum and hogsheads of claret and brandy for the ship's officers, as well as large kegs of beer for the sailors and passengers.

Warwick notices his son's saucer-sized eyes and says, "Did you know, Charles, that there are cattle, sheep, pigs, goat, geese, and chickens in the holds?"

When the boy shakes his head, even more amazed, Nathaniel chimes in, "It's a veritable Noah's Ark below deck."

"Did you see them yourself?" Charles asks.

Nathaniel nods. "They're tethered and in crates among the travel chests, trunks, and furniture of the passengers. I had to pinch my nose because the stench was so bad, and it will surely get worse en route."

"Can I go see?" Charles asks eagerly.

"I'm afraid not. The ship will depart anon," Nathaniel says, noting the boy's disappointment. "Maybe next time."

Warwick marvels how well his cousin can communicate with children. He wishes he had that ability. Rich has managed to thoroughly alienate his older son, Robert, because he can't stop ridiculing him for spending too much time at court. He hopes young Charles will turn out better. The last thing he wants is another royalist in the family.

As Warwick walks toward the group of investors, the sound of horses' hoofs on the cobblestones distracts him. It is a hired coach, and when it comes to a stop, John Pym and William Jessop step down. The earl greets them warmly. Pym, looking disheveled as always, seems to have recovered his good humor. He had not been pleased when Warwick had to announce during the last general meeting that additional funds were needed to outfit the *Seaflower* and pay for the voyage. Hire for the ship alone costs 130 pounds a month.

It was fortunate that a letter from the colony governor, John Bell, had arrived a week earlier at Warwick House. Rich had held onto it to use for just such an occasion. He rose and read it out loud to the company members: "By anyone's standards, Providence must be accounted for utterly beautiful. . . . This little spot of land will grow into one of the gardens of the world."

After that glowing testimonial, none could object to the call to dig further into their purses. For Warwick, his noble peers, and the wealthy squires it was a drop in the bucket. But Pym and a few others had to take out loans to cover their share. That they did so without hesitation and complaint earned them Warwick's respect.

Soon after the earl's party joins the larger group, a loud bell rings on the quarterdeck, signaling the *Seaflower*'s imminent departure. Everyone's attention turns to the ship, where the passengers appear at the railing. Dressed all in black, woolen garb and flat-top hats, they line the length of the main deck from bow to stern.

Several dockhands pull the gangplanks onto the quay. Others untie the thick mooring ropes and toss them toward the ship, where sailors haul them up. Meanwhile, tars on the ratlines and lower spars unfurl a few sails and lash them fast. As the wind catches them, the *Seaflower* slowly floats away from the pier.

A cheer rises from the group of investors. The passengers wave with their hats to the men gathered below. Warwick watches his son waving back eagerly. For a moment, he feels like a young man again, caught up in the excitement of adventure. Could it be that all his efforts to create a flourishing Puritan colony in the New World will finally bear fruit, and that his dreams of empire will be realized?

Watching the *Seaflower* glide downriver, he thinks of Elfrith and Bullard pursuing the Flying Dutchman and hopes that they will finally catch up with him.

11

SURPRISE

Virginia—March 1631

L ate winter in Virginia is not a time for romance. The weather remains dismal and cold during the day and often plummets below freezing at night. There is snow on the ground, and the wind off the Chesapeake Bay and James River is bracing and moist, chilling people to the bone.

Margaret has been thinking a great deal about what Katherine told her at the hog killing. She didn't see much of John the next day, returning early to Sheppard's homestead with Jason and Paul and the boat loaded with two brine barrels filled with salted ribs and pork chops.

Over the next weeks, she observes John with new eyes at Lawne's Creek Church and during his Sunday afternoon visits afterward and concludes that Katherine was right—he continues to look at her with ardent desire but stops short of getting closer to her beyond brushing against her or holding her hand. If their relationship is to proceed, she has to take matters into her own hands. Every time the thought enters her mind, however, it sends tremors of anticipation and terror through her body.

Unfortunately, there has been little opportunity. On the Sundays when John comes to visit, the weather is too cold to go for a walk outside unless they're both bundled up. The kitchen area and Lieutenant Sheppard's house are warmer, but with people around, they have little privacy.

Of late, even church offers them little time alone together. John is often preoccupied, engaged in serious conversations with Anthony.

When John raises the issue with Thomas Goodman that Michael, Katherine, and Mathew had no contracts of indenture, the plantation manager said it was probably an oversight and agrees right away that it should be remedied. But he doesn't feel comfortable making that decision on his own before checking with William Ewens in England. So he dictates a letter to John explaining the matter and sends it off with the captain of the merchant ship transporting their plantation's tobacco crop to London.

Things don't go as well for Anthony, Mary, and their family. When Anthony reminds John Upton of his promise to take care of their contracts of indenture when they came to him from Bennett's plantation, he claims to have no recollection of such a conversation. He agrees "out of the goodness of his heart" to take the matter under consideration—Anthony is much too valuable a worker to reject his request outright. His knowledge and experience in raising horses and cattle are invaluable to the plantation. But days and weeks pass without Upton bringing it up on his own, and whenever Anthony tries to remind him, he acts busy or distracted. It frustrates Anthony to no end. John feels just as much at a loss for how to put pressure on the landowner, who is obviously stalling. He goes to the library and does more legal research, but nothing he finds in the documents helps to breach the impasse.

The whole muddle reminds Margaret of what happened with John Chew, who conveniently forgot a similar promise he had made to her. It puzzles her that Upton would behave that way. He has always seemed like an honest man. She imagines he would sympathize with Anthony and Mary's aspirations, having been an indentured servant himself at one time.

She understands why John, with his sense of fairness and justice, pursues the matter with passion, and it doesn't bother her that he is less available. Since the hog killing, she and a number of the women from Ewens's plantation have become friendlier and enjoy each other's company. Following Katherine's lead, they treat Margaret as an equal and welcome her advice regarding herbs and medicinal concoctions for various ailments. When some heal from bouts of indigestion by drinking her chamomile tea, Margaret rises even further in their estimation.

When John announces a little more than a month later that the time has come to start smoking the meat he and Michael butchered, and that Margaret is welcome to come and participate in getting things ready, she is pleased. She looks forward not just to spending time with him but to seeing her new friends.

Early the following morning, Paul accompanies her through the forest to Ewens's plantation. Not that Margaret is afraid of wild animals or encountering Indians, but Lieutenant Sheppard insisted that she not go alone. It is an overcast day, and the woods are bare. None of the spring leaves are yet in appearance.

When she arrives at the main house, the women welcome Margaret, hugging and kissing her. Katherine greets her warmly, too, and catches her up on what has happened. During the five weeks that Margaret has been away, they have twice inspected the boxes containing the meat. As the salt dries out the meat, a dark brown liquid drains from the holes in the bottom planks. The women have replaced the salt as needed.

When they get to the smokehouse, John, Michael, and other men are already at work, taking the saltboxes out of the shed and emptying them. They remove the cuts of meat and place them on the wooden tables. Margaret joins the women in washing off with warm water what salt remains from each piece. The men tie strings around the ham and loin hocks and through holes poked through the slabs of bacon. Then they sprinkle them with black pepper and hang them up inside the smoking shed, making sure that none of the pieces touch each other.

When all of the meat dangles from the rafters and the horizontal poles are rigged inside, Michael hunkers down and starts a fire with corncobs and tinder. As it gets going, he adds larger branches of oak and cedar, as well as small apple wood twigs that others have collected and cut off the trees during the week. Many of them still contain sap. Soon thick clouds of smoke billow to the ceiling, filling the shed with a pleasing scent.

"We want more smoke than fire. That's why we use fresh branches," Michael explains. "The apple wood adds a sweet flavor to the meat."

"We'll let it burn all day and night for the next two weeks," John says.

"You have someone watching all the time?" Margaret asks.

"No. If the fire goes out overnight, it's no big deal," says Michael. "We just relight it in the morning."

Margaret is surprised at his lack of concern. She knows from experience how difficult it is to keep an untended fire going and has spent many an early morning in the cold hours before dawn trying to rekindle it.

When Katherine gives her husband a meaningful glance, he says to John, "I can take care of this on my own. Why don't you and Margaret get cleaned up before supper?"

Neither of them needs another invitation for an opportunity to be alone together. They quickly go to the creek and wash the salt and pepper from their hands. By the time they're done, their fingers feel like icicles.

"I've never seen the library where you spend so much of your time," Margaret says, shivering. "I'd like to."

Surprised and pleased, John puts his arm around her shoulder, pulling her close to him, then heads to the main house.

In contrast to the bone-chilling weather, it is cozy indoors. The mansion is considerably larger than Lieutenant Sheppard's house, with a large entry and a staircase leading to the second floor. Margaret can see the spacious drawing room through an open doorway, but John guides her down a small hallway to another room: the library.

Immediately upon entering, Margaret notices a musty odor and the sour smell of mold. Afternoon light coming through the two windows provides dim illumination, revealing a dark wood table in the center with a small pile of books on it. The walls are covered with shelves, most of them filled from floor to ceiling with books. In one section, scrolls hang from thin wooden rods. In another, there are bins with folders containing documents. The room feels a bit cramped, but there are more books than Margaret expected.

Her eyes are drawn to a small side table by one of the windows where a collection of inkwells, quills, sealing wax, and stamps lies on a dark green runner. It has been more than a decade since she has held a feathery pen in her hand and written anything but her name, much less read a book or document. She wonders if she could still do it.

"The books were brought here during the Indian uprising to keep them safe. This was one of the places that escaped relatively unscathed," John explains. "Since then, many in James City call this plantation College Land."

He points to the upper corner of one of the shelves and lowers his voice to a whisper. "I've hidden my money behind those volumes."

Margaret looks up. He has chosen a good spot, a dark nook no one would bother to disturb.

Indicating other areas, he says with pride, "There are the law books. Maps and atlases are over there, travel accounts here, and religious prayer and philosophy books against that wall." He goes over to them and brushes the sepia and dark brown spines.

Retrieving a folder from a bin and placing it on the table next to the stack of books, he continues, "Let me show you what I've been working on. These are the contracts of indenture for Ewens's plantation, except for Michael, Katherine, and Mathew, of course."

His face is flushed with pleasure as he opens the folder and takes out a piece of parchment. Margaret barely looks at the writing, signatures, and stamps, but focuses on how excited he is. It is obvious that, for him, this is a living, breathing document that determines the course of someone's life.

As he searches for his own contract to show her, she puts her hand on his shoulder and says softly, "John."

He looks up, startled, and turns toward her. Margaret, her eyes glistening, holds his stare for a moment. Then she takes his face in her hands and kisses him. John feels her mouth on his, soft, moist, and insistent. He wants to respond but draws back. Margaret smiles, takes his hand, and places it on her breast. Through the woolen dress, she can feel his grip tighten and her nipple harden.

"I want you," she says and nods to him ever so slightly.

He pulls her to him, enfolding her body in his arms, feeling her chest rise and fall rapidly. He covers her face with kisses and strokes her eager, yielding body.

The sound of a door shutting interrupts their passionate embrace, and they pull apart and listen breathlessly. When they realize it came from somewhere else in the house, they start to laugh. John quickly puts a finger to Margaret's lips, and they both giggle softly with relief and joy.

John gently kisses her and then draws away. "We must take care. Hester may come in before we know it," he says. "It's the time of day when she tidies up."

Straightening her ruffled dress, Margaret says, "Yes, we should get back or the others will wonder what we're up to." She smiles mischievously. "We have much to do and talk about anon."

As John restores the documents to their proper place, Margaret looks around the room. The light from the windows has dimmed even further. More time has passed than she realized.

By the time they rejoin the others outside, the sun is hovering above the forested banks on the other side of the James River. It is suppertime.

Everyone is busy getting ready to eat, but Katherine gives them a knowing look. She gestures Margaret over to her, embraces her, and whispers in her ear, "I am so happy for both of you."

Wondering how she knows, Margaret looks around and notices others glancing at her and John with barely disguised merriment.

"You both are all aglow!" Katherine says.

Margaret can't keep herself from grinning. The joyfulness inside her gushes over. "Yes, and for good reason," she burst out. "Thank you."

* * *

Having taken the big first step of acknowledging their feelings for one another, Margaret's and John's emotions run the gamut from sheer giddiness and unbridled joy to unhappiness about their situation. Others, both at Sheppard's farm and Ewens's plantation, note the buoyant changes in their demeanor—their sprightly gait as if they're walking on air, the special light in their eyes, the easy smile when people kid them or offer congratulations.

As the weather breaks and the early spring flowers appear, they go on longer walks, exploring the woods together. It gives them the privacy they've been craving to touch, hug, and kiss each other unobserved.

They also spend considerable time discussing the difficulties of their situation. Although eager to tie the knot, they know they will have to live in separate households for another five years. While both Sheppard and Goodman would be happy to have them as a married couple on their plantations, neither agrees to give up his servant without compensation. John considers using his money to buy out Margaret's contract of indenture, but he doesn't know if he has enough, and he can't think of a credible explanation to answer questions about how he obtained his stash.

They both want to start a family, but John points out that having children will add additional time to their indenture contracts— three or more years for every child—and it would be better to wait until they have their freedom. Margaret wonders what Michael and Katherine are doing to prevent getting pregnant. She has some notions already because when she worked as a midwife with Dr. Pott, several women asked what remedies there were to keep from having more children. Other than breastfeeding their newborns for a more extended period, perhaps as many as three years, the doctor mentioned drinking tea made from the dried blossoms of pennyroyal after lying with their husbands. Until then Margaret had known the plant only as a mintlike flavoring for stews, whose odor also kept insects away, but the flowers wouldn't be ready until summertime. She vows to ask Katherine the next time she sees her if she has any other ideas.

Margaret gets the opportunity sooner than expected. Two weeks later, when the smoking of the meat is done, all the participants in the hog killing gather to celebrate. Goodman invites Lieutenant Sheppard's household for the festive meal, and this time Jason draws the short straw and stays behind.

The dinner, held at the usual time in the early afternoon, is a lavish spread with samples of every smoked cut. Michael and John receive much praise for the sweet-flavored bacon, loins, and ham, both roasted and cooked. There is more dancing, and to Margaret's amazement, John grasps her hand and pulls her into the line opposite him for a rousing jig. He knows all the steps and performs them with confidence.

Afterward, she seeks out Katherine, who has been watching and clapping along. "He wanted to surprise you and practiced all week with Hester," she whispers, smiling.

"That he most certainly did," Margaret replies. "But I want to talk to you about something else."

Noticing her serious expression, Katherine takes Margaret by the arm and heads toward the creek, away from the others. "I am glad to see you and John so happy," she says. "But I can imagine it's difficult contemplating being married and living in two different places."

Margaret sighs in acknowledgment. "At least we're in the vicinity so we can see each other every week," she says. "My friend Frances was separated from the man she loves for many years."

"What about children?" Katherine probes gently.

"That's what I want to talk to you about," Margaret says eagerly and proceeds to share her dilemma.

Katherine listens carefully and says, "Michael and I are waiting to have children, too. We want to have more money saved up before we start our family." She smiles at Margaret with a conspiratorial gleam in her eyes. "Come with me."

When they get to her cottage, Katherine opens the pine chest under the window and finds a small linen bag. She takes out a pinch of dried dark kernels. "These are wild carrot seeds. Take them for four days after you lie with John and you won't get pregnant. It is best to chew them."

"I know the plant. It has a cluster of white flowers," Margaret says. "When they dry, they curl up and look like a little bird's nest."

"Yes. This summer after they bloom, we can go and harvest more together," Katherine says. "The flowers look just like hemlock, which, as well you know, is very poisonous. You have to be careful and learn how to tell them apart. I'll show you."

Margaret doesn't tell her that she knows the difference already. The green hemlock stems have purple blotches on them. The wild carrot's stems are hairy, and the root is quite tasty.

She hugs Katherine impulsively and says, "You're a good friend. What would I do without you?"

Katherine finds a small pouch and pours half of the seeds from her bag into it. Handing it to Margaret, she says, "Find a comfortable spot to lie with John. It will hurt a little the first time, and there may be a bit of blood, but it will get easier and feel good before long."

12
UNION
Early April 1631

T wo weeks later, Captain Jope arrives at Sheppard's homestead by boat. Just as the year before, he comes bearing gifts to "abduct" Margaret for a day. Once again, the lieutenant gives his permission readily. Margaret dashes to the kitchen, her heart thumping, and retrieves her pearl necklace from its hiding place. Just to make sure, she checks that the bag of wild carrot seeds Katherine gave her lies safely tucked away among the dried herbs and spices.

Keeping the necklace in her balled fist, she hurries down to the creek and nimbly steps into the waiting boat, barely touching the weathered hand Jope extends to her for support. As they cast off the wooden dock, Jason, Paul, and Mathew watch their departure, standing with arms folded like self-appointed sentinels, grinning.

When the boat rounds a bend in the creek, Jope at the tiller asks, "What is going on? The servants at Ewens's plantation smirked like the three coves we just left behind."

John, sitting next to Margaret, is busy helping her put the golden chain with the pearl drop around her neck. When he has fastened the clasp, she turns to him. "You didn't tell him?" John shakes his head no but looks like he is about to burst at the seams.

Jope stares intently at the happy pair, his sapphire blue eyes narrowing. "All right, out with it! What are you two up to?"

"We want to get married," they blurt out simultaneously.

Margaret quickly adds, "By you."

The sailors stop rowing and turn around in astonishment. For a moment, all that can be heard are the plops of water dripping from the raised oars and the screech of a hawk in the distance.

Jope looks thunderstruck. Then his face comes alive, opening like a blossom, with a dazzling smile. "Why, that's wonderful news!" he gasps. "Mary will be so happy."

The others mutter, "Congratulations," under their breaths, glance awkwardly at one another, and resume rowing.

For the remainder of the trip down the creek, the passengers keep silent, stealing shy glances at one another. John has already informed Jope about becoming a hog farmer—he has brought along one of his smoked hams as a gift—but he doesn't want to get too personal in the presence of the sailors. He and Margaret sit on the wooden bench, holding hands, leaning against each other, her head resting on his shoulder. Jope realizes that they both have grown a bit more in his absence—matured and filled out—and their ease with one another makes him happy. This is how he wants to remember them.

They're all pleased to see the tall masts of the *White Lion*, towering over the line of trees before they reach the sandy shore and the river.

When they climb aboard, Margaret and John find that little has changed, other than a few new, curious faces among the shipmates gawking at them, wondering who the visitors are. No doubt, as soon as the rowers climb up on deck, news of their nuptials will reach every nook and cranny of the ship.

After greeting Gareth and Samuel Teague, the navigator, John and Margaret head to Jope's cabin. They sit at the table and nibble at the biscuits and cheese laid out for them. Jope arrives in good time, takes off his leather overcoat, lays it on the bed, and joins them.

They start making small talk to catch up on what has happened in the year that has passed.

Much of it is mundane news. Mary and the children are well. She sends her greetings. In James City, Governor Harvey continues to annoy the wealthy planters who keep insisting that he can't go off half-cocked and pass edicts without their consent. John shares more details about his new trade. Jope is surprised that, unlike in England, he and Michael let the hogs run wild in the forest.

"No one wants to build fences strong enough to keep them from rooting in the fields," John explains. "Since tobacco requires new land every year or so, the boundaries have to be moved, and it's easier with the snake fences."

Jope doesn't fully understand and turns the conversation to why his guests want to get married. When he realizes that Margaret is not with child, he is even more pleased. She and John have come together on their own. There are so many ways in which their union makes sense, both practically and emotionally. For the first time in years, he feels confirmed in his destiny again, that rescuing John and Margaret was the right thing to do. Even if they are not head over heels in love, that may be a good thing: their affection will grow and deepen in time and maybe become that much stronger. It happened with him and Mary, two people as unlike as can be. Why not with them?

When there is a knock at the door, Jope checks who it is. Then he turns back to John and Margaret and asks, "Are you ready?"

Surprised, John and Margaret nod. They get up, unsure of what is about to happen, as Gareth and Samuel Teague enter warily, looking ill at ease.

The captain takes charge. He indicates a spot for John and Margaret to stand in the open area by the windows and takes his place before them, with Gareth and the navigator by his side.

Realizing that no one else knows what to expect, he starts out, "As you know, our faith doesn't hold with the extravagant display and vain marriage ceremony of the Anglicans, who are just Catholics in disguise. For us, marriage is a civil union between two people who come together in love and willingness to share each other's journey through life."

Looking at Margaret and John for a long moment, he seems to grow in stature. Then he intones solemnly, "Are you, John and Margaret, ready to enter into matrimony with each other, hold each other dear, help one another in times of happiness and periods of peril, and love each other as you stand before me?"

Margaret and John, holding hands, look at each other with glowing faces and nod as one. Then they turn to Jope together and say, "Yes."

He smiles and says, "Then, before these witnesses, I pronounce you husband and wife. May God bless your union and grant you a life that is happy, munificent, and fruitful."

To John and Margaret, their captain haloed by the afternoon sun pouring in through the windows appears like an otherworldly being, and they stand in silence, not wanting the moment to end. But when Jope holds out his arms, the newlyweds rush to him. He embraces them in a mighty hug and kisses them, John on the cheek, Margaret on the mouth. She feels his thick mustache more than his lips and hears him whisper for both their ears, "I couldn't be happier for you."

When he releases them, Gareth and Samuel Teague offer their congratulations. While they exchange hugs, handshakes, and kisses, Jope steals away. He soon returns with the cook and several helpers in tow. They are carrying trenchers filled with food, including slices of John's ham, filets of fish, and more biscuits. One of the sailors brings a large bowl filled with a savory stew. Another brings ewers filled with beer.

The five participants in the wedding ceremony sit down and enjoy the feast. They talk excitedly about mundane matters, but John notices that they treat him like an equal now—no more kidding him as a youngster, or stories about him as an awkward cabin boy. They regard him as a man.

There is only one moment that dampens the general mirth. When Gareth asks where Margaret and John are going to live, their faces fall, and they explain that their contracts of indenture require them to stay at their respective plantations.

"At least we know when we will gain our freedom, unlike some others who have no contract at all," John concludes, tight-lipped.

"You mean Anthony and his family," Jope asks, remembering their conversation from the previous year.

"Yes," John says, surprised. "I have been trying to help him, but his new master, John Upton, won't honor the promise he made when Anthony and his family were transferred to him."

Jope thinks for a moment. Then he asks, "Has Richard Bennett returned to Warrosquoake?"

"Yes," Margaret says. "The plantation lies farther to the east from us than some others, but he has come to Lawne's Creek Church once in a while." She adds, "Not for the service, of course, but to meet up with his constituents. He is the burgess for Warrosquoake now."

"Why don't you ask him to intercede with John Upton?" Jope says. "Surely he will verify the terms of the agreement he made with him." When John looks dubious, he continues, "Bennett comes from a family of devout Puritans. He won't shillyshally regarding Anthony's rightful claim."

Margaret chimes in: "I remember when he first came to Virginia and stayed with the Chews. He was always respectful to me, and he appreciated Anthony's loyalty, keeping the plantation going for the Bennett family after things fell apart following the massacre and the plague."

"It is worth a try," John agrees, looking more hopeful.

Teague changes the mood further by telling a funny story about being stuck in an unexpected coral reef for several days, and another round of beer restores everyone's high spirits.

By the time they finish there is little food left and the sun has set. Sounds of fiddle music waft through the window, the ship's crew taking the opportunity of a wedding ceremony aboard to dance and enjoy themselves after supper.

At a glance from Jope, Gareth and Teague offer their congratulations again and withdraw. While the cook's helpers return and clear the dishes, Jope lights a lantern and hangs it by the windows. He goes to the bed, picks up his coat, and puts it on.

Then he bows to the newlyweds with a flourish and says, "The cabin is yours for the night."

He is about to leave when Margaret asks, "But where will you sleep?"

"Don't worry. I'll find a suitable spot to bunk down," Jope assures her with a smile and departs, shutting the door behind him.

For the first time all day, Margaret and John are alone.

They look at each other for a long time in silence. Then Margaret goes to John and kisses him. When he responds, she is glad that his lips are soft and smooth, not surrounded by a scratchy mustache and beard.

She steps back, undoes her skirt, lets it drop to the floor, and draws her dress over her head. Arms at her side, except for her stockinged feet, she stands naked before John, inviting him to look at her.

It is not the first time John has seen a woman without her clothes. There have been a number of times in Havana and Port Royal when he accompanied his shipmates to local brothels. But it is entirely different with Margaret. There is no challenge, no attempt to seduce, only a frank invitation and acceptance. He examines her dark brown shoulders, full breasts, rounded belly, bushy-haired triangle below, and long legs. Her smooth skin reflecting the flickering light from the lantern takes his breath away.

He moves toward her to embrace her, but she holds up a hand and points at him. It takes him a moment to realize that he is still dressed and she wants him to strip off his clothes, too. He does so slowly, removing his coat and shirt, untying his leather belt and stepping out of his trousers until he faces her in his stockinged feet, just as bare.

Margaret lets her eyes roam over his dark brown body, sinewy limbs, muscular chest, stomach, and stirring manhood.

When Margaret finds his eyes again, they are glistening with desire. She holds out her hands to him, and John comes to her, sweeps her off her feet, carries her to the bed, and puts her down gently. Wrapped in each other's arms, they feel and caress each other's bodies and take in each other's scent. As their excitement mounts, their breathing becomes shorter.

At some point, Margaret guides him inside her and clutches his buttocks, squeezing them hard, encouraging him, urging him on until she feels a tearing pain and cries out. His release comes with a long groan of pleasure, and she starts to laugh, filled with unspeakable happiness.

When John draws back, confused, Margaret pulls him to her again and covers his face with kisses.

For the rest of the night they continue to explore each other's bodies—merging again and again until finally, all their youthful vigor spent, they drift off to sleep.

* * *

When Margaret and John get up in the morning and walk arm in arm on deck, the air is fresh and balmy. Jope, Gareth, and a few other sailors are there already discussing repairs they want to make to the ship before heading out into the ocean.

Jope looks them over and, satisfied by what he sees, says, with a roguish cast to his eyes, "I see you slept well. Ready for breakfast?"

"Starving," John says happily.

"Me, too," Margaret adds.

Pleased, Jope nods to Gareth and heads back to his cabin with them to enjoy porridge and eggs.

After breakfast, when it is time to leave, Margaret and John receive a surprise. As they go out on the main deck, the crew has lined up in two rows, creating an aisle passage for them. The seamen start to clap in unison and do not stop until Margaret and John reach the railing of the ship and get ready to climb down the rope ladder into the boat waiting below to take them back to Sheppard's plantation.

Everyone is so elated by the joyful occasion that, when they say their various good-byes, it crosses no one's mind—not Jope's, not John's, not Margaret's—that it is the last time they will see each other.

13

TRICKERY

Early May 1631

The positive atmosphere engendered by John and Margaret's wedding lingers on the *White Lion* for several weeks. There seems to be no grousing by any of the crew about courting ill fortune because a woman spent the night aboard. The winds that usually blow offshore in Carolina and Florida are favorable, allowing Samuel Teague to chart a direct southern and western course that skirts the Bahamas and heads straightaway for Cuba. During the trip, Gareth drills the new sailors in the captain's special way of raiding Spanish galleons when sailing in consort with another marauding vessel. By the time the *White Lion* reaches Havana, Jope is confident that ship and crew are battle ready.

On the second night in port, he meets a young Englishman in a dockside tavern. Roland Middleton, captain of the *Triton*, has a pleasant manner and light brown beard that hasn't entirely filled in yet. Newly commissioned in the Earl of Warwick's fleet, he seems unsure of himself. Jope attributes his nervousness to his lack of experience as a ship's commander, although he has been to sea for some time and has participated in several privateering raids. His hunch is borne out when he suggests sailing in consort, and Middleton relaxes right away, happy to team up with a seasoned buccaneer. Teague checks out his navigator and reports that Thomas Gilfoy has significantly more experience than the fledgling captain. It is considered good practice to pair an old seadog with a commander still in his salad days, green around the edges, and Jope appreciates the wisdom of whoever is in charge of the Earl of Warwick's navy.

When they meet up again, Gilfoy proposes heading into the Gulf of Mexico and lying in wait near the Yucatan Peninsula, where the major sea-lanes from the Spanish territories to the south converge and create a bottleneck. It is a sound plan. Jope and Teague continue to be impressed. They would have suggested the same plan.

Both ships take on extra provisions to be able to spend a longer time at sea without resupplying. Then they set sail, with the *White Lion* leading the way. The weather couldn't be better: clear skies, hot temperatures, and gentle, cooling breezes from the east.

Within days, they catch sight of a ship bearing the Spanish flag. It is a large merchant vessel, not a war galleon, and rides low in the water, indicating a hold filled with cargo—a promising target. As they unfurl all of their sails and pick up speed, Jope feels the thrill of the hunt again. How he has missed the creaking boards under his feet, the plumes of water crashing over the foredeck from the bow cutting through the waves, sending salty spray across the foredeck.

With the wind at their back and their ships lighter and swifter, they soon close in on their prey.

When the Spanish ship hoists the white flag of surrender, the *White Lion* smoothly moves between the merchant vessel and the *Triton.* Jope watches as sailors lower the pinnace and, after the boarding crew led by Gareth climbs down after it over the railing, casts off. But when he squints up to the crow's nest and his lookout, he sees the young man frantically waving his arms. Jope suddenly has a sick feeling in his gut. Peering across the gap, he realizes that the Spanish ship has a tarp hanging over the side near the front hull, covering the name. The men appearing at the railing don't look like Spaniards at all. None of them wear breastplates or Capitano hats.

When the Spanish ship opens its gun ports, cannon muzzles thrust out and aimed at the *White Lion*, there are desperate cries from the pinnace: "Go back, it's a trap! We've been tricked!"

From the lee side come frenzied shouts as well: "The *Triton* is aiming its cannons at us!"

Suddenly, loud shots issue from the ships on either side, their volleys crossing in front of the *White Lion's* bow, raising tall columns of water in the ocean.

Realizing he is trapped, Jope watches helplessly as the Spanish ship strikes its yellow and red standard, along with the white flag, and runs the British Union Jack up the mast to take their place.

From the *Triton*, a familiar voice bellows, "Ye might as well surrender, John, by God's nails!"

Looking across the gap, Jope makes out the singular figure of Daniel Elfrith at the rail of the quarterdeck. The young captain stands in back of him like an underling.

Jope's mind races as he considers his options. Elfrith must have stolen aboard before they left Havana and hidden below deck until now. This was a carefully planned ambush. Even if he manages to get away without being blown to pieces in the broadside crossfire, he'd be abandoning his men in the pinnace.

It is too late to escape anyway. Sailors from the *Triton* toss grappling hooks and swing across to board the *White Lion*. Some of his own crew descend by rope from the lower spars on the masts, men who have sailed with him for less than two years. When they reach the deck, they advance on his loyal shipmen. It takes a moment for Jope's men to realize that they are under attack from traitors in their midst and start to fight back. Gareth and the sailors from the pinnace climb over the railing and join them, but they are soon outnumbered.

A handful of the mutineers rush toward the stairs to the quarterdeck, with pistols drawn. Ambrose, one of Jope's oldest crewmen, blindsides their leader with a swinging cutlass. The blade hacks into the shoulder of the bearded lout with a scar on his cheek and blood gushes from the wound as he howls in pain. There is a gunshot, and Ambrose, his head knocked back, crumples to the deck.

Jope springs forward and shouts to the men below, "Stop fighting! Do not resist. Lay down your weapons! There is no need for further bloodshed!"

He has to bellow several times before his men comply. The sailors from the other ships start to disarm them and herd them around the mast of the main deck.

By then, the mutineers have climbed up the stairs and advance on Jope. Among the handful of men aiming their pistols at him is a young lug with a face like a weasel, and a bald ruffian with eyes shining like black coals.

"Time to surrender, Captain. I will have your sword," says the ferretlike man.

Jope answers contemptuously, "I will not bow to you."

"Then surrender to me," comes a coarse voice from behind him, along with the smell of sour breath.

Jope wheels around and recognizes Captain Bullard, the vile brute who is Elfrith's crony. The last time Jope encountered Bullard was some years back in Havana when they tussled in a dark alley because the lout tried to strike John, but Jope would recognize the flickering madness in his eyes anywhere. He must have climbed up the back of the ship to ambush him from behind.

"I will give my sword to none but Captain Elfrith," Jope says with as much dignity as he can muster.

"You're in no position to dictate terms," Bullard challenges.

He nods to the others, and they grab Jope, immobilizing his arms, and bind his wrists behind him with ropes.

When he is secured, Bullard steps up to him and says, "You certainly won't be needing this anymore," and rips the pearl drop from his ear.

The searing pain jolts Jope, and he reels for a moment in shock. As the men at his side steady him, he feels blood running down the side of his face into his beard.

Bullard pulls the sword from the sheath at Jope's belt and puts the blade under his chin. "You're mine now. You think that little black bastard is better than me? I have a mind to sail to James City after we're done with you and take care of him . . . and his black strumpet."

Jope's eyes blaze with hatred and his muscles bulge as he tries to tear himself free, but to no avail.

Smiling venomously, Bullard continues, "Aye, think I'll get a good taste of her before I cut her throat!"

"That's enough, Raymond. By God's blood, we are not barbarians!" Elfrith's booming voice comes from the stairs. He stands holding onto the railing, wheezing from the exertion of climbing the rope ladder to the *White Lion* and the stairs to the quarterdeck.

Bullard's eyes become pinpoints, but he pulls back and lowers the sword.

When he has recovered, Elfrith walks up to Jope. "Well, John, you're in quite a pickle. Will you promise to behave and not stir up any trouble?"

After a moment's reflection, Jope nods and says, "Yes." Tilting his head toward Bullard, he adds, "But if he threatens my children again, I will kill him."

"I don't trust the bastard," Bullard says, scowling. "We should finish him off now."

Elfrith holds up his hand, silencing him. "The captain is a man of his word, a gentleman." He turns to the sailors holding Jope. "Unbind him and get him a towel to staunch the bleeding. Then bring him to my cabin." Raising his voice, he barks to the others, "Secure his men, but make no reprisals!"

When the sailors have removed the ropes, Jope rubs his wrists to restore the flow of blood to his hands. Looking up, he sees Bullard grin. The ruffian's eyes glimmer with such malevolent hatred that it sends a shiver down Jope's spine.

As Bullard walks past Jope he hisses under his breath, "When I look up your black hussy, I'll make her squeal like a pig!"

In an instant, Jope snatches the dagger from the belt of the sailor next to him, leaps after Bullard, and before anyone can stop him, slashes straight across his throat.

For a moment nothing happens. Bullard stands still, the outline of his body slightly askew. Then a small gurgling sound escapes him, and he crumples to the deck. His body starts to twitch and shudder uncontrollably, and his eyes dart about in a desperate frenzy of disbelief as his lifeblood seeps away. Everyone watches in shock, rooted to the spot. Bullard's death throes seem to take forever until, at last, after a final tremor and rattle, he lies still.

Elfrith is the first to move. He snatches the pistol from his belt and cuffs Jope across the back of his head with the wooden handle. The captain falls unconscious to the deck next to his victim, the bloody knife lying between them.

Looming over him, Elfrith shakes his head and says with regret, "Wish you hadn't done that, John." He motions to the other men on the deck. "Take him to the brig and put him in irons." Gesturing toward Bullard, he adds, "And get him ready for burial."

Then he stalks off without a glance at his dead accomplice.

* * *

Jope awakens with a splitting headache and his ear throbbing. He groans and tries to feel his head, but his manacled hands are attached to a long, heavy chain, bolted to the floor. He is lying in a large cage enclosed by thick, wooden bars, dimly lit by a lantern. There is a dank stench of urine and vomit.

As he realizes that he is in the brig of a ship—not his own—he hears a voice. "He is awake."

Immediately, two men come and help him sit up. He recognizes Gareth and Samuel Teague. Their hands are not cuffed.

"Where are we?" Jope asks groggily.

"On the *Triton*," Gareth answers. "The rest of our crew—the ones who are still with us—are being kept on board the *White Lion*."

"So far, they've not been ill-treated," Teague says.

It all comes back to Jope in a rush—the ambush, Elfrith, Bullard. He takes a moment to orient himself and listens carefully. There is no sound of lapping waves. The creaking ship is not moving forward, just rising and falling, bobbing on the ocean waves.

"I don't know how much time we have and what they plan to do with us," Jope says with urgency. "But if any of us get out of this predicament alive, be sure to do what we talked about in Portsmouth."

Gareth starts to protest, but the hinged door from the deck above bangs open, and a man shaped like a large tub comes waddling down the wooden stairs. It is Elfrith, followed by four burly, glowering sailors. He walks up to the bars and peers inside.

"Ah, you've come to, and none the worse for wear, by God's nails," he says. "I had to whack you hard, but you've always had a thick skull. Perhaps now you'll come to your senses." He gestures to the sailors. "Bring him."

The men unlock the door to the brig and stand back. Jope has never seen them before, or the ones who stand back, pistols drawn, glowering at Gareth and Teague. After unbolting the chain from his manacles, two brawny lads grab him roughly under the shoulders and propel him forward. Jope falters at first, but by the time they climb the stairs, he has found his footing. Another flight up, and they emerge on the main deck. As they head toward the captain's cabin, every crewman they pass glares at Jope with hatred. A few even spit at him. It does not surprise him. Although he can't imagine them caring much for Bullard, who was no better than a beast, Jope killed one of their own.

When they get to the captain's quarters, they push Jope down in a chair by the table and position themselves by his side. The cabin looks much like his own on the *White Lion*, but without the altar and books.

Elfrith arrives and takes a chair opposite Jope. He waves to the guards and says, "You can go." When they start to object, he adds, "Don't worry. He's in handcuffs, and he won't do anything foolish while we have his men. Will you, John?"

Jope shakes his head, and the sailors reluctantly depart.

When they have closed the door, Elfrith sighs. "You have caused quite a commotion, John."

Instantly, Jope's eyes blaze with fury. "He threatened my ward—after I warned him!"

Elfrith holds up his beefy hands. "I know. I know. Never could understand why those two blackamoors mean so much to you. I'll admit, Bullard could be a menace. But here's my problem, besides what to do with you. He coveted your ship, and now that he's gone, there's no one to captain it."

Jope hears the implication in Elfrith's words and responds like someone with nothing to lose. "Well, then, all I can say is, 'I hope the sharks feast on him.' The thought of that bastard at the helm of my ship turns my stomach."

Elfrith gives him an exasperated glance. "The Earl of Warwick doesn't want the *White Lion* under his banner. It would raise awkward questions. No doubt your crafty brother would bring a lawsuit against him, and Rich would have to explain why he had an English subject killed. Trying to justify his actions would make him a laughingstock among his important friends and enemies—the man with the largest navy in England made a fool of by the Flying Dutchman! Warwick wants you bloody gone—not done away with for good, but definitely taken off the map."

When his face takes on a calculating expression, Jope realizes that Elfrith is in a quandary—the fat-kidneyed captain doesn't know what to do with him. He laughs at the absurdity of the situation.

Elfrith flares up in anger, "Zooterkins, I don't think you realize the gravity of your situation!"

"Oh, but I do, Daniel, I do. It's the irony of it all that amuses me. If you'd waited another season or two, you'd have been rid of me anyway. My eyesight has been failing for some time. I can't make out the wart on your nose, even though I know it's there."

Elfrith leans forward, squinting, and notes the filmy patches crowding Jope's pupils. Their milky blue color almost matches Jope's irises. Realization dawns on Elfrith's face, replaced briefly by pity. With his fleshy jowls, he looks like a despondent bloodhound.

Jope feverishly searches his mind for a way out and decides to be bold. "I have a proposal for you. Let Gareth, my second-in-command, take my place as captain of the *White Lion.* I will send him home with a letter to Joseph telling him to use the ship as a merchant vessel in the East Indies. That will satisfy Warwick. Take what munitions off the ship you will and let her go with the men who want to go with Gareth and Teague."

Elfrith runs his fingers through his greasy hair. He gets up and walks around the cabin, stopping several times to cast cunning glances at his captive. Finally, he comes to a halt and leans on the back of his chair. "That is actually not a bad plan, by God's nails," he says. "But what do I do with you, John?"

Looking at him steadily, Jope says, "You can do with me what you will. I know I can't go back to England." He tries to raise a hand, but the manacles won't allow it. "I ask only two favors."

Elfrith scoffs. "You're hardly in a position to ask for anything."

Jope continues as if he hasn't spoken. "Whatever you decide to do with me, leave my wards in Virginia alone. And make sure my wife, Mary, knows I'm gone for sure. Believe me, that will take some persuading."

Eyeing him shrewdly, Elfrith says, "It would be so easy to just throw you to the sharks and be done with it, but I owe you. You saved my hide in Virginia, and I am obliged to repay the favor."

Jope holds his breath, like a prisoner before a judge waiting for the verdict.

"Bullard's crew is out for blood, though." Elfrith's hangdog expression is tinged with regret. "I've got to give them something— at least an eye or a hand."

14
REPERCUSSIONS
Winter 1631–Late Fall 1632

It turns out that approaching Richard Bennett for help with indenture contracts for Anthony and his family is easier than John anticipated. Bennett shows up at a Lawne's Creek Church service one
Sunday soon after being appointed commissioner for Warrosquoake.
As a burgess with official duties, he tries to carry himself with the
dignity befitting his new role. But his youth is still in evidence—his
light brown beard is sparse, and the occasional glint in his eyes belies
his reputation as merely a serious-minded Puritan leader.

When Margaret and John approach him, he seems genuinely
pleased to see them. They congratulate him on his new appointment, and he asks after their well-being. At the mention of Anthony's
name, he says with some regret, "Now that my landholdings are
growing, I could use him. I was a fool to let him go."

He listens carefully to John making a case for his friend and
takes only a moment to think before he says, "I will be happy to
speak on Anthony's behalf. His cause is just, and it is the right thing
to do."

The following Sunday, Bennett is not in attendance, but Anthony
finds John right away. He is so excited that the words tumble from

his mouth like raindrops during a summer shower. Bennett came for a visit during the week. The following day, John Upton took Anthony aside and told him he remembered the conversation they'd had after all and would draft the appropriate indenture documents anon. Upton's eye had twitched and he did not look happy. Anthony affected surprise and gratitude without a hint that he had anything to do with Upton's change of heart. Margaret sneaks a glance at the plantation owner on the other side of the churchyard, seemingly immersed in conversation with John Uty. He does not look in their direction.

"Let me read the documents before you sign," John counsels.

When he gets a look at them two weeks later, it turns out that Upton has indentured Anthony and his family for another fifteen years, claiming time lost due to the children to justify the additional stint. It isn't a fair settlement at all, and John, outraged, wants to continue negotiating, but Anthony is content, his freedom assured.

* * *

The remainder of the year passes with minor victories for some and heartbreak for others—on both sides of the Atlantic Ocean.

Margaret and John's relationship deepens even though they live apart for most of the week. As the weather gets warmer, they spend many a Sunday afternoon in the forest, taking their pleasure on the soft ground, cushioned by leaves and pine needles. Margaret usually returns to her homestead alone with berries, herbs, or mushrooms in her basket to cover their assignations, but she fools no one. She always emanates a special luminescence after she's been with John.

The protective measures Katherine recommended work well. In late August, she and Margaret, now best of friends, collect enough wild carrot seeds and pennyroyal flowers to last them both for the next year, and then some.

* * *

The same month on the other side of the Atlantic Ocean, Gareth arrives by coach at Jope's estate in Tavistock. Following the captain's instructions to the letter, he stopped first at Sir John Glanville's mansion.

After Gareth gave his account of Jope's demise, Glanville looked at him for a long time. Then he asked, "Did the Earl of Warwick have a hand in any of this?"

Jope had warned Gareth that his wife's uncle was sharp as the point of a dagger but to stick to his story no matter what, so he said, feigning surprise, "No. What would make you think that?"

If Glanville seemed dissatisfied with his answer, he gave no indication. Gareth didn't even have to ask him to come along to offer emotional support to his niece when he would deliver the bitter news. He suggested it himself and followed him in his own carriage.

As they walk to the front door together, Gareth feels like turning back. He has met Mary only a few times but never had a long conversation with her. A servant answers their knock and shows them into the drawing room, where Mary is waiting for them, her body tense and her face unnaturally pale.

Without preamble, she says, "He's gone, isn't he?"

When Gareth nods, her hands fly to her mouth and an anguished moan issues from her throat. She starts to sway and Glanville rushes to her side. He leads her to the sofa and sits down next to her, holding her hands in his. Gareth stands awkwardly, unsure what to do next, until Glanville gestures to the chair opposite. By the time he sits down, Mary has managed to get control of herself.

"Tell me what happened," she says bravely.

Gareth delivers the fabrication Jope concocted—that he was struck by an errant bullet during a raid on a Spanish galleon. When the wound in his chest started to fester, the ship's surgeon tried everything he could to save him, but to no avail. The captain died three days later, and they buried him at sea.

Mary hangs on every word coming from his lips and keeps shaking her head as if refusing to believe what she hears. Gareth takes out a small box, opens it, and hands it to her. When Mary sees the pearl drop inside, her eyes widen in shock. Gareth forces himself to hold her stare, hating himself for uttering the lie Jope insisted he tell: "He died with his name on your lips."

Instantly, Mary bursts into tears and buries her head in her uncle's chest, sobbing. Glanville draws her close to him and holds her until her weeping subsides.

Gareth bears witness helplessly. When Glanville gives him a slight nod, he gets up and says softly, "I am very sorry, Mary. I wish there were something I could do." She looks up with tear-stained eyes, the bulging veins in her forehead distorting her beauty.

Sighing, he says, "It is time for me to take my leave."

Impulsively, she clutches his hand and kisses it, refusing to let go as if she could fend off the truth so long as she holds on. In the end, she moans softly, releases him, and says, "May God go with you, Gareth, and protect you."

A spasm of pain doubles her over, and Glanville takes her in his arms, letting her cry against his shoulder, stroking her blond tresses gently like a child's. He nods again to Gareth, dismissing him.

As he steps into the entry hall, Gareth hears keening from the kitchen where the servants are mourning their master. He feels like he is stealing away like a thief, responsible for robbing Mary of her happiness and causing her unbearable grief. Passing a doorway, he finds a young girl looking up at him with large, uncomprehending blue eyes. He realizes that it is Jope's daughter, Joane. The resemblance to her father nearly breaks his heart.

When he hurries outside, the air is balmy and it irritates him. He would prefer thunder and rain to match his black mood. Climbing into the hired carriage, he directs the driver to the mansion of Joseph

Jope. Along the way, Gareth fingers the letter in his pocket, dictated to him by the captain. It names Gareth captain of the *White Lion*, sets forth why the ship is no longer welcome in Caribbean waters, and suggests that it join the fleet of merchant vessels in the East Indies instead. He hopes the missive will suffice and convince the captain's older brother without further explanation to let Gareth keep his command.

* * *

In London at his house in Holborn, the Earl of Warwick has Alfred pour him a glass of his best wine when he receives news of the successful capture and death of the Flying Dutchman. Captain Elfrith has sent a letter with a westbound English merchant ship. Reading it, Warwick grunts with satisfaction and is surprised when he feels a pang of sorrow. Now that Captain Jope is no longer a thorn in his flesh, he can admit to himself that he actually liked the man. However, his brief self-reflection does not extend to shouldering any blame for their enmity, even though he initiated it by breaking his promise to protect the African children for Jope.

Warwick allows himself another sip to celebrate. Then he turns his mind to more pressing concerns. The success of Providence Island has hit a snag with many of the settlers complaining about the draconian regulations imposed by Governor Bell on behalf of the company. It will take considerable diplomacy and probably more money to appease them and put the enterprise back on course to create a thriving Puritan commonwealth. In the meantime, Rich also wants to obtain a patent from the king for a new colony in Connecticut. Then there is the mounting conflict with an influential member on the board of the Massachusetts Bay Company. Above all, he must continue quietly to fan opposition to Charles's foolhardy policies whenever possible.

As Warwick takes another sip, he relishes the feeling of being a man of power and influence. He smacks his lips like the loudmouthed, fat captain and laughs when Alfred frowns in surprise at his moment of juvenile audacity. Rich has earned it. He deserves it. Like few other men, he is in a position to right the English ship of state in its battle against the hated Spanish, found an empire based on the True Religion, and bring prosperity to his family and friends.

Perhaps it is time to commission Anthony van Dyck, the newly acclaimed Dutch court painter, to do a portrait of him.

* * *

As Margaret and John get ready for the coming winter, they grow closer to Katherine and Michael. John is determined to play a greater role in his second hog killing. In the meantime, they enjoy hearing the stories of ongoing political squabbling in James City. It is big news when John Harvey bows to the inevitable and officially acknowledges that the Governor's Council and General Assembly make the decisions for the colony. He must submit his proposals for a vote and abide by their pronouncements.

Of course, everyone understands that his acknowledgment doesn't guarantee Harvey will keep his promise. No doubt, he will continue to do things on his own whenever possible and work behind the scenes to get his way. Harvey has already managed to divide the Governor's Council and burgesses in the General Assembly into factions supporting and opposing him, leading to frequent, acrimonious debates. Prominent members working against him include Richard Stephens, George Menefie, John Uty, Richard Bennett, and Francis Pott. As a result, heated discussions regarding Harvey's abuses of power—real and purported—predominate conversations before and after church.

Margaret is not surprised to hear that John Chew belongs to the pro-Harvey contingent, even though she remembers the governor having a roving eye for Mrs. Chew when he came for supper at the merchant's house. Harvey can charm people as quickly as repel them. Still, little of the bickering makes sense to Margaret, and she is happy that none of it affects her directly.

She and John look forward to Captain Jope's next visit. Margaret hopes that he will come in the spring but knows from past experience that it may take longer.

15

JOPE

The Miskito Coast—1633

It may be the middle of winter, but Captain Jope suffers from the relentless humidity. Lying in a hammock strung between two trees and fanning himself with a palm frond helps only a little. It was worse in the summer and fall when daily rains soaked everything. He misses the cool ocean breezes aboard ship.

He swats a mosquito that has landed on his shoulder with the stump that is his right arm, which he misses badly. Although it is all but healed, after they hacked off his hand on the *Triton* with everyone watching, he keeps forgetting how useless it can be. Sometimes he reaches out to grasp something before remembering he no longer has fingers there. At other times, he experiences pain in his digits long gone as if they were phantom appendages.

A dark-skinned Indian girl brings him a gourd filled with fresh water. She is not much older than Margaret was when he rescued her. But unlike the slender, long-limbed African girl, this one looks like her mother and the rest of her tribe, shorter and squat. Still, she has a beauty all her own, and her disposition is sweet and kind. Jope takes two big gulps, emptying the vessel, and hands it back, thanking her with one of the handful of words and phrases he has learned of her language. She smiles and heads back to the nearby hut.

It has been nearly six months since Elfrith abandoned him to his fate on the sandy shore of the Central American mainland with nothing but a wineskin filled with drinking water, some biscuits, and a dagger hidden in his leather boot.

"I'm sorry, John. I wish I could do better," the fat tub of lard had said and made as if to wipe a tear from his grizzled face.

For a moment Jope had wanted to laugh out loud and embarrass him, but he remembered that he owed his life to Elfrith's sentimental streak, and he wasn't safe yet. Anyone else would have put a bullet in his head and tossed him overboard without a second thought. So, without saying good-bye, Jope had turned his back on Elfrith and started to trudge toward the line of coconut trees and dense greenery.

Much of that land, he discovered, was impenetrable mangrove jungle, so he kept to the edge of a large river where the forest lining the shore was less dense. He found some fruits on the ground—the Miskito Indians he met later call them "papaya"—took the risk, and bit into one. It tasted sweeter than anything he had ever eaten, and he experienced no ill aftereffects. So many of the plants and animals he encountered were unfamiliar—flocks of squawking parrots, chattering monkeys, and a giant, horselike, dark brown beast with a curved snout. Beset by sandflies and mosquitoes, he trudged on in the unbearable heat. At night he hardly slept, keeping his dagger at the ready.

Three days later, when he saw a group of Miskito Indians paddling their canoes downriver, he thought he was hallucinating. But when he shouted and waved his arms, they came ashore. Fascinated by his towering height, blond hair and beard, and blue eyes, they took him along on their fishing expedition. One of the younger men gathered some leaves and plants Jope had never seen and made a poultice for his oozing, cauterized stump. It was a foul-smelling concoction, but it worked and the wound began to heal. They also gathered red berries and smeared them all over him and themselves to keep the flies away. That remedy worked, too.

When they returned to their village farther inland, the older men engaged in an animated discussion, which Jope assumed was about him and would seal his fate, even though he didn't understand a word. From time to time, some of them would come and look at him curiously and with some sense of awe. In the end, they took him into their tribe.

Since then, he has tried to make himself useful. The big opportunity came when another tribe conducted a raid in the late afternoon. Jope gutted one attacker with his dagger and brained another with his stump. When he rose to his full height, his mere appearance struck fear in the assailants. They turned and ran into the jungle.

As a reward, the woman whose husband was killed during the battle invited him into her hut, and Jope has lived with her and her daughter ever since.

The Miskito have surprised him. They are kind and generous, smile and laugh easily, yet they are fierce fighters. They hunt, fish, collect berries, and gather roots diligently in the cooler early morning hours, then spend the steamy afternoons resting in swaying hammocks until sundown.

Jope hears a toucan calling and chattering high up in a tree, but when he squints at the canopy overhead, all he sees is a dim, filmy blend of greens and browns. He worries that, if his eyesight deteriorates, he won't be able to find his way on the jungle trails without help, unable to avoid venomous snakes, fire ants, and poisonous leaves on his own.

He is not confused about his prospects. He knows he will live out his days here among the Miskitos. As a Calvinist he does not believe in redemption—his fate is preordained—and he can no longer, in good faith, believe that he is one of the elect. But when he thinks of Margaret and John and his decision to rescue them, he fervently hopes that his act signified a more exalted status. Few others would have made that choice and subsequent commitment to protect and nurture them.

He wonders about Mary and his children and tells himself that they are well. He hopes that, at her uncle's urging, she has remarried and is building a new life for herself. Perhaps in time, she will find happiness without him. Although he misses her, it becomes harder to conjure up her image in his mind beyond her blond hair, the color of her eyes, and occasional flashes of her quizzical expression. It pains him that he can't picture his two children, Joana and John Jr., at all.

Margaret and John, on the other hand, are indelibly imprinted in his memories, more than anyone else he has met in his life. It gives him daily comfort to think of them, both when he first met them on the *San Juan Bautista* and, more recently, when he married them. Although he no longer plays a role in their destiny, he believes with all his heart that the concatenation of events he started on the Spanish slaver will matter long after they're all gone.

Jope often muses that, when he dies and the Indians bury him, no one from his earlier life will know where to visit his grave. On days when he feels despair creeping in on him, he wonders if anyone will remember him at all.

MONHEGAN
7/95

PART TWO

ENDINGS AND BEGINNINGS

16
NEW ARRIVALS
Virginia—1633

Following Governor Harvey's call for people to come to Virginia from England, it doesn't take long for newcomers to arrive in droves. The vast majority of the immigrants are impoverished young men. A few, encouraged by Harvey's special recruitment, bring useful skills with them—glassmaking, tanning, pottery, brewing. Others who hail from the countryside and know about growing crops and raising farm animals adjust quickly to the different conditions and circumstances of their new home. But most are unskilled and uneducated menials—poor, city-bred laborers—who have nothing to trade on but the brute strength of their bodies.

The influx does not affect Margaret and John directly, although some arrivals swell the ranks of the other plantations on the south side of the James River. The most immediate effect is that Lieutenant Sheppard gets called away to help in the fight against Indians who resist the newcomers as they push farther inland. As building begins on the six-mile palisade wall from the mouth of Queen's Creek near the York River to Archer Hope's Creek east of James City, more clashes take place. They occur mostly between Indians and the surveyors who lay out the lines of demarcation before the start of construction.

Lieutenant Sheppard usually returns from his campaigns tired and irritated. The struggle with the Indians never seems to end, and while he gets paid well for his services to the colony, he hates the disjointed approach to keeping the "heathen savages" in check.

"We're just sprinkling drops of water on a smoldering fire when it flares up. We should be dousing it for good," he complains when the subject arises.

But there are no easy solutions when Governor Harvey and his council officially promote friendly relations with the tribes. No one wants an all-out war. The colonists are in no position to do that. As a result, Sheppard's attempts to punish Indian incursions with his militiamen inflict little damage. More often than not, the Indians fade into the forest after a sneak attack, and their villages are too well fortified to assault them with the small forces Sheppard commands.

So, the lieutenant returns home in a bad temper, and it takes him awhile to regain his more amiable disposition. He becomes a petty tyrant, finding fault with how Margaret, Jason, and the others have run the plantation in his absence. Confident that they all perform their jobs capably, they let him gripe and criticize, knowing that his ill humor will soon pass.

Despite his frequent absences and contrary to his carping, his goals of making the farm self-sufficient, ready to expand into a bigger enterprise, proceed forthwith. But instead of taking the next step and increasing his property holdings, as many other planters are doing, Sheppard has other plans.

One evening at supper, after returning from James City, he pulls a letter from his doublet and announces, "I just received news from England that my future wife will be leaving and arrive here by ship in late spring. We must get things ready and make her welcome."

He looks around the table to gauge everyone's reaction. If he has any doubts about the venture, he hides it well. After congratulating him, Margaret and the others recover, bombarding him with a flurry of questions: What is her name? Where is she from? How did this happen? How will things change at the farm?

Sheppard provides what answers he can. Priscilla is the youngest daughter of a gardener in the city of Gloucester near the Severn River about a hundred miles east of London. The lieutenant's uncle who lives in nearby Cheltenham and raised him acted as an intermediary and made all the travel arrangement. Unlike most other immigrants, who ship out from London or Plymouth, she will be embarking from Bristol across the channel from Wales. The ship is named, appropriately, the *Hopewell.*

Of course, there will be adjustments to the living arrangements at the house. Sheppard plans to have carpenters build an addition to the house.

Margaret has a difficult time going to sleep that night. While she welcomes another person helping around the house, she looks on Priscilla's arrival with trepidation. She can only hope that her new mistress won't be another Mrs. Chew or Frances Piersey Matthews— haughty, privileged women both, who treat their servants with disdain.

That Sunday, the news of the lieutenant's impending marriage is the talk of Lawne's Creek Church. From there word travels quickly to James City, upriver and downstream. For a while, wherever Sheppard goes, he has to endure good-natured teasing for giving up on bachelorhood.

When Margaret confides her worries about Priscilla to John, Katherine, and Michael at church, they try to calm her.

"You're older, more experienced," Michael reassures her.

"I remember how hard it was to get my bearing when I first came to Virginia," Katherine says. "Priscilla will be much too worried how strange everything is to give you a hard time."

"She'll be like a fish out of water and will have to depend on you," John adds, smiling. "You'll be her lifeline."

It pleases Margaret that he is in such good spirits lately. The last hog killing was another success. John applied all he had learned the previous year and performed like a seasoned hog butcher. The demand for salt pork in James City is as great as ever, and when he and Michael bring another barrel of hog meat to the market there, they sell it in no time. Margaret can always tell how good his week has been by the quality of their conjugal Sunday visits.

When Sheppard hires carpenters in anticipation of Priscilla's coming, he asks them to put an addition to his house with two extra bedrooms. He wants some privacy for him and his bride and room to grow for when they start their family. With the help of Jason, Paul, and Thomas, the carpenters also build a large barn so that the male workers have a place for themselves to gather and sleep. It is large enough to accommodate additional servants and field-workers in the future. Margaret will continue to stay at the main house, to cook and to perform her other household duties. She is excited about having her own place and bed. It will make for a welcome change from sleeping on the floor.

By the time the carpenters finish, the trees are budding and sprouting leaves, and it is time to plant a new crop of corn and tobacco. The day Margaret moves into Sheppard's old bedroom, cleared of all furnishings except a bed and straw mattress, is an exciting time. That Sunday, she proudly shows it off to John. He is impressed. At Ewens's plantation, he has a cot in one of the workers' quarters and no real privacy.

Little else changes. Margaret weeds her garden, removing the herbs and flowers that died during the winter, and puts in seeds for new ones. With the ground no longer frozen, she starts foraging in the forest again for mushrooms, tubers, and roots, and she and John resume their Sunday afternoon walks.

With the passing of March and Priscilla's imminent arrival, Sheppard becomes increasingly flustered. He acts as if he is on tenterhooks, tormented and unable to sit still for any length of time. He stares out the window toward the creek every afternoon after dinner, hoping for news of his bride. He has asked a militia friend to send him word as soon as the *Hopewell* makes anchor at Point Comfort and before the harbormaster grants the ship permission to travel upriver. He wants to be at the James City docks to meet Priscilla when she steps ashore. It amuses Margaret to see a grown man, a soldier no less, act skittish as a cat.

He has considered taking Margaret along to help facilitate the first encounter with his betrothed, but she wisely persuaded him otherwise.

"It is important that you meet Priscilla on your own," she told him. "I can serve you better by making sure everything is ready here at the plantation." She didn't tell him that she had an ulterior motive for staying behind. She has no interest in becoming Priscilla's maid.

In early April when word finally reaches Sheppard that the *Hopewell* has arrived at Point Comfort, he experiences a moment of blissful relief, followed immediately by another bout of anxiety. Like any trained military leader, he springs into action, shouting orders at Thomas and Paul to ready the boat for travel to James City. He considers putting on his red uniform, but at Margaret's suggestion wears his best doublet and coat instead. He does take his sword.

At the dock, Margaret wishes him good luck and watches him leave, sitting rigidly upright in the boat like a military commander, only to collapse as the impact of the momentous occasion threatens to overwhelm him. Then he sits up straight again. She has never seen him so excited and tense at the same time, not even before embarking on any of his military missions.

Thomas and Paul strain at the oars to pick up speed and quickly disappear behind the bend in the creek. They will take Sheppard across the river, where he will spend the night at the house of Elizabeth and Richard Stephens. Sheppard has become friendly with the merchant during meetings of the Governor's Council about how to deal with the Indians and defend the colony against outside attack. Although Stephens is nearly twenty years older, they get along well and share a mutual contempt for Governor Harvey and his offensive manners. Margaret imagines they will do everything they can to calm the young bridegroom.

As Margaret returns to the house, she checks once more that everything is ready. The newly built wooden bed in the larger of the two additional rooms has a soft mattress, linen sheets, and a quilted comforter Sheppard bought in James City. Margaret wonders if he and Priscilla will get married right away. With newcomers to Virginia, the Anglican minister in James City often suspends the requirement that bans be read for a fortnight before the actual wedding ceremony, as long as both parties are in agreement.

After two days pass, Margaret and Jason begin to worry that something untoward has happened. Did the *Hopewell* not arrive as promised? Was Priscilla not on the ship? Perhaps she became sick during the voyage and needs time to recover. It's not unusual for ocean travelers to take ill.

The next day is Sunday, and they decide to skip the service at Lawne's Creek Church in case the lieutenant and Priscilla arrive. After a quiet midday meal together, with nothing better to do, Jason heads for the mouth of the creek to see if they are coming. Margaret busies herself in the kitchen.

When John arrives, wearing his doublet with his pistol at his waist, she seems distracted. He kisses Margaret in greeting. "Is everything all right? I was worried when I didn't see you at church."

To his questioning glance at the house, she shakes her head and says, "It's been two days and there is no sign of them yet. Jason went to the river. I'm on my own."

Surprised, John says, "Do you want me to leave in case they come?"

Smiling, Margaret draws him close. "No, silly."

She kisses him tenderly and he responds with pleasure. It is the first time they have been alone at Sheppard's, and Margaret would like nothing more than to go with John to her room and to bed, but if the others returned, it could prove embarrassing. So they sit on the front porch, kissing and caressing each other. They look out over the newly seeded tobacco fields and enjoy the warm spring breeze filled with the pungent odor of the turned soil.

Suddenly, Jason crashes through the low undergrowth where the creek makes a turn.

"They're coming. They're coming," he shouts from afar and hurries toward them. He is so winded that he has to bend over to catch his breath. When he recovers, he gasps, "I took the path through the woods. They'll be here within minutes."

John says, "I should be going."

Margaret grasps his hand for support. "Of course not. You'll be meeting Priscilla soon anyway. Might as well be now."

The three walk to the dock to wait. Margaret and John hold hands and stare downstream.

Before long, the rowboat rounds the bend. As they approach, Margaret can make out the people in the boat—Thomas and Paul pulling at the oars with all their might, Lieutenant Sheppard, and a young woman sitting next to him. She is wearing a gray woolen cloak around her shoulders and a white cap on her head, signifying that they are married. Relieved, Margaret waves to them. When the lieutenant notices John standing beside her, he points and whispers to his bride.

Jason grabs the rope Thomas tosses him, pulls the bow close to the dock, and lashes it to one of the thick wooden uprights. Paul secures the oars and ties up the rear. When the boat is as stable as it will get, the young woman stands up awkwardly. Lieutenant Sheppard holds her by the waist to steady her. She wobbles until Margaret and John take her hands and help her up onto the dock.

"Thank you," she says, straightening her dress.

Her skin is pale white, like someone who hasn't spent much time outside, and her mouth is small, with thin lips. She reminds Margaret of a fawn, with hazel eyes that flicker with apprehension.

"You must be Margaret," she finally says, her voice soft and shy.

"Yes," Margaret replies, curtseying, "and this is my husband, John."

Bowing formally, John says, "Pleased to meet you."

Priscilla smiles timidly. "Robert told me about you. I didn't expect to meet you here today."

By then, Lieutenant Sheppard is standing beside her. "Glad you're here, John," he says, meaning it. "This, dear," he indicates his foreman, "is Jason."

Jason bows awkwardly. "Welcome to Sheppard's Landing."

Blushing, Priscilla says, "Thank you. You're all being so kind."

Sheppard takes his young wife by the arm. "Come. Let me show you your new home."

He leads her up the slope and into the house while Paul and Thomas haul a travel trunk from the boat and carry it after them. Jason follows with the lieutenant's sword.

John brings up the rear and collects his pistol from the porch. He turns to Margaret. "Perhaps I should go."

"Nonsense, husband," she says. "You'll stay for supper."

17

PRISCILLA
Virginia—1633

With the men at Sheppard's plantation occupying their own living and sleeping quarters, the atmosphere in the main house becomes calm and peaceful. Only mealtimes, when everyone sits together around the table in the living room, interrupt the quiet. After the blessing, as people start to eat, conversations often become animated and, occasionally, boisterous. Margaret likes the change in living arrangement, being able to spend the late evenings and nights by herself in a place of her own. She is glad that Sheppard and Priscilla get along well and seem to like each other.

A bit timid at first, Priscilla soon warms up to the easygoing camaraderie of people who work together closely and have known each other for several years. She soon overcomes her initial shyness and begins asking a myriad of questions. The men indulge her curiosity about her new surroundings and answer her inquiries patiently. As she settles in, any worries Margaret had about what kind of mistress she would be dissipate like morning fog. Although delicate and not suited for the most physically demanding tasks on the farm, Priscilla pitches in as best she can. She doesn't object to performing the most menial chores, such as cleaning out ashes from the hearth in the living room. Eager to learn, she treats Margaret like an older sister and listens carefully to her explanations regarding what needs to be done. Margaret introduces her to the household duties gradually, starting with the simpler tasks—washing laundry at the creek, feeding the chickens in the pen out back, and collecting eggs for breakfast.

In the kitchen, she shows Priscilla unfamiliar staples, such as corn, squash, and pumpkins, and teaches her how to cook over an open fire and bake biscuits, corn pones, and bread. Priscilla doesn't always catch on right away, and Margaret patiently goes over again what to do. She remembers when she came to Virginia herself, ill prepared for plantation life after two pampered years at an English manor, and she remains tolerant when Priscilla doesn't learn things quickly.

Margaret enjoys introducing Priscilla to new tasks and places. Seeing them through the eyes of a tenderfoot allows her to perceive them in a fresh light. Marveling at the tobacco shoots that Paul and Thomas transfer from the growing trays to the fields, Priscilla says, "They're so tiny."

Margaret comments, "Wait until they are big as a house."

When Priscilla accompanies her teacher to the forest to forage for mushrooms and herbs, all of the shrubs and trees amaze her—long-needle pines, hickory trees, cypresses, and dogwoods. The small leaves of the live oaks surprise her, too. She is used to larger ones from England. The first time she sees a raccoon in a tree, with its black-rimmed eyes and nimble fingers prying open a chestnut, she finds it adorable, and Margaret has to explain to her about the dangers of vermin. But when an opossum scuttles across the forest path in front of her, she jumps in fright and squeals, "A rat!" Amused, Margaret can't tell which is more scared, Priscilla or the creature that charges into the bushes for safety.

When Priscilla first lays eyes on Margaret's vegetable and herb garden, she responds with astonishment. "My mother grew a few carrots, onions, and herbs in the back of our cottage in England, but it was nothing like this bounty," she says. "I wish I'd spent more time with her. I don't know much about it."

There is a hint of anguish in her voice, and Margaret realizes she is homesick. "You'll learn quickly," she says kindly. "We have to depend on what we can grow ourselves here for the winter."

She wishes Priscilla knew more about gardening, but when she asks what she learned from her father, who took care of the parkland on the country estate of a baron, Priscilla becomes subdued. "I didn't go there very often," she says quietly.

Sometime later, when she feels more comfortable with Margaret, she confides that one day the oldest son of the baron cornered her in the study, pushed her against the wood-paneled wall, and forced his hand up her skirt. "He stank of liquor and garlic," she says, wrinkling her nose in disgust. "Fortunately, two servants came down the hall just then and startled him. Otherwise, I might not have been able to escape." Her face reddens with embarrassment. "After that, I made excuses when my father asked me to come along with him, even though it meant missing out on a good meal. I think he knew what had happened and was disappointed with me that I did not yield to the baron's son."

Priscilla gives a dismissive laugh, but Margaret can tell how much it still upsets her. She has come to recognize, by the apprehension in her eyes and her rapidly blinking eyelids, when Priscilla feels uncomfortable or troubled.

The mention of her assailant's rank breath takes Margaret back to the time a drunkard assaulted her on the riverbank near the Chew house, threw her to the ground, and tried to rape her. Although she fought back, she was saved from harm only because William, the head butler, who had been looking out for her, came to her aid. He rushed to her side and bashed the brute over the head with a thick branch cudgel, driving him off. She still gets angry remembering how helpless she felt at the hands of the foul-smelling ruffian.

She realizes that Priscilla left England for Virginia for more reasons than the easy lure of a new life.

Priscilla manages to fit in well with the surrounding community, whose social life revolves around the Sunday services at Lawne's

Creek Church. The planters' wives are happy to welcome a new young member into their gossip circle. The population on the south side of the James River keeps swelling, and the congregation fills the small church to capacity. Some of the servants have to stay outside and listen to the service through the open windows.

Notable among the newcomers are William Spencer and his family. He is a good ten years older than Lieutenant Sheppard. Weathered-looking, with the first traces of gray hair in his full beard, he has sharp, inquisitive eyes that gleam with a wealth of experience. In contrast, his wife, Alice, seems staid and conventional, with the long, drawn face of a hardworking Englishwoman. Their pretty nine-year-old daughter, Elizabeth, has long, yellow-blond hair and a friendly, outgoing manner. Spencer patented land next to Lawne's Creek three years earlier but didn't move there until this spring when Governor Harvey appointed the new tobacco inspector for Hogg Island and its environs.

John Uty's wife whispers to Priscilla that Spencer owes his job to the bickering between Governor Harvey and the planters over tobacco. Sir John, demanding that they grow other crops, such as wheat, rye, and rice, has insisted that the General Assembly limit annual tobacco cultivation to two thousand plants per laborer. In return, the burgesses passed a law requiring inferior tobacco to be burned. They don't want crops of inferior quality to damage Virginia's reputation abroad, undermining its competitiveness in the English and Dutch markets against the harvests from Cuba, Jamaica, and Barbados. Spencer's job is to determine and certify which tobacco makes the grade.

Like the other women, Priscilla prefers gossip about important people in James City and elsewhere to the ins and outs of legal matters and talk about money and tobacco sales. "What I can't comprehend is why everyone complains about Governor Harvey," she says innocently. "Why don't people like him?"

In the ensuing silence, some of the women become tight-lipped, and others respond with hollow laughter. Priscilla, realizing that she has stirred up a hornet's nest, blushes and says, "I didn't mean to put my foot in—"

"That's all right, dear," says Mistress Uty, patting her hand. "We're all friends here."

As the group breaks up to leave, she stays close to Priscilla and hisses in her ear, "The man is a villain, a vile creature!"

Her hostility surprises Priscilla. On the way home, she tells Margaret, "She made him sound like a monster. I can't believe he is really that bad."

Margaret doesn't know how to respond. "I met him only a few times, but that was nearly a decade ago when he was heading a commission to investigate the Virginia Company," she says. "He came to dinner at the Chews' residence, but all I can remember is his nasal voice, which could be annoying, and that he had an eye for the ladies."

It is more than the other women told Priscilla and keeps her wondering if the governor did more than flirt with one of them.

Two weeks later, Priscilla has the opportunity to see the man for herself when Sheppard receives an invitation to a festive gathering at the governor's mansion. Upon arrival across the river, the lieutenant and Priscilla take a stroll around James City for the second time since her arrival. Once again, the settlement—the courthouse, church, and shops—disappoint her. After living in England, even in a small town, it seems hopelessly provincial.

Her spirits rise, however, as soon as they arrive at the governor's mansion. The great room with its tall ceiling, lit by candles and wall sconces, is impressive. The local burgesses wearing velvet doublets of different colors and their wives preening in fancy dresses bedecked with pearls and gemstones outshine any gathering Priscilla has ever attended. She wishes her outfit and the gold necklace Lieutenant Sheppard gave her as a wedding present were more expensive looking.

Waiting in line to meet Governor Harvey, she feels ordinary and has an impulse to bolt, but it is too late. Lieutenant Sheppard leads her before Sir John and presents her.

As she curtsies, Harvey lets his eyes roam over her and says, "So, we finally get to meet the elusive Mrs. Sheppard. Your husband has been doing you no favors hiding you from us."

Priscilla blushes. "It is an honor to meet you, sir. Thank you for inviting us to your lovely home."

Harvey wags his finger at Sheppard and admonishes, "You really shouldn't keep such a jewel from us." Turning back to Priscilla, he gestures around the room gallantly. "Consider this as a welcome to you and to honor your presence among us."

Flustered, Priscilla stammers, "I—I don't know what to say."

Harvey smiles roguishly and gives Sheppard another glance. "If your husband permits, allow me to whisk you away for at least one dance tonight."

As Sheppard bows in courtesy, Priscilla recovers and says, "It would be my honor, sir."

"You will do very well here, my dear," Harvey says, nodding to indicate that the audience is over, and turns his attention to the couple next in line.

Priscilla and Sheppard move farther into the room, and the lieutenant takes two glasses of red wine from a servant and hands one to her. She sees John Upton and his wife, who tips her coifed head to her, and recognizes Richard and Elizabeth Stephens, at whose house she stayed when she and Sheppard got married. During the evening they meet other couples, who welcome her warmly. There are so many that she has a hard time remembering all their names.

When the butler announces the first dance, a galliard, couples move to the center of the room and form two lines. Priscilla and Sheppard watch from the side. To the lieutenant's untrained ear, the musicians are more refined than the players at the hog killing, but they strike up as lively a tune, and many burgesses and their wives perform their hops and leaps with vigor. At times, the tapping of their shoes on the wooden floor sounds like raindrops on forest leaves. Priscilla feels her feet twitch in rhythm and can't wait to join in. She and Sheppard participate in the next dance, a reel, and Priscilla performs so energetically that several men come up afterward and ask her to dance with them.

At some point, Harvey comes to collect on her promise. He is an adequate dancer, but what he lacks in physical grace, he makes up in attentiveness. Priscilla feels as if he has eyes only for her, spinning a magical web of fascination around her. Rarely has she felt such intense interest from a man she has just met. She doesn't know what to expect, but when the dance is over, Harvey merely bows and says, "Thank you, my dear," releasing her from the spell.

After that, she watches him surreptitiously. To her surprise, his eyes keep drifting to Elizabeth Stephens for much of the evening. Elizabeth doesn't return any of his furtive glances, but Priscilla is certain that Sir John is infatuated with her.

Although Sheppard doesn't dance as much as Priscilla, he is smitten with her, happy she is making such an excellent impression. On their way to Richard Stephens's home to spend the night, he hugs her close to him and murmurs endearments in her ear.

When they return to the plantation the following day, Priscilla tells Margaret everything that happened, including Harvey's interest in Elizabeth Stephens. "The governor is a very charming man," she says. "But now I understand why he isn't married. He is pining for another."

Margaret does not contradict Priscilla but keeps her own counsel. She is not convinced that Priscilla knows enough about the world to be sure of the true meaning of what she witnessed. Considering the not-so-hidden enmity between Harvey and Richard Stephens, the governor may have other ideas when he looks at the wife of his foe.

She receives confirmation regarding Priscilla's limited experience in relationships the first time since her arrival that Lieutenant Sheppard is called away on military matters. He returns a week later, irritable and gruff, as always, and takes out his foul mood on his wife. He criticizes her appearance and behavior. When he orders her to ready his pipe for smoking and she doesn't respond quickly enough, he scolds her. Margaret watches Priscilla blanch and feels sorry for her. Unaccustomed to his ways, Priscilla thinks it is her fault.

Sheppard barely settles down when he participates in another campaign. During his absence, Priscilla gradually recovers her good humor. But when he returns and acts as mean-spirited toward her as before, she becomes upset.

The next day she joins Margaret to gather kindling in the forest. "What have I done that Robert treats me so?" she complains. "Why doesn't he love me?"

Margaret points to a twig Priscilla is about to put in her basket. "Not that one—it will make too much smoke in the kitchen." Then she answers her: "It has nothing to do with you. Believe me, he is like that after every campaign."

"But he doesn't criticize you or Jason, or the others," Priscilla complains.

"He used to, and we just ignored him. Trust me, we have known him a lot longer than you. He always behaves like this when he comes back from battle. It's his way." She presses Priscilla's hand. "Give him a little time, and he'll become his normal self again."

"Are you sure?" Priscilla asks.

When Margaret nods, Priscilla seems relieved. She walks on, picking up more small branches.

At some point, she asks, "What exactly does Robert do when he is gone that makes him so ill-tempered?"

"He fights and kills Indians," Margaret says matter-of-factly. "It's dangerous, bloody work."

Priscilla stops and puts down her basket. "In England, I heard a lot of talk about the 'heathen savages.' Our minister warned me to be careful. He said they were lurking behind every tree in the woods and would kidnap or kill me. But in all the time I've been here, I haven't seen a single one. Are they really so bad?"

Margaret, having had both agreeable and harrowing experiences with Indians, considers what to tell her. She decides it is best to warn her, or Priscilla might do something foolish on her own that will get her in trouble. So, Margaret relates what happened during the massacre over a decade earlier at Warrosquoake Plantation, sparing her only the most gruesome details. Priscilla's eyes grow big as saucers, and her eyelids flutter like butterfly wings as Margaret tells her how the Indians slaughtered men, women, and children and burned all of the houses to the ground.

By the time Margaret concludes, "It happened up and down the James River, and more than three hundred people were killed," Priscilla is in tears.

"How did you survive?" she asks in a small voice.

Margaret vividly remembers the ferocious Indian warrior, his face contorted and covered in red paint raising his battle-ax overhead and ready to strike, looking down at her and then turning away. But she says, "I hid in the bushes until they were gone." To lighten the mood, she adds, "There was one good thing that came out of it all."

"What was that?"

"When we finally returned to the plantation, Lieutenant Sheppard arrived to build a fort and protect us. That's how I met him," she says, smiling. "I wouldn't be here otherwise."

Priscilla responds with a small, tentative smile of her own. Then, impulsively, she throws her arms around Margaret and says, "I am very glad about that."

Margaret feels touched and pats her on the back.

True to Margaret's words, Sheppard reverts to being a doting husband, acting like nothing untoward ever happened. Priscilla remains on edge for a little while longer but soon relaxes, trusting that everything is well again.

18

JOHN

Virginia—1633

Under normal circumstances, many of the things Priscilla blurts out and the way she asks questions would offend others, but she utters them in such a sweet, guileless manner that people do not hold it against her. The fact that they treat her like a young girl who doesn't know anything yet and lacks social graces doesn't seem to bother her. Even Lieutenant Sheppard, who feels embarrassed when he hears about her latest blunder, can't stay angry with her for long.

Witnessing Priscilla's missteps in her eagerness to please others and to satisfy her curiosity amuses Margaret, even when it affects her directly.

After one of John's Sunday afternoon visits, Priscilla takes her aside and says, "I approve of your choice of husband. He is so courteous, calm, and reasonable."

Margaret, who knows how Priscilla suffers from Sheppard's temper, receives the compliment graciously.

The week after the planters' wives invited Priscilla into their gossip circle at Lawne's Creek Church, she surprised everyone after the service by approaching Margaret and her friends. Unaware of the startled looks of Ann Uty, Margaret Upton, and Dorothy Spencer,

Priscilla nodded to John and asked Margaret politely, "Won't you introduce me to your friends?"

At first, the African men were formal and a bit awkward with her, not knowing what to say to the young wife of the lieutenant. But Priscilla charmed them, saying something personal to everyone. She complimented Anthony for his expertise with cattle and horses, asked Mary about her children, mentioned to Michael how much she had been enjoying his smoked pork and bacon, and praised Mathew as an expert fisherman. Her engaging manner put everyone at ease. By the time Priscilla turned to Katherine, the older woman had accepted her genuineness as real and gave her a welcoming hug, which surprised Priscilla and pleased her.

They all continued to chat comfortably together, laughing occasionally, and Margaret was happy that everyone got along.

Sitting next to each other on the boat ride home Priscilla said to her, "I like your friends. They are nice. I had no idea there'd be so many men and women with dark skin here. They don't seem any different from the rest of us."

Margaret looked at her startled, but didn't say anything.

Priscilla happily prattled on: "Until I met you and John, I never encountered anyone from Africa. Oh, I heard about blackamoors in England once in a while. They worked as sailors on ships that came into Bristol harbor, but none ever visited the town where I grew up."

"And what do you think of us?" Margaret asked pointedly.

Priscilla cuddled up to her. "Oh, I like you and your friends better than many of the people I've met here who look like me."

She said it so ingenuously that Margaret couldn't help but smile and indulge her.

But there are times when Priscilla's curiosity turns to nosiness and becomes annoying. One afternoon, she emerges from the kitchen and, holding up Margaret's pearl necklace, says, "Look what I found in the crevice behind the hearth!"

Margaret, who is planting herbs in the garden, rises quickly and extends her hand. "That belongs to me."

When Priscilla gives her a questioning look, she insists, "I wore it on my wedding day, but it gets in the way of work, so I've taken it off."

"Why not keep it in your room?"

Margaret shrugs. "I forgot, figuring it was in a safe spot."

Inspecting the intricate gold setting for the pearl, Priscilla says, "It is very pretty. Where did you get it? Did John give it to you?"

"No. It was a wedding present."

Priscilla's face falls and she pouts. "Was it . . . from Robert?" she asks in a soft voice. "He has never given me anything so beautiful and precious."

Margaret shakes her head, irritated at her foolish vanity.

Feeling relieved, Priscilla examines the necklace further. Suddenly, she exclaims. "It's from that captain who comes here from time to time and whisks you away to his pirate ship for a day and night! How romantic!"

At first, Margaret is stunned that Priscilla knows about Captain Jope until she realizes that Lieutenant Sheppard must have told her. "Yes," she admits. "He married John and me on his ship, and we spent our wedding night there."

"You must tell me all about it," Priscilla says eagerly.

"Some other time," Margaret says. "I want to get this planting done before it's time to get supper ready."

Realizing that she won't say anymore, Priscilla acquiesces. "I'll just put it back in its hiding place." She leans close to Margaret and whispers, "It will be our secret."

But while Priscilla respects Margaret's desire for privacy on this occasion, she continues to pry and watch for opportunities to meddle. She checks the niche behind the hearth occasionally to make certain Margaret hasn't put the necklace in another hiding place. She observes her and John on Sunday afternoons when it is time for him to go back to Ewens's plantation. They walk out the front porch together, give each other a quick, affectionate kiss, and part. Margaret always lingers and looks after him until he disappears into the woods. But when she comes back inside, she seems a little melancholy.

One morning, as Priscilla helps Margaret carry the breakfast dishes down to the creek for washing, she asks, "Doesn't it bother you that you and John can spend so little time together?"

Margaret puts down her basket filled with cups, bowls, and plates and starts to rinse them in the cold water. "We don't have any choice. Besides, it's only a few more years before we fulfill our indenture and can do what we want. Anthony and Mary will have to work a lot longer before they get their freedom."

Priscilla demurs. "But they live together."

They continue washing in silence for a while, stacking the clean dishes in the baskets.

Then Priscilla says, "Why don't you ask John to spend the night here on Sundays? He can leave early the next morning and still get back to Ewens's plantation in time to start his day there."

Margaret looks at her in surprise, the plate she's holding dripping water on her skirt. "It would be most agreeable, but I don't think we can presume," she says. "What would Lieutenant Sheppard think?"

"Oh, I've checked with Robert already," Priscilla says nonchalantly. "He does not object." Then her eyes twinkle in mischievous delight. "A bed is so much more comfortable than the forest floor," she teases.

From then on, John stays over most Sunday nights, even when Lieutenant Sheppard is away. Margaret is quite pleased, although she finds the first time a bit embarrassing because Jason, Paul, and Thomas keep grinning at them during supper and send mock kisses to each other for her and John's benefit. Priscilla shoots the men angry glances, but Margaret and John endure the teasing amicably.

By the following week, everyone accepts the arrangement as normal, and for one afternoon and night a week, they feel like a true married couple. Margaret always looks forward to the time when

John stays over, even if they are both so exhausted from their busy week that they merely sink into bed and fall asleep. Spending the night in each other's arms is pleasure enough.

* * *

Late one Wednesday morning, Margaret and Priscilla are baking bread in the kitchen when John arrives from the forest and hurries toward the main house. Priscilla sees him first and pokes Margaret to get her attention. When she looks up, she notices that he isn't wearing his pistol at his belt, as usual. He doesn't respond to Paul and Thomas waving to him from the field where they are crimping the tobacco plants but rushes on like someone possessed.

Margaret feels her chest constrict. John has never come to see her during the week, except when he accompanied Captain Jope on his visits. She runs to meet him and stops, taken aback by his disheveled appearance.

"What is it?" she exclaims.

A tortured cry escapes him. "Captain Jope is dead!"

Margaret feels his words like a stab to her heart. For a moment it seems that the world has stopped. "How?" she says, faltering.

Recovering his breath, John manages to say, "Mary sent a letter. It arrived this morning on the *Charles*, William Ewens's supply ship."

From his coat, he pulls a folded sheet of parchment. The remnants of a broken seal dangle from the bottom.

"Read it to me," Margaret says.

When Priscilla approaches, unable to hide her curiosity, Margaret gives a quick shake of her head, warning her off. Then she and John go to the front of the house and sit on the porch, away from everyone's prying eyes.

As John unfolds the letter, Margaret puts her hand on his arm for comfort. She recognizes Mary's neat, careful writing. "Read it to me," she says again, more softly.

JOHN

With halting voice, he begins,

Dear John and Margaret,

It is with a heavy heart that I write this. A year ago, I received notice that Captain Jope died during a raid on a Spanish ship and was buried at sea.

I have remarried to make sure our children have a home. My new husband, Arthur Harte, a gentleman, is taking good care of me and John's children.

I hope you are well, too. I know John cared about both of you as if you were his own children, and he wished the very best for you. I know he would have liked nothing better than to see you married.

Margaret gasps, "She doesn't know he married us! He never returned home that year."

"I will write to let her know. There isn't much more," John says and continues to read.

I wish you both, with all my heart, much happiness and success in pursuit of your destinies in the New World. May the Lord keep you safe and sound.

Mary Jope Harte

John starts to sob quietly, and Margaret puts her arm around his shoulders. Taking the letter from his clenched fingers, she can only imagine Mary's anguish and feels a deep sadness for her. Yet her own heart beats calmly, and she is surprised that she feels no sorrow for the death of the captain. Instead, a growing sense of conviction fills her body with ineffable joy.

She pulls away from John and says, "He is not dead!"

John looks at her bewildered.

Putting her hand on her chest, she says, "I would feel it here, know it here," and repeats firmly, "He is not dead."

"Where is he then?" John asks softly.

"He may be lost somewhere, marooned, but he is still alive. I am certain of it." She puts her hand on his and squeezes it. "You must believe me, John. I will feel it when he dies—sense it, know it."

Looking at her mystified, John feels a glimmer of hope. "I believe you," he says quietly, feeling less bereft than when he first read the letter and rushed to bring her the news.

Sitting in silence with their arms wrapped around each other, they remain adrift in their separate thoughts and memories of their captain.

Then John pulls Margaret closer and says, "I must get back."

She nods and kisses him. When they stand up, they embrace again, unwilling to separate. Finally, Margaret lets him go. John expels a deep breath and leaves.

As Margaret watches him head toward the forest, she is glad to see him recover his forceful stride, and a feeling of serenity comes over her. *Captain Jope is alive.* If he weren't, she would feel it. It surprises her that she has such a deep connection with him, but she doesn't doubt it, not for a moment.

When she gets back to the kitchen, Priscilla asks tentatively, "Are you all right? John looked like he received some terrible news."

Margaret smiles, bolstered by her feelings of certitude. "No, everything is fine."

19

TWO NAMED FRANCES

Virginia—Summer-Fall 1633

The most shocking event of the year, with unexpected ramifications for many important people in the colony, is the death of Frances Grenville West Piersey Matthews. Without warning, she becomes bedridden with a burning fever, stabbing pains in her belly, and uncontrollable diarrhea. Despite every effort on the part of her doctor and stepdaughter Mary to nurse her back to health, she succumbs a week later. Word of her passing travels quickly throughout Virginia. Some say it was the flux; others believe it was due to some rotted pork she ate.

Margaret receives the news before most of the other settlers in the Hogg Island area when Lieutenant Sheppard returns from a meeting of the Governor's Council in James City. She immediately thinks of Frances, her best friend, who, coincidentally, bears the same name as her departed mistress. What will happen to her now?

At the Sunday service, John Uty gives a eulogy for the woman who was the closest to royalty Virginia had. The daughter of an English nobleman, Frances Grenville arrived in 1621 and, during her relatively brief time, married in short succession three of the colony's most prominent settlers. The first was Nathaniel West, the brother of Lord De La Warr, one of the founding members of the now defunct Virginia Company. After his early demise, Frances married Abraham Piersey, a successful merchant twice her age and the wealthiest man in Virginia at the time. The wedding at his plantation, Floridew, was a lavish affair with no expenses spared and everyone in the colony who mattered attended. For Margaret, who went as maidservant to Mrs. Chew, it was a rare opportunity to spend an afternoon with her Frances, who had worked as a kitchen worker at the plantation ever since her arrival in Virginia on the *White Lion*.

When Piersey died in 1628, his young wife settled his estate and set her eyes on Samuel Matthews and married him at Denbigh, his plantation close to the mouth of the James River. Margaret's friend Frances and her son, Peter, ended up there as well, far enough away that Margaret has not seen them in five years.

As far as Margaret is concerned, the only good thing about the resettlement was that it brought Frances closer to Emmanuel Driggers, the man she loves, from whom she had been separated even longer. An indentured servant, too, he has been working on a plantation close to Denbigh, owned by Dr. Pott's brother Francis. Margaret thinks about them often. She imagines that Frances and Emmanuel spend time with each other the way she and John do. Perhaps they have gotten married, too.

Now, depending on the division of Frances Matthews's estate, things may change again.

When Abraham Piersey died, Frances not only inherited part of his fortune, she also became the guardian to his two daughters and their shares until they came of age. For Elizabeth, who married Richard Stephens against her stepmother's wishes, that money has never been an issue. It is a different matter for her younger sister, Mary, who married Thomas Hill, a gentleman, earlier in the year with Frances's blessing. The newlyweds have been scraping by on Thomas's small plantation, Stanley's Hundred, just north of Denbigh. After caring for Frances during her illness, Mary was named the executor of her will.

Everyone else in Virginia is eager to find out the extent of the property and wealth left behind, and who will inherit what. Frances and Peter just might end up in the house of Elizabeth and Stephens in James City. Margaret would like nothing better so that she can see her friend again and spend time with her more often.

At the reading of the last will and testament of Frances Grenville West Piersey Matthews in James City, there are no unexpected revelations. The division of her estate into three equal parts is straightforward—one for Frances's son Nathaniel, who is at school in England; the other two for Piersey's daughters. But to everyone's shock and surprise, Samuel Matthews claims that there is no money left and that most of the property belonging to Frances has been abandoned or lies in disrepair. All funds have been used for land purchases that haven't yielded any profit, or for settling debts incurred as a result of poor management.

John relates to Margaret and Sheppard what he heard from his contacts in James City, that Mary was beside herself when she heard the news. In private, she was even more incensed.

"She called her stepmother a driggle-draggle whore and an obscenity that rhymes with blunt," he says. "She had choice words for Matthews, too—accused him of being a scobberlotcher and profligate wastrel."

Priscilla blushes and says, "I had no idea gentlewomen knew such language, much less made use of it."

Margaret hides her amusement. Having listened to Mrs. Chew's diatribes, she isn't shocked, although Mary's wicked tongue surprises her. Living next door to her, she remembers her as meek and decorous.

In no time, rumors about fraud, betrayal, and treachery are on everyone's lips. Abraham Piersey was a very wealthy man, and Matthews has a reputation as a shrewd investor and responsible plantation owner. The notion that he and Frances have squandered a fortune, and in such a short time, beggars belief. The general consensus is that Matthews is trying to cheat Piersey's daughters out of their rightful inheritance.

Mary and Elizabeth certainly believe it. Their stepmother has been a stingy guardian and doting mother to her son. She would not have wasted Nathaniel's inheritance. At Mary's instigation, the sisters hire a lawyer to contest the will and sue Matthews.

It is the kind of scandal that would occupy the English aristocracy and royal court in London for weeks on end. In Virginia, it becomes the topic of conversation for months around dinner tables, before and after religious services, and at other public events. Workers, servants, masters, and mistresses alike delight in sharing the latest tidbit regarding the legal maneuvers and how the warring parties clash in court.

For a while, the scandal eclipses the other favorite subject of gossips and rumormongers: Governor Harvey and his latest transgressions. At the same time, the presence of Sir John makes for confusing battle lines in the court case as participants and onlookers take sides. Thomas Hill and Matthews are opponents both in the legal fight and in their relations with the governor: Hill supports Harvey while Matthews can't stand the man or his policies. Richard Stephens finds the governor just as irritating but sides with his wife against Matthews on the legal front. Lieutenant Sheppard and John Uty, on the other hand, feel torn because they are Stephen's friends and usually find themselves allied with Matthews against Harvey in Governor's Council meetings.

Margaret enjoys hearing from John about the latest chicaneries, but she really wants to know how the court case is proceeding. She figures that, with his interest in legal matters, John would have insights others don't have. But when she queries him, he shrugs his shoulders apologetically.

"This is not an area in which I have any expertise," he admits.

He would like to be able to help, knowing how much Margaret worries about the fate of Frances and how the uncertainty of the outcome upsets her. Depending on how the suit is settled, Frances could be living just across the river or as far away as ever. Although John has no memory of Frances from the voyage on the Spanish slave ship and, later, on the *White Lion*, and has never met Peter or Emmanuel Driggers, John cares about what happens to them. He feels as if he has a personal stake in their well-being because it concerns what matters to him most, besides his love for Margaret: the freedom of Africans in the colony.

Just as frustrating is that the legal wheels grind slowly. There is so much information to track down, gather, and document. Taking an inventory of all the possessions Frances owned for herself is a long, drawn-out process, especially since Matthews is not very cooperative and forthcoming.

To everyone's surprise, Governor Harvey inserts himself into the proceedings by offering to help Elizabeth and Mary with their suit. Town gossips discussing his possible motives wonder if, perhaps, he means to mend bridges with Richard Stephens or repay Thomas Hill for backing his initiatives. The sisters accept, believing that the governor's high standing will aid their pursuit of justice. With Mary living far away from James City, Harvey starts to counsel Elizabeth at his mansion.

Still, as the case drags on, some self-proclaimed legal authorities predict that it will take several years to settle the matter, and most people in the colony lose interest and turn their attention elsewhere.

* * *

In the late fall, John Harvey announces to the Governor's Council that his program of diversifying crops has been a sterling success. Not only have planters been able to store plenty of grain for the winter, Virginia has sent five thousand bushels of wheat to the Massachusetts Bay Colony, earning a tidy profit for those who complied with his demands to grow other crops besides tobacco. Many of the plantation owners, who participated under protest, are not impressed, however.

At the meeting, John Uty is heard to mutter, "I could have earned tenfold the money with tobacco."

Others share his discontent.

Margaret doesn't pay much attention to the political wrangling. With the weather turning crisp and cool, and the musty smell of decaying leaves in the air, she works hard to help finish the harvest and get ready for the winter.

When Lieutenant Sheppard leaves on his last military excursion of the year against the Indians, Priscilla frets about how to deal with his foul mood when he returns. But by the time he arrives by boat two weeks later, she no longer has to worry. Running to him expectantly as he steps onto the dock, she throws her arms around his neck and kisses him.

Surprised, he pulls back. "What is it?"

"Oh, Robert, I have great news," she exclaims and catches her breath. Beaming, she announces, "I am with child."

For a moment, Sheppard stands still and stolid as a tree trunk. "Are you sure?"

When she nods happily, he sinks to the ground and puts his hand on her belly. Looking up at her with shining eyes, he says, "My dearest, you've made me so happy."

20
ANOTHER ARRIVAL
Virginia—1634

For Margaret, Priscilla's pregnancy has immediate consequences. Much as the news delights Lieutenant Sheppard, he also worries about his wife's health. Although work on the plantation has made Priscilla stronger—she is no longer the frail young girl who arrived nine months earlier—he is concerned that her constitution won't hold up under the strain of her daily household chores while their child is growing inside her.

After his first midday meal home, he makes a point of cornering Margaret alone in the kitchen. "Make sure she performs no heavy labor," he orders. "At the first signs of her growing tired, relieve her and let her rest."

Margaret understands that he is overreacting as usual, coping with his inability to guarantee Priscilla's safe delivery by trying to control everyone else. But she assures him she won't burden her unduly.

At first, Priscilla continues to pitch bravely as before with all tasks, despite the bouts of morning sickness that send her dashing outside, so that the smell of her vomit doesn't pervade the house and kitchen. But as she gains weight and becomes visibly bigger, she tires more easily and finds it difficult to bend over and move about. Some days, she stays in bed until breakfast is ready, joining the others and nibbling at a biscuit. At other times, her appetite is so prodigious that everyone is amazed at the quantities of food she can consume.

Reducing Priscilla's load means extra work for Margaret, but she fulfills her promise to Sheppard without complaining. When she mentions at church what is going on to John, Katherine, and Michael, they are not sympathetic to Priscilla's situation. Katherine has not yet had children of her own. But other servants at Ewens's plantation have, and they toiled around the house and in the fields right up to the time they went into labor and gave birth, and returned to work a few days after delivery.

"Of course, they are servants like you and me," she says pointedly. "I don't know about the wives of the plantation owners, but I imagine their lot is much easier."

Anthony and Mary, who speak from experience, echo her comments. The practice is different for mistresses and their maids, leading up to giving birth and afterward. Servant mothers must take care of their babies on their own, in addition to doing their usual household chores and farm duties. The wives of the planters have nursemaids and, in some cases, wet nurses to look after their newborns and children.

At some point, Sheppard asks Dr. John Woodson, the military surgeon stationed on the south side of the James River, to come and examine Priscilla. The lieutenant has known him for a number of years and trusts him implicitly. Margaret has met the doctor several times herself and found him to be full of good humor, unlike the dour-faced Dr. Pott. Woodson has a good ten years on Sheppard, and his full, graying beard makes him look even older. He also likes to eat and drink, attested to by his rather sizeable belly and the red veins in his cheeks and bulbous nose. He knows that Margaret helped pregnant women deliver babies under Dr. Pott's supervision.

Upon arrival, he greets her warmly and says, "I am confident you'll know what to do when the time comes."

Although not quite so certain herself, Margaret nods with more assurance than she feels, wanting to look trustworthy for Lieutenant Sheppard's sake.

Dr. Woodson checks Priscilla's pulse, feels her forehead, and looks into her eyes. Then Margaret brings a small bowl filled with urine. Knowing from experience that he would be asking for it, she had Priscilla provide it ahead of the physician's visit. Dr. Woodson makes much of swirling the pale-yellow liquid and sniffing it and announces, "You are in excellent health."

His avuncular presence relaxes the young mother-to-be and allows her to voice her fears. "What if something unforeseen happens?" she asks, her eyelids fluttering.

The doctor smiles indulgently and says, "You're not to worry your pretty little head. The baby will be born at an ideal time of year, late April or early May, when the weather is warm but the summer heat and humidity haven't set in yet." Indicating Margaret, he adds, "And you could not have a better helpmate by your side."

Priscilla seems comforted.

Her husband is not as sanguine. After he pays the physician, he says, "A word, John." Outside on the porch, he asks, "Are you sure Margaret can handle things in your absence? While I respect her ability as a housekeeper, I am not persuaded of her expertise as a midwife."

Knowing a nervous, fussing husband when he sees him, Dr. Woodson strokes his beard as if giving the matter serious thought. Then he fixes his brown eyes on Sheppard and says firmly, "I meant what I said about Margaret, Robert. She is quite capable, and Priscilla will be fine. The rest is God's will."

He clears his throat and walks to the waiting boat to be ferried back to his plantation.

ANOTHER ARRIVAL

* * *

On a balmy day in early May, Priscilla and Margaret are cleaning the table in the common room after breakfast. Heading to the kitchen, she hears Priscilla cry out. She quickly puts down the dishes and hurries back. The petrified young woman is standing next to a stool and staring at the puddle of water at her feet, unaware that she is holding a wooden spoon in her clenched fists.

"It just happened," she says bewildered. "What does it mean?"

"The baby is coming," Margaret tells her.

She runs outside and from the porch calls to the fields, where Lieutenant Sheppard is tending to the young tobacco plants with the other men. It doesn't take long for them all to come running.

The lieutenant immediately takes charge. "Go get Doctor Woodson," he tells Thomas.

Meanwhile, Margaret has led Priscilla to the bedroom and made her comfortable. When Sheppard tries to follow, she stops him and says, "Get Jason to boil water in case the baby arrives before Dr. Woodson can get here."

Suddenly rattled, Sheppard asks, "How long will it take?"

"She could be in labor for several hours or much, much longer," Margaret says. "It's impossible to tell at this time."

Sheppard rushes to his wife and takes her hand. "How are you, my darling?" When Priscilla tries to smile, the terror in her eyes arouses his ire. He turns to Margaret and yells, "Do something! Anything!"

He gets up and starts to pace, stomping around the room in his heavy boots.

Without giving it a second thought, Margaret confronts him. "You must listen to me, Robert. This is not like one of your military campaigns where you can give an order to your men, and they will do what you say. Priscilla's baby will come in its own time."

Sheppard stares at her, incredulous. "How dare you talk to me like that? What do you know? You're useless!" he yells frantically, his voice on the edge of hysteria.

"Stop your shouting!" Margaret yells back, matching his intensity. "I know that you can't control this, but you can make it worse. The important thing right now is not to upset Priscilla."

Sheppard's face drains of color. For a moment, he wants to fight back, balling his fists. Then he acquiesces. "Do what you have to do," he says and strides from the room.

Fortunately, it is an easy birthing. Between contractions, Margaret dabs the sweat pearls from Priscilla's forehead with a moist cloth. She takes the time to show Jason where the hyssop is in the kitchen so that he can brew a tea that will help relax Priscilla and offers it to her in small sips. With no birthing stool at hand, Margaret uses one of the wooden stools from the living room when the time for delivery grows near. Shortly before the doctor arrives, the baby is born. Margaret ties the umbilical cord with a string and cuts it with a knife the way she remembers Dr. Pott doing. The newborn starts to cry after two slaps, and Margaret places the child at Priscilla's breast. With one last push, the tired young mother delivers the afterbirth. Margaret puts it into a bucket and has Jason bury it outside far away from the house.

Sticking her head out of the bedroom door, Margaret nods to Lieutenant Sheppard, who has been pacing outside to escape from Priscilla's screams and in the living room during the quiet interludes. He looks haggard and exhausted. When she beckons to him, he rushes into the bedroom to Priscilla's side.

"Oh, dearest, are you . . . are you . . . are you all right?" he stammers. "I have been so worried."

A sense of serenity emanates from the tired young mother. She shifts the baby so that Sheppard can see the ruddy little face. "Look, Robert, look!" she says. "We have a daughter."

Doctor Woodson arrives an hour or so later by boat. Paul and Thomas, who have done everything in their power to bring him to the house as quickly as possible, sit at the oars, utterly spent. Jason brings them some biscuits and beer.

After examining Priscilla and the baby, he shakes Sheppard's hand. "Congratulations, Robert. You have a fine, healthy baby girl."

Then he turns to Margaret. "You did an excellent job, Margaret." He adds with a humorous gleam in his eyes, "I don't expect you'll need me again until next time."

Margaret nods, pleased that he acknowledged her.

"A glass of wine in celebration, John?" Sheppard asks, relieved.

"Don't mind if I do," Dr. Woodson says.

Escorting him into the common room, Sheppard says in passing, "Margaret, would you get us a bottle?"

Margaret fetches two glasses and a bottle of port from the cupboard and puts them on the table. Not expecting to be invited to join them, she goes back to Priscilla and the child.

She wets the cloth in the bowl of water and wipes Priscilla's tired face.

As she bends over, Priscilla whispers to her, "Thank you. You'll be next."

Taking the baby from her arms to put her into the wooden crib by the bed, Margaret smiles at her and says, "Get some rest."

Meanwhile, Sheppard and Dr. Woodson imbibe more than one glass of wine. With mother and daughter well, their discussion turns to what they consider masculine matters—the affairs of the colony. When they have finished their second glass, Sheppard indicates the bottle and asks, "Can you stay a bit longer?"

Although sensing the younger man's need for company, Dr. Woodson says, "I'd like to, Robert, but I must get back home before dark. You know, you are fortunate to have Margaret. She is very proficient and will take care of everything."

When the doctor looks in on Priscilla and the baby, Margaret puts her finger to her lips. Mother and child are both sound asleep.

Margaret joins Sheppard to head outside with Dr. Woodson and watch from the porch as he departs by boat, Paul and Thomas rowing at a more leisurely pace. Margaret closes her eyes and expels a deep breath, relieved that everything went well. She feels the afternoon sun's rays warm her face like a blessing. Although it has been a surprisingly quick birthing, it seems like she's been up for days. When she opens her eyes, Sheppard is looking at her. She wonders how long he has been studying her.

Gradually, his boyish smile replaces his serious expression, and he says, "Thank you, Margaret. I should not have doubted you."

Margaret understands that it is as close to an apology as he can manage. "I'm just glad everyone is all right," she says.

* * *

Priscilla recovers her strength in just a few days. After watching Margaret swaddle the baby a few times, she takes over all aspects of care for her daughter, from nursing to washing out the diaper linens at the creek. She also resumes helping Margaret with the many household chores that need to be done. As a military man who values the ability to perform one's duty under trying conditions, Lieutenant Sheppard is pleased how his wife measures up to the challenge and goes about her work without complaint. He doesn't let on that he is a little disappointed that the baby isn't a boy.

Ten days later, everyone in Sheppard's household travels to Lawne's Creek Church for the Sunday service to have the baby baptized. Since the lieutenant is considered a gentleman and military man of rank, Reverend Faulkner, the Anglican minister, has made a special trip from James City for the occasion. Priscilla carrying her baby daughter enjoys being the center of attention in the circle of the plantation owners' wives, who make appropriate cooing and clucking sounds. Sheppard receives hearty backslaps of congratulations from their husbands. No one pays any attention to Margaret, which allows her to spend uninterrupted time with John and her other African friends.

After everyone files into the church, the service commences with a hymn. Then the Reverend Faulkner reads and expounds on Psalm 127:3–5:

Behold, children are a heritage from the Lord, the fruit of the womb a reward. Like arrows in the hand of a warrior are the children of one's youth. Blessed is the man who fills his quiver with them! He shall not be put to shame when he speaks with his enemies in the gate.

The actual ceremony is brief and to the point. He anoints the child and intones, "I baptize you in the name of the Father and of the Son and of the Holy Spirit, Priscilla Sheppard."

When he sprinkles some water on her face, the baby starts to wail, her indignant protest echoing through the church to the amusement of the assembled crowd.

When the service is over, Priscilla hands her daughter to Margaret and goes out to join the celebration, a feast of pies and cider.

Margaret doesn't mind remaining behind for a spell. Holding the baby close and comforting her feels good, and she wonders when she and John will have the opportunity to welcome their first child.

21
MARYLAND
Virginia—Summer 1634

Ry the time the General Assembly convenes in James City in
July, little Priscilla smiles at her parents with such delight that
Lieutenant Sheppard is loath to leave her and his wife even for a day
or two. He is not looking forward to a meeting filled with partisan
bickering over every law or regulation Governor Harvey wants to
enact. He shudders to imagine the shrill, impassioned voices of burgesses on either side reverberating through the rafters of the large hall
of the church where the gathering takes place.

This year, Harvey can boast of some genuine accomplishments.
After declaring the session open, he launches into a long speech
detailing the progress being made in attracting craftsmen to ply their
trades—notably an apothecary, a glassmaker, a blacksmith, and a
brick maker—to allow Virginia to be more self-sufficient. The last
occupation is important because the wealthy merchants and planters
want to build fancier houses in James City. In his nasal voice, Harvey
also touts the establishment of regular quarterly meetings for the
colony's principal court in James City, as well as the authorization of
monthly subsidiary courts in other parts of Virginia. He takes credit
for all of it even though a number of burgesses on his Governor's
Council drafted the appropriate legislation.

Saving the best for last, he turns to the successful completion of the six-mile palisades wall across the peninsula from the York River and James River. "It will offer protection against the Indian tribes for all the new settlers pouring into Virginia," he proclaims, gloating. "I am pleased to report that our colony is thriving entirely due to my humble efforts."

But his moment of self-appointed glory is short-lived.

William Tucker, a wealthy planter, rises and says, "Rumors have floated across the Atlantic Ocean that the King has plans to make the tobacco trade a royal monopoly and prohibit us from selling to the Netherlands."

"I know nothing of that," Harvey replies in a dismissive tone.

But his answer does not satisfy those fearful of the monarch's greed.

"That is where our largest profits come from," says John Uty. "We must petition the King accordingly."

Despite the murmur of approval from the attendees, the governor says, "I don't think that will be necessary. These are idle speculations."

"Notwithstanding, we must inform him of our needs and wishes!" Uty insists.

When most of the forty-six burgesses voice their agreement, Harvey gives in. "Very well. Get me the signed document, and I'll convey it to His Majesty."

Just when he thinks he has weathered this challenge, William Clairborne, a frequent thorn in his side, presents him with another. "What are you going to do about Lord Baltimore's renegade settlers north of the Potomac River?" he demands with a booming voice.

Immediately, a chorus of aggravated supporters joins in his outburst.

Two years earlier King Charles granted a patent for a colony to the north called Maryland on territory Virginia's gentry considered their own. The recipient, Cecil Calvert, second Baron of Baltimore, wasted no time. Eager to colonize his new acquisition, he sent to America two ships, the *Ark* and the *Dove*, with seventeen men of noble birth and two hundred other immigrants, mostly servants. Led by Leonard Calvert, his younger brother, they made landfall in March of this year at St. Clement Island in the Potomac River. Their leaders established contact with the Piscatawny Indians and, after purchasing land from the natives, started to establish a settlement at St. Mary's City on a tributary farther inland.

Leonard Calvert also sent representatives to James City to meet with Governor Harvey. He received them in the presence of several burgesses who generally support him. The newcomers presented a letter from King Charles, affirming their rightful claim to Maryland, and asked the governor for help to get their footing there. Harvey didn't tell them that the monarch had sent him a letter as well, ordering him to assist them in their new venture. Thus, he sounded magnanimous when he pledged Virginia's full support and assured his visitors that he would do everything in his power to provide them with the food, supplies, and tools they needed.

Of course, what transpired at the meeting soon became public, as was bound to happen in a town where no secrets keep for long. Just as predictably, most of the other burgesses and many of Virginia's lowborn citizens reacted with outrage.

Heated conversations and arguments ensued throughout the colony, including at the Sunday gatherings at Lawne's Creek Church. With John Upton supporting the governor, and Lieutenant Sheppard, John Uty, and William Spencer opposing him, discussions were lively. Since there was no easy solution to the conflict, the bickering parties departed for their respective plantations churning with resentment, only to resume arguing the following Sunday.

Margaret is surprised that John agrees with the Harvey contingent, although he keeps quiet about it. While not a monarchist, he believes in honoring the rule of law. He also thinks helping newcomers is a good idea. When he puts it like that, Margaret feels the same way.

Priscilla, unhappy that everyone is so upset, voices the same sentiment on the way home. "I don't understand what all the fuss is about. There is plenty of land for everyone."

"It's quite simple," Sheppard informs her, with a condescending tone of voice. "That land belongs to us, and now it will be occupied by Catholics!"

"But aren't they English like us?"

"That is not the point!" Sheppard says crossly. "The Catholics follow the dictates of the pope, who has been consorting with Spain for years. He would like nothing better than to make us part of the Spanish empire!" He adds, "And I'm afraid our King, being a Catholic himself and under the sway of his French wife, only makes things worse."

That is the general view of most Anglicans and Puritans, who have suffered from prosecution under the Stuart monarchs. But at the General Assembly, Harvey pulls out the letter from King Charles and conveys the royal demand that Virginia help and support Maryland to make sure the new colony thrives. He ignores the initial grousing coming from the attendees and announces stridently, "We shall send food and other supplies. It is an order from the King!"

The result is pandemonium.

Jumping to his feet, Samuel Matthews roars, "These provisions are needed here in Virginia."

"They belong to us!" William Tucker shouts even louder.

"I would rather knock my cattle in the head than sell them to Calvert," George Menefie yells.

"It will be war if they dare touch my property," William Claiborne cries out. He is especially upset because he built a trading outpost on Kent Island two years earlier. It lies miles to the north in the middle of the Chesapeake Bay, surrounded on both sides by the territory Maryland now claims as its own. He figures it is only a matter of time before the new settlers there will want to take it over.

Other burgesses voice their protests as well. They are afraid that the King will invalidate their land titles, the way he did in Ireland.

But Richard Stephens is the loudest and most vehement critic. Along with Claiborne, Matthews, and Francis Pott, he wants to restore the old Virginia Company, or some version of it, because he made his biggest profits under its regime. He and Harvey are cut from the same cloth—irascible, quick to anger, prone to emotional outbursts, and eager to heap abuse on opponents. Annoyed by Harvey's haughty manner, he launches a personal attack.

"You are nothing but a lackey for the King," Stephens fulminates. "You do not care for this colony or its inhabitants one whit."

Stung, Harvey defends himself aggressively. "I have championed Virginia since I first came to these shores," he shouts. "Unlike you, who's gotten rich by gouging your customers."

With the meeting threatening to descend into chaos, cooler heads prevail long enough to call for adjournment. Reluctantly, the others agree—nothing of value will be accomplished in the throes of such roiling emotions. Calling for the assembly to reconvene the next day, Harvey gavels the meeting to a close.

But tempers continue to flare afterward. When Harvey leaves the church, Stephens confronts him in the open square outside.

"You are a vile, scheming knave," he shouts.

A small crowd gathers quickly as Harvey retaliates, "You, sir, are a dastardly poltroon!"

"Whoremonger!"

"Lily-livered rapscallion!"

"Say that again, you miscreant, and I'll—"

In response to the challenge, Harvey does a little jig, flapping his arms like a bird and warbling, "Cuckoo, cuckoo."

Stephens charges Harvey, his face flushed red as a beet, veins throbbing in his forehead, but his punch glances off the side of his opponent's head. When he cocks his fist again, Harvey whacks him across the face with his walking stick, sending several of his teeth flying from his mouth. Reeling from the blow, Stephens crashes to the ground. Several men—John Uty, Samuel Matthews, and Lieutenant Sheppard—step between the adversaries. As if unaware of his injury,

Stephen rears up like an enraged boar and struggles to continue, but the other men hold him back. When he has calmed somewhat, Sheppard helps him to his feet and supports him on the way to his house.

Bleeding from the mouth, he looks back over his shoulder and sputters, "This—this—this is not the end of it!"

Harvey watches them go, a small, victorious smile playing about his lips.

News of the altercation quickly travels all over James City and across the river. The nastier tongues claim that Stephens had it coming. As a wealthy merchant, proud, arrogant, and hot-tempered, he is not well-liked in some circles. Memories are long in the colony, and his detractors point to the time a decade earlier when he fought a duel with George Harrison, his rival over a pretty damsel. Stephen's pistol shot wounded his opponent in the leg then, and Harrison died two weeks later of the injury. In the eyes of his enemies, Stephens is finally getting his due. Others think that there are long-standing political issues that has caused bad blood between him and Harvey. Still others lay the blame at Elizabeth's door, for meeting with Harvey in private at his mansion.

John shares the latter view, and he expands on his notion with Margaret on their next Sunday afternoon walk in the forest. The tall oaks, hickory trees, and sycamores provide a shady canopy that offers relief from the burning heat and humidity. Margaret is wearing her pearl necklace. Since Priscilla discovered it, Margaret puts it on whenever John comes to visit.

As they meander through the woods past nattering squirrels and chirping birds, John tells Margaret that he thinks what really caused the fight is that Stephens thinks Harvey is trying to seduce his wife, Elizabeth. Since the governor has been helping her with the lawsuit against Matthews, they have spent considerable time together at his mansion, going over documents and developing a legal strategy. According to John's sources, when Harvey made advances toward her, she didn't rebuff him.

"One of the servants saw him take her hand and kiss her, and then she kissed him back," John says. "How Stephens found out, no one knows, but when Harvey imitated a cuckoo, calling him a cuckold for everyone to see, he went berserk."

Margaret is shocked. She can't imagine the aloof, arrogant Elizabeth, mother of two young children, being enamored of Harvey, despite Priscilla's account of how charming he was at the dance gala. She fingers the pearl between her breasts, trying to make sense of it.

Suddenly, a scream of terror followed by cries for help disturb the stillness. They come from deeper in the woods, and Margaret and John rush in the direction of the shrieks. Stumbling over roots and past brambles, they soon come upon a horrifying sight. Two Indians have overpowered a young, blond girl and are holding her captive. One of them has clamped a hand over her mouth while the other one is wrenching her arms behind her. The two braves are naked from the waist up, their sinewy muscles bulging. Their chests and faces are covered with red clay war paint.

"Stop. Let her go," John yells, pulling the pistol from his belt and aiming it at the two braves.

Alarmed, they scowl at him but hold on tight.

Margaret recognizes their captive. It is Elizabeth Spencer, the young daughter of William Spencer. Heart pounding in her chest, she wavers for only a moment. Then she takes several steps forward, arms extended from her sides, palms facing them, in a gesture of peace.

"Margaret," John warns her.

Not heeding him, she advances slowly on the trio. "Keep still, Elizabeth. It will be all right," she says softly to the girl who has clamped her eyes shut as if expecting a blow.

Margaret is counting on the fact that the Indians consider Africans benign ghosts because of their dark skin and bear them no ill will. At least that was true a decade ago during and after the big massacre, and she prays that ten years have not changed their beliefs. Seeing the eyes of the Indian braves flicker uncertainly strengthens her resolve. She moves a few steps closer still, slowly reaches up behind her head, and unclasps her necklace. Holding it by the golden chain, she offers it to them. The pearl gleams in the shaft of sunlight slanting through the overhead canopy, catching the Indians' attention.

"Margaret, don't—" she hears John from behind her.

Undeterred, she takes another step forward, and then another, until she is within touching distance and can smell the pungent odor of sweat emanating from the two natives. The older, who has his arm around Elizabeth's neck and mouth, grasps the necklace with his other hand. He examines it, then gazes at Margaret in wonder. He says something to his companion in a guttural language Margaret doesn't understand. With their eyes locked on Margaret's, they let Elizabeth go and slowly back away. John keeps his pistol trained on the departing Indians until they disappear into the dense, green underbrush.

When Elizabeth no longer feels their hands on her, she opens her eyes. Seeing Margaret beckoning to her, she rushes to her and collapses into her arms, sobbing with relief.

Margaret hugs her tight. "It's all right. You're safe now," she says in a soothing voice. "You'll come home with us, and we'll let your father and mother know where you are."

"What happened?" John asks, worried that there may be other Indians nearby who might be planning to launch an attack.

In a halting voice, Elizabeth explains how she chased after a butterfly, paying no attention to her surroundings. When she no longer recognized where she was, she wandered around the forest, lost.

"Suddenly, the two Indians jumped out from behind a walnut tree and grabbed me. If you hadn't come along—" she gasps, and tears fill her eyes again.

"Let's get you back to our house where you'll be safe," Margaret says gently.

Elizabeth nods, and the three start off toward Sheppard's plantation. Walking under the canopy of oak, pine, and hickory trees with nuts and twigs crunching under their feet, Margaret finally realizes what danger they faced and starts to shiver. When they reach the snake fence on the outskirts of the tobacco fields, she takes a deep breath to get her feelings under control.

Closer to the main house, John's calls for help bring everyone running. While Margaret and Priscilla take Elizabeth inside, John informs Lieutenant Sheppard and the others about the encounter with the Indians. Sheppard immediately gets his muskets and sends Thomas to the Spencers' plantation to reassure the parents that their daughter is safe and to warn them to be on the lookout for Natives in the vicinity. Jason and Paul arm themselves with axes and knives.

Priscilla brings a cup of cider for Elizabeth, who gulps it down greedily.

"Would you like to see little Priscilla?" she asks, to take the young girl's mind off her ordeal.

Elizabeth nods eagerly and follows her into the bedroom.

By the time William Spencer arrives, out of breath and looking terror-stricken, Elizabeth has recuperated to the point where she is smiling again, sitting at the table in the common room and chewing on a biscuit. When she sees her father, her eyes light up and she hurries to him. He picks her up and crushes her to his chest.

"Oh, Elizabeth, we were so worried!"

Throwing her arms around his neck, she cries out, "I'm sorry, Father. I won't do it again."

As he strokes her hair, he says to Sheppard, "Thomas told me she was captured by two Indians and nearly carried away. I don't know how to thank you, Robert."

Sheppard points to Margaret and John, who are standing nearby, watching the reunion. "You must thank them. They rescued your daughter from the two Indians who were kidnapping her."

Surprised, Spencer turns to them and says with genuine emotion, "I thank you both from the bottom of my heart." Then his face takes on a puzzled expression. "But how—?"

"John chased them off with his pistol," Margaret says, squeezing John's hand covertly to ensure he won't contradict her.

Spencer grasps John's hand with his free hand. "You are a brave man," he says. "Thank you again. I am in your debt."

John tries to wave him off. "I am happy Elizabeth is all right."

Priscilla and Sheppard suggest they spend the night, but Spencer says, "I must get home. Dorothy is beside herself with worry." He glances at Elizabeth, who has fallen asleep on his shoulder.

Sheppard nods in understanding. "We must be careful for the next few days. Paul will go with you. Godspeed."

After they have left, John says, "I must go, too, and warn everyone at Ewens's. If I hurry, I can get there before nightfall."

Margaret accompanies him to the edge of the forest. The late afternoon sun casts a golden sheen on the upper leaves of the trees ahead.

They walk in silence past the corn and tobacco fields until John stops and says, "That was a brave and foolhardy thing to do, Margaret. Promise me you won't risk your life like that again."

She looks at him searchingly, sensing the desperation of losing her behind his demand. "You know I can't do that, John. But I promise you I won't do anything foolish."

He reaches out and puts his hand to her cheek. "I'm sorry you lost your pearl necklace."

"Me, too," she says and kisses him tenderly.

On her way back to the house, tears well up in her eyes. This is the second time she has lost a pearl to the Indians. The one her mother gave her was taken during the massacre. This one was her only keepsake from Captain Jope. That it, too, is gone reminds her that he is gone from her life and leaves an ache in her heart.

22
NEW LIFE
Virginia—Fall 1634

King Charles continues to seek to govern the colonies through his Privy Council and other committees. In early September, Governor Harvey receives an official notice from the monarch to divide Virginia into eight shires. He shares the royal edict with his own council at his mansion, which has a room large enough to accommodate the eight members. Although the burgesses resent the King's efforts to meddle in Virginia's affairs, this suggestion makes sense. Most of the territories in question already have large enough cities to use as local county seats, like James City, Charles City, and Elizabeth City near the mouth of the James River. With burgesses and military planters acting as homegrown officials, communications throughout Virginia would improve.

At its next meeting, the Governor's Council draws up a map to present to the General Assembly in November. To Harvey's dismay, John Uty also presents a document for King Charles that protests his plan to establish a royal tobacco monopoly, so that every attendee can sign it at the larger gathering. A look passes between the governor and Richard Kemp, the colony secretary.

By then, Richard Stephens has recovered enough to come to the council meetings again. Dr. Woodson had to pull the three tooth stumps left in his jaw from Harvey's assault. The extraction was so painful that it took three men to hold him down.

Elizabeth cared for his wounds but refused to stop meeting with Sir John over legal matters. "He is giving Mary and me good advice," she insisted but agreed to take along Mrs. Chew as a chaperone to make her husband happy.

At subsequent gatherings of the Governor's Council, Stephens and Harvey sit at opposite ends of the table as far away from each other as possible and avoid looking at one another. Their enmity and rumors of an affair between Sir John and Elizabeth provide ongoing grist for the gossip mill in James City. Margaret hears the most delectable tidbits from John but still finds it hard to believe that the rumors are true.

Fall is a busy time, and she and John are fully engaged at their respective plantations in the harvest of corn and tobacco and preparation for winter—repairing cracks in the houses and making candles and soap. Priscilla takes care of her baby daughter, who has started to crawl when she is not nursing or asleep.

One night, Margaret has a dream. She is standing on the quarterdeck of the *White Lion*, alone. The vessel moves across the water on its own like a ghost ship, with no crew in sight. The sails flap in the wind. The cloudless sky is robin-egg blue, and the afternoon sun beating down feels hot on her face. When she looks around the ship again, she suddenly finds herself on the poop deck. Captain Jope stands at the railing, arms akimbo, smiling at her. He looks younger, the way she remembers him when he rescued her and John, his blond, leonine beard showing no gray and his blue eyes bright and blazing. Her heart beats faster and she starts to run to him but can't move her feet. They are rooted to the deck.

Jope doffs his wide-brimmed hat and bows to her. Then he shrugs regretfully and lets himself topple over backward over the wooden railing. Shocked, Margaret rushes to the railing and looks down, but there is no splash in the wake. A sea eagle floats in the breeze high above. It calls out once with its high-pitched caw and flies away in the opposite direction of the ship's course. As Margaret watches it become a mere speck and disappear, a deep sadness overtakes her.

When she awakens, the feeling lingers like a disturbing scent. There is a dull ache in her chest, and she knows that Jope is dead. Wherever he ended up for his last two years on earth, he is no more. Although she knows that he believed that his fate—whether he is one of the elect—was predetermined, Margaret offers up a prayer for him and hopes he is with God.

That Sunday afternoon she and John take a walk. The air is crisp and filled with the sound of the turning leaves susurrating in the breeze. When they get to their favorite clearing, surrounded by cypress trees and live oaks, she stops and says without preamble, "Captain Jope is dead."

Surprised and stunned, John remains silent for some time. Margaret hears a flock of birds taking off to head north for the winter.

"How do you know?"

"I dreamed about him earlier this week," she says.

They sit on the fallen tree trunk at the edge of the clearing, and she takes his hand. The simple certainty with which she relates her dream convinces John. Since Jope has not visited for over two years, he hasn't been holding out hope for his return. But preparing himself for the inevitable is not the same as facing Margaret's conviction and accepting it. He closes his eyes, and a host of images and memories of Jope inundates his mind. When he opens them, between his tears he sees that Margaret's dark brown eyes are misty, too.

"I hope he didn't suffer at the end," he says quietly.

Margaret, trusting her vision of Jope smiling, says, "I think he died in peace."

"But we will never know."

Nodding her agreement, Margaret says, "We must honor his life by making something of our own."

Continuing to clasp each other's hands, they start to talk about their captain, sharing their memories of him.

That night, they make love with a desperate kind of passion—gripping, clutching, embracing each other as if they need to affirm that they are alive. Afterward, they lie entwined like the sprouting limbs of two bushes, their fates entangled, and cry softly until they are asleep.

* * *

Seven weeks later, Anthony's wife, Mary, is the first to notice that Margaret is with child. On Sunday after church, she observes that Margaret standing next to Priscilla seems to have a special glow. When she mentions it to her husband, Anthony promptly seeks out John, who is talking to Katherine and Michael.

"So, you're going to be a father soon," he says, slapping him on the shoulder. "Congratulations on starting your own family."

When he sees John looking utterly befuddled and his friends equally bewildered, Anthony stammers, "I didn't realize. I . . . I thought you knew."

John quickly recovers and gives a forced smile. "Of course, thank you, Anthony. I didn't realize at first what you meant. Margaret and I are thrilled."

At first, Katherine responds with jubilation. Then her eyes narrow. "Why didn't you tell us?"

"I—we wanted to wait for the right moment to announce it to everyone," John fabulates. "Please don't say anything yet."

"Of course, John," says Michael. "You can count on us."

Meanwhile, Mary has approached Margaret, who is just as startled when she discovers that her condition is visible to others already. She has been certain for less than two weeks that a new life is growing inside her, but she held off telling John, worried about how he would respond to the news.

That afternoon when John arrives at Sheppard's plantation, he is irate. As soon as they enter the forest, out of earshot of the main house, he explodes, "How could you not tell me, Margaret! I had to find out from Anthony."

Margaret looks down embarrassed. She picks up a fallen maple leaf and twirls it nervously in her hand. "I am very sorry, John. I have suspected it for less than a fortnight, and I wanted to be sure before I told you." She adds in a pleading voice, "I didn't expect this any more than you did."

John paces and kicks at the fallen leaves. They crackle and flutter in the air in a cloud of brown dust before settling back on the ground. "You know what this means, don't you?" he snarls. "We both will have years added to our indenture. How could you?"

"Are you accusing me of getting pregnant deliberately?" Margaret responds. "I used all the safeguards. You know as well as I that they don't always work."

He wheels on her, his feeling of helplessness driving his passionate outburst. "You should have been more careful."

In a soft voice, Margaret answers, "It happened the night I told you about our captain."

He stares at her, the wind knocked out of him. Unable to hold on to his fury, he drops down on the log and puts his head in his hands.

Margaret approaches him cautiously. "This child is a gift from God, John. We will be a family. Isn't that what you want?"

He rubs his forehead, then looks up at her, pained. "Of course it is. I just hoped it would be under different circumstances, that we'd have our freedom by the time it happened."

He sighs as she steps closer and puts his hands around her waist, resting his head against her belly. "You're right, Margaret. The child *is* a gift from God, and I am happy that we are having it together."

He spends the night at the house with her but has a hard time going to sleep. Early in the morning on the way back to Ewens's plantation, he goes over his options again and again in his mind. It vexes him that he has not earned enough money raising hogs to buy their freedom without raising suspicions. Besides, Sheppard would not let Margaret go—she is too important to his household, especially now that Priscilla has a baby to take care of, and with more likely to come. By the time he reaches the snake fence at the edge of the plantation, he has made a decision. He will be pragmatic and accept his fate for now.

When the workers John passes greet him with knowing grins, he realizes that Katherine and Michael did not keep their promise to be quiet. In a way he is glad—he won't have to make a big announcement himself. Over the next few days, many take the time to come up to him and offer their congratulations. The reality of what is happening starts to sink in. His life will be irrevocably changed.

That evening after supper, John heads to the main house and asks Thomas Goodman if he has time to meet. The plantation manager invites him into the library. He brings a taper and lights the candles on the table. John's eyes stray to the upper corner of the bookshelf where he has hidden his pieces of silver.

When they are seated, John says, "I suppose you have heard by now that Margaret is with child."

Breaking into a rapturous smile, Goodman says, "I have, John. Felicitations to you and your wife! If there is any way Dorothy and I can be of help, let me know."

"Thank you, Thomas. I will."

Goodman's face turns serious. "You realize, of course, that we have to amend your contract of indenture to make up for the time you're going to spend with your wife and child."

John nods. "That is why I came to see you."

"I think the usual three additional years will suffice," Goodman says matter-of-factly. "Why don't you prepare the document—you already know how—and we'll settle the matter?" He indicates the shelf where the contracts are filed away.

It galls John that he will have to write the agreement extending his own servitude, but he says, "Yes, of course."

* * *

Things don't go as smoothly at Sheppard's, although when Margaret first announces that she is pregnant, Priscilla claps her hands in delight and embraces her like a sister.

"Oh, that is wonderful news," she says and laughs. "We'll both be young mothers together!"

"Yes, I am very happy for you and John," Sheppard says with a smile. "We must celebrate next Sunday."

Margaret accepts the congratulations from the others at the farm, but later Sheppard takes her aside and says, "We must discuss your contract of indenture."

Having expected as much, Margaret maintains her composure and says, "I understand, Robert. But I would like John to be present."

Sheppard readily agrees. "Of course, that makes sense. He is your husband."

The following Sunday afternoon, the three of them sit down at the table—Margaret and John across from Sheppard—while Priscilla hovers nearby, feeding her daughter.

As a military man used to making quick decisions, Sheppard comes to the point right away. "I think we need to add five more years to Margaret's contract of indenture," he says.

Margaret gasps and stares at him as if seeing him for the first time.

John says. "I believe three years is the norm, Robert. That is what Thomas Goodman and I agreed to."

Sheppard scratches his nose in irritation. By settling his own term of indenture already, John has forestalled him taking advantage of the situation. He pretends to think it over and says, "But you won't be taking care of the child day to day. It seems only fair that

Margaret has to account for that. I am prepared to be reasonable, however—four years."

John forces himself to stay calm. "I have written five such contracts at Ewens's plantation at Goodman's behest, and husband and wife have always had the same number of years added," he says firmly. "I think three years makes more sense."

Sheppard's face hardens. "I don't think so."

Margaret is about to speak when Priscilla interjects, "Please, Robert, it seems only fair."

Flushing red, Sheppard wheels on her and thunders, "Quiet, woman! This is no concern of yours!"

Startled by the angry shouting, the baby starts to cry. Priscilla soothes her and withdraws to the bedroom, pouting. Sheppard returns to the negotiation, but his wife's interruption has tilted the scales against him.

"All right, three years," he says. "But your child will be indentured to me for the requisite twelve."

A look passes between John and Margaret. Much as they hate these terms, they both know that this is as good a bargain as they can get.

Margaret stares at Sheppard as if he were a stranger. "Very well, Robert. That is agreeable to us."

Leaning back from the table, Sheppard says casually, "All right. John can draw up the document and I'll sign it."

It is a deliberate insult, relegating him to the role of a scribe. Margaret, sensing John bristling next to her, speaks up. "No, not unless you pay him for the service, and I will want him to read the document to me before I sign it."

Tight-lipped, Sheppard says, "Fine. I will have someone else take care of it."

He rises from the table and stalks into the bedroom. Margaret and John go outside and head down to the creek. When they get to the dock, they hug to comfort each other.

Looking at the dark green water flowing toward the James River, she says, "I am disappointed with Robert. I thought better of him, but he is just like Chew: greedy, devious, and mean-spirited."

John's response is more measured. "You shouldn't be surprised. Robert is like every other plantation owner, out for what is best for him and what he can get. You'll see, in a day or two he'll be over it."

Given the tense atmosphere in the house, however, he knows better than to stay for the night. He excuses himself before supper and heads back to Ewens's plantation. Margaret hears Sheppard and Priscilla arguing in their bedroom before she goes to sleep.

If Sheppard feels bested in the negotiations, he doesn't let it show. True to John's prediction, he behaves like a practical soldier and moves on. Just a day later, he smiles at Margaret and compliments her for cooking an exceptionally tasty meal, and the next time he sees John, he greets him with a friendly smile.

With things returning to normal, John resumes spending Sunday afternoons and nights with Margaret whenever he can.

23
OUSTED!
Virginia—Spring 1635

As Margaret starts to feel the changes taking place inside her body, she calls on Priscilla for help. Unexpectedly, their roles reverse. Priscilla becomes the teacher. She explains to Margaret that what she experiences is normal, that she felt the same way—from the nausea overtaking her in the morning to the odd cravings for berries and briny pork, from the bewilderment of her belly growing to the surprise the first time the baby kicks. Priscilla's excitement at every new development assures Margaret that her pregnancy is proceeding without mishap, and she actually looks forward to giving birth.

She wishes she could share her joy with John, but as Margaret pays attention to the changes in her body, she also notices a change in him. He seems distant, as if her growing belly and the new life inside her is an unhappy reminder of the additional time of servitude he has had to take on. He puts his hand on her stomach only reluctantly. At times he looks at her as if she were a stranger. When she asks him about it, he denies having any negative feelings and acts more solicitous toward her, but soon his faraway look returns.

When she shares her concern, Priscilla tells her, "Don't worry. Men aren't comfortable around expecting mothers. He'll be different once the baby arrives."

Margaret hopes she is right. She wants to believe that, when that time comes, John will be as taken with their child as Lieutenant Sheppard is with his baby daughter.

* * *

In the meantime, the disagreement between John Harvey and the burgesses about how to govern Virginia has come to a head. By now, it is clear to everyone that the King's representative won't change his ways—his arrogant, overbearing announcements; his secretive meetings with the men who support him; and his high-handed ways of springing his decisions on the council and General Assembly.

Harvey's continued support, both in word and deed, of the Catholic settlers pouring into Maryland further alienates many of the important planters in Virginia, especially those whose landholdings lie in Charles River County, close to the border with the new colony to the north.

Matters come to a boil in April after a clerk in the office of the colony secretary discovers the letter to King Charles protesting efforts to create a royal tobacco monopoly. Apparently, Harvey never sent it.

When word leaks out and Richard Stephens confronts Richard Kemp about it, the secretary says, "You must ask the governor about that."

At the next council meeting, Samuel Matthews raises the issue. Even before everyone is settled around the table at Harvey's house, he asks the governor, "Why did you not see fit to send the General Assembly's letter of protest to the King?"

Rather than dissemble or deny it, Harvey puffs up his chest and answers, "Such a petition must come from the people of Virginia and needs have many more signatures to give it the appropriate weight. Short of having them attached, there was no reason to send it."

"You had no right to make that decision," John Uty says in an icy voice.

"I had every right," Harvey reacts heatedly. "I am the King's substitute here and the appropriate conduit to His Majesty in all matters regarding the colony!"

The other burgesses at the table who disagree exchange glances but say nothing more. Harvey proceeds with the meeting, not realizing that their frigid response signifies more trouble than angry outbursts would have.

The news of the governor's disrespect of the General Assembly quickly travels throughout Virginia, creating ripples of discontent that swell to outrage and vocal demands for justice. Even those burgesses who generally support Harvey think that he has gone too far this time.

There is talk of nothing else at the Sunday get-togethers at Lawne's Creek Church. Servants and masters alike weigh in on the matter. John, considering the governor's course of action an illegal usurping of power, voices his opposition loudly. The dissident plantation owners—Uty, Spencer, and Sheppard—huddle to discuss how to respond.

In York on the Charles River, a group of wealthy planters holds a secret meeting at the house of William Warren. They include William English, the sheriff of Charles County; Nicola Martian; and Francis Pott, the younger brother of Dr. John Pott, who sits on the Governor's Council. After delivering impassioned speeches, they draw up a petition to the King for redress of the wrongs done by Governor Harvey. The next day Francis Pott starts to circulate printed versions in the southern parts of Virginia.

When Harvey hears about the meeting, he becomes apoplectic. Not only does he take it as a personal affront to himself, but as an insult to His Majesty, King Charles. Threatening the participants with dire reprisals, he sends out warrants for the arrest and jailing of Francis Pott and his coconspirators. He also dispatches letters calling for a special meeting of the Governor's Council.

When the news reaches Sheppard's plantation, Margaret worries about how it will affect her friends Frances and Emmanuel Driggers, who belong to Francis Pott. She knows too well how workers and servants get buffeted about when their masters suffer misfortune.

The missives to Governor's Council members arrive late the next morning. That afternoon, John Uty and William Spencer show up by boat at the main house, surprising everyone. They have never set foot on Sheppard's plantation before of their own accord, and their serious expressions when they ask to speak with the lieutenant in private puts everyone on edge.

They decline Priscilla's offer of refreshment and take a stroll outside with Sheppard to talk out of earshot of the others. After half an hour, Sheppard sees them off at the dock.

Margaret, washing linens at the creek, watches them shake hands and hears Uty say, "I'm glad you are with us, Robert."

When Sheppard returns to the main house, Priscilla asks, "What did they want, Robert?"

Although his lips tighten, he responds casually, "They wanted to discuss matters regarding the council meeting the day after tomorrow. It is nothing to worry your pretty head about."

But she persists, "Don't treat me like a child, Robert. Tell me what is going on!"

"All right. It is a serious business, but I can't say. I'm sworn to secrecy."

Priscilla pouts, but Sheppard remains immovable.

The tension mounts when the lieutenant leaves for the Governor's Council meeting the next day, looking even more serious than when the other planters visited.

At his departure, he warns Priscilla, "I may not be back for several days."

He kisses her and his daughter good-bye and has a quick word with Jason. Then he leaves carrying one of his muskets with him as Thomas and Paul row him down the creek.

When he is gone, Jason pulls out the remaining weapons to clean them and get them ready, further alarming Priscilla and Margaret.

* * *

By the time the council convenes around the large oak table in Harvey's house the next afternoon, all the members are present, including Richard Kemp, Dr. John Pott, John West, George Menefie, John Uty, John Harwood, Samuel Matthews, Thomas Purfoy, and Lieutenant Sheppard. A dark cloud hovers over the start of the proceedings because Francis Pott, Nicola Martian, and William English have been apprehended, brought under guard to James City, and are being held at the governor's mansion.

Sir John calls for an investigation of their activities and has the protesters brought before the council one by one. He questions them himself. The other attendees remain silent. Martian and English offer little of substance to counter his accusation and blame Francis Pott as the main instigator. It sounds like a ploy they concocted to deflect attention away from them, figuring that Dr. Pott will not let his younger brother bear the brunt of Harvey's fury.

When it is time for Francis Pott to be examined, two soldiers bearing muskets bring him into the large room. Standing before the assembled burgesses in a brown leather doublet, he stares defiantly at Harvey, his bearded lips curled in a contemptuous sneer.

When the governor challenges him to produce the letter in question, Francis shrugs and says nothing. But when his older brother gives him a small nod, he pulls out a piece of parchment and unfolds it. The letter is the size of a broadside. "What would you like me to do with it?" he asks blandly.

"Read it out loud," Harvey snarls.

In a clear, steady voice, Francis complies, reiterating the circumstances of Harvey refusing to send the letter from the General Assembly to King Charles and keeping it a secret. The language is factual and matter-of-fact, and Harvey listens in silence, his eyes shooting daggers at Francis.

But then his nemesis reads, "We address this missive directly to your Royal Highness, uncertain of our ability to get justice from the governor."

In an instant, Harvey leaps to his feet, blood rushing to face, and shouts, "That is an outrageous accusation!"

The others jump up from their chairs as well, and the meeting threatens to descend into chaos.

Richard Kemp tries to cool things down. "Perhaps we should adjourn for the day," he says in a moment of quiet. "We have received a great deal of information and must digest it with reason in order to proceed. Let us adjourn and reconvene tomorrow."

He fixes his eyes on Harvey. As the governor's crony and chief supporter, his word carries weight with him, and Harvey acquiesces.

"I believe you're right, Richard," he says. "Take the prisoner back to jail," he orders the two guards.

As they march Francis Pott from the room, the other council members exchange furtive glances. Samuel Matthews, acting as spokesman for the group, says, "We agree, as well." He adds significantly, "I hope everyone here will act with reason next time we meet."

*　*　*

His words fall on deaf ears. Usually, wiser heads prevail after a good night's rest, but during the delay, everyone's position hardens. When the council reconvenes, it becomes clear that Harvey has brooded all night and much of the day. If anything, his desire for revenge has reached blistering proportions.

After calling the meeting to order, he launches into a tirade: "This is a crisis the likes of which the colony has not seen since the Indian uprising more than a decade ago. Then the threat came from the outside. Now it grows from within, and we must take steps to root out the cankers gnawing at our divine institutions. To that end, we must issue a proclamation declaring martial law throughout Virginia in order to ensure the safety of all our citizens." He finishes, his nasal voice strident and scathing. "As for the traitors imprisoned here in James City, I demand the council immediately approve an order to execute them for high treason!"

But when he looks around the room, he is met with a row of stony faces.

Even Richard Kemp, usually eager to please him, says, "I can see you are all in a passion, Sir John, which makes men go to extremes they later regret. Perhaps the punishment you seek is too harsh for leading citizens who have merely expressed their opinion, albeit in not the most decorous manner."

Speaking for everyone else, Samuel Matthews adds with finality, "Under no circumstances will the council consent to such draconian measures."

"Surely you don't think this atrocious behavior should go unpunished?" Harvey snarls in disbelief.

"That is our view."

Seeing the determination of the men sitting at the table, Harvey's eyes narrow. "In that case, what do you think the prisoners deserve for inveighing against the government and their affront to the authority of the King's substitute? I want each of you to tell me individually!"

George Menefie, recently admitted to the bar, rises and confronts Harvey. "This is just another example of your personal vanity," he opines. "You offer nothing but disrespect to the General Assembly, but when you perceive the shoe being on the other foot, you lash out. 'Tis not becoming, sir!"

By now the governor's face is dark red with fury. Spittle spraying from his mouth, he screeches, "You are a good-for-nothing miscreant!"

"And you are not fit for the office of governor of Virginia!"

Harvey advances on Menefie as if to strike him, then grabs him by the shoulder and shouts, "I arrest you upon suspicion of treason to His Majesty."

Immediately, the other council members jump to their feet. Samuel Matthews and John Uty put their hands on the governor. Matthews says forcefully, "No, Sir John, we arrest you on suspicion of treason to His Majesty!"

Kemp tries to mediate again, "Sirs, he is the King's lieutenant, and what you're doing is more than you can well answer for. I pray, give a small respite to your anger and recover your reason."

Uty answers firmly, "No, you toadying lackey. The governor has been long past reason, and it is time we put an end to this farce!"

He nods to Dr. Pott, who signals Lieutenant Sheppard. Brushing past a startled servant, the lieutenant opens the front door and gives a shout. Instantly, a troop of musketeers rises from the embankment to the river and marches to the entrance. Another detachment emerges from behind the trees in the fields in back of the houses lining the street and surrounds the governor's mansion.

When Sheppard returns, Uty says, "You are under arrest until further notice. You will not leave these premises, or you will be conveyed to jail."

Kemp, standing at a window looking out at the soldiers, rebukes them, "It is not fit you should have men carrying weapons near the governor's house."

Sheppard can't help grinning at his impotent complaint. "We have arms and are in charge, and Sir John knows it!"

* * *

After a sleepless night, during which the conspirators meet and hatch further plans, reaction to Harvey's ouster pours in from other parts of the colony. Some Governor's Council members have traveled to their respective counties and told their constituents directly what happened. Thomas Purfoy brings reactions from the eastern, most populous parts of Virginia. Taking their will into account, the council meets at the church in James City and chooses Samuel Matthews to convey their decisions to Harvey.

At first, the governor is anything but chastened. Seething with rage, he starts to shout and threaten Matthews, "I'll see you all hanged!"

Lieutenant Sheppard signals, and two armed musketeers enter. At their sight, Harvey quiets down.

"You will listen and act with respect, Sir John, or go to jail," Matthews says drily.

With Harvey bowing to the inevitable, Matthews informs him, "Feelings against are running high among people, and there is the danger that some will try to commit violence upon your person—" he hesitates for effect, "—unless you agree to your deposition from office."

When Harvey starts to flare up, Matthews raises his hand, silencing him. "The council will call for the General Assembly to meet and install John West as temporary governor while the matter is to be settled in England before King Charles. It is best you leave the colony for a while. If you do not consent, the council will not protect you. You will be on your own."

Sobered, Harvey asks a few questions for clarification. It becomes clear to him that he is the victim of a well-organized campaign against him and that his best course of action, for the moment, is to retreat.

"I consent to the deposition proceedings," he says.

* * *

The General Assembly meets ten days later in James City. As promised, the members elect John West as governor. They gather all charges against Harvey and draw up a calendar of grievance against him to be sent to the commissioner of plantations on the King's Privy Council in London. They entrust the document to John Harwood and Dr. Pott, who will accompany Harvey there and plead the case for the colony.

Two days later, the three men set sail for England.

Harvey's departure sets off celebrations throughout Virginia. The few supporters he still has keep their opinions to themselves. Various accounts of what happened pass from mouth to mouth, often embellished to make Harvey seem like the jester in a Shakespearean comedy,

Margaret and Priscilla are fortunate that Lieutenant Sheppard and John Uty witnessed all the activities surrounding Harvey's ouster. Both men are happy to provide extensive and exhaustive testimony. Over dinner at the plantation and at the Sunday service, they tell the story of what happened as often as people wish to hear it.

John, with his contacts among servants, adds information from inside the governor's house. After his ouster, Harvey got drunk every night and wandered from room to room like a sleepwalker, bemoaning his cruel fate.

Shortly before Sir John embarked for England, Elizabeth Stephens came to visit him under the guise of getting a last bit of advice on her court case against Samuel Matthews.

"They were quite busy," John relates cheerfully, "but they spent more time holding hands and kissing than discussing legal matters."

24

MIHILL

Virginia—Summer–Winter 1635

For the next six weeks, Virginia's new leaders bask in their free-dom from Governor Harvey's interference. But then a letter arrives bearing grim news from Dr. Pott for Acting Governor John West. Pott and Thomas Harwood have been imprisoned in London awaiting the outcome of an investigation into the deposing of Governor Harvey. When their ship docked at Plymouth Harbor in Cornwall, Sir John somehow managed to debark ahead of them. He arranged an audience with the mayor of the city, impressed him with his bearing and credentials from the King, and persuaded him to arrest them as criminals.

Then he made his way to London and pleaded his case before the Privy Council. King Charles was outraged that the people of Virginia had flouted his authority and treated his appointed repre-sentative with disdain.

The inquiry before the Star Court Chamber is progressing slowly, but Dr. Pott feels that the deck is being stacked against them. He and Harwood are doing their best to rally nobles and influential mer-chants to their cause. Surprisingly, the Earl of Warwick has offered his support even though he has neglected his Virginia plantation for some time because of the many Anglicans living there. Apparently, his colonial venture on Providence Island has been running into difficulties. Spanish forces tried to invade the island and were repelled, but the settlers chafe under regulations imposed by the investment company, and experiments with slavery are not translating into good financial results. Warwick, still looking for a strong foothold in the New World from which to attack Spain, wants to keep all his options open. Dr. Pott and Harwood are glad to have him on their side, even if it is a mixed blessing. Although the earl is a powerful ally with many prominent friends, he is also a Puritan whose motives the colonists view with suspicion.

While the news from England gives momentary pause to the burgesses responsible for Harvey's ouster, it does not stop them from pursuing their aims. With the majority of the Governor's Council and John West of like mind, they proceed apace to undo some of Sir John's most unpopular regulations, in particular, the limits he set on tobacco production.

Still, every time a ship from England moors at the dock in James City, George Menefie or John West's secretary checks with the captain if he carries any official letters from the royal court. But when no communication from the King or the Privy Council arrives for some weeks, everyone relaxes and hopes for the best.

As John Uty points out at one of the Sunday church gatherings, "The longer it takes to settle things in London, the better it is for us."

* * *

Later in July, after the main meal of the day, John and Michael are mending a section of snake fencing at the southern edge of Ewens's plantation. It is an oppressively hot, humid day with hardly any breeze blowing for relief. Suddenly they hear an unfamiliar voice calling from afar. Looking up, they recognize Paul from Sheppard's plantation hurrying toward them.

He stops, swaying from exhaustion, sweat pearling off his ruddy face. "I've been looking for you, John—they told me. . . . I would find you here," he manages to get out breathing heavily. "I got here as fast as I could—"

Instantly alarmed, John calls out, "What is it?"

"It is Margaret, your wife," he gasps. "She's having the baby!"

Without a word, John takes off running. By the time he locates Thomas Goodman at the main house, the plantation manager has already heard the news. "Go, go!" he says, making shooing motions with his hands. "Good luck!"

John takes only a moment to get his pistol before rushing off in the direction of the woods. Hurrying past fields dense with tall, green tobacco plants and cornstalks, several times he wipes the sweat pouring from his forehead. He doesn't perceive that it is cooler in the forest and pays no attention to brambles lashing his face as he cuts through the undergrowth when it intrudes on his path. Nor does he notice when he disturbs birds nesting in the bushes, and they fly up into the trees and chirp and chitter angrily at him from the branches above.

As he comes within sight of the main house of Sheppard's plantation, a long shriek stops him in his tracks, and he almost wants to turn back. It must be Margaret, although her voice sounds like nothing he has ever heard.

Suddenly the screaming stops and he hurries on, grateful for the silence. Getting closer, he is surprised to spot Anthony standing on the porch in conversation with Lieutenant Sheppard, Thomas, and Jason.

When Anthony sees John, he comes quickly down the steps to greet him. "I brought Mary to help," he explains. "Margaret asked for her."

"Is something wrong?"

"No, everything is fine."

John feels a moment of relief. "Thank you. I want to see Margaret!"

He brushes past him, but Sheppard steps in his way. "I don't think that's a good idea right now," he says firmly. "Priscilla and Mary told us to go away and leave them to it." He turns back to Thomas. "Get John a cup of water and a cloth. Your forehead is bleeding."

"It's nothing."

Another horrific scream issues from inside the house. It pierces John like a knife, and he grimaces. His jaw tightens. "How long has it been?"

Jason looks up at the sun, calculating. "She went into labor this morning, but it's been like this only for the past hour," he says.

Suddenly, the exhaustion from racing to get there catches up with John. A feeling of helplessness threatens to overwhelm him, and he sits down heavily on the porch steps. Thomas hands him a cup and moist rag. The water feels cool in his mouth and throat. When he dabs his forehead, there are only a few spots of blood on the white linen.

Sheppard, who went through Priscilla's delivery just a year earlier, understands some of what John is experiencing. He puts a hand on his shoulder and says, "It will be all right."

For the next hours, the men stand around awkwardly making small talk, pace on the porch, and wander aimlessly down to the creek and back. Whenever Margaret screams, John flinches and holds his breath, unnerved. At some point, Paul returns from Ewens's, walking slowly and with a slight limp, as if he pulled a calf muscle.

Shortly after the sun sets, Margaret's shrieks come at ever shorter intervals until there is a grueling scream that seems to go on forever and makes John want to punch his fist through the wall of the house. When it finally subsides, everyone sighs with palpable relief.

Suddenly, high-pitched, almost indignant cries puncture the stillness, startling the men. They turn toward the house as Priscilla comes out on the porch. She looks tired but pleased. "Congratulations, John. It's a boy," she says.

John rushes up the steps into the house and into the birthing room. The air is heavy and pungent with the odor of sweat and blood. Margaret has returned from the makeshift birthing stool to her bed, and Mary is daubing her forehead with a moist cloth. She is lying propped up against a pillow, a small, swaddled bundle at her breast. John can make out a light-skinned head and black hair.

In a weary yet happy voice, Margaret says, "Come here, John. Say hello to your son."

John looks at the little scrunched-up face with a broad nose, eyes closed, and lips making a sucking movement. He is overcome by a welter of feelings—joy that Margaret and the baby are all right, wonder, bewilderment, and confusion.

Sheppard and the other men crowd into the room behind him and have a look until Mary says forcefully, "We must give Margaret and the baby some rest."

As they file out, John kisses Margaret on the forehead and says, "Get some sleep. I'll be here in the morning when you wake up."

Dazed, he heads outside where the other men offer their congratulations. He thanks them as if in a dream. Sitting on the porch with his head in his hands, he tries to make sense of what has happened. Unsure of what he's supposed to feel as a father, he seems at a loss. He wishes he could talk to Captain Jope. He would have known.

Mary and Anthony leave early the next morning to return to John Upton's plantation, and the Sheppard household settles back to normal as best it can. Priscilla makes a special effort to provide breakfast for everyone, and the men show their appreciation, praising the porridge even though it is too dry and salty.

When John looks in on Margaret, she seems much recovered from her labor. The baby is in her arms.

"Would you like to hold him?" she asks. "Careful, don't wake him."

John suppresses a moment of panic and takes the sleeping baby from her. Holding him awkwardly in his muscular arms, the child seems to weigh almost nothing. Because of the tight swaddling, John can't feel his body. He searches the tiny face as if seeking some sign or mark of recognition, but the baby still looks like a strange creature to him.

Watching him gaze so serious-minded and concerned at his child, Margaret says, "It will get easier."

She holds out her hands, and John gives the baby back to her, feeling relieved.

When he sits down on the bed next to her, she asks, "Have you thought about what name to give him?"

John doesn't respond right away.

Margaret realizes it hasn't crossed his mind and says, "We could name him John Jr. after you and in honor of Captain Jope."

Gazing out the window at the tobacco fields hazy in the afternoon sunlight, John ponders. The name doesn't feel right. He would be reminded of the captain's death every time he looks at the boy. "Too many Johns," he says, reviving his old joke. "It would be confusing."

Margaret thinks about other important people in their lives and suggests, "What about Mihill?"

The name is a version of Michael, and John considers it and its implications, then nods. "It is a fine name." He scratches his head. "You know, I should return to Ewens's plantation. I'll be back as soon as I can."

He squeezes her hand, kisses her lips, kisses his son on the forehead, and departs.

Margaret looks after him, puzzled. This is not how she imagined it. John seems a bit distraught by the whole thing. Perhaps he feels overwhelmed and just needs more time. Mary did warn her that some men don't know how to relate to babies and don't really warm up to their children until they grow older and start to talk.

As she cradles the baby boy in her arms, he opens his eyes. "Hello, Mihill—Mihill, Mihill, Mihill," Margaret says, trying on the name and likes it. "Mihill."

* * *

When Michael and Katherine hear that John and Margaret have chosen Mihill as the name for their son in his honor, they are thrilled. Their joy seems to rub off on John, and he becomes a more genial father. In addition to his regular Sunday visits, he spends another day during the week at the Sheppardses' as well, with Goodman's blessing. But when he realizes that the baby sleeps most of the day, he returns to his regular schedule.

The baptism at church is not as lavish an affair as for Priscilla and Sheppard's firstborn. Fewer people from the area attend, and the minister in James City does not make a special trip across the river. William Spencer performs the rite in his stead. He still feels thankful to John and Margaret for saving his daughter Elizabeth, and this is a small way to repay them. The dinner afterward with everyone contributing dishes is a happy gathering, as Virginia's settlers never miss an opportunity to share a good community meal. The weather cooperates as well, with clear skies instead of the afternoon showers typical for this time of year.

With much cooing over the newly christened baby and compliments and congratulations coming from all sides, John feels for the first time that becoming a father is a good thing. He experiences good-natured, teasing comments like, "When will the next one be along?" as a sign of affection.

That night he nestles up to Margaret in bed and whispers to her, "I am very glad we have Mihill."

But his elation is short-lived. First, Lieutenant Sheppard reminds him that, with Mihill having been baptized, the boy's contract of indenture needs to be settled. While acting like a kind and sympathetic friend during and immediately after Margaret's delivery, he reverts to being an unsentimental, hard-driving plantation owner, insisting that Mihill be indentured for twelve years, as agreed. John understands that the lieutenant seeks to tie Margaret to his household for a longer period than her own contract. But since Sheppard agreed to reasonable terms for Margaret, he readily accepts, planning to buy out his son's contract long before that time elapses.

His mood darkens when a week later the *Charles*, a ship belonging to William Ewens, arrives with a hundred new settlers. Although tired from the ocean crossing, they have eager faces, having been told how hospitable Virginia is to newcomers. Little do they know that a number of them won't make it past the "seasoning," the six-month period of adjustment to the colony's climate and environment when illness claims the lives of the sickly and weak. Fewer than a quarter of them are female, mostly household servants. The men are primarily unskilled riffraff who loitered and begged in the streets of London, unable to find work. But Ewens's plantation is growing and needs every extra hand.

In preparation for their arrival, Goodman had two more barns built for them to use as their living and sleeping quarters. John has the task of collecting and sorting out their contracts of indenture, which they've brought with them. As he examines them in the library, he realizes that many are written for less time than he has served already himself. He understands that three-year contracts are appropriate for workers who paid their ocean voyage in part or for all of it, or had someone else assume the cost. But there are five-year agreements for people who have few skills in comparison to his. The unfairness of it galls him.

He vows never again to put himself in a situation in which he yields up what limited control he can exercise over his destiny. He certainly will make sure not to add time to his servitude.

As a result, he restrains himself when he feels sexual desire for Margaret. Lying next to each other in bed, when she caresses his chest and he feels himself stir, he pulls away or turns his back to her, pretending he is too tired until his desire subsides.

At first, Margaret thinks nothing of it. Caring for little Mihill while performing her household duties is exhausting for her, too.

But when several months pass, she realizes that something is wrong. She wishes she could ask advice from someone she can trust. Like John, she misses Captain Jope's sure-handed guidance.

Margaret considers confiding in Priscilla, but she is too young and childlike in her understanding of men. Besides, she is preoccupied, having discovered that she is pregnant again. Mary, who acted as midwife when she had Mihill, is another possibility, as is Katherine at Ewens's plantation. Both are older, more experienced women and have been married longer than she and John. But they also have lived together with their husbands for many years, never suffering weekly separation. On the other hand, because John sometimes confides in Katherine, she might be able to offer insights into what's bothering him.

What Margaret wishes more than anything is that her old friend Frances were available. As far as she can tell, Frances and Emmanuel Driggers have a similar arrangement as she and John, living apart on nearby plantations and seeing each other only occasionally. No doubt Frances would have helpful advice for her situation. Margaret prays for Frances's well-being at night before she goes to sleep.

25
FRANCES
Virginia—1635–1636

In December, the suit Elizabeth Piersey Stephens and Mary Piersey Hill brought against Samuel Matthews is settled. The court holds for the sisters, finding that the plantation owner has unfairly deprived them of their rightful inheritance. It orders Matthews to hand over lands, including the plantations of Piersey's Hundred, Weyanoke, and Boldrup and to return to them all indentured servants and workers who belonged to their stepmother. In addition, Matthews must pay the sisters a sum of fifteen hundred pounds.

The verdict is a stunning victory for the Piersey sisters, as welcome as it is unexpected, and all of Virginia talks about it for days.

John, who was in James City when the court's decision was read, tells Margaret, "Elizabeth came out of the building well satisfied and proud as a peacock. Mary followed as if in a daze, though she was obviously pleased, too."

Margaret laughs. She can imagine the arrogant older sister strutting about town triumphantly with Mary in her shadow. But her heart beats faster when she realizes the verdict may also be an answer to her prayers. Frances might return to the Stephens household in James City just across the river.

For the sisters, it is fortunate that the verdict comes when it does. By the time Matthews has made over the deeds to all lands in question and sends the servants and workers to them, news reaches Virginia that John Harvey has been acquitted by the Privy Council's Star Court Chamber in London of all charges and reinstated as Virginia's governor by King Charles. The decision affects Matthews personally.

The official letter from the Crown to John West conveys the extreme displeasure of His Majesty that the people of Virginia dared to scorn his authority and depose his imperial substitute. By order of the Privy Council, the chief perpetrators of Harvey's ouster—John West himself, John Uty, George Menefie, and Samuel Matthews—are to travel to England and stand trial for their actions. Surprisingly, none of the agitators from the southern plantations, notably Francis Pott, appears on the list.

Meanwhile, Margaret's hopes that Frances will come back to James City are dashed when Richard Stephens's health worsens. He never fully recovered from the blows he received at Harvey's hands and often feels dizzy and weak. Dr. Woodson—doing his best to stand in for Dr. Pott, who remains in England—advises him to move to a more restful place than his residence amid the noisy bustle of James City. So, Richard, Elizabeth, and their son relocate to Boldrup Plantation, where Frances and other servants join them. Being close to her sister Mary somewhat mollifies Elizabeth for having to live in the countryside. At least, they can get together more easily and make plans for their inheritance.

Margaret is very disappointed when she hears that the Stephens household has moved away. It doesn't help that John is preoccupied with preparations for hog-killing day and making sure the newcomers to Ewens's plantation fit in. At least he seems glad to see her and little Mihill whenever he can make time for them.

* * *

In April 1636 Sir John Harvey returns from London to take up the mantle as Virginia's governor again. Planning to stage his arrival as a triumphant spectacle, he borrowed one of King Charles's royal ships to convey him back to James City. But the vessel sprung leaks and would have taken months to fix. Unwilling to wait, Harvey booked passage on a small merchant ship. Weighed down with cargo, it lies low in the water, and debarking requires him merely to walk across a horizontal gangplank—hardly the imposing entrance he would have preferred from the main deck of a galleon down to the dock. Nor does his arrival attract the large, welcoming crowd he desired. Only a handful of his supporters, led by Richard Kemp, are in attendance.

Undaunted, Harvey returns to his own residence and wastes no time in assuming office again. Armed with an impressive-looking document from the King authorizing his reinstatement as governor, he relieves John West of his duty. He also replaces his adversaries on the Governor's Council with burgesses more to his liking, including Richard Bennett from Warrosquoake County and John Upton from the Hogg Island area. He compiles a list of measures the interim government took in his absence that he means to repeal. But the first item on his agenda is sending his enemies to England to stand trial.

Harvey personally sees them off at the James City dock with a small contingent of armed guards to make sure everyone under-stands that they are criminals—traitors in the eyes of His Majesty. It rankles him that more people show up for their departure than came to his arrival. But he takes satisfaction in watching the subdued good-byes between the conspirators and their families and friends, and the glum faces of the accused as they climb aboard the ship that will take them to England and an uncertain future.

For Samuel Matthews, who has no one seeing him off, there is a small benefit. The court has granted his petition for a reprieve, postponing the payment of the money he owes Elizabeth and Mary until his difficulties with King Charles are settled.

As the ship casts off and heads downstream, those left behind wave after it. They avoid looking at Harvey, who, chin held high, basks in his victory and waits until the vessel disappears around the bend in the river at Hogg Island.

Margaret pays scant attention to the goings-on in James City because she has her hands full delivering Priscilla's second child. This time, Lieutenant Sheppard trusts in her skills, although he hates having to listen to his wife's agonized screams throughout the night from behind the closed door to the bedroom. The delivery takes longer than the first time, but everything goes smoothly, and late the next morning the happy parents welcome another daughter. They name her Susannah, after Sheppard's favorite aunt in England.

While Priscilla recovers, Margaret cares for all three young children in addition to performing her regular household chores. By the time of the christening two weeks later, she is exhausted.

Although the baptism ceremony at Lawne's Creek Church is as lavish as before, the celebration is overshadowed by the news that Richard Stephens is at death's door. Apparently he has contracted the flux and has become bedridden with ague, shivering fits, and diarrhea. Everyone offers prayers for him, but few hold out hope for his recovery and wonder what his wife, Elizabeth, will do when he is gone.

Days later, his constitution weak from the beating he received from Harvey, Stephens plunges into a sweat-drenched delirium. During his fits of babbling and yelling, he accuses his wife of being an unfaithful hussy and worse.

When he finally expires, Elizabeth almost feels relieved and buries him at Boldrup Plantation. Never having cared much for country life, she returns to James City with a retinue of servants, many only recently reacquired from Samuel Matthews.

In the will, read in the court at James City, it becomes clear that Stephens did not hold a grudge against his wife or exact posthumous revenge, despite his feverish jabbering. He makes their seven-year-old son, Samuel, primary heir of his estate, including the two large plantations and the house in James City, but grants Elizabeth lifetime rights of use and a dower of a third of all his property. Within days, Elizabeth has the titles to the plantations transferred to Samuel's name.

Meanwhile, Margaret is overjoyed to find out that Frances is among the servants in Elizabeth's household. Although keen to see her, there is little opportunity for her to get away. While Priscilla is back on her feet and takes on most of the care for the three young children, leaving Margaret to handle the rest of the tasks, there is not enough free time, even on Sunday afternoons, for a trip across the river to visit with her friend.

John, however, still goes to James City from time to time, so Margaret asks him to meet up with Frances and find out how she is faring. Having heard a great deal about her from Margaret already, he has been curious for a while to meet her.

"It will be my pleasure," he says.

The opportunity comes sooner than expected when John makes the trip across the James River to file an application at the court on behalf of William Ewens. Based on the number of new workers recently transported to the colony, Ewens claims five thousand acres of land to the south of the plantation.

After John registers the document with the clerk, he walks downriver to the new town section of James City where Elizabeth Stephens has taken up residence again. The two-story brick house her deceased husband built is not as ostentatious as John Harvey's mansion farther on, but it is one of the more beautiful homes in the area, with a large property out back extending far into the interior to where the forest begins. Cattle graze and low in the fenced-in meadow.

It is still morning when John knocks on the dark wooden front door. A heavyset, middle-aged woman with a pinkish face answers. Squinting into the sun, Elizabeth's head of household peers at him in surprise.

"Who is it, Grace?" Elizabeth Stephens's voice comes from inside the house.

"It's John, the young African from Ewens's plantation who supplies us with hog meat from time to time," Grace calls back over her shoulder.

"Well, ask him in."

John steps inside the house, puts his hat and pistol on the oak side table near the entrance, and follows Grace into the living room. The curtains are not drawn as would be customary in a grieving home, and light pours in from the large windows. Elizabeth Stephens sits on a sofa wearing a black dress befitting a widow in mourning. A book she's been reading lies half open next to her. Although she looks tired, her face shows no signs of crying or grief. Her son, Samuel, sits on the floor playing with a small wooden horse and wagon.

"Hello, John. What brings you to my house today?" Elizabeth asks, looking at him with curiosity.

He bows formally and says, "I am here to offer my condolences for your loss on behalf of Thomas Goodman, his wife, myself, and everyone at Ewens's plantation."

She nods graciously. "Thank you. Please convey my thanks to the others as well."

"I will," he replies. "I also bear a message for one of your servants, Frances." Seeing Elizabeth frown, he quickly continues, "It's from my wife, Margaret. They are good friends but have not seen each other for a long time."

Elizabeth thinks for a moment. "I suppose that's all right. Where is she, Grace?"

"Helping out in the kitchen."

"Show John where. They can talk outside. And get him something to eat." She turns back to him. "Take as long as you like. You are always welcome here."

John bows again. "Thank you. You are very kind."

If Grace is surprised by her mistress's generosity, she doesn't show any sign of it as she takes John to the rear of the building. John is still digesting his unexpected encounter with Elizabeth. She seems kinder than he expected, and without airs. Perhaps the pain of losing her husband has tempered her pride and arrogance.

The air in the kitchen is hot from the open fire and pungent with spices and the odor of stewing meat. An ebony-skinned woman is cutting up string beans and tossing them into a metal pot. When she raises her eyes, John sees that she is somewhat older than Margaret, attractive but not as beautiful, and a bit plump. The beginnings of worry lines crease her forehead.

"You have a visitor, Frances," says Grace curtly. "If the cook can spare you, you may talk out back with him."

The younger woman's curious gaze turns to puzzlement.

A bearded man wearing an apron keeps dicing carrots on a wooden board. "It's fine with me. We are in good shape for dinner," he says without looking up.

"All right then," Grace says and withdraws into the house.

Frances takes off her apron and gestures for John to come with her. She leads him outside to a wooden bench near the fenced-in chicken coop. Taking a seat, she looks him over and waits expectantly.

Feeling awkward because of her frank scrutiny, he blurts out, "Margaret asked me to say hello."

Understanding dawns in her eyes, and then again when she looks at him more closely. "You're John!" Frances exclaims. "Margaret's John." She claps her hands together and laughs in delight. "The last time I saw you was when we all came here with that captain who rescued us. You were just a small boy. Then you sailed with him for a spell, and now look at you—a fine, handsome young man."

John feels himself flush, disconcerted by her recollections. But her manner is so genuine and caring that he relaxes. When she pats the bench beside her, he sits down without a second thought.

As they talk, John quickly realizes why Margaret is so taken with Frances. She has a way of listening and asking questions that draws him out, and he tells her more than he expected to reveal. At the same time, she seems remarkably well informed. She already knows about Margaret and him, that they are married, have a son named Mihill, and live apart on separate plantations. It surprises him. She must have been making inquiries about them as soon as she came back to James City.

As if reading his mind, Frances says, "We're *malungu*." She smiles enigmatically. "We have our ways of keeping up with the news about the people we love." Although John is mystified, she continues, "I know what you're going through. My husband and I are in a similar situation as you and Margaret. We lived on different plantations near each other, too, but now we're far apart."

"So, you and Emmanuel Driggers got married!" John exclaims.

Frances smiles wanly. "Yes."

"Margaret will be so pleased."

"You can tell her Peter is well, too, but working on another plantation," Frances says in a melancholy voice. "I wish we could all be together." Then she brightens. "Emmanuel is working on getting all of us free." She leans close to him and whispers, "He says it's important for us to be free from bondage to the white owners so we can live our lives the way we want to."

John feels his heart beat faster. He understands that Frances is taking a risk telling him that so early in their encounter. It means she trusts him. Her comment speaks to what he has been thinking for some time. He is glad that others among the Africans besides Anthony a share his ideas. He would like to meet Emmanuel and hear more of what he has to say.

As they continue to talk, neither notices the time passing until the cook calls, "Dinner is ready."

John joins the household servants sitting around a table in a room next to the kitchen. Frances introduces him to the men and women, African and white. Most have spent the past seven years at Matthews's plantation and wonder if life is any different south of the James River. John answers their questions and assures them that their experiences are similar.

When it comes time to leave, Frances gives him an impulsive hug and says, "This is as much for Margaret as for you. Tell her how happy I am that she is well and that I can't wait to see her."

"Me, too," John says and leaves.

During the trip across the river, his head is aswirl with thoughts and ideas. He has a lot to share with Margaret.

26
ANOTHER WEDDING
Virginia—Summer–Fall 1636

Emboldened by the mandate he received from King Charles and the Privy Council, John Harvey proceeds as if nothing problematic happened the previous year. If anything, he antagonizes his opponents even more with his arrogant ways of making decisions on his own. When he gets excited, his insistent, nasal voice rises even higher, irritating everyone. But Virginia's leading citizens expected nothing less from him and hope their representatives in England, although in serious legal trouble, will sway the King with the support of their powerful relatives and friends. So, they bite their tongues and bide their time.

Meanwhile, Sir John still has the ability to surprise them. He extends an olive branch to his enemies by issuing formal pardons to all participants in the "mutiny" against him, although he exempts the men he sent to England for trial. Some appreciate his implicit call for unity after a divisive time, but most dismiss it as an empty gesture, a ploy to garner support that costs him nothing.

But then in late August, to everyone's astonishment he announces that he and Elizabeth Stephens are engaged and will be married in the fall.

The news dumbfounds just about everyone in Virginia. Yes, there were rumors that Harvey had a closer relationship with her than mere legal counselor, but while many enjoyed the gossip, they didn't really believe it to be more than tittle-tattle. Now the proclamation that the governor is about to marry the widow of his bitter enemy, and so soon after Stephens's death, creates more buzzing than a swarm of bumblebees.

One acid-tongued wag opines, "Well, they're kindred spirits—vain and haughty."

Another jests, "It gives 'court*s*hip' a whole new meaning."

That quip is much repeated throughout the colony.

As the news settles in, there is much commentary about Harvey's age—a bachelor all his life, he is nearly twice as old as his bride. Elizabeth's willingness to forfeit a good portion of her inheritance from Stephens receives considerable attention, too, as does the persistent rumor that she is pregnant with Harvey's child.

Yet, after the bans are read and posted at the church in James City, people wait eagerly to find out who the bride and groom have invited to the wedding and reception at the governor's mansion. It promises to be the biggest social affair of the year, and not receiving an invitation would be a humiliating snub.

To Harvey's credit, he doesn't wear his grudges on his sleeve but invites everyone of standing: burgesses, merchants, and gentlemen alike, and their wives, of course. Although few are fond of him, only a handful decide not to appear. The opportunity to show off their own wealth and rank, mostly in the form of their spouses' sumptuous dresses, does not come along often, and not in such an extravagant setting.

Of course, Priscilla and Lieutenant Sheppard are among the many couples planning to attend. The word at Lawne's Creek Church is that none of the remaining plantation owners in the vicinity will miss out either, including Richard Bennett, John Upton, and William Spencer. Even Thomas Goodman and his wife will go, representing their absentee owner, William Ewens.

Margaret would love to go, too, not to witness the ceremony but to finally see Frances again. Unfortunately, with three young children to take care of, someone needs to stay behind.

She feels melancholy while helping Priscilla mend and improve her best dress, a dark blue velvet outfit. They arrange the gown on the living room table and work in the bright sunlight coming into the windows, adding some jewels near the shoulders and sewing more lace on the sleeves and at the neckline. Priscilla's prattling on about how excited she is and who she expects to see there lulls Margaret into a sense of subdued acceptance.

So, she doesn't pay attention when, out of the blue, Priscilla asks, "How would you like to come to the wedding?"

As the words sink in, Margaret asks, "What do you mean?"

"Come to the wedding," Priscilla goes on. "You'll go as my maid, but you can spend as much time with your friend as you like." She adds in a conspiratorial whisper, "It is Robert's and my way of saying, 'Thank you,' for all you've done for us."

Margaret is astonished. The suggestion is so unexpected, she sputters, "But—but—but who will take of the children?"

Priscilla smiles slyly. "Elizabeth Spencer will come and mind them. Jason is staying behind, of course, to make sure everyone is safe. I've worked it all out with Robert and Elizabeth's father."

Amazed, Margaret realizes that Priscilla has addressed all of the details. Since Elizabeth was attacked in the forest, she has become a responsible young girl, and she likes children. She has been spending time minding Mihill and Priscilla's children after church to give the parents time to talk among themselves.

All Margaret has to do is say, "Yes," and she doesn't have to think about it. "I would love to."

"It will be fun!" Priscilla says, pleased. "John can join us, too, if he wants to."

When Margaret asks him the following Sunday, he makes a big deal of acting surprised before saying casually, "Sure, I guess I'll go, too."

He doesn't fool Margaret for a moment. "You've been in on this, haven't you?"

"Well . . . yes. I've been informed about it," John admits, looking as if he's about to burst.

"Was it your idea then?"

He shrugs in an offhanded way, but Michael, Katherine, and Mathew standing behind him grin from ear to ear.

Margaret slaps him on the arm in mock anger, then gives him a long kiss.

* * *

Crossing the James River, Margaret enjoys the cool morning breeze caressing her face. The clear blue skies promise another warm, late October day, perfect weather for a wedding. Margaret is wearing her Sunday best—a simple cotton blouse, dark skirt, and white cap—that pales beside Priscilla's fancy blue velvet gown. For a fleeting moment, she wishes she still had the pearl necklace Captain Jope gave her, but it doesn't bother her for long. Feeling elated and apprehensive, her mind is a jumble of thoughts about what will happen when she and Frances meet. How much time will they have alone together? Will it be enough to catch up on all that has transpired since they last saw each other? Will they still be as close as in the past? Will she be able to share her worries regarding John and get the advice she needs?

John, sitting next to her, yawns occasionally, but Margaret can tell that he feels on edge. He arrived the evening before and spent a restless night. It is the first time he will mingle with Virginia's most prominent citizens, and he worries what to say when he has no apparent reason to justify his presence among them. Dressed in his usual Sunday outfit—leather doublet, belt, and dark brown trousers, but no pistol—he looks around out over the waves and fidgets with his fingers.

Lieutenant Sheppard in uniform occupies the seat next to Priscilla and indulges her enthusiastic jabbering.

As the boat comes within view of the dock, Margaret's thoughts turn to Elizabeth Stephens. The last time Margaret saw her at a wedding was over a decade ago when her father got married to Frances Grenville West at Floridew Plantation. Margaret remembers Elizabeth and her sister, Mary, at the ceremony, wearing matching lavender dresses and looking none too pleased. Considering the subsequent disagreements with their stepmother, it seems natural in retrospect that they were unhappy already. Margaret wonders how Elizabeth feels getting married today, now a recent widow herself.

By the time they arrive at the church, a large crowd is already milling at the entrance. Sheppard and Priscilla join a group of burgesses and their wives heading into the church. Margaret notes that, on this occasion, Priscilla's dress more than holds its own among the other gowns. The interior of the church has room enough only for Virginia's elite. The servants gather in the open area between the entrance to the building and the public whipping post, stocks, and pillory.

Margaret eagerly searches the crowd for Frances, but John notices her first. "There she is," he says, pointing.

But when Margaret follows his gaze, she sees a tall, gaunt black man. Catching her breath in disbelief, she squeezes John's hand.

"What is it?" he says, surprised.

"It's Emmanuel. Emmanuel Driggers!"

The man's eyes lock onto hers in recognition. Forgetting all decorum, Margaret rushes over to him, and his muscular arms engulf her. When he lets go, Frances is standing next to him, her eyes luminous.

"Hello, Margaret," she says. "It has been quite awhile."

For a moment it seems to Margaret like no time has passed at all. Frances looks just as she remembers her—her soft, round figure, the gentle expression on her face. Then she notices the beginning of crow's feet at the corners of her eyes.

"Oh, Frances," she says, her lips quivering.

Frances opens her arms and enfolds Margaret in a prolonged embrace.

"It is so good to see you," Margaret whispers in her ear.

By the time they let go, John and Emmanuel are already deep in conversation.

They stop talking, and there is a moment of awkwardness when no one speaks, waiting for the others to start. Then the beginning of a hymn from inside the church captures everyone's attention. Everyone surges to the building, crowding around the entrance. One of the older servants goes up the steps and listens at the door. For the remainder of the service, he relays what is happening inside, from the minister's sermon and advice he doles out to the bridal couple to their wedding vows. In between, everyone joins in singing the familiar hymns as best they can.

At last, the service is over, and Harvey's servants carry around baskets filled with kernels of corn to toss at the newlyweds to wish them prosperity and good fortune. Everyone takes some. Margaret remembers the ritual from the big wedding she attended at Floridew. As people form two lines to make a long walkway, she joins others crowding in back. They don't have to wait long before the bride and groom emerge from inside the church and stand at the top of the entrance steps. Harvey is wearing a fancy black doublet covered with silver embroidery while Elizabeth looks radiant in a traditional red gown with round sleeves, made especially for the occasion. She is carrying a bouquet of myrtle and orange blossoms.

Margaret thinks she looks happy and is pleased for her.

Sir John and Elizabeth wave to the cheering crowd. Then, as they walk down the pathway, people pelt them with corn kernels from both sides. The newlyweds endure the drubbing good-naturedly. The rest of the wedding party follows close behind them on the way to the governor's mansion. Margaret recognizes Elizabeth's sister, Mary, with a man who she imagines is her husband. Thomas Hill seems an amiable fellow, although his sparse facial hair can't cover up the fact that he has a weak chin. It surprises Margaret that Mary has aged more than her older sister. The boy at their side must be Samuel, Elizabeth's son by Richard Stephens. He looks unhappy and troubled, like someone who wishes he were somewhere else.

The rest of the retinue consists of burgesses, plantation owners, merchants, and their wives. They're chattering about how lovely the ceremony was, all expectations to the contrary. Everyone seems to have decided that a truce on all political quarrels is in order to celebrate the union and enjoy the festivities.

Frances nudges Margaret and smiles mischievously, pointing at some of the wealthy women who walk clumsily up the street, lifting their skirts so the bottom hems of their fancy dresses don't drag in the dirt.

"As elegant as a herd of cows," Frances whispers, making Margaret laugh.

"I have missed your wicked humor," she says.

The last to leave the church is the Reverend Faulkner, looking pleased with himself. As he heads to Harvey's mansion, the host of servants and workers brings up the rear.

At the mansion, everyone repairs to the meadow in back. There are tables filled with plates of roast pig, beef, and venison; bowls of vegetables of all kinds; and cakes, pies, and other sweets for dessert. Servants keep bringing out tankards of beer and pewter cups filled with red wine. Musicians play lively jigs and reels, and as the day wears on, the wedding attendees dance with ever increasing abandon.

After partaking in the cornucopia of food and drink, Margaret and her friends find a quiet spot away from the bustle, a wooden bench shaded by an oak tree.

Emmanuel nods to Frances and Margaret and says, "We will leave you two alone. You have a lot to catch up on."

Touched by his generosity, Margaret grasps his arm and says, "I truly appreciate it, Emmanuel."

"You and I will find another time." He winks at her and adds, grinning, "Your husband and I have manly things to discuss." He puts a hand on John's shoulder and takes him off to another part of the meadow.

Frances and Margaret sit on a wooden bench and look at each other for a while. The silence between them deepens as neither can decide who goes first until, finally, they both burst out laughing. Once the dam is broken, their conversation flows smoothly. There is so much to tell about what has happened in the intervening decade. Like Margaret and John, Frances and Emmanuel did get married even though they lived on different plantations and saw each other only occasionally. Now that Frances is back in James City, they once again live apart. Fortunately, Emmanuel's hard work has paid off. As an indispensable servant to Francis Pott, he will accompany his master on trips to James City. He and Frances are making plans for the time when they're both free and can live together as man and wife.

When Margaret asks about Peter, Frances becomes subdued. "He is sixteen now, and a handsome young man," she says in a low, bitter voice. "But he works on another plantation because of a deal Samuel Matthews made with George Menefie for some horses. I miss him every day."

Margaret takes her hand, and they sit quietly for a while. Then she starts to tell Frances all about Captain Jope, the last time she saw him when he married her and John, her certainty that the news of his death was premature, and the dream that confirmed for her that he was finally gone.

Frances gives her an odd yet meaningful glance and says, "He was very important to you. I heard about others in Africa who had such powerful connections with those they love. It is a rare gift."

Feeling acknowledged and accepted allows Margaret to unburden herself further and share some of her deepest concerns. She talks about how angry John was when he found out she was with child because it would add years to their indenture, and that, since Mihill came into the world, he has been reluctant to lie with her. "He starts to respond to me but then draws back," she says plaintively.

Frances smiles empathetically and says, "Emmanuel has the same concerns and does it, too. That is why we don't have children yet." She thinks for a moment. "Does John love the boy?"

"I suppose so," Margaret says. "He holds him but doesn't play with him much."

"Give him time," Frances counsels. "Men are not good with children, not until they're older."

Again, Margaret feels reassured and gives Frances a grateful hug. Time passes quickly, and before they know it, the sun is riding low in the sky.

John and Emmanuel return, comfortable in each other's presence.

As they get close, John announces, "Lieutenant Sheppard is ready to go home."

"So soon?" Margaret says, disappointed.

"We will get together more often now that we live just across the river from each other," Frances promises.

They say their good-byes quickly, hugging and shaking hands. Margaret and John leave first. When she glances back, Emmanuel and Frances are looking after them with their arms affectionately around each other.

On the way home, traveling across the James River and up the creek to Sheppard's house, Margaret and John lean against each other, happy to relax. They listen amiably to Priscilla going on about the wedding and the reception and what she thought of Harvey and Elizabeth as a couple. It has been a most satisfying day for everyone.

When they are finally alone in her room, Margaret says, "Thank you, John, for making this day happen. It means a lot to me. What did you and Emmanuel talk about?"

"Indenture and freedom," John says with enthusiasm. "It's amazing, but he and I have similar views. He says that planters pay lip service to the sanctimony of marriage, but their desire for making money is more important to them. They will separate us whenever it suits their needs, which is why we must work to gain our freedom as quickly as we can so we can determine our lives ourselves." He adds fervently, "I want to speak with him again as soon as possible."

"I'm glad you two like each other," Margaret says, happy he is so passionate. It amazed her how different his conversation was from what she and Frances talked about. She can't wait to see Frances again, too.

Exhausted from a full, long day, they sink into bed without undressing and spend the night in each other's arms.

27

SETTLING IN

Virginia—1637

Ll those who thought that being married to Elizabeth would
temper John Harvey's domineering ways quickly realize that
they were mistaken. If anything, the governor becomes even more
aggressive and vindictive. He continues to work for a royal tobacco
monopoly even though, in the face of nearly unanimous opposition
by Virginia's planters and their influential friends, not to mention
the urging of his Privy Council, King Charles has backed away from
his demand, at least for the time being. But Harvey manages to rein-
state regulations to limit the growing of tobacco in favor of cultivat-
ing other crops. To check up on how well people observe his edict,
he has the General Assembly create an office that will keep a record
of all exports of tobacco and other commodities from Virginia.

But what sends shock tremors throughout the colony is how
openly the governor abuses his power to take revenge on the leaders
of the rebellion. After extending an olive branch earlier, he confis-
cates their properties and adds them to his own holdings or gives
them to his few remaining friends and cronies. Richard Kemp especially benefits from the forced land distribution. Harvey starts by
seizing Denbigh Plantation, having championed his wife Elizabeth's
cause against Samuel Matthews, who is still in England. Then he

goes after the properties of Dr. Pott, John Uty, and John West. In the process, he more than doubles his property holdings throughout Virginia.

Sir John and Elizabeth continue to hold lavish dinners, parties, and dances at the governor's mansion. Harvey even invites certain former opponents, hoping to bring them to his side. Remembering the role of the militia in his ouster, he makes sure to request the presence of Lieutenant Sheppard and other military leaders as often as possible.

Margaret continues to accompany Priscilla to these events, acting as her lady's maid. It raises Priscilla's standing in the eyes of the wives of wealthy burgesses and merchants who can afford several personal maidservants. Margaret is not impressed by the opulent interiors of the governor's mansion—the fancy hardwood furniture, expensive wall hangings, paintings, and silver plates on display. Unlike the decorations at Aldwarke, which felt like they were a part of Aunt Isabel, these adornments merely reflect Harvey's power and the position in society to which he aspires. They don't convey the character of a lived-in home.

Margaret is happy to play her role, however, because it gives her many opportunities to meet with Frances. In their conversations they trade gossip and recipes, share intimate feelings and knowledge about their husbands' quirks, habits, strengths, and preoccupations— what annoys them, puts them at ease, and stirs them. Margaret finds Frances's practical yet joyful approach to life inspiring. Her bawdy sense of humor and mocking of the pretensions of others provide them both with no end of amusement.

One afternoon, Margaret brings Mihill with her, dressed in a child's gown. When Frances holds out her hands to him, he pulls away and refuses to smile. She chucks him under the chin and says, "He will be a fine young man, as stubborn as his father." Then she lifts him up into her arms and nudges him with her finger until he gurgles with pleasure and adds, "See, that wasn't so hard. All you have to do is tickle his fancy." Her sly sideways glance toward Margaret suggests she has more in mind than enticing a child.

When Emmanuel Driggers comes to James City at the side of Francis Pott, besides spending time with Frances, he usually meets up with John as well. Weather permitting, they take walks along the river or to the harbor docks. John enjoys the conversations with the older, more seasoned man who not only shares his concerns but broadens his understanding of the world. Their discussions tend to be less personal, concentrating on social and political issues, from slavery in the Massachusetts Colony and on Providence Island to living conditions in Virginia to the future of Governor Harvey and his policies.

When the news reached England that Sir John confiscated the property of the men he sent there for trial, they were outraged. By then Uty, Matthews, West, and Pott were no longer in prison, and they immediately filed a complaint with the Privy Council. Matthews, especially, called on his many friends to use their considerable influence on his behalf. Approaching King Charles directly and petitioning his advisers, they obtained an order commanding Harvey to restore all the land in Virginia that belongs rightfully to Matthews to his agents. But when the document arrived in James City, the governor ignored it.

"Mark my word, that will be the end of him," Emmanuel predicts. "Property ownership is the foundation of wealth in Virginia. Take it away from a man unjustly, and you will make an enemy for life!"

Like John, he worries that slavery will come to Virginia as well. "We are fortunate in our current situations," he says one time. "So many servants are mistreated by their masters. I've seen the bruises from the beatings they received, even when they try to hide them at the church gatherings on Sundays."

Above all, they talk about their prospects. On one of their outings, they watch a ship carrying passengers from England to Virginia dock and unload. The newcomers, mostly men, look tired and undernourished, and their clothes are threadbare. Their eyes have none of the curious sparkle of the well-fed citizens of the colony.

"Another group of uneducated, unskilled workers who've been sold a bill of goods that they would have a life of ease and leisure here," John muses.

But Emmanuel says, "These are times of expansion, John, times of change, and we should welcome the opportunities they bring for us. All that's holding you and me back is that we are not yet free!"

John returns from his conversations with Emmanuel feeling exhilarated, irritated, and preoccupied all at once—elated that he has a friend who shares his ideas, annoyed because he feels tied down by his family obligations, and brooding about his future. He no longer blames Margaret and Mihill for being indentured longer than he anticipated, but he often wishes he could move out on his own and make his way in the world. On the other hand, he doesn't know yet what he wants to do when he attains his freedom. He decided to come to Virginia because he thought he wanted to have a family like Captain Jope and Mary, and because he loved Margaret and wanted to live with her, but now he realizes that things are not so simple.

Anthony has plans to raise horses and cattle on his own farm, and Emmanuel wants to become a plantation owner and cultivate tobacco. But John has no interest in dealing with livestock or crops that require constant tending. One of the reasons he likes raising hogs is that they forage for food in the forest on their own and don't need much attention.

Although he is acquiring the necessary skills to become a plantation manager like Thomas Goodman, the job doesn't interest John. It would mean doing all the work without reaping the financial benefits. When he and Emmanuel talk about it, his older friend astutely points out that in Virginia most men of means, power, and independence are merchants or plantation owners—their wealth is the result of owning property or ships. Although John can't deny the truth of that observation, he doesn't want to take that path for his own future. It frustrates him that there seems to be no alternative for him, some profession that allows him to combine his love for books and the law. Sometimes he wishes he had a trade he could pursue.

He understands why Michael and Katherine are content to stay at Ewens's plantation. Goodman treats them well, and they are comfortable with their situation. But John is torn. He knows that no other place like it exists in Virginia, with a substantial library and a manager who appreciates his skills. At times, he imagines that perhaps he, Margaret, and Mihill can live there for a good while and grow their family within a community that includes a small core of Africans. But then the thought comes unbidden: *I can't be a pork monger for the rest of my life.*

Margaret follows Frances's advice to listen to him patiently and respond with sympathy when he chafes and tries to discuss his concerns with her. She would like to be more helpful but has no answers either, not for him nor for herself. And so they both feel stuck, muddling along from day to day.

They have no idea what unexpected twists and turns their destinies are about to take.

* * *

Priscilla and Sheppard have been writing letters to their respective relatives in England, extolling the benefits of life in Virginia—the warm climate; the abundance of fish, fowl, wild animals, and land; and the many economic opportunities. The insatiable demand for tobacco in England and other parts of Europe continues to create wealth beyond anything imaginable in the old countries for enterprising people like John Upton.

Sheppard is thinking about expanding his land holdings, too, and being employed by the colonial government to keep the peace gives him a unique advantage. With the influx of new laborers from

England, planters throughout Virginia cultivate more than their existing tobacco fields. On the York Peninsula, they want to move beyond the palisade between them and the Indians. They already breach the wooden barricade at will to hunt, gather roots and berries, cut down trees for timber, and graze their horses and cattle. Feeling provoked, the Indians retaliate with raids of their own across the defensive barrier, and the ensuing skirmishes require Sheppard and his troops to intervene to restore an uneasy peace. The lieutenant gets well paid for his service and has every reason to expect that the tussles will continue for some years, guaranteeing him a steady income. Using the money, he plans to expand his property southward. It's easy to create new fields by girdling trees, but he will need more help to take care of the increase in crops.

Early in the summer of 1637, he receives word from his uncle in England that his two cousins, Agnes and Dorothy, excited by the glowing promises of his letters, want to immigrate to Virginia. With no likely marriage prospects where they live, they are willing to take the risk of seeking their fortune in the New World. They plan to stay with Sheppard until they can find suitable husbands. Feeling obligated to act as their guardian, he agrees.

After a flurry of letters back and forth across the Atlantic Ocean to work out details and seal the deal, Sheppard announces the news at supper to everyone on the plantation. His cousins will arrive in the spring along with more workers to clear and expand the fields to the south. Priscilla chimes in about how wonderful it will be to have more people around. Margaret, although she keeps her thoughts to herself, feels less enthusiastic, worrying about having to take care of another two women unused to the demands of plantation life. Hearing that Agnes and Dorothy will bring their own maidservant makes the news more palatable. An extra person around the house to assist with chores and help mind the children will make up for the extra work required to feed all the newcomers to the plantation.

Practical as always, Jason asks, "Where will they all stay?"

"I will have another addition built to the house—two rooms for my cousins and their belongings," Sheppard answers. "We'll also increase your living quarters to accommodate the additional workers. Margaret will share her room with the new maidservant."

Margaret feels as if she received a slap. Although she doesn't let it show, she feels both hurt and angry for being unvalued and unappreciated.

When supper is over, she clears the dishes in silence until Priscilla asks, "Is anything the matter?"

Margaret forces herself to remain calm. "I'm just wondering what will happen when John comes over?"

"I wouldn't worry about that," Priscilla says casually. "I'm sure things will work themselves out."

Surprised that someone she thought of as a friend would show so little regard and compassion, Margaret holds her peace and gets on with her work.

But the following day, Lieutenant Sheppard seeks her out when she is alone in the kitchen. Priscilla has taken the children for a walk. Margaret is kneading dough, getting ready to bake bread for the week, and looks up only briefly.

"I wanted to speak with you about your living arrangement," he says, giving her a slight smile. "Sharing your room with someone else will only be for a short while. I want you to stay on after you fulfill your contract of indenture. If you agree to do so, we can build a separate place for you, John, and Mihill."

As Margaret continues to dig her fingers into the dough, something John told her that Emmanuel said comes into her mind: "Until you are free, you will always be at the beck and call of the plantation owners." Out loud, she says, "That is very kind of you, Robert. Let me talk it over with John."

Sheppard nods. "Of course. Take all the time you want to make your decision," he responds and leaves.

Alone, Margaret considers her options. Her indenture will be finished in another year. What she really wants is for John to buy out Mihill's contract with the money from his privateering days, so they can all be at Ewens's plantation together. Surely, Sheppard will agree since her son is too young to be of use around the farm. Mihill wouldn't be of any value to him as a worker for some years.

But when she proposes it to John, he stares at the ground. "It is too soon," he says.

"Don't you want to be with us together as a family?" Margaret asks.

"Of course I do," he replies straightaway. "But people would talk, wondering where I got the money from. No one would believe I earned it from the hog trade. They would think I stole it and accuse me of being a thief!"

A wave of sadness comes over Margaret. "When then?" she asks in a small voice.

"I don't know!" John shouts in anguish. For a moment, he looks like a lost boy. Then his features harden and he says harshly, "I don't want to talk about it!"

When he storms off in anger, Margaret realizes that she has hurt his pride. He feels as powerless as she does.

The following Sunday, John acts as if nothing happened between them. He smiles as if he is genuinely glad to see her and Mihill. Margaret returns his smile, acquiescing for the moment but hoping that they can talk further soon and find a solution. In the meantime, she accepts the inevitable and tells Sheppard that she will share her room, but she does not look forward to the arrival of his cousins and their maid in the spring.

MONHEGAN
7/95

PART THREE

EXPANSION AND GROWTH

28

AGNES
AND DOROTHY
Virginia—Spring 1638

Whom Samuel Matthews's friends find out that Governor Harvey ignored the order to return the lands he confiscated to their rightful owners, they petition King Charles and his Privy Council with renewed resolve. The monarch, annoyed that his representative would disregard his decree, issues a more forceful pronouncement. That imperial order, a weighty scroll with official-looking crimson-red seals reaches Virginia in late March on the *Guiding Star*, the very ship that carries the passengers who will alter the course of Margaret's and John's destiny once again.

Margaret knows that big changes are coming, but nothing prepares her for the upheaval her life is about to undergo.

Sheppard's announcement that his two cousins are on their way from England has turned the plantation topsy-turvy, and for much of the winter and early spring, Margaret has been diligently at work to prepare for their arrival. But there is more to the arrangement. Sheppard's uncle, along with sending his two daughters across the Atlantic Ocean, also assembled a crew of laborers eager to make a new start in Virginia. He paid their fare and indentured them to

259

Sheppard, which will allow the lieutenant to claim 650 additional acres for his plantation, according to the headright system that allots 50 free acres to landowners per taxable person on their property. Tripling his land on the south side of the James River will increase his yield and earnings from tobacco and raise his standing in the community.

For Margaret, it means sixteen more mouths to feed.

In anticipation of the expansion, Sheppard hired carpenters who, with the help of Jason, Thomas, and Paul, have built another addition to the main house—two rooms overlooking a section of the creek. They also put up two more sleeping barns for the new male workers. The two young women besides Sheppard's cousins, their maidservant and a kitchen wench, will share Margaret's room.

Although she isn't happy with the sleeping arrangements, Margaret actually looks forward to their arrival. Having someone to help with cooking and other household duties is long overdue. It has been challenging to perform all the extra work to get ready—sewing pillowcases and mattresses, stuffing them with straw, and making bed comforters in case the cousins don't bring any.

Then there were the carpenters. When they first got started, they tracked so much dirt through the house that Margaret and Priscilla could hardly keep up, washing the floors and cleaning after they left for the day. The hammering and sawing woke up the children and baby from their naps. Coughing from the sawdust in the air, they cried inconsolably, adding to the general din.

When Priscilla complained that the workmen didn't take enough care, Sheppard, whose nerves were frayed by then, too, almost lost his temper. Margaret wondered why he was making such a fuss about the accommodations for his cousins, two women he hardly knew. They hadn't been born yet when his uncle sent him away to a military school, and by the time he left for Virginia, they were still young children. The few times he visited his uncle's estate, he hardly took notice of them.

But then Priscilla told Margaret something about Robert's past she didn't know. He was orphaned at an early age when his mother and father were executed as heretics for their extreme Puritan faith. Sheppard's uncle rescued him and took him into his household.

"He did not hold the radical religious views of his parents, yet he treated Robert like a son," Priscilla explained. "Robert feels that he owes everything to his uncle. He wants to do whatever he can for Agnes and Dorothy to have a good life here."

Margaret knows how important loyalty is to Sheppard. It is one of the qualities she values about him. But when she mentions what she heard about him to John, he doesn't seem very impressed. "So, Robert comes from a privileged background, which gave him a big advantage when he wanted to make a fresh start," he scoffs. "He got a second chance, untainted by his family history."

"I think you're being unkind," Margaret says softly. "It speaks well of him that he feels indebted to his uncle and is so keen to repay him for his support."

"Now that he'll benefit from it once again," John replied. "Let's see how loyal he is toward you for all you've done for him."

His words echo in her mind when the carpenters put the final touches to the new rooms before starting on the workers' barns. They construct bed frames with ropes pulled tight between the two side rails to support the mattresses. Two go to Agnes's and Dorothy's room, the other two end up in Margaret's already small bedroom, sitting there as a reminder of how confined her sleeping quarters will be.

The first time he sees the crowded room, John contemplates the empty bed frames with bemusement, too. He is not looking forward to sharing the room with two maidservants during his Sunday visits. But when Margaret tries to talk to him again about buying out the remainder of the indenture contracts for her and Mihill so they all can live together at Ewens's plantation, he remains adamant that it is yet not the right time.

The carpenters finish in late March, just in time. Only a week after they pack up their tools and leave, the *Guiding Star* arrives at Port Comfort. Once again, a messenger Sheppard paid to be on the lookout for the ship brings the news. Since the vessel is carrying important documents from King Charles, it will be cleared quickly to travel upriver and dock at James City the next day.

Immediately, the plantation becomes a flurry of activity. To get the two new rooms ready, Margaret sweeps up the dried rosemary and thyme she spread around to counteract the smell of the fresh pine timbers. She fluffs the pillows and places mint leaves under them. While Jason and his men put a large eating table in one of the new barns, Margaret and Priscilla spend the rest of the day in the kitchen preparing food, using extra supplies they bought in anticipation of all the new mouths to feed. Fortunately, they had just baked bread earlier in the week.

The next morning, everyone is up before dawn. It promises to be a chilly spring day, and Margaret stokes the fire in the hearth to warm up the living room. Sheppard, Jason, Thomas, and Paul gobble up their breakfast. No one mentions that it is probably the last meal they will share at the same table.

By the time the men row the boat down the creek, swollen from the melting winter snow, to head for James City, dawn has broken. Everything seems dipped in gray, even though the sun has risen above the treetops to the east. The sky remains overcast all day.

Priscilla and Margaret feed the children and dress them in newly washed gowns. Then they start to prepare the welcoming dinner. Since they don't know the exact time when Agnes, Dorothy, and the new workers will arrive, they have planned a collation of roast meats, bread, and cheese with a porridge that has been simmering all night over a low fire in the kitchen.

The tension of anticipation in the house is almost palpable. By the early afternoon everything is ready, and the women get impatient. Margaret has set plates, pewter cups, and silverware on the dining table, and rearranges spoons and knives to keep busy. She puts another log on the fire in the hearth and joins little Priscilla and Mihill who are playing with a rag doll and a small wooden ship in the corner of the living room.

"What could be taking them so long?" Priscilla frets, as she changes Susannah's diapers.

Suddenly, Thomas comes running up to the house shouting, "We're here, we're here!" He catches his breath. "I stepped ashore downstream and ran here to warn you they're coming."

Margaret goes to the kitchen and lowers the crane hook with the large iron pot over the flames to reheat the porridge. When she returns to the sitting room, she and Priscilla take one last look around the house to make sure everything is in order. Then Priscilla cradles Susannah in her arms while Margaret grabs the other children by the hands. Together they step outside and head down to the creek.

By the time they get there, Sheppard's boat is within sight, making its way to the dock. It hasn't warmed up any since the morning, and the women shiver in the cold breeze. Margaret puts her arms around Mihill and little Priscilla. As they wait, more skiffs round the bend of the creek. One carries travel trunks and furnishings. The others bring the workers, young men who huddle close together against the chill and gawk at the surroundings. One points excitedly ahead toward the main house.

The arrival of Sheppard's boat with a loud thud against the dock startles Margaret and the children. They watch as Paul tosses a rope to Thomas, who lashes it tight to the wooden post farthest upstream, leaving room for the next skiff. While Jason steadies the boat, Sheppard gets out and helps the passengers step up onto the platform.

Two women dressed in gray travel coats climb on land. They straighten their cloaks and walk unsteadily toward the small welcoming group as if they don't entirely trust that they're on solid ground again. They look like sisters, having the same long, narrow noses and thin lips. Their eyes are the same gray as Lieutenant Sheppard's. Margaret realizes that they are younger than her and Priscilla.

Sheppard makes the introductions. "Priscilla, these are my cousins, Agnes and Dorothy," he says.

Priscilla and the sisters curtsy to each other. Dorothy ventures a tentative smile, but Agnes remains stern-faced, her lips drawn tight.

When Sheppard says, "This is Margaret, who is in charge of the household," the new arrivals are taken aback and stare at her.

Margaret can't tell if it's because he introduced her as an equal to Priscilla or that they don't know what to make of her dark skin. She figures that the lieutenant told them she is African, but the reality of meeting her in person seems to have come as a shock.

Undeterred, Margaret curtsies and says in an affable voice. "This is little Priscilla and my son Mihill. We all are happy you made it here safe and sound."

"And this is Susannah, my youngest," Priscilla adds, indicating the baby in her arms.

The two women nod politely as a young girl emerges behind them. Her brown travel cloak is threadbare. She has pretty features and the whitest skin Margaret has ever seen. Her cheeks and forehead are dotted with light-brown freckles. Unlike the two sisters, the girl gapes at Margaret wide-eyed and open-mouthed.

Finally Dorothy speaks up. "This is Jane Hemlock, our maidservant."

"I've never seen a blackamoor before," Jane bursts out. Before Margaret can react, she embraces her and says, "I hope we'll be good friends."

Her simple gesture disarms Margaret, as does Jane's crouching down, smiling at the children, and chucking them under the chins.

"Mind your manners, Jane," Agnes says. "You are not a nanny."

Her nasal tone of voice reminds Margaret of Mrs. Chew. She feels pity for Jane, whose face turns red as a ripe strawberry in embarrassment.

Standing up awkwardly, she says, "Yes, mistress."

Priscilla breaks the tension. "Why don't we go inside? You must be famished from your long journey. Margaret and I have prepared a meal. Come, Priscilla. Come, Mihill."

She leads the way uphill toward the house.

Sheppard turns to Margaret and says, "Get the food ready for us, then feed the other arrivals." He doesn't wait for a response but finds Jason to give him orders regarding the new workers. "Show them their living quarters and bring the travel trunks of my cousins and their maid up to the house."

Meanwhile, Margaret and Jane watch as the second and third skiff dock and the men inside climb up on land.

"There is Lucy," Jane calls out, pointing to a girl even younger than she at the back of the boat. She waves to get her attention, then gestures for her to come to them.

A plain-faced, haggard-looking wench soon joins them. She seems to have none of Jane's spark and looks bewildered.

"Meet Margaret, who runs the household," Jane says. When Lucy doesn't move, she adds, "Go on, then. She won't bite!"

Margaret is relieved when a small, tentative grin breaks out on Lucy's face. Perhaps the girl is just shy. Margaret smiles and says, "Welcome, Lucy. Why don't you come with me to the kitchen? We have a lot of hungry people to feed."

She leads her and Jane around the house to the rear. When they get to the kitchen, Lucy looks inside and breathes in the smells with pleasure. There are baskets of bread and cheeses, and wooden tren- chers covered with linen cloths to keep flies away. Jane lifts one of them, revealing a heap of turkey and venison pieces. Margaret checks the iron pot filled with porridge and decides it is hot enough. She stirs it with a wooden ladle and fills four porcelain bowls.

While Jane and Lucy carry the bread and cheese into the sitting room, Margaret brings the bowls on a tray. Sheppard, Priscilla, Agnes, and Dorothy are sitting at the table in the living room. The lieutenant has opened a bottle of port. He and his guests are sipping the dark red liquid gingerly. The baby is back in her crib. Little Priscilla is sitting at a small table nearby. The sisters have shed their travel cloaks, revealing gowns that, although unadorned, are made of fine cloth. Margaret can imagine what the dresses in their trunks look like.

As she serves the bowls, Margaret hears Agnes complain, "I hardly slept during the voyage. I thought I was going to die!"

"She got the seasickness bad," Dorothy explains with a slight smile.

When Margaret sets the porridge before them, Agnes looks at the kernels of corn in it, wrinkles her nose, and sniffs at it like a finicky cat.

"Margaret is a marvel with spices," Priscilla assures her.

Dorothy dips into the porridge and starts to eat it without hesitation. Agnes scoops up just a bit with the tip of the spoon and tastes it with pursed lips. She makes a face but decides to take another bite. Then her hunger gets the better of her and she eats heartily just like the others.

On their way back to the kitchen, Lucy maintains a stoic expression, but Jane smirks and rolls her eyes. Margaret smiles to herself. She likes Jane already.

Jason and Thomas are waiting for them, looking at the food trays with longing. "We've finished unloading the travel trunks and showed the men their quarters. We'll bring the skiffs back tomorrow," Jason reports.

Thomas adds, "They're all hungry as wolves. And so am I."

"I have plenty of food ready for them," Margaret says, indicating jugs of cider, the baskets, trenchers of meat, and the big pot of porridge. "Take Lucy with you to help you carry them. You'll have to make several trips. When they have finished their meal inside, they will want the trunks brought to their rooms."

Margaret and Jane take the largest trencher and a bowl of bread pudding into the living room and help the children eat by cutting up the meat for them into smaller pieces. By the time everyone is done, Jason has returned with several of the new workers to the kitchen. Margaret brings him to the living room and introduces him.

Sheppard, leaning back comfortably in his chair, asks Dorothy, "Would you like to rest now? We'll get your rooms ready."

Dorothy nods gratefully.

"Bring their trunks," Sheppard orders.

Jason bows and withdraws.

"Jane," Agnes orders. "Help us change out of these travel clothes."

"Yes, mistress," Jane says, curtsying.

It takes the men awhile to lug the heavy travel chests inside. They leave the cabinet and wardrobe on the porch. Meanwhile Jane looks after Agnes and Dorothy. Margaret clears the table, and Priscilla takes care of the children, who are long past their nap time. After another hour, the sisters are settled and asleep.

When Jane finally tiptoes from Agnes's room, Margaret brings her to the kitchen. They sit on wooden stools and eat in silence, watching the sky outside slowly darken.

Before dusk settles, Lucy and Paul come carrying several baskets filled with the pewter bowls, cups, and spoons that the workers used. They are neatly stacked and clean. Lucy must have eaten with the men because she looks more alert.

"Paul and others helped me wash them at the creek," she announces, smiling.

Margaret is pleased. "That was very good of you."

Grinning, Paul says, "Always happy to help." He adds, "Well, a fine evening to you all," winks at Lucy, and trudges toward his sleeping quarters.

By the time the women have cleaned up the kitchen, it is pitch-dark outside. Margaret lights a candle and brings Jane and Lucy to her room. As they enter, she puts her finger to her lips and points to the crib at the foot of her bed.

Nodding in understanding, Jane whispers, "Where is his father?"

"John works on Ewens's plantation up the river and west of here," Margaret whispers back. "You'll meet him this weekend."

Jane looks around. Her small, wooden travel trunk sits at the foot of her bed.

Noticing that Lucy is swaying from exhaustion, barely able to stay on her feet, Margaret says, "Why don't you get some rest, both of you? I'll take care of things in the meantime."

Gratefully, the two girls lie down on their beds without removing their dresses and immediately fall asleep.

Margaret goes to the crib. In the flickering light, she looks at her son, who lies there with his eyes closed and a serene expression on his face. She smiles, then sighs, remembering how lost she felt when she first arrived in Virginia and didn't know anyone. Everything looked different from what she knew. She can imagine that for the new arrivals—women and men alike—having left behind family and friends, stone houses with well-appointed rooms, and familiar villages and cities, this must be a strange and daunting experience. And they haven't encountered the wilderness and backbreaking work in the tobacco fields yet. Aware of how hard life can be in Virginia, she wonders how many will survive.

29
INITIAL TENSIONS
Virginia—Spring 1638

If Agnes and Dorothy had hoped to live the pampered life of highborn ladies, they quickly realize that Virginia is not the idyllic paradise they imagined. On Sheppard's plantation everyone has to contribute. Perhaps Priscilla explained the reality of heading a small household in the colony, or the lieutenant had a word with them. In any case, they adjust to their situation without complaint. Although they rely on Jane to help them get them dressed in the morning, they do not demand her services all day long and let her assist others with their chores.

They, themselves, use their sewing and embroidery skills to darn and mend clothes. Agnes willingly feeds the chickens out back and collects their eggs. Dorothy, it turns out, likes children and is happy to spend time with them, freeing up Priscilla to do other things. She, in turn, relieves Margaret of some of her duties, allowing her to give her undivided attention to the most challenging task—preparing meals for a group of people that swelled overnight from six to twenty-two. Lucy turns out to be a great help in the kitchen, as is Jeremiah Bridges, a young lad of fifteen who assists her in carting the food to the workers in the fields. He has the face of a street urchin, with a stubby nose and a mop of reddish, unruly hair, but he is eager to lend a hand and proves quite capable.

All things considered, the transition goes surprisingly smoothly. The sisters soon follow Priscilla's lead and defer in domestic matters to Margaret as the most senior member of the household. The only moment of tension happens at supper the day after Agnes and Dorothy arrive. Margaret sets a plate for herself and Jane at the table. The meal, consisting mostly of leftovers from dinner early in the afternoon, doesn't require much preparation, and Lucy has started to eat with the workmen already.

Jane feels uncomfortable at first, but Margaret encourages her. "Don't worry. This is how we do things here."

But when they set the food on the table and draw the chairs back to sit down and join Sheppard, Priscilla, and the sisters, Agnes, barely able to contain her anger, hisses, "Servants do not eat with their masters and mistresses."

Jane flinches as if bitten by a snake and, flushing bright red, takes a step backward. Dorothy looks down at her plate. Priscilla holds her breath. Margaret stares in surprise at Agnes, then looks at Lieutenant Sheppard, challenging him to say something.

After exchanging a glance with Priscilla, he offers in a quiet voice, "I know that is the custom in England and in some homes in James City, but here we do things differently. Margaret has been a part of this family since she came here with me."

"Surely, Robert, you don't mean to—" Agnes starts to interrupt but, meeting Sheppard's determined expression, thinks better of it.

When the lieutenant continues, there is steel in his voice. "Margaret has lived here longer than anyone else at this table but me. She has always eaten with us, as has her husband, John, when he visits, and that will not change."

Agnes bows her head slightly. "As you wish, Robert. But my maidservant will not join us. I insist upon it!"

Jane quickly says, "I'll eat with the children," and pulls her chair to the table where Mihill and little Priscilla sit.

For the remainder of the meal, the air in the room is thick with tension despite Sheppard and Priscilla doing their best to keep the conversation light. The sisters barely poke at their food, but Margaret eats quietly and deliberately. She still finishes ahead of the others and gets up, excusing herself. When everyone is done, she and Jane clear the table as if nothing had happened.

For the next two days, Agnes treats Margaret with icy politeness and scolds Jane for the slightest mishap. Dorothy, who seems to be the more easygoing of the two sisters, continues to act friendly toward her. Still, Margaret wonders what it will be like when John comes by on Sunday afternoon.

She finds out soon enough because word of all the new arrivals at Sheppard's plantation quickly spreads throughout Hogg Island and the south shore region. John, figuring that everyone is busy adjusting to the newcomers, decides to bring the lieutenant's share of the smoked meat from the hog killing to the farmstead himself, rather than waiting for a time when Sheppard can send men to pick it up. He and two helpers travel midweek by boat from Ewens's plantation, with an assortment of hams, pork loin, and ribs, along with two barrels of meat pickled in brine.

In gratitude, Sheppard invites them all to stay for dinner—John at the main house and the oarsmen with the other workers. The sisters are surprised, but John's courtesy and well-mannered conversation soon win them over. The fact that he is now holds the position of assistant manager at Ewens's plantation, overseeing more than 150 people, impresses them. That he is responsible for the delicious ham Margaret serves helps, too. Even Agnes thaws a bit when he talks about how difficult the adjustments were for him when he first came to Virginia.

"I didn't know anyone at Ewens's plantation," he says.

"How did you manage?" she asks.

He reaches for Margaret's hand and squeezes it. "I've been fortunate." Then he quickly adds, "Everyone is very helpful here.

You'll see that when you meet all your neighbors this Sunday at church."

Afterward, he spends some time with Mihill and Margaret. She introduces him to Jane, Lucy, and Jeremiah.

When John takes his leave and heads outside to pick up his men, Sheppard joins him. "I'd like to buy additional meat from you, John. We'll need it with all the new workers to feed."

Pleased, John scratches his chin. "I'll check with Michael how much he has besides what's already promised to folks across the river, but I think we can accommodate you with whatever you need." He looks at the new section of the house with its newly thatched roof and stained timbers, and continues, "You should build a smokehouse of your own for turkey and venison. The hog meat will keep better there, too."

Sheppard considers the suggestion. "I think you're right," he says. "As we keep growing here, we will want to be self-sufficient."

* * *

That Sunday at Lawne's Creek Church, just about everyone comes from the surrounding plantations. Although John Uty is still in England, his wife, Anne, puts in an appearance, as do the Spencers and Uptons and their servants and field-workers. Even Richard Bennett shows up from Warrosquoake. They all want to get their first glimpse of Lieutenant Sheppard's cousins from England.

The other newcomers draw plenty of attention, too. Jane, with her simple, engaging manner, easily makes friends with other servants, both black and white. Her sincere interest in Anthony's children endears her to Mary. Lucy, reluctant to mingle, stands off to one side at first. But being young and unattached, she soon attracts a number of male plantation workers who flirt and vie for her attention like drones buzzing around a queen bee.

With Margaret at his side, John makes a point of seeking out Agnes and Dorothy to pay his respects. The sisters greet him politely—Dorothy says something complimentary about little Mihill at his side—but they barely acknowledge the rest of the Africans or menial workers. They prefer to mingle with the wealthy landowners and their wives instead, pleased by the gracious welcome they receive.

After the initial pleasantries of getting acquainted, the conversation turns to John Harvey's response to the strongly worded order from King Charles. Realizing that he overplayed his hand, the governor has started to return the property he confiscated to its rightful owners and their agents. It is a bitter pill for him to swallow, not only because of the implicit admission of wrongdoing but also because of the considerable reduction in his income. His cronies, notably Richard Kemp, who have to give up land they considered their own are unhappy, too.

But Harvey is not the kind of man who allows his spirit to sag for long. To let everyone in Virginia know that he considers this development only a small setback, he and Elizabeth have announced a large social gathering in a fortnight to celebrate the coming of spring.

When Dorothy wonders, naively, whether she should attend, Mrs. Uty touches her arm and says, "Oh, my dear, you and your sister must go! No one here likes Sir John—after all, he had my husband imprisoned in England—but none of us would miss one of his parties for the world!"

* * *

The day of the festivities a warm breeze accompanies Agnes, Dorothy, Sheppard, Priscilla, Jane, and Margaret on their way to the river. Flocks of migratory birds occupy the oaks and walnut trees. Margaret listens to their chatter and enjoys the ride. She muses about the frenzy of the last few days. All week long, the sisters have harried Jane to get their dresses ready, cleaning them, fixing the lace trimmings, and fastening the pearl decorations. Fretting over the slightest details, they'd driven nearly everyone to distraction. Even Priscilla, who always makes sure to look her best for these social gatherings, found their fussing excessive. Margaret can't wait to tell Frances all about it.

Arriving at Harvey's mansion mid-afternoon, Agnes and Dorothy are not disappointed. They find the interior furnishings as sumptuous as in any English manor they've visited. The governor gives them an effusive welcome and examines them with the appreciative glances of an old rake who has married but can't help stray with his eyes. As unattached, young women of some means, they quickly attract a crowd of the colony's eligible bachelors, sons of burgesses and planters. The young men fawn over the sisters, invite them to dance, and hang on their every word. Impressed by the lavish surroundings and reception, Agnes and Dorothy feel cherished. For the first time since their arrival in Virginia, they are joyful and glad that they left England and made the trip to the colony.

Margaret introduces Jane to Frances—Lucy has stayed behind to take care of the children—and then encourages her to have a good time, confident that she can take care of herself. Frances has heard from her own sources plenty about the coming of Sheppard's cousins, of course, but Margaret catches her up in detail, especially on Agnes's inconsiderate conceit.

"It sounds like you have another Mrs. Chew on your hands," Frances comments. "But you're more expert now. You can deal with her."

When Margaret voices her doubts about being able to handle such a large household, Frances berates her with kindness. "You're the oldest and most experienced woman there, with more abilities in your little finger than the five others put together," she teases, making Margaret laugh.

By the time she leaves, Margaret feels better and more confident.

On the way home, the night air is pleasantly cool, and the lantern at the bow throws a small cone of light on the waves ahead.

The bright moon illuminates the treetops on the other side of the river as a jagged black line and leads them to the entrance of the creek. Everyone feels tired but happy. Margaret is pleased that Jane enjoyed herself after a trying week. Agnes and Dorothy chatter like excited children about the young men they met, elaborating on their physical qualities and prospects. Priscilla adds her own knowledge of them, and they gossip contentedly, making the time getting to their plantation pass quickly.

When John visits the following Sunday, things go more smoothly than Margaret expected. Agnes and Dorothy welcome his presence at supper without complaint, and he continues to charm them with his affable manner.

Later that evening as they are cleaning up in the kitchen, Jane and Lucy announce that they will spend the night in the living room.

"You and John deserve to have the bedroom to yourself," Jane tells Margaret with a meaningful glance.

Margaret is touched by their generosity and accepts their offer. Although the opportunity is wasted as far as Jane's innuendo, she and John enjoy being able to talk in private and get a good night's sleep.

* * *

With Margaret and John assuming new responsibilities, their summer is busier than ever. As Goodman's assistant, John has to spend longer hours supervising the new workers and teaching them how to care for the growing tobacco and corn plants. When he does show up at Sheppard's, he is often irritated and tired. Margaret is just as preoccupied managing the household, keeping Sheppard's cousins satisfied, and spending enough time with Mihill. She and John both look forward to autumn after harvest and winter when things slow down a bit.

Most of the new workers at Sheppard's spend their time clearing fields for tobacco farther to the south. As a result, Margaret doesn't meet everyone right away. With Jane, Lucy, and Jeremiah helping, she actually has more time to tend to her herbal garden than she anticipated and to grow peas, carrots, beans, and other root vegetables to vary the meals she cooks for everyone.

Lieutenant Sheppard has been considering John's suggestion to build a smokehouse. When he mentions it to his foreman, Jason says, "I think we can manage that on our own. I'll see if any of the new workers have any carpentry skills."

Two days later, Margaret is alone in the kitchen when she notices Jason and four young men standing in a grassy spot nearby, leaning on hoes and shovels, talking. He walks off an area the size of a small room while one of the men follows him and uses a mallet to hammer pegs in the ground at the corners. Margaret recognizes two, George Griffin and Randall Whitley. The others are unfamiliar to her. They must have been spending their time working in the fields farthest to the south.

When she walks over to them, George and Randall nod to her respectfully.

Jason looks up and says, "These men are going to build you a smokehouse, Margaret."

"Lieutenant Sheppard told me last night," she says. She measures the longer side of the marked-off rectangle by walking heel to toe between the pegs at the corner. "I think it needs to be a little bigger to accommodate the fire pit."

"We can do that," Jason says. He points to the third man. "This is Joseph Spering."

"Pleased to meet you, Margaret," a thin youngster says awkwardly.

By then, the fourth man, who has been kneeling on the ground, joins them. "I'm Robert Swett," he says, wiping his brow. "Thank you for all the good food you've been cooking for us. I never ate that well in Cornwall."

Margaret looks at him in amazement. His eyes are bright blue as the summer sky. An image of Captain Jope aboard the *White*

Lion gazing at her flashes through her mind, followed by a pang of anguish that he is gone. She never thought she would see such azure eyes again.

Jason interrupts her reverie. "Well, Margaret seems to know what's required, so I leave you in her able hands."

As he walks away, Randall tells her, "Just tell us what you need, and we'll take care of it."

"I will," Margaret promises. "I'll check with my husband, too, when he comes by. He'll know what's required for sure."

"Is he the one whose hog meat we've been eating?" Swett asks. His voice is brighter than the gruff, commanding baritones she remembers from Jope, but it has the same Cornwall inflection.

"Yes."

"Well, he knows what he's doing. I've never tasted better."

Pleased, Margaret smiles. "I'll tell him. He'll be happy to hear it."

"I'll tell him myself when he comes," Swett says. He rubs his hands together and calls to the others, "All right. Let's get to work."

Until that moment, Margaret hadn't realized that he was the leader of the group. It surprises her. Although he appears to be a few years older than the others, he doesn't have the qualities she associates with someone being in charge, Except for the blue eyes and blond hair, there is nothing about him that seems anything like Jope. As she returns to the kitchen, she wonders what brought him from Cornwall to Virginia—what he left behind.

30
A WALK IN THE WOODS
Virginia—Spring–Fall 1638

John and Michael are trudging through the forest beyond the tobacco fields of Ewens's plantation to check on the hog population after the sows have farrowed. It is late spring and the tree canopy overhead has not yet filled in with leaves, allowing sunlight to stream down in bright beams and sheets of luminescence. It rained earlier in the day, a quick, intense shower that drenched the ground and left the air heavy and humid, redolent with the musty undercurrent of fermented leaves and pine needles.

Although they left their overcoats at the plantation, the two men are sweating in their white linen shirts. From time to time, they sweep their sleeves across their foreheads to wipe away the beads of perspiration. John is carrying his pistol along with a dagger in his belt while Michael has a large knife strapped to his side. His two hounds are straining at their leashes, but he keeps them tightly reined, lest they bark too soon and chase their quarry off. The men have taken them along as much to sniff out the hiding places of the wild hogs as for protection in case they encounter any Indians. The expansion of the plantation's tobacco fields southward, with snake fences as barriers, has driven the hogs deeper into the woods and encroached on territory the Quiyoughcohannock Indians consider their hunting grounds. Some are not happy about sharing the land with their new neighbors.

So Michael and John are wary as they look for places where the wild pigs have rooted for mushrooms and tubers, and track them to their lairs and hollows in the dense shrubbery. They have already managed to stir two sows with litters, one with sixteen piglets, the other with twelve. While the dogs held the mothers at bay, the two men used their knives to mark the offspring's small ears with three parallel angled cuts.

Soon they come to a small pond surrounded by oaks and cedars. Willows line the banks, their boughs reaching out over the water. The place always reminds John of the small lake in the woods behind Captain Jope's house in Cornwall, especially in winter when the tree branches were bare. Now, with light green leaves on trees unlike any John saw in England, the illusion is not as strong.

He and Michael round the raised banks until they come to a spot where an open stretch of shore slopes gently toward the water. It is muddy and covered with tracks from a variety of wild animals who've come to slake their thirst there. They recognize the imprints of deer and hogs and let the dogs sniff around for a while. At some point, one of them raises its head and proceeds to follow a set of tracks back into the forest. John and Michael follow at a leisurely pace.

For a while, they walk in silence, each wrapped in his own thoughts. John recalls the last conversation he had with Emmanuel Driggers, shortly after a ship arrived at James City carrying Africans taken from a Spanish slave ship. The men and women aboard came on land only long enough to be traded for tobacco by the waiting planters and their agents. Unlike the white immigrants from England who came to Sheppard's and Ewens's plantations, none of them received a contract of indenture.

"They call it indenture for life, but it's nothing short of slavery," Emmanuel said when they met and John expressed his disapproval. "The Africans don't speak English and are frightened. No one informs them of their rights."

Emmanuel had traveled to James City on behalf of Francis Pott to pick up provisions for building an addition to the plantation's tobacco barn in anticipation of a bigger harvest in the fall. Like Sheppard, Francis has brought on more workers—he, along with other owners in the area, got them directly from ships at Point Comfort when they first arrived—so Emmanuel knew firsthand what happens and it infuriates him. It rankles John, too, and he vows to do what he can for the new arrivals in James City.

When Emmanuel informed John of his coming, John delivered the last barrel of pork to John Chew's house, using the opportunity to get together with his friend. They met late in the afternoon near the governor's mansion where Emmanuel was spending time with Frances. They greeted each other like two men who liked each other but hadn't become close friends yet.

Emmanuel first asked after Margaret and Mihill—Frances would want to know every detail—and John obliged, happy to report that they were doing fine.

When he asked about Frances in turn, however, Emmanuel's face fell. "I am worried about our future," he volunteered. Then he leaned closer to John and said softly, "No one else in the colony has heard about this yet. Francis Pott just received a letter from his brother in England. All charges against the men Harvey accused of treason have been dropped. They're coming home soon. But Dr. Pott has decided to remain in London to continue plotting with his influential friends against the governor. He wants to have him permanently removed."

"I guess Harvey never realized what enemies he made, on both sides of the Atlantic Ocean," John said. "From what Margaret told me, Dr. Pott can be as tireless as a beaver and as tenacious as a bulldog."

Emmanuel laughed but quickly turned serious again. "I doubt that Harvey will last another year, and I worry what will happen to Frances if he decides to head back to England. What if she has to go with him and Elizabeth?"

John thought for a moment and ventured, "I don't think they legally can take a servant indentured in Virginia with them, especially one who came here directly from Africa. I'll check in the library when I get back to the plantation to be sure and will let you know what I find."

Emmanuel nodded gratefully, and soon after, they parted warmly.

Returning to Ewens's plantation, John did not feel as confident, however, as he had pretended to be with Emmanuel. He worried about his and Margaret's future, too. He wished he knew how to best proceed. He had almost asked Emmanuel's advice about what to do with his hidden stash of money but shied away at the last moment. Perhaps the next time they meet, he'd feel he can trust Emmanuel with that secret. In the meantime, he'd decided not to alarm Margaret about Frances's possible fate. No reason to worry her until there was definitive news about Harvey's future.

The dogs' barking brings John back to the present. Michael checks to see if they found something, but it turns out to be just a squirrel they chased up a tree. Sensing that his friend is distracted, Michael says, "Why don't we take a rest?" He ties up the dogs and sits down on a thick oak branch that has fallen on the ground.

John hunkers down on the roots of a hickory tree opposite him. He closes his eyes and thinks about the last time he was with Margaret. When he arrived Sunday afternoon at Sheppard's, he found her in the back of the kitchen in conversation with two workers he had not met. One of them had blond hair and said something that made her laugh. John was surprised. He had not heard her laugh like that for some time.

When they noticed him, Margaret beckoned him over and introduced them. "This is Randall Whitley and Robert Swett, two of the workers who are building our new smokehouse. My husband, John."

Pleased that Lieutenant Sheppard decided to heed his advice, John came closer, only to be startled by Swett's bright blue eyes.

As if she could read his mind, Margaret said, "Robert is from Cornwall, just like Captain Jope, but he never heard of him or his family."

"I grew up near Penzance, far to the east of Tavistock," Swett said in explanation, his bearded face open and friendly. "I understand you are the man who provides us with our delicious hog meat. I'd welcome any advice you can give us on the construction of the smokehouse."

He'd led the way to where six upright posts, four in the corners and one each in the middle along the sides were held in place with narrow crossbeams and ceiling joists from which the curing meat would be hung. The roof rafters, angled upward from either side, met at the central ridge board, the highest point. None of the walls had been covered yet. The skeleton building looked simple, solid, and big enough to accommodate meat for a plantation twice Sheppard's size.

John walked all the way around the long, narrow shed. "This will do quite well, but it is bigger than you need for now, unless you mean to go into the hog business yourself," he commented with a grin. He indicated a spot little more than halfway on the long side. "I'd put in a partition here and close it off; that way you can keep a small fire going as the meat cures. You can take it down when the plantation grows and you need more room."

"That is an excellent suggestion," Swett agreed immediately. "Isn't it, Randall?"

The younger man blushed, too bashful to contribute anything.

Looking closer at one of the mortise-and-tenon joints held together with wooden pegs, John said, "The joining shows excellent craft. Your work?"

Swett looked pleased at the compliment. "My father was in the shipbuilding trade, and I learned some skills from him," he said. "But it's really a team effort with Randall, George, and Joseph."

John appreciated Swett sharing credit with the other workers. Noticing that Margaret observed them with interest, he asked, "Where is Mihill?"

"Taking a nap. Dorothy and Priscilla are watching the children," she answered.

Swett excused himself. "I'm heading back to the barn. There is a card game I don't want to miss. I'm sure you two have plenty to talk about. Come, Randall."

He nodded to them and sauntered off, the youngster in tow.

Thinking back on the encounter, John reflects that there was something appealing about Swett. He liked his easygoing, yet confident manner. Margaret didn't have anything more to say about him, except to confirm that his eyes reminded her of Captain Jope, too.

When one of the dogs barks, John blinks and squints at Michael.

"It's nothing. He saw another squirrel," his friend says. "Ready to go on?"

John gets up, brushes off his pants, and repositions the pistol in his belt. Checking the angle of the sun, he figures that there is plenty of daylight left. "Let's find the next sow."

"If all the litters are as large as the first two and the fall crop is good, too, we'll have another superb year," Michael says.

"Let's hope so," John says. But following his friend who has taken the lead, he wonders if it will be enough to justify buying out both Margaret's and Mihill's contracts.

* * *

For Margaret, much of the rest of the year passes like any other. As Agnes and Dorothy settle into the daily routines, everyone relaxes. By the middle of July, it is apparent that Priscilla is pregnant yet again. The cousins are happy for her and solicitous of her condition, pitching in even more with household tasks when she gets nauseated in the mornings.

Swett continues to find ways to make himself useful, earning both Sheppard's and Jason's respect. More articulate than most of the other men who arrived with him, he can explain what needs to be done to his fellow workers better than Thomas or Paul.

When Daniel Walton stirs up a nest of copperheads while clearing the underbrush for a new field, he is fortunate that only one of them bites him in the calf just above his boot. By the time his terrified screams bring everyone running, the snakes have slithered away. Swett immediately takes off his belt and wraps it tightly around Daniel's thigh. Thomas cuts a cross into the bitemarks with his knife and sucks out the poison as best he can. Then they carry the terrified youngster to the main house, where Margaret takes over. She makes a poultice of mayapple ointment and lemon balm for his leg and gives him a draft of sassafras tea when he starts to shiver with ague. Daniel's leg swells and he spends a rough, painful night, but his fever breaks in the morning and he recovers quickly. Lucy's plentiful ministrations seem to help, too.

Swett receives many compliments for his quick reaction. "I'm just glad Daniel is all right," he says.

It turns out that he is a good storyteller, too, entertaining everyone at the special Sunday afternoon dinner with fanciful yarns. Lieutenant Sheppard has instituted the practice of having everyone on the plantation eat together once a week, weather permitting. As a military man, he knows the importance of keeping up the spirit of his men, and he doesn't trust Jason yet to know how to do that on his own. Since he is often away, both in James City and dealing with Indian attacks, Sheppard believes that personal contact between his family and his workers is important.

He appreciates Swett's verbal facility, which eases the potential awkwardness between the laconic workers and his cousins and

Priscilla. Agnes seems rather taken with Swett, too, although he doesn't encourage her in any way, no doubt thinking that she is above his station, certainly while he is still an indentured servant.

* * *

When Samuel Matthews, John Uty, George Menefie, and John West finally return from England in the late summer, they receive a hero's welcome, like veterans returning from a victorious battle. Just about everyone in James City comes out to meet the ship at the dock, and people send up cheers as each man descends from the main deck, waving, happy to be home.

At Lawne's Creek Church the following Sunday, Uty gets another rousing reception. Basking in the congratulations and good wishes from all those attending, he gladly satisfies everyone's curiosity about his time in England. William Spencer, acting as minister for the occasion, devotes his sermon to divine justice served.

If John Harvey realizes that the return of his enemies marks a sea change for his administration, he does not let on in any way.

Of course, he has his hands full dealing with another problem. Leonard Calvert, the governor of Maryland, has sent troops to seize the trading post on Kent Island in the northern Chesapeake Bay, belonging to William Claiborne. Although Harvey despises Claiborne, having removed him as colony secretary to appoint his crony Richard Kemp in his stead, the blatant aggression demands an answer.

While the governor considers what to do—an official protest to the King and Privy Council perhaps, a demand for compensation at the least—Kemp argues publicly that Harvey should ignore the matter.

This upsets a close friend of Claiborne. The Reverend Anthony Panton, the first Anglican rector of York and Hampton Parishes, starts to rail against Kemp in his sermons, calling him a "jackanapes," ridiculing his "unkempt" appearance, especially his elaborate hair-style, and accusing him of incompetence. Outraged, Kemp convinces Harvey to arraign the reverend on the charge of treason. With the governor presiding, the trial in James City is swift and predictable, resulting in a guilty verdict. Harvey sentences the Reverend Panton to pay a fine of five hundred pounds, requires him to publicly apologize for his speeches, and banishes him from Virginia upon pain of death, should he ever return.

While the matter of Kent Island remains unsettled, Harvey and Kemp are satisfied to have struck a permanent blow against their most vocal opponent. Neither realizes that a much bigger crisis looms on the horizon for them.

In December, the relentless agitating by Dr. Pott and other influential men, including the Earl of Warwick, to get rid of Sir John once and for all finally bears fruit. King Charles, tired of hearing complaints about the irascible governor, listens to his advisers and removes Harvey from office, appointing Sir James Wyatt in his place. The royal decree does not reach Virginia until more than two months later, in February of the following year, but Harvey's fate is sealed.

31
TROUBLE AND WOE
Virginia—Spring 1639

The hog killing in late January is not as bountiful as John and Michael had hoped. The fall litters were smaller than in the spring, resulting in a reduced harvest. While there is enough meat for both Ewens's and Sheppard's plantation, their personal shares are not as plentiful as in previous years. Michael takes it in stride—he has been in the hog trade long enough to know that there are good and bad years—but John is disappointed. It means he will have to postpone his plans to spend his own money freely for even longer.

He doesn't get a chance to mope for long because Katherine announces that she is with child. Although the pregnancy is not planned, Michael copes with it better than John did when he found out about Mihill. Bowing to the inevitable, he says, "We've always wanted to have children. Now we are going to, just a little sooner than expected."

John is amazed and decides to keep a discussion of the inevitable indenture issues to himself until after the child is born.

When John relates the news to Margaret, along with Michael's sanguine reaction, Margaret does not remind him of his own, for which he is grateful.

The next time she sees Katherine at church, Margaret gives her a hug and says, "I am so happy for you!"

Katherine, still elated by all the congratulations that have come her way at Ewens's plantation, says, "Thank you. I want you to be there to help when the baby comes."

Margaret clasps her hand. "You can count on me."

* * *

The arrival of King Charles's order dismissing John Harvey as governor eclipses all other news in Virginia for some time. His replacement, Sir Francis Wyatt, seems an excellent choice because he served as Virginia's governor before, during the Indian uprising of 1622. Many older settlers remember him as a forceful leader who took charge during that time of crisis, rallying the colony and helping it survive. They look forward to his arrival, hoping that he will act to unify the divided factions and restore reasonable discourse again. But Wyatt won't arrive for some months because he needs to put his affairs in order before setting sail for Virginia to assume the office.

In the interim, Colonel George Reade steps in as acting governor. He is just thirty-two years old, rather young for such an important office, and has ties to Harvey. But most of the colony leaders think him harmless, unlikely to cause any more trouble, and they accept him as a surrogate until the real governor arrives.

The most immediate change for Sir John is that he and his wife are forced to vacate the governor's mansion, even though he used some of his own money to build and furnish it. Rather than move into his wife's house in James City and endure the snide looks and mocking whispers of his neighbors, who all delight in his misfortune, he and Elizabeth withdraw to Boldrup Plantation on the Warwick River closer to the Chesapeake Bay. Although it now belongs to her son from her former marriage, as his guardian—Samuel Stephens is only ten years old—Elizabeth has the right to live there until he comes of age. Returning to a place that bears few happy memories for her, she decides to make the best of an unpleasant situation. Although quiet and secluded, the plantation lies close to the property of her sister, Mary, and her husband, Tom, who has supported Harvey throughout his tenure, assuring the outcasts at least two friends in a sea of enemies.

Harvey and Elizabeth make the move so quickly that it comes without warning for most members of their household. Frances barely has the time to convey a message to Margaret that she is leaving before climbing aboard the pinnace that will take her downriver. Margaret is dismayed that her friend departed without the chance to say good-bye to her in person. As the truth sinks in of what it really means, that she has once again lost the only person with whom she could be herself, Margaret feels a gaping loneliness in her heart.

Margaret was unhappy already when she heard about Harvey's successor. She remembers Francis Wyatt as a humorless, spiteful man, who resented her because she caught him unaware in a moment of weakness and self-doubt. She suspects he has not changed and can only hope that, after more than fifteen years, he has no recollection of her and the incident.

She knows Frances would have reassured her somehow, but now she is gone. Not one to feel sorry for herself too long, Margaret concentrates on the benefits that might come from this calamity. Frances will be living near Emmanuel again, and he will likely continue to come to James City with Francis Pott. On those occasions, Margaret will hear more news about Frances than when she was gone previously.

Thinking about how close a bond Frances and Emmanuel have had, even during their times of separation, Margaret realizes that she and John are going through a rough patch. She wishes they could be just as close, but since the hog killing, he has been even more preoccupied with matters at Ewens's plantation and concerned about the increasingly unequal treatment of Africans in Virginia. When she tries to point out that, for them and the other Africans in the vicinity, things are not so bad, he gets irritated with her and closes her out further.

Perhaps John is right. While the change in governors throws the colony administration into a crisis, it doesn't prevent the General Assembly from performing its legislative duties. At the first meeting of the year in James City's church, the burgesses pass a number of bills further regulating the tobacco trade, making it illegal to sell arms to the Indians, and prohibiting Africans from carrying any weapons—muskets, pistols, and knives—in public.

The Sunday after the acting governor signs the bills into law, John arrives at Sheppard's in a cloud of fury. He bursts into the main house and strides into the sitting room where Priscilla, Agnes, and Dorothy are knitting and doing needlepoint. Margaret and Jane are clearing away the last dishes from the midday meal, while Sheppard is at the hearth lighting his tobacco pipe with a burning twig. He looks up as John marches forward and plants himself in front of Sheppard.

Forgoing any greeting, John challenges the lieutenant, "Did you have anything to do with this outrage, Robert?"

Taken aback, Sheppard straightens. "What are you talking about?"

"The law forbidding me to carry my pistol and dagger!"

The women sitting on the sofa and chair look at one another in shock. They have never seen such rude and brazen conduct.

Margaret takes a step forward to intervene. "John—"

But John holds up his hand and hisses, "Not now, Margaret." He stares hard at the lieutenant. "Well?"

Sheppard shakes his head, containing his irritation, and says, "This is not the place, John. You're upsetting the women!"

John looks around as if coming out of a trance. He sees Agnes and Dorothy, cowering like frightened deer, fearful of a sudden outbreak of violence. Priscilla holds her round belly with a pained expression on her face.

Embarrassed, he says, "I am very sorry. My apologies, ladies. I don't know what came over me."

As he stands there uncertain, Sheppard gestures for him to go outside and beckons to Margaret to come as well. She quickly wipes her hands on her apron and follows them onto the porch, avoiding eye contact with Agnes, Dorothy, and Jane.

By the time she gets there, the two men are walking toward the creek. She catches up to them standing at the dock. The creek has risen high on its banks from the melting snow and spring rains, and there are eddies in the gurgling waters. The air is heavy with the smell of an approaching storm. John is tight-lipped. Sheppard takes a puff on his pipe and lets the silence settle.

Finally, he says, "I do not agree with that bill, John, and did not vote for it. Someone's been selling pistols and muskets to the Indians. In the last two encounters with them, they fired upon me and my men." His smile has no mirth in it. "Fortunately, they are terrible shots . . . as yet."

John looks at him, confused. "What does that have to do with this law?"

"The rumor is that it's the Africans doing the selling."

For a moment, John stands there stunned. Then he flares up. "Even if that were true—and I don't believe it for a moment—that's no reason to punish the rest of us."

"I don't like it any more than you do, John," Sheppard says unhappily.

"How am I going to protect myself when I go out into the forest looking after my hogs?"

"I wouldn't worry about that. Surely no one who sees you there will care one way or another."

"That is but small comfort," John replies bitterly. He hesitates before continuing in a contrite voice, "I'm sorry that I was so hot-mouthed, Robert. I'm very upset, but I shouldn't have brought this into your home."

Sheppard waves off his apology. "It's all right. Why don't you and Margaret spend some time together while I smooth things over with the ladies?"

John nods gratefully and lets Margaret take his arm. They amble toward the rear of the house.

"I wonder what Emmanuel will make of this," John says. "There must be more of a purpose to this law."

Sheppard looks after them, scratching his head, and takes another puff on his clay pipe. He starts to head back when a cry of distress comes from the house, so heart-rending it freezes all three in their tracks. Dorothy appears on the porch, wild-eyed.

"It's Priscilla," she cries out. "She's having the baby!"

For a moment they all stand there like girdled trees. Then Margaret springs into action. Hiking up her skirt, she dashes up the porch steps and rushes into the house.

Priscilla still sits in the chair, a big splotch of water staining her skirt. She looks upset, her doelike eyes terrified.

Margaret hurries to her side and takes her hand in hers. "Let's get you into the bedroom."

As Dorothy comes to her aid, Margaret turns to Agnes. "Go fetch a bucket of water and have Lucy boil it in the kitchen. Then bring it to me."

Agnes bristles. "How dare you order me about!"

Margaret says firmly, "I'm sorry, Agnes, but this is not the time. Have you ever helped bring a baby into the world?"

"No, but—"

Lieutenant Sheppard has joined them and interjects, "Please, Agnes, do as she says. This isn't the first time Margaret has assisted with birthing."

Agnes hesitates, but he has already forgotten her, hurrying to Priscilla and taking Dorothy's place at her side. "Oh, my darling, let me help you to our room."

Priscilla smiles gratefully. "I'm all right. I was just startled."

But she lets her husband and Margaret guide her into the bedroom and put her to bed. When they have settled her between the sheets, Margaret murmurs to Dorothy, "Find Jane and send her to me." As Dorothy leaves, she turns to Sheppard. "Thank you, Robert. Now, if you would—"

He smiles bravely. "I know. It's time for me to go. I'll send for Dr. Woodson." He kisses Priscilla on the forehead and walks out of the room.

Margaret gets linen cloths from an oak cupboard. It has started to rain hard, with drops drumming against the window, and the room is dark and gloomy. She calls for Lucy to bring candles.

By the time Jane arrives with a bowl of cold water for compresses, Priscilla has had her first contractions, minor twinges, but a welcome sign that things are progressing well. Both times Priscilla went into labor before, the babies came quickly. Margaret hopes that this birth will go smoothly also.

Then Dorothy brings a small candelabra, which lights up the room and raises everyone's spirits.

But as the day and evening wear on and the contractions come with greater frequency, Margaret gets worried. Priscilla labors through the night, her piercing screams echoing as far as the workers' barns, keeping everyone awake and anxious, but the baby won't come. Jane, Lucy, and Dorothy try to help, rubbing Priscilla's temples with spearmint and having her take sips of chamomile tea, but nothing relieves Priscilla's agony for long.

In the flickering candlelight, the room is heavy with the smells of her exertions and sweat. During a moment of calm when Priscilla lies back exhausted in the drenched sheets, Margaret feels for the baby and is horrified. It is positioned upside down, feet first. A feeling of dread and utter helplessness washes over her. She has never dealt with a breech birth but knows that that, at this late stage, the chances of a successful delivery are slight. She tries to put up a brave front for Priscilla's sake and makes her as comfortable as she can.

When Dr. Woodson finally arrives—the storm delayed his trip across the river—he notes the desperation in Margaret's face. When he takes her aside to ask about the progress of the delivery, Margaret says in a tight, low voice, "I'm afraid the baby is stuck. It's not in the right position."

The doctor strokes his beard. "Have you told anyone yet?"

Margaret, near tears, shakes her head.

Woodson goes to Priscilla and, with a forced smile and ebullient voice, says, "Well, let's have a look, shall we?"

He feels Priscilla's belly and works for a long time to right the baby, ignoring Priscilla's desperate screams. Finally, he stops. He pats Priscilla's hand and gets up, his shoulders sagging.

When he turns to Margaret, his expression is grim. "Keep her comfortable," he murmurs for no one but her to hear. "I must speak to Robert. Perhaps we can save the child, but there is no hope for the mother."

Margaret feels a stab of pain in her chest. She closes her eyes for a moment. Then she grits her teeth, goes to the washbasin, and wets another linen cloth. She sits down on the bed beside Priscilla, whose eyes are closed. Her face has the pallor of ashes. When Margaret gently wipes her forehead, Priscilla's eyes flutter open. For a moment, she seems not to know where she is. Then comprehension dawns on her pallid face and she asks in a small voice, "Am I going to die, Margaret?"

She sounds so forlorn, Margaret nearly breaks down in tears. To stop herself from crying, she takes Priscilla's hand and says firmly, "We're doing everything we can, Priscilla. God willing, everything will be all right."

When the next contraction comes, Priscilla scrunches up her face and screams at the top of her voice. She clenches her fists so hard that Margaret has to hold on with all her strength to prevent her hand from getting crushed.

As Priscilla's shrieks subside, there is a howl of anguish in the sitting room, and suddenly Lieutenant Sheppard stands at the foot of the bed, his hair disheveled and face wild, looking at his wife's wracked body.

As she starts to relax, he turns on Margaret, points to the door, and with eyes ablaze, shouts, "Get out! This is all your fault! You and John's!"

Margaret rises, shocked, "I am so sorry, Robert, but I—"

"Out! Now! And tell your husband never to set foot on my land again!"

He stumbles to the bed and collapses at Priscilla's side. Taking her into his arms, he starts to rock her and sobs like an inconsolable child.

Leaving, Margaret barely notices Dr. Woodson at the door making small placating hand gestures to her. She walks past Agnes, Dorothy, and Jane in the sitting room like a condemned prisoner on her way to execution.

Outside, she sees the first glimmer of dawn above the tree line. The air is clear and chilly. All the plantation workers have assembled in front of the porch, keeping a silent vigil. They look up at her with anxious, questioning faces. Margaret searches for John but doesn't see him anywhere. A collective shudder sweeps through the crowd as another series of tortured screams come from the house.

As Margaret walks down the steps, Jason and Swett come up to her.

"How is she?" Swett asks and flinches when Margaret shakes her head.

Jason says quietly, "I sent John away last night. I thought it best."

Margaret nods, but when she takes another step, she falters. Swett and Jason rush to her side to steady her.

Recovering her balance, she whispers, "Thank you. I'm all right. Please let me be."

The line of glum-faced men parts to let her proceed. Walking to the back of the house, Margaret has a metallic, bilelike taste in her mouth. She passes by the garden as if in a fog, paying no attention to the first green shoots of spring flowers poking through the musty soil. When she gets to the kitchen, Lucy is stoking the embers in the hearth, keeping the fire going under the cast-iron pot filled with water. Jeremiah looks on helplessly.

Margaret sits on a stool and buries her head in her hands.

Priscilla dies later that morning, hemorrhaging when Dr. Woodson cracks her pelvis to save the baby and ruptures a blood vessel. The child, a boy, is stillborn, choked by the umbilical cord wound around his neck.

The next day, they both receive a burial in a small clearing behind the main house. Everyone on the plantation attends the brief ceremony. A few neighbors come to pay their last respects as well, including Elizabeth Spencer and her parents. Lieutenant Sheppard, supported by Agnes and Dorothy, is too shattered by grief to speak, so it falls to William Spencer to say a few words and read from the Bible. Margaret watches from the back of the small assembly, a dull ache in her heart.

Despite Dr. Woodson's insistent explanation to Sheppard that she did nothing wrong and isn't to blame, the lieutenant acts as if Margaret does not exist. When he encounters her by accident, he doesn't say a word and looks through her. Agnes and Dorothy treat her as a pariah, too.

Lucy, Jane, and Jeremiah serve all the meals in the house while Margaret keeps to the kitchen, until it is time to go to bed. When Lucy gives her the all-clear sign, she sneaks into the house and tip-toes to their room.

She spends as much time with Mihill as she can. One afternoon, he helps her dig in the garden to plant bluebells in memory of Priscilla.

32
DISAGREEMENTS
Virginia—Spring-Summer 1639

For the next two weeks, Lieutenant Sheppard spends several hours each day sitting at Priscilla's grave. He stares at the simple wooden crosses staked in the dark earth mounds of Priscilla and their son with a forlorn expression and remains deep in mourning. When he walks about the plantation, he hardly utters a word and mumbles only curt replies in response to questions. He continues to ignore Margaret. On the occasions when their paths cross and their eyes lock briefly, she feels such hatred issuing from him, it strikes her with fear. In the face of his wordless fury and his cousins' dismissive attitude toward her, Margaret goes about her duties with stoic determination, but she is hurting inside, too. Priscilla was her only friend at the plantation, and Margaret feels bereft, pained by the thought that she was somehow responsible for her death. In her mind, she goes over obsessively what happened but can't find anything she did wrong. Still, the possibility that, had she only known more about birthing, there might have been a way to save Priscilla and her child keeps gnawing at her. How she misses Frances.

John wonders as well if he bears some of the blame, but he doesn't feel comfortable sharing his doubts with Margaret because she is so troubled herself. When he mentions his qualms to Katherine and

Michael, however, they disabuse him of any guilt he might feel, even if he caused Priscilla to go into labor. They support Margaret as well. But when Katherine encourages her to talk, Margaret remains silent, unable to find words for the jumble of her distraught emotions.

"Give it time," Katherine counsels her. "The lieutenant will get over it, and things will return to normal." She adds, "By the way, this changes nothing for when I have my baby. I want you there taking care of me."

Her bigheartedness and compassion almost move Margaret to tears.

They also give her the courage to approach Sheppard after supper to talk about rescinding his declaration that John is not to set foot on his property. The lieutenant turns red as his uniform and doesn't let her finish before shouting, "I meant every word of it. I will get my musket and go after him if he shows his face here."

The following Sunday, when Margaret tells John of Sheppard's pronouncement, he responds with righteous indignation.

"That is despicable," he explodes, heedless that others startled by his outburst look at him in disapproval. "I have a right to see you. What happened was not my fault, nor yours!"

"I know," Margaret says, putting her finger to her lips and pulling him aside among the trees. "He has dark moods and is irritable with everybody."

John bristles. "Has he put a hand on you?"

"He would not do that," Margaret says with a confidence she doesn't quite feel. There are times when Sheppard's anger has frightened her.

John feels reassured, but after the service he confronts the lieutenant, "A word, Robert."

Sheppard freezes and eyes him with disdain.

"I am very sorry for your loss," John starts. "I can't begin to imagine what you're going through, but I will come to see my wife. You have no right to prevent me."

Aware that the other churchgoers are watching, Sheppard gazes at John for an uncomfortable spell. Then he says in a tight voice, "You may visit Margaret, but you are not to step inside my house. You are not welcome there." He turns away and stalks off.

After that encounter, Margaret spends most Sundays after church with John at Ewens's plantation. It gives her a reprieve from the strained atmosphere at Sheppard's, and she welcomes the opportunity to play with Mihill unencumbered by Priscilla's children.

For part of the afternoon, Katherine and her husband keep an eye on the boy so that Margaret and John can have some time to themselves. They usually take a walk to the river or the outskirts of the plantation, along the snake fences protecting the farthest tobacco fields from wild animals. They note the changes in the growing plants and the forest—the maturing leaves of the hickory and chestnut trees and the flourishing, dense undergrowth. Taking comfort in each other's presence, they try to enjoy these moments of respite, untouched by concerns about the past or future. When they talk, their conversations deal with mundane matters, although John continues to be vocal about his resentment of the burgesses in the General Assembly and of Sheppard for supporting the law prohibiting him and other Africans from carrying weapons in public. Margaret lets him rant without commenting. She understands why it is so important to him, even if it seems to her that he is overreacting.

Since there is no place for her to spend the night in privacy, she returns with Mihill to Sheppard's plantation before dusk. On occasion, John finds someone to help him row them home, but most of the time, Margaret and the boy tromp back through the forest on their own. It is a long walk, and Margaret keeps him engaged by pointing to squirrels leaping among the branches and having him imitate the calls of different birds they encounter. Although Mihill does his best to march along like a little soldier, he tires and Margaret has to carry him for the last mile or so. She doesn't mind. Alone with her thoughts, she readies herself for the despondent mood at

Sheppard's house. If it weren't for Mihill, she would consider moving into one of the barns with the workers.

Around the time Sheppard finally starts to emerge from his cocoon of grief, Indian clashes in Henrico County across the James River call him away. Everyone is relieved when he is gone. In his absence, the melancholy fog that has covered the plantation like a shroud lifts. Workers start to smile, tell jokes, and sing again while laboring in the fields. Even Agnes becomes less judgmental. Everyone hopes that military action will cure the lieutenant of his gloomy disposition and restore him to his former self.

But when Sheppard returns a week later, for a while, things are actually worse. With Priscilla gone, there is no one to help him transition back to civilized life, and he unleashes his anger on Margaret, criticizing her at every turn. Margaret tries not to take it personally, but his words sting. When he recovers after a few days, he does not apologize nor relent, resorting to stern-faced civility and irritability, leaving her feeling miserable.

Fortunately, some of the other workers—notably Jason, Thomas, Robert Swett, Jane, and Lucy—try to make up for Sheppard's conduct by treating Margaret with kindness and compassion. They express frequently their appreciation for her cooking, especially when she serves up new dishes. Lucy and Jane pitch in with chores that Margaret usually does on her own.

* * *

One Sunday afternoon in the middle of the summer, as Margaret returns with Mihill from Ewens's plantation, she is surprised to find Robert Swett waiting near the oak tree whose fallen trunk reaches across the creek to make a natural bridge. Although tobacco fields have encroached southward, this area is still surrounded by lush, virgin forest, and Swett is alone, sitting on a smaller log nearby and whittling away at a branch.

Margaret is carrying Mihill on her shoulders, and when Swett sees her, he smiles, gets up, and waves hello. He approaches her quickly.

Perspiring from the oppressive humidity, Margaret wipes her forehead and adopts a teasing attitude. "Why, Mr. Swett, fancy meeting you out here in the middle of the wilderness."

"I figured you could use a hand if you came this way," he says, taking Mihill from her.

Grateful, Margaret smiles at him. She sits down on the log to rest and says, "You should be careful out here by yourself. The Quinyoughcohannock Indians sometimes come this far when they hunt and forage, and they could cause you trouble."

Swett remains standing and gives her a big grin. "The same could be said for you, a woman out here alone."

"I have Mihill to protect me and keep me company," she replies with a comical expression.

Glancing at the sleeping boy in his arms, Swett chuckles. "I don't think he'd be able to protect you while he's asleep."

"I don't need protecting," Margaret says. "The Indians don't bother me."

"Really? And why is that?"

"They think we dark-skinned Africans are ghosts and leave us alone."

Swett's amazed expression and the penetrating stare of his blue eyes tell Margaret that she has perhaps said too much. She hopes he won't question her further and is relieved when he just raises his eyebrows and nods his head.

But then he says, earnestly, "I would never think of you as a ghost."

She flushes. "Shall we get back to the plantation?"

"Very well," he says, almost disappointed.

Margaret rises and brushes leaves from the back of her skirt.

Carrying Mihill close to his body, Swett steps onto the tree trunk and deftly crosses the creek. On the other side, he puts the boy on his shoulders. Mihill is so sleepy that his head rolls forward, his chin resting on his little chest. Swett extends his hand to help Margaret to get down from the trunk. She takes it, jumps, and lands smartly on her feet. As they head toward the plantation, she is surprised how comfortable it feels to walk beside him.

By the time they get to the edge of the first tobacco field, the sun has almost set. The last rays swathe the top of the tobacco plants and cornstalks in a golden haze. The growing green crops contrast with the dead trees among them, the girdling notches visible on their black trunks. Margaret has a sudden notion of life existing in the midst of death, and she draws in an involuntary breath.

"The lieutenant is back," Swett says, jolting her from her musing.

Margaret sighs. She is not looking forward to his irritable moods. Out of the blue, she asks, "How long is your indenture, Robert?"

If her question surprises him, he doesn't let on. "Three years," he answers candidly. "I came into a little money when my father died and used it to pay for part of my passage."

"Oh, I am sorry about that."

"Don't be. He was a hard, miserly man who turned every farthing over twice before he spent it. I was surprised he left me anything at all."

"What do you aim to do when you've fulfilled your contract?" Margaret asks.

Swett shrugs. "I figure I'll take the fifty acres that are my due and stay in the area. I've got some skills and should be able to do work I like." He adds casually, "What about you and John?" From her silence, he can tell that it is not an easy subject for her. "I don't mean to pry," he follows up quickly. "That's your business and his."

"It's all right. I don't mind you asking," Margaret says.

By then, they are close enough to the house that she is spared the need to answer. "I appreciate you helping me," she says. "I'm obliged to you."

"Don't mention it," Swett says, smiling. "No bother at all." He lifts Mihill over his head and deposits him in Margaret's arms. The sleeping boy puckers his lips but doesn't wake up. "Anytime I can help, let me know." He turns and walks off toward the workers' barn.

Margaret looks after him, puzzled. Then she heads toward the kitchen and gently puts Mihill down on a blanket in the corner. She goes to the fire pit and stokes the embers. They are glowing bright red. She puts on more logs to make sure the fire will last through the night. Then she sits on a stool and watches as flames start to lick at the black bark of the wood. She plans to stay there until it gets dark before taking Mihill into the house and bedroom and go to sleep herself. She can only hope that Sheppard relents at some point and acts like a decent human being again.

* * *

But the lieutenant remains adamant and distant as ever, locked in his angry resentment toward her. In late summer, Indian troubles call him away to the York Peninsula, and when he returns a week later, he acts as if he, not the Indians he fought, were on the warpath. He goes out of his way to find fault with everything Margaret does, from her meals to her gardening to the way she folds the laundry. At times he looks at Mihill with resentment, and he never addresses the boy directly.

The constant verbal assault—abetted by Agnes and Dorothy, who add their own snide comments—takes its toll on Margaret. Many a night after an especially vicious onslaught, she has a difficult time going to sleep, and when she does, her dreams turn into nightmares.

One Sunday afternoon at Ewens's plantation after a particularly difficult week, Margaret and John head to the James River while Katherine watches Mihill. They walk past stands of oak trees with Spanish moss swaying from the branches. The air is thick with humidity, and the slight offshore breeze provides little relief.

When they reach the wooden dock with the large shed at the far end where tobacco hogsheads are stored prior to shipping, Margaret finally speaks. "His verbal abuse never stops, John. He has not an ounce of kindness in him. I can't stand it any longer."

It is not normal for her to complain, and her pained tone of voice alarms him. "I wish there were something I could do, Margaret," he says sympathetically. "I really do."

"You can, John," Margaret insists, putting her hand on his arm. "It is time to use the money Captain Jope gave you and buy out the contracts of indenture for Mihill and me."

John reacts as if stung and moves a few steps away from her. His mind reeling, he grips a wooden post to calm himself. As he feels Margaret coming up behind him, he sighs and murmurs, "You know I can't do that."

"Why not?" Her challenge is filled with anguish.

"It's too soon. You know how people talk and rumors fly."

She turns him by the shoulder to face her. "That just an excuse."

Unable to meet her eyes, he pleads, "I can't take the risk, Margaret, especially not now that I have a position of responsibility here. It's not the right time. Not yet."

Anger wells up inside her. "With you, it'll never be the right time."

"That's not fair!"

"I can't believe you'd put your reputation above the well-being of your family." Her voice is scathing.

"It's a dangerous time for all of us Africans," he retorts, incensed. "The burgesses are trying to limit our rights. We have to tread with care."

"I thought you cared for me. Some husband you are!" she hisses and stomps off.

"Margaret!" he calls after her. "Don't go."

But she feels too furious, too hurt to stop. As she trudges to the houses for the plantation workers, she feels miserable and abandoned, and her eyes fill with tears. Why couldn't John recognize how wretched she is and do something about it? She feels as if he doesn't see her at all.

When she reaches Katherine and Michael's cottage, she wipes her tears on the sleeve of her blouse and puts up a good front. Katherine is playing a game of quoits with Mihill, watching him toss the ring made of rope at an upright wooden stick in the ground. It lands a foot short, but Katherine claps her hands in encouragement. When Margaret's shadow falls across the playing area, she looks up, surprised to see her alone.

"Thank you, Katherine, for taking care of him," Margaret says with a small, forced smile. "Come, Mihill, it's time for us to go home."

When he starts to pout in disappointment, she gives him a sharp look. He gathers the rope rings and, handing them over, says, "Thank you, Aunt Katherine, for playing with me."

Katherine pinches his cheek affectionately. "We'll play again next time."

Without further explanation, Margaret propels Mihill forward by the shoulder toward the main house. As they approach the fork where a path branches off toward the forest, they encounter John. She stops long enough for him to say good-bye to his son, but when he tries to approach her, she turns away, unyielding.

"Time to go," she says to Mihill, takes him by the hand, and walks away.

John looks after them. He feels hurt and angry with Margaret for being so obstinate, and furious with Sheppard for putting him on the spot. He knows that he let Margaret down, even if he had to refuse her. If only Emmanuel would come to James City soon. He is the only one John trusts to tell about his hidden stash and ask for advice. Katherine and Michael are helpful and kind, but he can't rely on them to keep his secret.

As Margaret and Mihill hike through the dense woods, she despairs of what to do. She never imagined John would be more concerned with his reputation than doing right by her. How can she trust him or be close to him if he doesn't have the best interest of her and their son at heart? A thought crosses her mind that it would be nice if Robert Swett met them by the creek. But when they get to the fallen tree, he isn't there, and she feels disappointed.

33
ROBERT SWETT
Virginia—Summer 1639

When Swett first laid eyes on Margaret, she took his breath away. He had heard from sailors in Cornwall about Africans in the colonies, but he'd never actually seen a dark-skinned person before, and he thought she was beautiful. Then he met the others from the nearby plantations at church, including Margaret's husband, John. They were all hardworking and intelligent. Although they tended to keep to themselves, when he sought them out, they were warm and sociable, and treated him with respect. Anthony's knowledge of cattle and horses, and Michael's and John's understanding of the hog trade were impressive, and Swett recognized them as like-minded peers. They were eager and determined to gain their freedom and make something more of themselves than becoming lifelong field hands.

But Margaret fascinates him most. It isn't just her attractive, full-figured body and naturally regal bearing that appeals to him—she is tall compared to most women—but also her expressive face, which suggests intelligence and curiosity, and kindness and sensuality, too. When she gets excited about something, her eyes sparkle in a way that makes him want to share her enthusiasm. Although Priscilla's death and Lieutenant Sheppard's shameful treatment of her have dimmed her good cheer for some time, her perseverance in the face of relentless censure impresses him. He wishes he could get to know her better.

His work on the plantation makes it possible to see her with some frequency in ways that draw no attention. Being handy with all kinds of tools, Swett has become something of a jack-of-all-trades around the plantation, relieving him of the long, tedious hours and backbreaking work of tending the tobacco and corn plants. He fixes snake fences where wild hogs damage the rails trying to gain entry to the fields. In the spring, he reinforced the dock at the creek where the surges of water from the melting snows threatened to unmoor some of the older support pilings. During the summer downpours, the roof of the main house springs a leak. Rooting around in the attic, he finds a hole in the wooden planks, probably caused by raccoons, nails it shut, and replaces the thatch covering.

His ability to organize and manage the men required for the various repairs and projects, and get the jobs done efficiently, makes him invaluable to Jason and Sheppard, and they come to rely on him for other matters as well. As a result, he spends more time at the main house, and his friendly manner charms everyone there, especially Dorothy. Even Agnes, who thinks of herself as a serious-minded person, smiles in his presence. His sunny demeanor, good humor, and handsome appearance, enhanced by his blue eyes and dashing, straw-blond locks of hair, add to his appeal.

When Margaret was banished from the living room during the day, Swett always poked his head in the kitchen during his visits to the main house and said something to cheer her—or he searched her out in the garden and engaged her in conversation about various herbs and flowers.

Swett knows he took a risk meeting up with Margaret and her son at the creek that Sunday she returned from Ewens's plantation. She might not have shown at all or welcomed his attention. Spending too much time alone with a married woman is improper, and he has no intention to upset Margaret's relationship with John. The few times Swett has talked with John, Swett has found him to be perceptive and likable. But he is drawn to Margaret with such force that he can't help himself and continues to create occasions that allow him to spend brief moments with her.

As summer arrives and plants thriving in warmer temperatures grow, Margaret takes more frequent trips into the forest—sometimes alone, sometimes with Lucy—to look for herbs, roots, berries, and mushrooms. When Swett sees her leave, he makes sure to inspect the fences at the edge of the plantation fields so he can encounter Margaret as if by accident when she returns and exchange a few words with her.

One afternoon, he visits Margaret in the kitchen. She is cutting up one of the smoked hams to put into a batch of soup simmering in a large iron pot over the fire.

Swett approaches her with hands behind his back and, when she looks up, says almost bashfully, "I've made a present for Mihill."

Margaret gives him an odd look, which turns to amazement when he brings his right hand forward. He holds a small, carved wooden duck, its beak and some feathers blackened with charcoal. It looks remarkably lifelike.

"I made it from butternut wood. It will float in water," Swett says happily.

Margaret gazes at him, mystified. "It's beautiful, but I can't accept your gift. It is too special."

Anticipating her objection, Swett smiles and shows his left hand, revealing another, similar duck. "I made one for little Priscilla, too."

Margaret feels bewildered—he has anticipated that others might construe him playing favorites—and marvels at his thoughtfulness and consideration. "In that case, I thank you kindly," she says and bows slightly. "I'm sure the children will be delighted."

She takes the duck and runs her hand over the smooth surfaces. A welter of emotions plays over her face—joy, pleasure, melancholy, and sorrow—and it moves Swett deeply. He imagines that it is the first time Margaret has received a gift in a long time, even if it is for her son.

"I hope Mihill will enjoy it," he says, keeping his voice steady. "I'll just deliver this one to the lieutenant for Priscilla." Then he quickly leaves to go inside the house.

For the next several days, to the amusement of everyone, including Sheppard and his cousins, thin, high-pitched quacking sounds echo through the house.

* * *

But Swett's fascination with Margaret does not flag, and he soon gets the opportunity to spend more time with her. For a fortnight, in the depth of summer, heavy morning and early-afternoon rain prevent the gatherings at Lawne's Creek Church and make it impossible for Margaret to visit with John at Ewens's plantation afterward. Instead, during lulls in the downpours, Lieutenant Sheppard conducts services on the porch of the main house, leading the small congregation in prayer and passages from the Bible. Not having to travel to and from the church gratifies the plantation workers because it gives them more free time in the afternoon.

The second week, after the dinner meal, when the skies start to clear, Swett takes a chance. As Margaret prepares to go for a walk in the forest, he asks, "May I go with you?"

For a moment, she looks at him with suspicion, but the smile accompanying his request is so guileless, she consents. "I'm pleased for the company."

While Lucy cleans up the dishes and Jane takes care of the children, Swett and Margaret use the break in the weather to head out, ambling past the tobacco fields into the woods. Margaret is wearing her white linen cap and has brought a basket along to collect berries and mushrooms. Swett has put on a brimmed hat. Insects buzz around them, and the air is thick and steamy after the morning downpour, under the tree canopy. From time to time, drops of water fall on them from the leaves overhead.

Swett tells Margaret about growing up in Cornwall, in the town of Ilfracombe at the mouth of the Bristol Channel. Many ships take advantage of its sheltered harbor, and as a boy he dreamed of going to sea and visit faraway places. Being the second son in the family, he would not inherit his father's shipbuilding business, and he didn't want to work for his older brother. He considered immigrating to the Massachusetts Colony but heard that it was filled with Puritans whose religious fervor wouldn't suit him. When he read a notice from Sheppard's uncle seeking able-bodied men to go to Virginia, he jumped at the chance.

Margaret finds Swett easy to talk to. When he asks if she really meant her warning about Indians—he has yet to meet one—she tells him what happened during the Indian uprising. It is the first time Margaret has talked at length about that terrible time to anyone but Frances. Swett's thoughtful questions lead her to share her memories of the plague and her time at the Chew residence as well.

She tells him about her confrontation with the merchant when he tried to cheat her by adding extra years to her contract of indenture, which resulted in her coming to Sheppard's plantation. Swett looks at her with admiration. "That was courageous of you and smart," he says. "What last name did you put down on the written document?"

"Cornish. Margaret Cornish."

Swett surprises her by roaring with laughter. "Margaret of Cornwall," he calls out in delight. "Why, that practically makes us kin."

She joins in his merriment, but when he asks, "Why did you choose that name?" she hesitates. Although Captain Jope cautioned her against speaking about that part of her history, she feels that enough time has passed and decides she can trust Swett.

So, she says, "I actually spent time there and liked it."

Now it is Swett's turn to be surprised.

Margaret talks to him at length about her time in England and Jope's role in her life but omits the Earl of Warwick from her account. In the telling she remembers things she hasn't thought of for twenty years—the evening of heavenly music at the mansion in Aldwarke; the ice flowers on the window panes in winter; Aunt Isabel's parting words to her; Mary Jope, her hair as golden as Swett's, waving good-bye from the entrance of her home. Feeling no more than a pang of sadness, she realizes that the wounds of leave-taking against her will have all but healed.

Amazed at the wealth of her experiences and how long she and John have known each other, Swett feels apprehensive. Prying further seems like trespassing on sacrosanct ground.

As they return to the plantation, he carries the basket heaped with herbs and wildflowers for Margaret's garden. Near the workers' barns, he leaves her to head to the main house by herself. Margaret walks on, happy that she has been able to unburden herself and baffled when she grasps that someone has actually paid attention to her for the first time in years.

So, she is secretly pleased when it rains the following Sunday morning again, allowing her and Swett to take another stroll together and resume their conversation.

The forest is just as humid after the morning rains as before, but shafts of sunlight cut through the dim atmosphere. As they make their way carefully among the wet bushes, Swett bends the branches aside for her. In the open section of the path, they walk side by side, occasionally bumping against one another.

Swett tells her about his mother, who died when he was eight, and his father remarrying soon after to have someone in the house to take care of the children. "She was a stout, hardworking woman who had her hands full," he says of his stepmother. Blushing a little, he continues wistfully, "She had a beautiful singing voice, and she loved us with all her heart."

It has been twenty years since Margaret saw her mother for the last time, and she can't remember the sound of her voice. "I am glad for you," she manages, giving him a little smile.

But when Swett asks her, "What happened to your parents?" her face clouds over and he adds quickly, "You don't have to tell me if you don't want to."

Tentatively, Margaret starts to talk about Pongo, her village in Africa. Once she decides to loose the restraints, she doesn't hold back. She tells Swett about her father, who was a chieftain; her mother, who gave her a pearl on her birthday in honor of her name; the Imbangala raiders, who surely killed her parents and enslaved her; the long walk to Luanda, yoked to John; being branded at the docks; traveling chained in the belly of the Spanish slave ship across the Atlantic Ocean; and being rescued by Captain Jope.

This time, her memories overwhelm her and she breaks down in tears. Swett takes her into his arms, holds her, and gently strokes her hair while she sobs and shakes uncontrollably.

As she starts to recover, he whispers, "I can't imagine the horrors you went through, but you're here now, safe, and with me."

When he turns her face toward him and she looks up at him shyly, he kisses her, and she responds.

Realizing what he is doing, he pulls back. "I'm sorry, I shouldn't have—"

But she wraps her hands around his head and draws him to her. Her lips are soft and eager.

They grasp each other and run their hands up and down each other's backs. Swett puts his hand on her breast, feeling her nipple swell through the fabric of her dress. Margaret gasps and he pushes her up against a chestnut tree. She raises her skirt while he loosens his belt and lets his trousers drop to the ground. As they come together quickly in a prolonged shudder of passion, it starts to rain again, the patter on the leaves accompanying their feverish union.

By the time they pull apart, they are thoroughly drenched, but neither of them cares. Laughing, they strip off their clothes, spread them on the ground and lie down together to explore each other's naked bodies more slowly. Swett finds the scar in Margaret's side where the branding iron left its mark. He kisses it gently before returning with his lips to her belly, breasts, and dark nipples. She draws him on top of her, and the warm rain caresses them as they make love again.

* * *

That night tossing in her bed, Margaret can't go to sleep. She keeps seeing Swett's blue eyes locked on hers as the two of them moved in unison, molding their bodies to each other's desire. In all the time she has been with John, she has never experienced such ecstatic joy. She loves him, she knows, but this is different. There has been only one other person in her life who has made her feel that he saw her for who she really is, and that was Captain Jope. And now Robert—dear Robert—in his eloquent silences, with his loving words, and through his passionate actions.

From deep inside her, she hears a whisper like a sigh, "It is your destiny."

She sits bolt upright in the darkness and listens, but hears only the beat of her heart pounding in her ears.

In the morning, Margaret eats wild carrot seed and brews a tea of pennyroyal flowers to prevent getting pregnant. After breakfast, when she, Jane, and Lucy clean dishes and prepare for the dinner meal, Robert walks by the kitchen on his way to a meeting with Lieutenant Sheppard. When he looks questioningly at her, she gives him a surreptitious smile and watches him relax, then straighten and walk on with eager strides.

For the rest of the week, they act as if nothing happened between them.

34
WYATT
Virginia—Fall–Winter 1639–1640

The following Sunday dawns with clear, sunny skies. After a month's hiatus, nearly everyone at Sheppard's looks forward to catching up with friends from other plantations at Lawne's Creek Church. During the boat ride, Margaret worries that John might notice a change about her: her growing anxiety.

When they arrive, a large crowd has gathered already in front of the church—so many people that there won't be enough seats inside for all of them.

Margaret avoids Swett.

Then she sees John with the other Africans from Ewens's plantation. For a moment, she wants to run away, feeling that she will be so transparent that he will know what happened, or at least ask about a change in her.

But when she approaches, he greets her publicly as befits their relationship. "I'm very glad to see you, Margaret," he says and kisses her as if their argument never happened.

Then he picks up Mihill and gives him a kiss on the cheek. "I haven't seen you in a quite awhile. You've gotten heavier."

Watching John relate so easily to the boy brings a smile to Margaret's face, covering the sudden anxiety she feels about what she has done.

317

After the service and during the midday meal at Michael and Katherine's cottage, the conversation remains easygoing. But later on, at Ewens's plantation, John launches into what seems foremost on his mind. Another English ship that raided a Spanish slave galleon docked at James City during the week. All eighty black Africans aboard were sold to various planters and merchants.

"George Menefie and Richard Kemp both purchased some of them, the very councilors chosen to uphold and enforce the laws of Virginia. Yet they placed them under no contract," John fumes. "None of the Africans received a contract of indenture."

John comes back to the subject several times until Margaret feels that he is trying to tell her how fortunate she is, having a contract at all. To keep things light, she agrees with him, but inwardly she resents him trying to manipulate her feelings.

At some point, Katherine, who has watched Margaret increasingly withdraw as she and John keep talking past one another, takes Margaret aside. "You know, John is very upset that he can't help you with Sheppard, but he is too proud to admit it," she explains. "He hates feeling like a failure to you. It's why he won't look you in the eyes."

When Margaret realizes the truth of what Katherine is saying, all anger disappears from her being, and her heart goes out to John. When she returns to the cottage where he is playing with Mihill, she goes to him and puts her hand on his cheek. Startled, John looks up. Seeing forgiveness in her eyes, he takes her hand, gratefully, and kisses it.

For the remainder of the afternoon, they sit together comfortably on the stoop of Michael and Katherine's cottage and watch the sun descend on the other side of the river.

When it is time to leave, John says, "I have organized a crew so I can row you and Mihill to Sheppard's," he says.

"Thank you, kind sir. I accept," she says, with a humorous smile.

Once they're on the way, they enjoy the breeze on the river before they reach the entrance to the creek to Sheppard's plantation.

Margaret, sitting with Mihill on her lap, points to fish jumping and enjoys watching him clap his little hands with joy. But she is troubled. She feels torn between her duty to her husband and son, and her growing relationship with Robert Swett, which, although she doesn't understand yet how, could very well be her destiny.

After that conciliatory Sunday with John, Margaret almost ends her budding relationship with Robert. But at night in bed, she can't stop thinking about him. She shivers as she remembers the touch of his hand on her breast, that taste of his hungry mouth, the adoring stare of his dazzling blue eyes. The next time he asks her to come with him when there is an opportunity to sneak away, she follows him into the forest as if under a spell.

* * *

Fall is the busiest time of year, filled with candle and soap making for the winter and the harvesting of tobacco and corn. Everyone is preoccupied and tired from work, and Margaret and Robert have little time to get away together.

Having made up, she and John resume their Sunday visits, but the quality of their relationship has changed. The worst damage has been repaired and they get along well, but something remains unresolved between them. As a result, they are cordial and friendly but not intimate. Without a place to spend the night together and be physically close, they continue to live what feels like distant lives.

Frequently now, when Margaret returns through the forest, Robert waits for her and helps her carry Mihill back to Sheppard's plantation. She is always happy to see him, but in her son's presence, their exchanges are pleasant without being overly familiar. Robert makes no demands on her and gives no hint that he wants to do more than be helpful.

One positive development in the Sheppard household is that the lieutenant has grown less angry with the passing of time since

Priscilla's death. While he doesn't act any warmer toward Margaret, at least he stops disparaging her. As she gradually feels relieved of the emotional burden she's been carrying, her dreams of getting away from Sheppard's plantation diminish and her resentment of John for his betrayal of her all but disappears.

When Katherine goes into labor, she asks John to get Margaret right away. John races to Sheppard's in record time. Margaret, in turn, hurries to Ewens's plantation and the cottage where Katherine is experiencing the early stages of contractions. Anne Goodman and several female servants and field-workers who have had children of their own are with her. They have started all the necessary preparations, bringing cloths and starting to boil water, but Katherine relaxes visibly when she sees Margaret. After examining her, Margaret reassures her that everything is in good order and begins the long vigil into the night. She does not leave Katherine's side, keeping her as comfortable as possible.

Although routine, it is not an easy delivery. Katherine lies in labor for twenty hours. John does his best to keep Michael on an even keel. It is an impossible task. For someone who is normally imperturbable, he vacillates between ecstasy and terrified despair. John finally asks Mathew to get them when the baby comes, and takes Michael to the most distant fields on the plantation, out of range of his wife's screams.

By the time Katherine delivers, she is completely drained. She can't keep the infant at her breast without help and hardly recognizes Michael when he arrives, tired but jubilant. Margaret is exhausted, too, but her spirits are high. Successfully guiding her friend through the birthing has restored her confidence in herself and her abilities. She feels euphoric and grateful.

Two weeks later, she and John stand as godparents at the baptism of Katherine and Michael's daughter, Rebecca.

* * *

On December 10, Sir Francis Wyatt finally sets foot on Virginia's soil. More than fifteen years earlier, after the demise of the Virginia Company, he was installed as the first royal governor of the colony, and now he has been recalled to serve again. No one doubts that his mission is to assert King Charles's prerogative and put an end to the rebellion caused by Governor Harvey's mismanagement. The question on everyone's minds is: will he be as tyrannical as his predecessor, or will he work with the General Assembly and Governor's Council to further the interests of the colony?

Warned by a letter from King Charles's Privy Council of Wyatt's coming, George Reade makes extensive preparations for the new governor's arrival. When news reaches him that Wyatt's ship has been sighted at Point Comfort, Reade sets his plans in motion. The next morning, a welcoming committee consisting of burgesses, important merchants, and a large crowd of spectators assembles at the docks. A militia honor guard, carrying muskets and looking dapper in red uniform, stands by. The weather is unseasonably warm, with not a cloud in the sky, which pleases the wives of the wealthy attendees because it allows them to display their fancy gowns to the fullest. Everyone is eager with anticipation, but the excited chatter soon dissipates, and people get restless and bored waiting for Wyatt to arrive.

It takes another two hours before the tall galleon rounds the harbor entrance and approaches the main pier. At the first sighting, everyone perks up. A few boys race to the far end of the jetty for a better look. As the ship docks, sailors and dockhands secure a long gangplank between the main deck and the wharf. When Wyatt appears high up at the guardrail, a cheer rises from the crowd, and the soldiers of the honor guard snap to attention. The new governor acknowledges everyone below with a slow wave of his hand. Then he directs a sweeping gaze across the town. Much has changed in the fifteen years he has been absent from James City. New, larger homes have been built along the shore, some of brick, the harbor has been expanded, and there seem to be many more people milling about in the public areas.

Those who remember Wyatt from before whisper to each other that he does not look any different. Even though he professes the Anglican faith, he is dressed like a Puritan, all in black. As he descends the ramp, the soldiers salute as one. The welcoming ceremony is formal and brief. Reade takes off the chain of office with the large gold pendant and places it over Wyatt's head. The Reverend Faulkner offers a prayer of thanks for his safe journey. Then Reade and the other dignitaries accompany Wyatt to the governor's mansion, his new home, while his servants bring his travel trunks after them.

At the reception in his honor, Wyatt is cordial yet distant, nothing like the voluble Harvey or his interim replacement. Agnes and Dorothy, whom Sheppard has brought with him for the occasion, are pleased to attend, even if the gathering is nothing like the celebrations they're known. There is no music or dancing, and Wyatt soon pleads exhaustion from the long voyage and asks to be shown his rooms upstairs.

The party breaks up with many of the attendees leaving dissatisfied, unsure what to make of their new governor. When, later that night, the full moon turns dark red for more than an hour, many Virginians are frightened and troubled. The most superstitious among them interpret the lunar eclipse as a warning sign from heaven that darkness will descend on the colony during Wyatt's tenure.

* * *

Lieutenant Sheppard and his cousins return to the plantation earlier in the afternoon than expected. Having eaten and drunk their fill at the welcoming party for Wyatt, they forgo supper, and Margaret uses the opportunity to get away to spend time by herself. Lucy and Jeremiah are happy to serve the workers on their own. Jane promises to look after the children while Margaret steps outside. When it gets dark outside, she puts Mihill to bed and kisses him goodnight.

While the other workers gather by the porch, hoping to glean news about their new governor from Sheppard and his cousins, Margaret sneaks out through the kitchen and heads for the forest. She will learn everything there is to know about Wyatt's arrival from the gossips at church the next day. She thinks about her encounters with the new governor after she witnessed his shameful loss of faith. Wyatt deliberately ignored her whenever they met on the street afterward. Although she can't imagine he would remember her so many years later, she has no intention of crossing his path again, not if she can help it.

The night air is still mild and the full moon is bright in the dark blue sky, lighting her way. Margaret walks to the clearing in the forest, hoping that, surrounded by trees rustling in the soft breeze, she can leave her concerns behind and experience a sense of calm and freedom.

But when she gets there, the sky has grown dark and the moon is halfway obscured by a ruddy shadow. Margaret sits down and watches in amazement as a translucent layer the color of red wine covers the entire lunar disk. She does not feel frightened, only curious, marveling at the beauty of the strange phenomenon.

When she hears noise in the underbrush and sees a flickering torch in the darkness, she doesn't feel worried. It must be one of the plantation workers. No Indian would make so much noise.

As the light comes closer, a voice calls out, "Margaret. Are you here?"

She recognizes Swett and replies, "Yes, Robert. Over here."

Emerging at the edge of the clearing, he says, "Oh good, I found you. I saw you walking toward the woods and was worried when the moon turned red."

Margaret feels oddly comforted. That he cared enough to come looking after her fills her with gratitude and yearning. "I'm obliged to you, but I'm not ready to go back yet," she says.

As he approaches, he extinguishes the torch. The smell of tallow is overpowering and dissipates slowly as he sits down next to her on the dry ground. They gaze at the moon together in silence and wonderment. With the lunar orb obscured, the stars surrounding it are visible again. The nighttime sky looks like a carpet strewn with diamonds.

"What do you think is going on?" Margaret asks.

"I don't know. It's a mystery and very beautiful, like you."

It is too dark for him to see Margaret flush with pleasure. She leans toward him, and he takes her into his arms. They kiss and start to make love unmindful of the hard ground. They move unhurriedly, letting their desire build slowly until, gasping and crying out, they reach orgasm. By the time they are satiated, the moon has almost returned to its normal color, as if its incarnadine coating has been washed away.

As Margaret rearranges her clothes, she says, "I suppose it's time to head back."

Swett agrees. "Yes. And it is bright enough that we won't need the torch."

They walk through the forest holding hands. The tree trunks on either side of the path loom like ghostly shadows. Margaret feels a close connection with Swett.

When they get back to the edge of the plantation, she says, "Thank you for coming to get me, Robert. I like spending time with you."

"Me, too, Margaret," he replies and kisses her.

They separate as in the past to make it look like they're coming back from different directions.

Margaret looks after Swett as he walks away and disappears into the darkness. She goes back to the main house and enters through the kitchen door to go to her room and bed. She listens to Jane's and Lucy's even breathing as her mind swirls with images of the evening and her heart tries to sort out her conflicting emotions.

* * *

Over the next few weeks, as people meet with Wyatt, officially as well as casually on the street, they still consider that the lunar eclipse the night of his arrival might have been a troubling omen. No smile ever seems to grace his face, and his dark, aquiline eyes fix on people who encounter him with such an intent stare that it makes them uncomfortable and they can't wait to be out of his sight.

Yet Wyatt's initial actions also endear him to many colonists. The day after he stepped foot on Virginia soil, he sent for Sir John Harvey to come to James City. Upon Harvey's arrival, Wyatt arraigned him before a court to answer all the charges against him, brought in England and Virginia, including his exiling the Reverend Panton from the colony. Harvey promised to mount a vigorous defense, leading to predictions that the trial would drag on for some time. That pleases the gossip mongers, as it provides them with ample fodder for months. Meanwhile, Wyatt makes sure that the last of the confiscated properties are returned to their rightful owners, bringing most of Virginia's gentry to his side.

But the colonists soon learn that, while their new governor has aged a good deal—the furrows in his forehead have deepened and the lines around his mouth increased—neither he nor his agenda have changed. When it comes to his religious views, Wyatt may be even more extreme than during his first tenure.

When he discovers that observance of the Sabbath has become lax because of Virginia's rapid growth, he starts to enforce rigorously the laws for mandatory church attendance in James City. News of offenders being put in the stocks and pillory and whipped for other transgressions, such as blasphemy, quickly travels throughout the colony.

The impact on the plantations across the river isn't as severe. None of the owners or managers are religious zealots, and they frequently make allowances for people being absent from church or cursing in frustration while at work. Still, the people attending the services at Lawne's Creek Church come with ears peeled, eager to hear about Wyatt's latest conduct and pronouncements. Gathering around recent visitors to James City for the latest news, Margaret and Swett keep their distance in public. She congregates with the African adults and children, while he joins the white servants listening to the smaller group of white planters and their wives chitchatting.

It is a different matter at the hog killing in early January, which brings members of Ewens's and Sheppard's plantations together. During the day, men and women have separate tasks. But in the late afternoon and evening, everyone gathers to eat and celebrate. This season's hog harvest has proved unexpectedly successful, with a large number of wild pigs butchered, and everyone, happy that there will be plenty of meat to go around in the coming year, gets ready for carousing and merrymaking. Beer and cider flow freely around the fires, and the smell of freshly roasted pig wafts in the air.

As the feast progresses, men and women start to dance, and Margaret watches them with envy. Her feet twitch in time to the drumbeat of tabors accompanied by fifes, fiddles, and bagpipes, and she would like to join them. But that would require coaxing John to participate, and he is content to lean back and relax after a long, hard day's work.

When the musicians take a short break, Swett comes over to where they are sitting with Mihill and their African friends. He bows formally and asks, "Margaret, would you do me the honor of joining me in the next jig?" He quickly turns to John and adds, "Only with your husband's permission, of course."

Margaret feels mortified. Swett has put her on the spot, drawing unwarranted attention to her. But John grins and waves his hand in approval.

Katherine comes to her rescue, unaware of what is going on. She smiles and says, "Go on. We'll come, too." When she looks at her own husband, however, Michael puts up his hands in protest. Undaunted, she turns to Mathew sitting next to him and, with a gesture that brooks no refusal, insists, "Come on, it's our turn."

When Mathew shrugs good-naturedly and gets up, Margaret can't very well object. Her friends all know she is the best dancer among them and eager to participate. So she accepts Swett's invitation and together the two couples walk to the edge of the dance area where a spirited hornpipe is in full swing. As they wait with others, clapping in rhythm to the music, Margaret gives Swett an irritated look, but he smiles back, unperturbed.

When the music finishes to generous applause, many couples return to their sitting places, while a few intrepid dancers stay on. The onlookers join them, lining up women on one side, men on the other, until the musicians strike up a lively jig. At first, Margaret holds back, but soon the music invades her body, and she leaps and twirls with abandon. Holding hands with Swett in public makes her tremble with pleasure, and she can only hope that the vigorous dancing disguises her feelings.

When the jig is over, Robert leads her back to John and says, "Thank you."

Then he walks away to where Sheppard and his cousins sit with Thomas Goodman and his wife. To Margaret's surprise, Swett asks Agnes for a dance and she accepts, looking gratified as she takes his hand. Margaret feels a pang of jealousy, but when John says, "That man's a dancing fool," she realizes that Swett is making the rounds deliberately. By showing everyone that he just wants to have a good time, he is protecting her reputation.

When she glances at Katherine, whose sensitive nose usually itches at the slightest suggestion of indiscretion, she sees no hint of suspicion, just an acknowledgment of how much she is enjoying the feast. Relieved, Margaret tousles Mihill's hair and puts her arm around John's shoulders. When she draws him close, he responds in kind and nuzzles her neck affectionately. As the evening wears on, she feels curiously happy and content.

Two weeks later, she discovers that she is pregnant.

35
RUPTURE
Virginia—Spring-Summer 1640

Margaret agonizes for several days before she gets up the courage to tell Swett about her condition. She weighs numerous possibilities in her mind on how to respond to him, depending on his reaction to the news—whether he is angry like John, unhappy, calm, indifferent, or perhaps even pleased. Finally, she goes on a walk carrying her basket, for all intents and purposes to gather new tubers and roots now that the soil has softened. But she makes sure to pass him and give him a small hand signal before she heads directly to their secret meeting place deep in the forest. The clearing surrounded by bare trees and leafless shrubs still has patches of snow on the ground. Robert arrives soon after, eager to spend time with her.

He immediately senses that Margaret is worried about something and asks, "What is it?"

"I am with child," she says right away and looks at him searchingly, waiting for his response.

To her amazement, Robert exclaims, "That is wonderful news! I can't tell you how happy I am." He embraces her, lifts her off the ground, and spins around several times.

When he puts her down, Margaret takes a moment to recover her balance and asks, "You're not angry?"

"Why should I be angry?" He takes her hands and kisses them. "A child is a gift from God!"

Margaret is taken aback. Those are the very words she said to John when he found out that she was pregnant with Mihill.

Robert looks at her, smiling. "How long have you known?"

"A week . . . I don't know. . . ." As he places his hand on her stomach, she adds plaintively, "But what shall we do? I'll start showing in another month and won't be able to hide it anymore."

"We will figure it out together," Robert says with assurance.

She marvels at his elation and confidence. For the first time since she realized what her fatigue and nausea in the mornings meant, she is free of worry and fear.

But her anxiety returns immediately when he says, "Of course, you must tell John."

That is what she has been dreading most of all—John finding out. She doesn't know how he will react, but she can't imagine the conversation going well. Nonetheless, Robert is right. "I will talk to him after church," she says.

But that Sunday, John seems preoccupied and Margaret gets cold feet and postpones telling John for at least another week.

It is Katherine who lets the cat out of the bag the following Sunday, before Margaret gets a chance to warn John herself. Heading by boat to Ewens's plantation, her daughter Rebecca in her arms, she faces Margaret sitting next to John on the wooden bench with Mihill between them. Comprehension dawns on Katherine's face when she notices Margaret's radiant glow, but she waits until they reach land before saying anything.

When they get to her cottage, she takes Margaret and John by the hand and bursts out happily, "Congratulations to both of you."

John looks at her baffled.

"I hope it is a girl this time," Katherine continues blithely. Then she notices Margaret's horrified expression. Mistaking it as irritation because she wanted to tell John herself, Katherine lets go and claps her hand to her mouth. Then, she says, "I'm sorry. I didn't know you hadn't told him yet."

Margaret manages to whisper, "That's all right."

Realizing what is going on, John looks with shock at Margaret.

But before he can react further, Michael puts his arm around John's shoulder and exclaims, "That is wonderful news! I am so happy for both of you."

John smiles uncomfortably, and Katherine signals to her husband to stop and let him go. She tells Margaret, "Why don't I take Mihill for a spell so you two can have some privacy? I'm sure you have a lot to talk about."

"We certainly do," John says with forced joviality.

He and Margaret head toward the woods, relieved they no longer have to feign good cheer. Walking in silence along the barren fields, John rushes ahead with such determination that Margaret has a hard time keeping up. She is familiar with his behavior. When something troubles him, he guards his feelings by holding them in and throws himself into work or intense physical activity. Now his world has collapsed and he has no idea what to do.

When they enter the forest, John continues to hurry on until he reaches the small pond. The willows on the raised banks are bare. At the lower embankment, transparent sheets of ice line the shore.

John stops at the water's edge, picks up a pebble, and tosses it hard, shattering a delicate ice pane. As Margaret catches up, breathing heavily, he turns and stares accusingly at her. In a constricted voice he says, "What have you done?" For a moment, his face betrays anger and anguish, but then he clenches his jaw, concealing all signs of emotion.

Margaret stands there distraught. When she has caught her breath, she says softly, "I don't know, John. It just happened."

A flash of anger crosses his face. "Who is the father? It certainly isn't me!" When she doesn't respond, he continues with a sarcastic edge to his voice, "Let me guess. It's Robert Swett, isn't it?"

As his eyes glare with rage, Margaret lowers hers and gives a small nod.

In an instant, John explodes. All the pent-up emotions burst forth in a long howl of accusations. "How could you? You have ruined my life! Our life together! Why? Tell me! Is it revenge because I didn't use my money to buy your and Mihill's contract?"

Margaret shakes her head. "I am so very sorry, John. I never meant to hurt you. You must believe me."

Furious, he raises his hand as if to strike her. When Margaret rears back like a frightened horse, he clenches it into a trembling fist and lowers it to his side. Horrified by how close he came to hitting her, he turns away. Suddenly he doubles over. Dropping to his haunches, he squeezes his head as if trying to contain the unbearable pain.

Approaching carefully, Margaret stands over him and says, "It's not your fault, not my fault."

He looks up with tears in his eyes. "I have loved you with all my heart, and you've broken it into pieces."

Hunkering down in front of him, Margaret takes his hands. "I love you, too, John."

"Then why?" His voice is small like a hurt child's.

Margaret says, "I believe Robert is my destiny!"

He searches her face for any sign that she is fabricating or making an excuse, but her eyes are steady, conveying the certainty he has seen in them only when Margaret is sure of herself. His emotions overwhelm him, and he starts to sob in deep, heavy gasps. Margaret puts her arms around him, tears spilling from her eyes as well.

The wind gently shakes the branches and twigs of the surrounding trees.

When no tears are left, Margaret gives John's shoulder a squeeze, and they slowly separate. Standing up, they rub their stiff legs and wipe their wet faces. John looks around as if waking from a nightmare, recognizing the place for the first time. Margaret is deep in thought. It is a moment of respite for both of them.

Finally, John asks, dejected, "What do we do now? This is a terrible muddle."

Margaret takes a deep breath. "I have a favor to ask of you," she says in a tentative voice.

Bewildered, John turns and looks at her.

She meets his eyes. "Please don't tell on me," she pleads.

His face clouds and he feels rage bubble up inside him again. Between clenched teeth, he says, "I don't know if I can do that."

"You know what will happen if I'm found out." Margaret's face is open and vulnerable.

For an instant, he wants to smash it. Then he realizes that, no matter how angry he is with Margaret, he can never hate her. "If I say yes, how would it work?" he asks carefully.

"I don't know. But it will buy us time to figure it out."

He shakes his head. "I don't promise anything."

Margaret understands that he can go no further now. Gazing into his eyes unafraid, she says, "Thank you."

* * *

During the next week, John returns to the pond several times at different hours of the day and once late at night. His emotions swing wildly, like a mad pendulum. Every time he thinks of Margaret and Swett in each other's arms, rage and pain overcome him, and he screams at the top of his voice, cursing at the crowns of the silent trees. But he also experiences brief interludes of serenity and even pleasure, thinking about how he and Margaret survived together, how she took care of him on the way to Luanda, in the bowels of the Spanish slave ship, and at Aldwarke until he went to sea with Captain Jope. Since his arrival in Virginia, there have been so many good times—and, of course, their son, Mihill. He just can't believe it's all over between them.

As the first leaves emerge on the branches and crocuses start to break through the black earth, he reaches a decision. He will protect

Margaret for as long as he can, even if it means living a lie, keeping up appearances, and smiling at the other workers on the farm who slap him on the back and congratulate him—even if it means having to endure discomfort and pain, being close to her when she visits with Mihill. He will insist on one condition: that they meet only at Ewens's plantation. Except for church, he does not want to lay eyes on Robert Swett.

When John tells Margaret of his decision, her obvious relief followed by a look of love and gratitude wounds him deeply. But he swallows his anguish then, and every time when it wells up later. As promised, he acts the loving husband during her Sunday afternoon visits, spending extra time with Mihill. He takes him along when he goes fishing with Mathew or inspects fences. In the late afternoon, John accompanies Mihill and Margaret to the edge of the forest. After they leave for home, he heads to the pond to walk off the tension that built up inside him during the visit. Sometimes he unwinds by the shore, watching the frogs and birds that have returned with the warming weather; at other times he breaks down and sobs until he has no more tears left to spill on the ground.

* * *

After Margaret starts showing, Swett becomes increasingly solicitous, so much so that Jane takes her aside and warns, "People are starting to talk about you and Robert, the attention he pays you. Be careful. You know that Agnes has set her sights on him."

The revelation surprises Margaret—she hadn't known. But when she watches Agnes blush and smile every time Robert shows up at the main house, she can't deny it. Robert is just as astonished when she tells him. He has been oblivious to Sheppard's cousin's feeble attempts to flirt with him, unaware that when he asked Agnes to dance at the hog-killing celebration, it awoke amorous feelings in her. With no experience in men, it took only a few exchanges of pleasantries during his visits to the main house for her to think he was in love with her. The possibility made her heart beat faster. When Swett did not follow up, she imagined that he was too reluctant to court her and reveal his true feelings because he believed that she would consider him beneath her and reject him.

But Agnes has met a number of the sons of merchants and burgesses at church, and during the parties John Harvey gave when he was still governor. The young men all seemed shallow and untutored to her. None had the maturity of Robert Swett, nor his abilities and ambition, which set him apart from the other indentured workers. She sees him as a young John Upton, a man who has prospects. To convince him that she regards him worthy, she smiles at Swett and touches his arm as if by accident whenever she can. But her efforts to be more congenial in his presence don't bear fruit. He continues to be pleasant but stops short of expressing more interest in her.

It bothers Agnes that he seems to show more consideration to Margaret, a common servant girl as far as she is concerned. But her jealousy disappears when Margaret's belly grows rounder. Once Agnes realizes that Margaret is pregnant again, she thinks she has nothing to worry about and waits for Swett to turn his attention to her. The fact that he comes less often to the house doesn't bother her. As spring advances, there is more work to do on the plantation. Little does she know that he stays away because Margaret told him about her desires.

36

DEPARTURES AND ARRIVALS
Virginia—Early 1640

In late March 1640, the trial of John Harvey reaches its much-anticipated conclusion. Margaret is interested only insofar as it will affect her friend Frances. She had hoped that Elizabeth Harvey would come to James City to visit her husband and bring Frances along, so that Margaret could get together with her and unburden herself. But Elizabeth has remained at Boldrup Plantation, even as the trial finishes. Rumor has it that she is pregnant with Harvey's child and doesn't want to travel.

When the jury returns its verdict, it finds Harvey guilty on all counts. Wyatt as presiding judge wastes no time in pronouncing the sentence: he reverses the order that forced the Reverend Panton into exile, acquits the cleric of all charges, refunds the five-hundred-pound fine he had to pay, and sends him word that he may return to Virginia at his leisure unharmed. All of Harvey's property is to be sold to satisfy his creditors.

To everyone's astonishment, Sir John's financial liabilities are immense. It turns out that King Charles has not paid him a farthing for his second term in office, and Harvey has run up massive debts to support his lavish lifestyle. Wyatt orders his Charles River estate and

James City mansion to be sold, along with his servants and workers. He allows Harvey to keep eight cows, four breeding sows, and his house furnishings, provided he stays in the colony. If he decides to leave Virginia, he will be able to take with him only those few things the court permits.

When Margaret hears of the outcome, she has mixed feelings. She is happy that Frances will stay in the colony but worries that she will be separated from Emmanuel again. She anxiously awaits news of who will receive Harvey's properties.

Richard Kemp, the former governor's crony and party to many of Harvey's misdeeds, suffers a similar fate. Wyatt has him convicted for conspiring against the Reverend Panton, too, and does his best to destroy Kemp financially.

There is nothing Harvey and Kemp can do except complain bitterly about their fates. Sir John seeks sympathy by portraying himself as unfairly persecuted and impoverished—a wretch to be pitied—but few take his side, and no one comes to his aid. After writing a letter to King Charles pleading to pay the salary owed him, Harvey asks to leave the colony before utter financial ruin descends on him. Kemp, finding himself in a similar situation, makes the same request. Wyatt graciously grants them both their wishes, figuring that they will make less mischief once they're gone. He can't imagine the possibility that the two will agitate against him in England. So, when they leave Virginia with their meager belongings—Harvey and Elizabeth at the end of May—most people in the colony welcome their departure with a "Good riddance" and pay them no more mind.

Margaret spends hardly any time thinking about it because the farewells of Harvey and his wife coincide with the one-year anniversary of Priscilla's death, which once again plunges Lieutenant Sheppard into gloomy despondency. Wracked with sorrow, he lashes out at Margaret whenever she crosses his path, just like the year before, and makes her life miserable. With no end in sight to his despair and angry outbursts, even Agnes and Dorothy, usually quick to take their cousin's side, feel that his wrath is self-indulgent and unjust. Robert, Jason, Lucy, Jane, and Jeremiah do their best to support Margaret as before, but no one at the plantation dares to take the lieutenant to task for his behavior.

John is no help either. While he keeps to his bargain and even expresses sympathy for Margaret's situation, he has no interest in committing any of his money to solve her woes. Margaret accepts his reaction. She does not see him struggle with his conscience or bury his pain as best he can when he is alone. As a result, her Sunday afternoon visits to Ewens's plantation give her little joy, and the only relief comes when Lieutenant Sheppard is called away to settle yet another altercation between settlers and the Indians.

* * *

In July, a court case reaches the Virginia Governor's Council, the colony's highest court, presided over by Governor Wyatt himself, that stirs considerable interest throughout Virginia. The trial concerns three indentured servants who ran away from the plantation of Hugh Gwyn, located on the Charles River on the York Peninsula across from James City. Gwyn, a wealthy burgess and former justice, is a cruel, brutish landowner who beats his workers whenever they don't fulfill his demands.

In late June, a Dutchman named Victor; a Scotsman, James Gregory; and an African, John Punch, having endured enough of Gwyn's maltreatment, decided to escape to Maryland. Under cover of a late spring rainstorm, they stole away from his plantation, hoping to get a head start before anyone noticed their flight. Unfortunately for them, the downpour made the ground soft and muddy and some of their footprints on the forest floor and in the swamplands remained visible, making it easy for those hunting them to follow their tracks. Captured in Maryland a few weeks later, they were returned to James City and held in the jail there until their trial.

Although the courtroom proceedings in early July don't attract the kind of interest John Harvey's trial did, a good number of local citizens attend when the Governor's Council hears the case. All three servants attest to the brutal treatment at the hands of the planter, including being punched, beaten, and scourged.

When Hugh Gwyn is called to the witness stand, he doesn't deny their accusations. "So I try to knock some sense into their thick skulls. What of it?" he says. "As long as they're indentured to me, I can do whatever I want."

The court does not take the testimony of the workers into consideration and holds for Gwyn. The verdict handed down seems a routine matter—runaway servants have been captured, convicted, and punished before—and no one expects the sentences to be out of the ordinary. That is what happens with Victor and Gregory, the two white men. As expected, they are sentenced to receive thirty lashes each and have their indenture extended for four years beyond their contractual term—one year in recompense to Gwyn for the loss he sustained due to their absence and three additional years to serve the colony.

But when it is John Punch's turn, Wyatt pronounces a more severe sentence. In addition to thirty lashes of the whip, he orders him to be indentured to Gwyn for the rest of his life.

The outcome provokes much discussion throughout the colony. Most white plantation owners and merchants are satisfied that the verdict is just and will discourage other servants from running away. They pay no attention to the unequal punishments the court meted out. Africans south and north of the James River are upset, however. They chafe at the unfairness of the verdict and interpret it as a deliberate attempt to intimidate and deprive them of their rights as citizens of Virginia.

For the Africans in the vicinity of Hogg Island, John Punch's harsh sentence heightens their sense of fear, suspicion, and mistrust regarding the motives of their white masters. Anthony worries about his plans to have his own horse and cattle farm when he gains his freedom. Even Michael and Katherine, whose contract of indenture was extended when they had their first child, are apprehensive about their future.

John is most outraged. "They made him a slave," he seethes while taking a walk with Emmanuel Driggers along the James River, far enough away from the town so that they can speak freely.

Emmanuel, who came to James City to conduct business on behalf of Francis Pott, agrees. "It is a disgrace, though hardly unexpected. The planters will do whatever they can to keep us submissive."

But he can marshal only so much indignation because he knows from personal experience that not all plantation owners are alike. Before John Harvey and Elizabeth left for England, Francis Pott paid them to sign over to him the contracts of indenture of all their servants. Then he sent his newly acquired workers to his plantation on the eastern shore of the Chesapeake Bay, all except Frances. In gratitude for Emmanuel's loyal service, Pott reunited him with his wife. They are expecting their first child.

"That is wonderful news," John exclaims. "Margaret will be so pleased." Then a shadow crosses his face.

Emmanuel misunderstands the reason. He thinks it concerns John and Margaret still being indentured and having to live apart. John is reluctant to tell him about Margaret and Swett. Instead, he mentions what has been on his mind for some time, ever since Margaret raised the issue of buying out her and Mihill's contract—what to do about his secret stash of money.

Emmanuel doesn't hesitate. "You should use it as soon as possible," he insists. "You and Margaret must be free to determine your own course."

"But what if people say that I have stolen it?" John asks. "I was hoping to keep at the hog trade long enough to make it seem believable that I have extra money."

"Talk to Thomas Goodman. From what you've told me about him, he will understand and support you. The fact that your money is in pieces of eight and doubloons will convince him," Emmanuel counsels. "Few people in the colony have actual cash on hand. Everybody gets paid in tobacco."

John trusts Emmanuel's judgment but remains doubtful. Crossing the river on his way back to Ewens's plantation, he thinks about what he wants to do for himself and Margaret. As much as she has hurt him, he can't bring himself to bear her ill will. She is still his wife and the mother of his son. As a member of the African community, she needs and deserves his help. Even with Swett at her side, no one else in Virginia can look out for her the way John can.

* * *

For Margaret, the happy news regarding Frances and Emmanuel provides a welcome respite. Although she is in her last two months of pregnancy, she and Swett still have no credible plan for what to do when the baby is born. As her belly has grown bigger, the humid, sultry Virginia summer heat has become increasingly oppressive. Unable to walk any distance without getting winded, she hasn't visited John at Ewens's plantation for some time. Instead, he has agreed to come spend time with her and Mihill at Sheppard's. On those occasions, Swett stays away from the kitchen and the creek where Margaret, John, and Mihill like to walk. It is an awkward arrangement that satisfies no one.

Fortunately, Lieutenant Sheppard's period of angry mourning has not lasted as long as before. Since regaining his spirits, he doesn't mind John visiting although he still forbids him entry into the house.

The talk with Emmanuel has helped John evaluate his options more clearly, and he reaches a decision. The next time he sees Margaret, he makes a point to talk to her alone while Lucy watches Mihill. They walk along the creek toward the James River. Surrounded by marsh elders and sumac, he tells her, "If you like, we will stay married in name only, and I will treat the child as my own.

When your contract of indenture is finished, you can do as you wish. If that means going off on your own, I won't stand in your way."

Margaret is deeply moved. "That is very generous of you, John."

"I owe you my life. It is the least I can do," he says.

But when Margaret replies, "Let me talk it over with Robert," his name burns like a glowing lump of coal in John's heart.

"You do that and let me know," he says tersely.

When Margaret shares John's offer with Swett later that evening, he is just as astonished and pleased. "That is great news," he says, relieved. Then he becomes pensive and muses, "I don't think I could be that forgiving if I were in John's shoes. He is an unusual man."

* * *

When Margaret goes into labor in September, it is difficult for Swett to stay away. With Lucy and Jane taking care of her, he knows she is in good hands. Still, he would like to be at her side. It pains him to see John arrive with Katherine in tow. They hurried through the forest as soon as they heard the news.

For the first time in over a year, Lieutenant Sheppard makes an exception and invites John into the house. Margaret is happy to see him and Katherine. She can rely on her older, more experienced friend and doesn't have to guide Jane and Lucy through the process while struggling to give birth herself. John showing up means a lot to her. He takes Mihill for a walk, out of earshot of her screams when the labor pains become excruciating. The boy looks upset, and John does his best to reassure him that his mother will be all right.

As they pass the workers' quarters, John sees Swett behind one of the barns, pacing and pulling nervously at his blond locks. His drawn face indicates a sleepless night spent worrying. On the spur of the moment, John walks over to him. When Swett sees him approach, he draws back, unsure of his intent. Seeing Mihill by his side gives him some assurance that John means him no harm.

It is the first time they have spoken to each other since the revelation that Margaret was with child. John looks at Swett, wondering what makes him so attractive to her. Perhaps it is the faint resemblance to Jope. Eventually, he says, "I'm not here to make trouble. We both love Margaret, in our own way. I ask only one thing of you: take good care of her when the time comes and I am gone."

Swett looks at him bewildered. That is not what he expected John to say. He run his hand through his disheveled hair and says. "I give you my word."

John nods, gives him a final glance, takes Mihill by the hand, and walks away.

Five hours later, when Margaret finally delivers a healthy boy, John steps back inside the house with Mihill. They go into her room, unsure of what they will see. Lying in the sweat-stained sheets of her bed holding a small bundle in her arms, Margaret looks drained but happy. When she notices John, she closes her eyes for a moment. She would like nothing better than to share this moment with Robert, but this will have to suffice.

Turning the swaddled bundle so John and Mihill can see the scrunched-up baby face, she says, "Say hello to your brother, Mihill."

John puts on a joyful smile, but he feels miserable. Although he acts like a happy father, taking Margaret's hand, reaching out to touch the baby, he feels nothing for this child. At some point, an agonizing pain burrows in his gut. Tears well up in his eyes as he realizes that the child means the end of his and Margaret's marriage. Whatever deception they will continue to carry on as man and wife, their life together is over.

Margaret sees how he is struggling and squeezes his hand. When he looks at her, she mouths, "Thank you."

Her gratitude doesn't make him feel any better.

They are both relieved when Lucy bustles in and says cheerfully, "Come, Mihill, time for supper. Your mother is tired and needs her rest."

It is hard for John to tear himself away. So much of his life has revolved around Margaret, even when they were not together, that he is reluctant to let her go and face a future without her. He kisses Margaret on the forehead and leaves.

In the sitting room, Lieutenant Sheppard waits for him. "You're welcome to stay the night, John," he says.

Much as he would like to get away, John accepts his offer graciously but does not share Margaret's bed.

37
DISCOVERED
Virginia—Fall 1640

It is difficult for Swett to stay away after the birth of his son. When he receives word, along with the other workers on the plantation, that Margaret had a boy, he can't celebrate the way he would like to, only express how pleased he is that everything has gone smoothly. He doesn't visit Margaret while John is still with her at the main house. So, three days pass before he sets eyes on his child. By then Margaret is up and working in the kitchen again.

It is an early fall afternoon when Robert pokes his head in and finds her sitting on a stool, paring and cutting up string beans. Lucy stands at a table nearby chopping a smoked rabbit into pieces for a stew. The open fire provides a cozy atmosphere, warmer than outside, and the pungent smell of herbs and the smoky meat hangs heavy in the air.

"I'm here to speak with Lieutenant Sheppard, but I wanted to offer my personal congratulations first," Swett says and then asks tentatively. "How are you, Margaret?"

Seeing him makes her feel happy, and she gives him a beaming smile. When she gets up and goes to him, ready to embrace him, he looks cautiously in Lucy's direction.

"It's all right. She knows," Margaret says.

Lucy looks over her shoulder and nods reassuringly. Then she returns to her task, acting as if there were no one else in the kitchen.

Swett stands there uncomfortably, not knowing what to say, until Margaret asks, "Would you like to see him? I keep him here with me. It makes it easier when he gets hungry."

"Yes, very much," he says eagerly.

Margaret goes to a wooden cradle standing in the corner under a table stacked with plates. She lifts out a small bundle wrapped in linen cloth and presents it to him. "Say hello to your son."

All Swett can see is the baby's face. He still has his pallid color, and for a moment Robert worries that everyone who sees the baby will know the truth about Margaret and him.

As if reading his mind, Margaret says, "All babies are born white. His skin will turn brown over the next few years." She extends the swaddled child toward him. "Would you like to hold him?"

Swett takes the sleeping child from her and rests it in the crook of his arm. The baby breathes softly. Noting the tiny face, the stumpy nose, the small mouth, and the tiny ears, a feeling of happiness wells up inside him. "What name shall we give him?" he asks.

Margaret whispers, "I'm thinking of Robert, but we can talk about that later, when he has made it through the next week or so. In the meantime, let's figure out how to see each other undisturbed. Lucy will come and tell you when."

Swett hands the baby back to her, feeling elated. He steps closer and brushes his lips against hers before he leaves.

To justify his visit, he stops in the house to speak with Sheppard about repairs that need to be made at the plantation before the winter. He also calls on Agnes, who is in the sitting room embroidering a dress with Dorothy. When she lays eyes on Robert, he is still exuberant from seeing Margaret and his son. His blue eyes sparkle and his smile is captivating. Mistakenly thinking it is intended for her, Agnes is pleased. For the next half hour, she and Robert engage in small talk that means nothing to him, but further fans the flames of her passion. When he excuses himself and departs to return to work, Agnes looks out the window after him, her heart pounding.

For the rest of the week, he finds reasons to come by every other day, and Agnes becomes increasingly ardent, looking forward to spending time with him. On Sunday when John comes to visit for the afternoon following church, Swett stays away. But he soon returns, and Agnes is convinced that he is finally courting her seriously.

But when she gives a rapturous description of their get-together to her sister, Dorothy purses her lips. Pulling Agnes aside to make sure no one can hear them, she tells her, "I didn't want to say anything, Agnes, but there is something odd going on. Robert is spending an inordinate amount of time with Margaret and her baby."

Taken aback, Agnes's thin lips become a taut line. "What do you mean?" she finally says.

"It has come to my attention that he visits Margaret in the kitchen or the garden and comes to see you afterward. He cuddles the baby and coos over him as if it were his."

"But . . . but it is John's child. He rushed here with that Negro wench when he heard that it was about to be born, and he's just been here again this Sunday."

"Yes," says Dorothy carefully. "But he doesn't seem to be very happy about it."

At first, Agnes dismisses her sister's warning. Swept up in the afterglow of her encounters with Robert, she wants to believe what her heart tells her. But Dorothy's comments lodge in her mind like an unwelcome visitor. After supper, in the quiet of her bedroom as Jane combs her hair, Agnes asks if she has noticed anything going on between Margaret and Swett.

Jane stops for a moment as if to think. Then she resumes combing Agnes's tresses and says, "Not that I know of, m'lady. Why do you ask?"

"No particular reason," Agnes says, feeling reassured.

But the worm of doubt Dorothy put in her mind continues to turn and burrow. For the next few days, Agnes perches herself at the window overlooking the approach to the house from the workers' quarters, on the lookout for Robert's arrival. The next time he walks casually up the path, she watches him head to the outdoor kitchen and disappear inside. Sometime later, he enters the main house looking for her.

When it happens again two days later, her suspicion yields to angry despair. The next time she sees Swett making his way toward the house, she sneaks to the door that leads to the kitchen. It is ajar, allowing her to listen to the conversation taking place inside although she can't see what's happening. The way Robert and Margaret laugh and talk so naturally with each other fills her with dismay, but she doesn't let on, later, when Swett comes to see her.

Her jealousy drives her to take desperate measures to listen in on their meetings. When she overhears Swett and Margaret arrange a tryst away from the house, her ears burn with resentment and she hurries to the living room. Upon Swett's arrival, she rubs her forehead, pleading a headache, and withdraws to her room. She can't be certain, but he seems relieved as she departs.

That evening after supper, Agnes sneaks out of the house long before Margaret leaves. She wants to get to the site ahead of time where they plan to meet. She doesn't have to go far to reach the stand of oaks and pines a few hundred yards behind the smoke shed. Since the arrival of the baby, Swett has suggested that he and Margaret meet closer to the house so that she doesn't have to walk far. They know they are taking a risk, but their desire has made them reckless, and they feel reasonably secure that John accepting the boy as his own offers them good cover.

By the time Agnes reaches the thicket, it is dark night, but a silvery half-moon provides plenty of light. There are dense bushes among the trees, and she decides to hide behind them at the edge of a small clearing. As she pushes deeper into the shrubs, burrs prick at her hands, and she bites her lip so as not to cry out.

Before long, the lovers arrive, first Swett and then Margaret. He listens for the crack of breaking branches and calls out softly, "Margaret? Is that you?"

"Yes." Margaret emerges from the darkness and rushes to him. They embrace passionately, kissing each other as if they have been apart for months.

"How I've missed you," Robert says fervently.

"Yes, my love, it has been too long."

The words pierce Agnes like a knife, and she moves abruptly, brushing the leaves.

Margaret hears the rustling. "What was that?" she says, instantly alert.

Holding her breath, Agnes keeps stock-still and doesn't relax until she hears Swett say, "Probably a deer or opossum."

Reassured, Margaret says, "I brought a blanket."

They spread it out on the ground and lie down side by side, kissing and caressing each other. Before long, their entwined bodies shift and move, rising and falling, consummating their union. It is torture for Agnes to hold still. She closes her eyes but can't escape hearing the moans and gasps of pleasure.

It seems like an eternity to her before Margaret and Robert finish. For a while, they lie next to each other, spent. Then they get up slowly and brush each other off. Robert picks up the blanket and folds it. Margaret tucks it under her arm and gives him a parting kiss. They leave, heading in different directions.

Agnes remains in the bushes for some time, her mind reeling. Her emotions vacillate between anguish and fury. Pulling away carefully to limit the tearing of the brambles, she realizes how chilly it is and shivers. Then she sinks to her knees, buries her head in her hands, and starts to cry. But her despair doesn't last long. As she gets up and brushes off her skirt, she grits her teeth, feeling rage and fury surge inside her. What Robert and Margaret are doing is illicit, forbidden, and sinful. Their betrayal has driven a dagger into her heart, and she will make them pay.

* * *

Margaret is wary when Jane seeks her out in the kitchen and tells her that Lieutenant Sheppard demands to see her. He has sent Jeremiah on the same errand for Swett. Stepping inside the living room, she realizes right away that there is trouble brewing. The lieutenant and Dorothy are waiting with grim expressions on their faces. Agnes stands next to them, scowling. No one says anything until Swett gets there. His eyes briefly catch Margaret's for reassurance, but neither knows what to expect.

Sheppard doesn't beat around the bush. "I have received word that you are carrying on an affair!" He doesn't give either a chance to respond before plunging on angrily, "Don't try to deny it. You were seen committing a shameful, immoral act. Your deed is unconscionable, against the commandments of God, and a grave breach of my trust in you!"

Margaret and Robert glance at each other. Considering the venomous look on Agnes's face, neither has any doubt about who divulged the information. They have talked about the possibility of being discovered and decided that they would face the moment with their heads held high. Neither feels sorry for what they have done, even if the consequences are dire. If anything, Margaret experiences a sense of relief, as the secret that has been gnawing at her is finally out in the open. She feels bad for John, though, who will be ridiculed as a cuckold. He does not deserve that.

"Have you nothing to say?" Sheppard's voice betrays his frustration.

Margaret looks at him, seemingly calm, although her emotions are in disarray. She gathers her courage and says, "It is true. Robert and I love each other."

"Yes, we do," Robert adds simply.

As Dorothy looks at them disdainfully, Agnes's scowl deepens and her gray eyes flash with hatred. Sheppard snorts with derision but seems almost disappointed. He did not expect them to admit their guilt so readily. Their confession spoils the opportunity for him to display righteous anger. He has never been a religious zealot, and while he does not condone what Margaret and Swett have done, it doesn't really shock him. He attempts to rekindle his fury by accusing Swett of treachery. "You have made a fool of me by leading Agnes on, making her believe you were serious about her."

Robert bows his head. When he looks up, he gazes at Sheppard but his words are for Agnes. "I never made any promises, but if anything I said or did persuaded the lady otherwise, I am truly sorry for it."

Agnes's cheek twitches, but she says nothing in return.

"What about the child?" Sheppard addresses Robert. "Is it yours?"

"That is of no concern here," Margaret interrupts. "It is a matter between me and John."

Sheppard stares at her hard, but she looks back at him without flinching. Although her statement is vague and leaves much unanswered, he decides not to pursue it any further.

"What will happen to us?" Robert asks.

Sheppard expels a deep breath. "I would have preferred to deal with this matter here on my own, but it is out of my hands," he says almost regretfully. "Agnes informed the Reverend Faulkner in James City, and he will take measures to bring you before the Governor's Council, where you'll be held to account for your misdeeds."

38
JUDGMENT
Virginia—October 1640

Two days later, on a Saturday morning, two constables, officers of the court, come by boat to the plantation to arrest Margaret and Swett. They got an early start, arriving shortly after breakfast at the dock on the creek. The two men, not much older than Margaret, dressed in dark brown doublets, caps, and pants, with swords at their side, walk up to the house and knock on the front door. When Lieutenant Sheppard answers, they bow almost apologetically. Margaret and Swett are his servants, after all, and he is an important member of the community.

The older man, holding up a folded piece of parchment, says formally, "We have a warrant to arrest two servants of yours and convey them to James City for trial."

The younger constable adds, "We're also to bring your cousin, Agnes Sheppard, to testify."

The lieutenant nods and says, "I understand." He gestures to Lucy. "Go and fetch Robert Swett from the workers' quarters."

Margaret is thankful that the waiting is finally over. She has prepared herself for this moment, giving Lucy and Jane instructions how to take care of the baby in her absence and readying her travel coat. Earlier, she asked Jason to notify John of what was happening, but he has not responded.

While everyone waits, Margaret says, "You must be hungry. Won't you come inside? Would you like something to eat?"

The constables decline, embarrassed, and continue to stand at attention on the porch until Swett arrives. Margaret puts on her overcoat and joins him. The older officer repeats that they are under arrest.

"We will go with you willingly," Swett says.

As Agnes and Dorothy step out on the porch, dressed for travel as well, Lieutenant Sheppard says, "My cousin and I will follow you in our boat."

"Very well," says the older constable.

It is one of those crisp fall days with perfect weather, not a cloud in the sky. Flocks of migratory birds heading south accompany them across the James River. To Margaret, it almost seems like the beautiful surroundings mock her. She holds Swett's hand for reassurance. From time to time, they glance at each other, smiling wanly. Physical contact between prisoners is usually not permitted, but the constables turn a blind eye.

When they get to the docks at James City, the officers help them climb out of the boat and escort them to the church where Virginia's Governor's Council will sit in judgment. A sizable crowd of spectators is already milling around the entrance in anticipation of the trial. The large number suggests that many shopkeepers have closed their stores early and suspended work in order to witness the proceedings. They consider it as much entertainment as the administration of justice. When Margaret and Swett walk toward the church, people start to gawk and whisper. Some of the women point them out to their young children.

The constables hustle Margaret and Robert into the church and take them to a wooden enclosure. "You will wait here until the trial commences," says the older man and gestures for his fellow officer to stand guard.

There are no chairs or benches inside where Margaret and Robert can sit. The only other time Margaret had set foot inside a court was the time John Chew was arrested for not paying his bills, and Dr. Pott sued him. She had to testify at the trial, and although she was nervous beforehand, she handled herself well. This time she feels mortified.

Looking around, Margaret notes a number of burgesses and their wives already sitting toward the front. She recognizes several merchants and their families, including George Menefie and his wife, John and Anne Uty, and Mister and Mistress Chew and their children. Soon, Sheppard, Agnes, and Dorothy arrive and occupy front-row seats. The workers who rowed them across the river, Jason, Thomas, and Paul, sit farther back. As the rest of the crowd comes in, John among them, Margaret holds her breath. She did not expect him to show up and can't imagine why he did. He does not look in her direction and finds a spot on the other side of the aisle. His face is stern and unreadable.

It takes the spectators awhile to settle down, but they all rise again as seven burgesses, wearing dark, formal clothing, file in from a side door and take their seats on the high bench. Governor Wyatt, dressed all in black, as usual, brings up the rear. As he sits down at the center with three justices on either side, the older constable intones. "Oyez! Oyez! All persons having business before the honorable Virginia Governor's Council Court are admonished to draw near and give their attention, for the court is now in session."

The spectators in the room sit down as well.

Wyatt strikes the wooden bench three times with his gavel and says, "We have before us a case of fornication by a female Negro servant belonging to Lieutenant Sheppard and a male worker on his plantation." He turns to the constable standing near Margaret. "Are the defendants and witnesses present?"

"Aye, my lord," the young man replies.

"Let the defendants approach."

When Margaret and Robert stand before the bench, Wyatt narrows his eyes and continues, "Please identify yourself for the court."

Robert takes a step forward and says, "I am Robert Swett."

"You will address me as 'my lord,'" Wyatt says, glowering. "You are a skilled worker and have lived in the colony for several years?"

"Yes, my lord. I came from England three years ago."

"How do you plead?"

"Guilty, my lord."

Low murmurs emanate from the crowd.

Wyatt scrutinizes him for a moment and says, "Very well." Then he fixes his eyes on Margaret, giving no indication that he has seen her before. "And you are?"

"Margaret," she says in a low, constricted voice, her heart pounding in her chest.

"Speak up for the court," Wyatt barks at her.

If he means to cow Margaret, his tone produces the opposite effect. She straightens and with a firm voice says, "I am Margaret. Margaret Cornish, my lord!"

Taken aback, Wyatt clears his throat and says, "How do you plead?"

Margaret takes a deep breath and says, "Not guilty, my lord. It was an act of love."

There are loud gasps from the spectators followed by considerable tittering.

Wyatt slams the gavel down on the bench and the crowd quiets. He glares down at Margaret. "Your reasons are immaterial. What concerns us here is the crime you have committed against God and the strictures of the church." He pauses and looks at the paper in front of him. "You are a married woman?"

Margaret swallows and says, "Yes, my lord."

"And you have two children."

"Yes, my lord. A five-year-old son and another, newly born, less than three weeks old."

Frowning at her, Wyatt says, "So much the worse for you." He gazes at the men sitting to his right and left, inviting them to add to his questioning, but they decline with small shakes of their heads.

Wyatt nods to the constable, who says, "You both may step back."

Margaret and Robert return to the enclosure. The rest of the trial passes quickly. Agnes testifies in clipped sentences, confining herself to the barest outline of what she overheard and saw, and how she went to the Reverend Faulkner to apprise him of what happened. As she leaves the witness chair, she glances in the direction of Swett, and a small, triumphant smile plays on her lips.

Normally, the justices would withdraw to consider the verdict, but Wyatt turns to the constable and says, "Bring the Negro woman before us again."

When Margaret faces the bench, he asks, "I understand that you are married. This baby, who does it belong to?"

Margaret hesitates and lowers her head. "I'd rather not say, my lord."

Again, Wyatt is taken aback and his scowl intensifies. But before he can speak, Swett calls out from the enclosure, "The child is mine, my lord."

That revelation causes such gasps and loud muttering among the spectators that Wyatt has to gavel several times and yell, "Order in the court," to quiet them.

When the crowd finally hushes, he resumes, "So, you have been committing adultery for some time."

When Margaret nods, he leans over and shouts, "Speak up, woman!"

Margaret meets his eyes, holding his piercing stare. "Yes, my lord," she says.

Wyatt pulls back with a haughty expression and announces, "The Court will now deliberate and reach a verdict."

The bailiff gestures for Margaret to return to the enclosure. The justices huddle around Wyatt and talk quietly among themselves.

Margaret, gazing out over the spectators, notices John looking at her. His expression is stone-faced, betraying no reaction. At some point, he looks away. Margaret turns to Swett, wishing for some eye contact to comfort her, but he is gnawing at his lip, worried.

The justices take barely five minutes to deliberate. When they return to their seats, everyone in the church leans forward, not wanting to miss a word of the verdict.

Wyatt gestures in the direction of the wooden enclosure. "The defendants will come forward and face the Court."

Margaret and Robert look at each other, trying to give each other courage, and stand side by side before the bench with their heads held high.

Like a minister promising fire and brimstone in hell, Wyatt proclaims, "Whereas Robert Swett has begotten with child Margaret Cornish, a Negro woman servant belonging unto Lieutenant Sheppard, the court therefore orders that Margaret Cornish shall be given thirty lashes at the whipping post and Robert Swett shall tomorrow in the forenoon do public penance in the pillory for his offense at James City church in the time of divine service according to the laws of England. Until then, the defendants will be remanded to the James City jail."

Then he raps the gavel three times.

To Margaret, the sounds feel like slaps in her face. She is shocked. Her mind is in a whirl. Why didn't she and Swett receive the same punishment? Why is hers more severe? Did Wyatt single her out because she spoke up for herself? Did he remember her from before, after all, and this is his revenge?

She feels as if she is surrounded by a mist and only vaguely registers Swett looking at her guilt-ridden, devastated, and remorseful.

* * *

After the spectators have cleared the church, the constables take Margaret and Robert to the jail, a small, one-story building near the military quarters for the soldiers of the fort. The two guards there, an older, bearded fellow and his younger assistant, take the prisoners and put them in adjoining cells. Light seeps in through a window high up on the wall on the spare furnishings—a wooden stool, a small table, and a mattress with a blanket on the floor. Margaret pads the bedding and feels cornstalks poke up through the cheap linen. The mattress hasn't been washed for some time, and the faint, sickly smell of vomit and urine rising from it nauseates her.

A knocking at the wooden wall partition startles her. She hears Swett's muffled voice, "Margaret, can you hear me?"

"Yes, Robert," she calls out in response. "I'm here."

"Oh, Margaret, I am so sorry."

"Don't be. We've done nothing wrong."

"But thirty stripes!"

The reminder tightens the knot in Margaret's stomach. She pulls the stool to the wall and sits. "Perhaps it is better this way. We won't have to sneak around anymore."

"I love you, Margaret."

"I love you, too."

For the rest of the afternoon, they talk through the wall, trying to stay connected.

As it gets dark, the sound of a key turning in the lock disrupts their conversation. The young guard comes into Margaret's cell carrying a trencher with a pewter soup bowl and a hunk of bread on it. "I've brought you some supper," he says, setting the plate on the small table and handing her a spoon. "Knock on the door when you're finished."

After he leaves, locking the door behind him, Margaret tastes the warm, thin liquid. It is a watery soup with bits of corn and carrots and two small pieces of gristly meat. The bread has a hard crust and is not much tastier, but Margaret hasn't eaten since breakfast and devours it all, mopping up the remnants of the soup with the last bit of bread.

After the guard returns and takes the tray away, she and Swett continue to talk. As darkness falls, it gets chilly, and Margaret wraps the blanket around her shoulders.

When the sky in the window and the interior of the cell have turned pitch-black, the older guard knocks on the doors and barks, "Time to go to sleep!"

Robert waits until he's gone and says, "I wish I could be with you and kiss you goodnight."

It brings a smile to Margaret's lips. "Soon, Robert, soon," she says. "Goodnight."

Then she feels her way to the mattress and sits down. It is the first time since the verdict that she has had the opportunity to think about her situation on her own. Is the punishment just? Have she and Robert committed a crime as everyone insists? She can't imagine that her baby was born in sin and worries about him, hoping that he is all right without a day and night of her milk. She considers Agnes's vindictiveness, Sheppard's conflicted expression, and Wyatt's unforgiving countenance, and decides that the only sense of guilt she feels is toward John. He has always been more sensitive than he lets on, and he has done nothing to bring any of this to pass. To be in charge is important to him, and in this matter, he can do nothing but respond. Having spent much of her life reacting to circumstances, she knows what it feels like to be helpless and simply have to endure. Her thoughts drift to Ndongo. It bothers her that she can no longer recall what her mother and father looked like. Then Captain Jope's face appears to her: tanned, bearded, laughing. The vision of his bright blue eyes brings her back to Robert lying in the cell next to hers and their dire situation. She dreads what will happen to her tomorrow.

Suddenly, she hears Lady Isabel's voice, imparting words she hasn't heard for a long time: "There is no fear in being afraid, but the decisions you make in fear can bring you shame. . . . Rely upon your faith. . . . The Lord will not betray you because you have been chosen by him."

In her mind, Margaret sees Isabel's face with her gentle yet fierce eyes surrounded by wrinkles and wispy, white hair. She is smiling at her with affection as she tells her, just as when she said good-bye, "Remember, you are special."

For a while, Margaret feels at peace. She will face with courage come what may.

39
PUNISHED
Virginia—October 1640

Startled by a knock on the cell door next to hers, followed by a shout, "Wake up! Breakfast," Margaret realizes that she fell asleep after all. The sky in the window is the dull gray color of dawn. By the time she orients herself, gets up from the mattress, and stretches her body awake, the door to her cell opens, and the older guard enters. He holds out a pewter cup, and Margaret takes it from him. It is filled with water.

When she looks at him, puzzled by the meager fare, he says gruffly, "That's all you get this morning. You wouldn't want to puke later on."

Suddenly, it all comes back—the trial, the verdict, and her punishment to come—and she feels the knot in her stomach tightening painfully as never before. She gasps and takes a few deep breaths to calm herself.

After the guard leaves, she sips the water. Then she calls out through the wall, "Robert, are you there?"

His hesitant "yes" is tense and apprehensive. She can tell that he feels just as anxious.

"We will survive this," she says firmly and is glad when he responds, "Yes, we will."

Margaret thinks about how to further encourage him and says, "When we get back to the plantation, I most definitely want our child to bear your name."

His reply, "That is wonderful," sounds tentative.

For the next hour or so, they talk about mundane matters. Then she hears boots clomping on the wooden floor outside, followed by a key rattling. The door to Robert's cell creaks open, and the older guard says, "It is time."

Robert tries to sound brave when he responds, "I am ready," but his trembling voice betrays how panicked he feels.

Then Margaret hears retching sounds and the terse, accusatory grumbling of the guard, "Waste of good food." She puts her ear to the wooden barrier between them as Robert calls out for her benefit, "Don't worry. I'm all right!"

Moments later, she hears the door close and footsteps passing her door and receding.

"Be strong," she calls after him. "There is no shame in it."

Alone, she realizes how upset Robert must be to have to stand in the pillory, exposed to the ridicule of all passersby on their way to church. For a moment she forgets her own impending ordeal.

Time passes slowly as the sky in the window turns blue and gradually brightens. Margaret rests on the stool and tries to find comfort in Aunt Isabel's words.

The sound of the key scraping in the lock at her cell jolts her. The door creaks open, and the older constable enters while the younger guard remains outside. Margaret stands up and faces him.

Giving her an evaluating glance, he asks, "Are you ready?"

Margaret feels bile rise in her throat, but she nods bravely and follows him out of the cell and down the dark corridor. After the dinginess of the jail, the blinding sunlight makes her squint. When her eyes adjust, she looks at the cloudless sky. From the angle of the sun, she can tell that it is shortly before the time when church lets out.

As Margaret and the constable start walking, the street is quiet and empty, but when they turn the corner, there is a throng of people by the church. A youngster noticing her approach points at her and calls out, "There she is!" All eyes turn to her. The crowd parts to let her through, creating a narrow alleyway. Spectators on both sides crane their necks to get a better look, their faces eager with anticipation to witness her punishment.

Margaret sees the whipping post up ahead at the end of the passageway, and everything slows down for her. She enters the open area around it as if in a trance. Robert is standing locked in the wooden pillory, his head and hands sticking out between two dark-brown, upright boards. He looks miserable but perks up when he sees her. She registers the faces of Lieutenant Sheppard, Agnes, Dorothy, workers from the plantation, and attendees of Lawne's Creek Church, but none of her African friends. She has a fleeting thought, wondering if John has come to watch. Then she sees Governor Wyatt standing on the church steps next to the Reverend Faulkner, their expressions stern and pitiless.

The young constable steps forward. Margaret is so intent on the whip in his hand with three cords dangling from the long grip that she barely notices the older bailiff shackling her wrists in the iron manacles attached shoulder high to the wooden post, rendering her helpless.

As the young constable moves behind her, the crowd quiets. In the tense silence, Wyatt's harsh voice rings out, "Lay on."

Margaret closes her eyes, anticipating the first blow of the whip, and is surprised that, when it comes, it hardly stings. The second stroke is just as light on her back, and the third as well.

The spectators who have been counting along become restless. Shouts of displeasure echo across the square. Someone yells, "Put your arm into it, you lily-livered poltroon!" Another hollers, "The stripes must be well laid on!"

The older constable grabs the whip from his assistant and tries to scourge him across the face. The young man absorbs the blows on his arms and staggers off as the crowd cheers and applauds.

Unable to see what's going on, Margaret relaxes and doesn't expect the next lash of the whip. It feels like a burning slash across her back. She cries out in pain and arches her body, her straining arms pulling against the shackles. She grits her teeth as the next several blows rain down on her like white-hot coals. It feels worse than a burn from a boiling iron pot, worse than the pains of childbirth because those stop from time to time. The flogging doesn't. By the tenth stroke, she loses count. Her arms are shaking from the strain, but she refuses to cry out.

When the beating finally stops, she is hugging the post and a moan escapes her, but there is no relief from the burning pain. If anything, her back hurts even more, feeling like it is on fire. Then her blurred vision clears, and she sees Robert in the pillory, tears streaming down his face. It revives her spirit: she will not give her tormentors the pleasure of watching her falter.

As the constable unlocks the shackles, she steels herself and slowly walks away from the whipping post. Every step is agony, but she keeps putting one foot in front of the other, not knowing where she is going. It heartens her when she hears a voice saying, "She took it well."

Suddenly, hands grab her on both sides under the shoulders, and she feels arms reach around her lower back to offer support. Margaret recognizes the black faces to her right and left and frowns. She feels disoriented. What are Frances and her husband, Emmanuel, doing here?

Frances's voice is soothing. "You are very brave, Margaret."

"Let us take care of you," says Emmanuel.

Margaret allows them to guide her down the street to a brick house. As she lumbers up the steps to the front door, she recognizes it as the home of Dr. Pott and dimly understands. Frances and

Emmanuel belong to his brother, Francis, who stays with him when he visits James City.

As they enter the house, Frances says, "We have arranged with Lieutenant Sheppard for you to stay here until you can travel."

"But I need to go back for my baby," Margaret says.

"The boy is in good care," Frances insists. "Your Robert is on his way back with the lieutenant and will look after him."

They take her to an empty side room. Emmanuel leaves, closing the door behind him, and Frances helps Margaret take off her dress. Blood has seeped through the fabric where the whip cut into her. The skin on her back is bruised and has started to swell.

Frances indicates a stool. "Sit here," she commands.

When Margaret complies, Frances puts a plaster on her back. After the initial stinging, it feels cool on her skin and moist, and it eases the pain ever so slightly.

"I made the ointment from comfrey," Frances explains. "Do you have that at Sheppard's to change the poultice as needed?"

Margaret nods.

"Good," Frances says, as she wraps a linen bandage around her breasts and back to secure the poultice.

"How did you come to be here?" Margaret asks, bewildered.

"When Dr. Pott sent his brother word that you were going to be put on trial, we had a pretty good idea how it would end. Fortunately, Francis Pott is a kind man, and he let me travel here with Emmanuel. We will take you to the dock later this afternoon to go back to Sheppard's. Unfortunately, we can't stay long enough to come with you. I will have to see the baby another time."

Tears come to Margaret's eyes not because of the pain she feels but because the care and generosity of her friends overwhelm her.

As Frances helps Margaret put her dress back on, she gives a small smile and says, "You certainly got yourself in a heap of trouble, but knowing you, I have a feeling he's worth it."

Her forthright acceptance is balm on Margaret's wounded soul. "I feel about him the way you do about Emmanuel," she says.

Just then Frances's husband returns. "I knew that as soon as I left the room, you two would start jabbering about me," he says, holding a cup out to Margaret. "Here, drink this. It's burdock tea and will reduce the swelling."

As Margaret sits back down on the stool and sips the somewhat sweet and earthy-tasting liquid, Dr. Pott puts his head in the door. "I see you are in good hands," he says. "I hear from Dr. Woodson that you are continuing your excellent work as a midwife and that you've just become a mother again. Congratulations on your new baby."

Margaret works up a small smile. "Thank you for your good wishes, Dr. Pott, and for opening your home to me in my time of need. I won't intrude on your generosity very long."

"I wish it were under kinder circumstances," says Pott. "Stay as long as you must." Before things get awkward, he continues, "I must be off. George Simmons's wife has come down with the flux."

After he leaves, Emmanuel says, "We better get going, too, if you want to make it to Sheppard's before nightfall."

Margaret rises laboriously. It is agonizing for her to move—her back continues to burn and hurts with every step—but with Emmanuel's and Frances's help she manages to hobble toward the docks. Along the way, people stop and watch them pass. Most look at her stone-faced but several nod to her and tip their caps. Although she doesn't know any of them, the fact that they seem to recognize and accept her gives her a good feeling.

At some point, she stops and asks Emmanuel, "Have you spoken with John yet?"

A look passes between him and Frances. Then he answers, "No, but I will meet with him after we see you off."

"Please help him and tell him how sorry I am," Margaret pleads. "I know he listens to you."

Emmanuel squeezes her hand. "I promise."

When they get to the docks, to Margaret's surprise, Jason and Thomas are waiting in the small rowboat. They greet her as if nothing unusual has happened. For the second time that day, tears come to Margaret's eyes unbidden.

Frances and Emmanuel kiss Margaret good-bye and help her climb down the ladder, where Jason and Thomas take her into the boat. Margaret winces with pain as she settles on the wooden bench. When they cast off, she watches her friends waving after her.

40
AFTERMATH
Virginia—Fall–Winter 1640

For the next three days, Margaret lives in torment. The slightest movement brings stabs of pain to her back. She spends most of her time sitting up in her bed, doing nothing other than feed her baby. At night, she catches some sleep lying on her stomach, but when she turns ever so slightly, she wakes up in agony. The plasters Jane applies to her back help, but it still takes two weeks before her bruises heal. The places where the whipping drew blood take longer. As she slowly mends, her ability to accomplish household tasks remains limited for some time because she cannot lift pots, carry trays filled with dishes, or take baskets of laundry to the creek. Fortunately, Jeremiah proves a dedicated helper.

Swett spends as much time as he can with her, but the day after Margaret comes back from James City, he has to return to performing his duties on the plantation and doesn't get back until supper. At least he and Margaret no longer have to hide their relationship and can express affection for each other openly. At first, the other workers cast furtive glances in their direction when they see them together, but they soon accept their devotion to each other as nothing out of the ordinary.

To everyone's surprise, Lieutenant Sheppard has a change of heart regarding Margaret. His attitude toward her changes, as if witnessing the punishment she endured because of her love for Swett has put him in touch with his better nature and erased any lingering anger and blame over Priscilla's death. He becomes downright solicitous toward her. "Take as much time as you need to recover," he tells Margaret early on. "When you are well again, we can talk about how the child affects your position and Robert's indenture on the plantation."

While others help out around the house, Agnes tries to hinder Jane's attempts to aid Margaret. Although she took pleasure in Swett being publicly shamed in the pillory and Margaret getting whipped, her mood and temper remain sullen and peevish. It irritates her that Margaret receives so much attention and she demands that Jane spend more of her time serving as Agnes's personal maid. Dorothy goes along with her sister even though it means that the household suffers. But when meals aren't ready in time and dirt dragged into the house piles up in the sitting room for days, Sheppard finally puts his foot down and orders Jane to help with the chores.

Aid comes from an unexpected quarter. The first Sunday back at Lawne's Creek Church, William Spencer and his daughter Elizabeth seek out the lieutenant after the service. The older man puts his hand on Sheppard's arm and says, "A word, Robert." After they move to a quiet corner of the building, he continues, "I understand that, due to recent circumstances, you are a bit shorthanded. Elizabeth has never forgotten Margaret and John saving her from the Indians that tried to kidnap her, and she wants to be of assistance. She has my permission to spend a fortnight at your house to help out. Just say the word."

Sheppard looks at Elizabeth standing next to her father with interest. He has paid little attention to her in the past, considering her a mere child. But now he sees a sixteen-year-old girl in the first blush of womanhood. Her figure is filling out, and she has a pretty face, surrounded by long, blond curls. Her attractive, blue-gray eyes are curious and do not wilt under his scrutiny. "I can cook, clean, sew, and do whatever is needed," she says eagerly.

Sheppard doesn't have to think twice. He has always respected Spencer as a fair, upstanding burgess and imagines his daughter is like a branch cut from the same tree. Besides, an extra pair of hands will ease the situation at home. "I thank you for the offer, William," he says and shakes Spencer's hand. Then he turns to Elizabeth and bows formally. "I'm pleased to welcome you to my house and would appreciate any help you can give us."

That afternoon, to everyone's surprise, Elizabeth travels back with him to his homestead. She fits in easily and charms everyone except Agnes. Having grown up on a plantation herself, she is not afraid of physical work and quickly demonstrates her value. Soon after she takes over Margaret's duties, the household returns to its normal routines, and her friendly, outgoing manner lifts the dour mood that had pervaded the residence.

Elizabeth also endears herself to Sheppard by making him feel comfortable and important. She mends his shirts and makes sure his room is clean. After supper, she brings him his clay pipe, tamped with tobacco, and lights it for him.

But she reserves her greatest care for Margaret, helping to change her bandages and bringing her extra food at mealtimes. When Margaret protests against the special treatment, Elizabeth enlists Swett's aid. "She must regain her strength," she says, encouraging him to help persuade her.

It turns out that Elizabeth is also good with the children, happy to play games with little Priscilla, Mihill, and Susannah, both indoors and outside. By the time Margaret recuperates enough to take up her duties again, and Elizabeth leaves to return to her father's plantation, everyone except Agnes is sorry to see her go. Sheppard personally escorts her home.

With Elizabeth gone, the house reverts to its dreary, tense atmosphere, and Margaret makes a crucial decision. After discussing the matter with Swett, she approaches Lieutenant Sheppard to talk about her future on the plantation. The two get together in the living room after sending Agnes and Dorothy out for a walk. It is the warmest place in the house, and Sheppard takes the armchair close to the fire. When he offers Margaret the chair opposite, she chooses to remain standing, earning her a calculating glance. It may be uncommon for a woman to negotiate on her own behalf, but the lieutenant has come to expect nothing less from Margaret, and her expression indicates that she is dead serious.

Margaret starts in without preamble. "As you know, I finished my indenture with you two years ago, and you are about to extend Robert's contract because of our son," she says. "I will gladly stay for the duration, but I no longer feel comfortable living in this house."

Sheppard's eyes narrow. He did not anticipate this development. "What do you propose?" he asks carefully.

"I want the fifty acres due to me so Robert and I can build a house for ourselves. I will continue to work here as before, but I will have my own place to go home to at night."

Leaning back, Sheppard crosses his arms. "It is an unusual request."

Margaret takes a step toward him. "Whatever terms of indenture you negotiate with Robert, I will abide by them."

Seeing the determination in her eyes, he looks toward the fireplace and the flames licking at the logs. "It is an interesting proposal. Let me think on it."

Margaret, realizing this is not the time to push any further, says, "I really appreciate it, Robert," and leaves for the kitchen.

* * *

The following Sunday, Margaret and Swett bring their baby, now four weeks old, to church to be baptized. It is the first time since her recovery that Margaret has ventured out among people away from the plantation, and she is unsure of how they will receive her. She need not have worried. There are a few curious glances from the wives of the burgesses and workers from other plantations who don't know her well, but for the most part, people treat her politely. In their eyes, she has served her punishment and it is time to welcome her back into the community.

Anthony and Mary receive her with open arms. Even Katherine and Michael greet her warmly and coo over the baby. Margaret is glad that she asked Jason to inform John of her plans ahead of time so that he could stay away.

The ceremony is brief but well attended. Even Agnes is there, standing stiffly next to Dorothy and Sheppard. Although the Reverend Faulkner refused to travel from James City to baptize a child "conceived in sin," John Upton has no such qualms and officiates in his place. During the baptism, Robert positions himself by Margaret, who is holding the baby, with Mihill standing by her side. Upton sprinkles water on the child's head and makes the sign of the cross on his forehead. When he calls out for everyone to hear, "I baptize you 'Robert Cornish-Swett,' in the name of the Father and of the Son and of the Holy Spirit," Margaret and Robert beam with pride.

Afterward, a number of people come up to congratulate them. They include both familiar faces and men and women Margaret hardly knows. She feels touched that so many have accepted her back into the fold.

When Katherine reaches the head of the line, she takes a long look at Robert Jr. and says, "He has both of your features." Then she offers, "Why don't Michael and I take Mihill with us for the afternoon so he can spend time with John? I promise we will bring him home by nightfall."

Margaret says, "Thank you," and impulsively hugs her.

By the time she and Robert return to Sheppard's plantation, Margaret is exhausted. She didn't realize how much she dreaded facing everyone, afraid that they would reject her. Feeling relieved that all went well, she sits quietly on the porch with Robert and their son, enjoying the afternoon sun. Letting the tiredness wash over her, she wonders when the lieutenant will get back to her about her request for a place of her own.

* * *

For John, the weeks of Margaret's recovery have brought neither relief nor resolution. Unbeknownst to her, he did go to James City to see her and Swett receive their punishment, but he kept to the far back of the crowd so she would not notice him. It gave him no pleasure to see Margaret suffer under the whip. Now that she is gone from his life, he feels at a loss, adrift with no sense of purpose to anchor him.

His talk with Emmanuel Driggers didn't help as much as he would have liked, other than to reassure him that Emmanuel was not going to take sides against him just because Frances is Margaret's best friend.

As they took their usual walk along the river, Emmanuel said, "What happened with Margaret is not your fault, and there is nothing you could have done differently to change it. You must believe that, John."

John looked out over the waves rippling the river and the puffy, gray-bellied clouds drifting low in the sky. Sad-faced, he whispered, "It is hard."

"I know," Emmanuel said with compassion. "But we must not let disagreements come between any of us. None of us can afford to."

John shivered involuntarily and asked, "What do you mean?"

"There are too few of us Africans and too many wealthy white planters who don't have our interests at heart. That's why we must look out for one another, come what may."

Although those words did little to make him feel better at the time, Emmanuel's presence provided some comfort. When the sun started to sink lower in the sky, John did not want their time together to end, even though it was time to head back to Ewens's plantation.

As they said their good-byes at the dock, Emmanuel took John by the shoulders and looked him in the eyes. "Remember," he said, "above all, the most important thing is to gain our freedom."

John has ruminated on Emmanuel's words repeatedly since then, both while taking long walks in the forest and before going to sleep at night. He knows Emmanuel is right, but whenever he thinks of Margaret, he feels his heart clamp shut. At times, he chastises himself for not listening to her when she asked him to use his money to help her, and Emmanuel's words absolving him of any responsibility provide no comfort.

In public on the plantation and during trips to James City, John maintains an unruffled exterior, but his closest friends, Katherine and Michael, can see how desperately he is struggling, overwhelmed by melancholy and hopelessness. They want to help but understand that nothing—not words or actions—can diminish his sense of loss. So they try to do the next best things they can. Katherine invites him for supper whenever possible. Michael suggests going on forays into the woods to assess the hog population more often than necessary. John knows what his friend is doing but gladly accepts the opportunity to distract himself, and they trudge along in the winter forest, bundled up against the bracing cold and examine the spoors in the snow. It promises to be another good year.

The first time John encounters Margaret and Swett at church, he feels a twinge of pain but hesitates only slightly. Aware that everyone's eyes are on them, he walks up to them and says more calmly than he feels, "Hello, Margaret, Robert. How are you?"

Margaret responds with similar formality, "It is good to see you, John," while Robert, who is carrying the baby, nods to him.

Noticing Mihill by her side watching them uncertainly, she bends down and says, "Go with your father. We will see you later tonight."

John puts his arm on Mihill's shoulder and heads into the church. He finds a spot for them on a bench in the rear and at the far side of the central aisle. When Margaret and Swett enter, they look around until they see them. Then they take their seats toward the front, close to the opposite wall. After the service, John and Mihill leave quickly for Ewens's plantation to avoid further contact while Margaret and Robert wait awhile. By the time they exit the church, there is no sign of John and Mihill.

In time, the encounters become less stilted. The main topics of conversation between Margaret and John concern arrangements regarding their son. When John has to go to James City early in the week, he often asks Margaret to take Mihill home with her. If one or the other is unable to attend church, they let each other know by messenger ahead of time.

Margaret appreciates that John takes a real interest in Mihill, not just letting Katherine take care of him. The first time she becomes aware of how much attention he pays to his son's education occurs when Michael returns Mihill late on a Sunday afternoon.

The boy crosses the natural bridge across the creek, full of excitement. When he gets down, he runs to her, crowing proudly, "I can count to five!" He holds up one hand and spreads his fingers. As he points to them one at a time, he says, "One, two, three, four, five."

Michael shouts from across the creek, "John taught him that," before leaving.

As Margaret watches Mihill, an image of John as a six-year-old at Aldwarke, counting numbers for Lady Isabel, comes into her mind, and she feels deeply moved.

Over the next few days, to everyone's amusement, Mihill arranges all sorts of objects in groups of five and counts them— stones, branches, pillows in the house, peas in the kitchen, pieces of meat in his stew.

At some point, he asks Margaret, "Mom, what comes after five?"

The following Sunday, Margaret compliments John for what he has done, and says, "That was very clever. Are you going to teach him how to write as well?"

John laughs for the first time in many months in her presence and says, "Maybe. But you'll have to teach him the next five numbers."

For John, the encounter has another consequence. Margaret's teasing comment reminds him of his time at Aldwarke, too, when he was not much older than Mihill is now, and he starts to think about his son's future. Recalling his last conversation with Emmanuel regarding freedom, he starts to hatch a plan.

41

ANOTHER COURT CASE

Virginia—Winter–Spring 1641

Two weeks after the hog killing in January, Margaret meets John before the Sunday service at Lawne's Creek Church to hand over Mihill for the rest of the afternoon. Unexpectedly, John moves close to her and says, soft enough so that only she can hear it, "I need to speak with you alone. When can we meet?"

The urgency in his voice alarms Margaret. "Is something the matter?"

"Not to worry. But not here," he murmurs. "Not enough time and too many people."

Margaret thinks quickly. "Why don't you bring Mihill back early? We can talk near the creek."

During the ceremony and on the way home, she wonders what could be on John's mind. Swett, accompanying her to pick up Mihill, has no idea either but ventures, "He must have a good reason."

It is a cold winter day and the light from the lead-gray skies gives the forest a twilight atmosphere. Margaret and Swett wait at the creek, stamping their feet and shivering, until they see John and Mihill emerge on the other side from among a stand of birches.

Walking briskly, their breaths create misty clouds. After they cross the large, fallen oak branch that spans the water, Swett takes the boy to the plantation, leaving Margaret and John alone.

Walking in the snow to keep warm brings back memories for both of them. Margaret glances at John, waiting for him to begin, but his face remains determined and serious.

Finally, he says, "I know you have made an arrangement with Sheppard regarding your and Robert's son. Unfortunately, that leaves Mihill out. He still belongs to Sheppard." He breaks off a twig from a larger branch lying on the ground. It makes a sharp crack. "A while back, I spoke with Emmanuel. We talked about how important it is for us to attain our freedom. I want that for you and your children, and I have come up with a plan for Mihill."

Margaret watches him warily and says, "Go on."

"This year's hog harvest has been good," he continues. "I have saved enough money by now to negotiate Mihill's freedom from Sheppard, so I can use some of the stash from my privateering days without raising any eyebrows."

Margaret notes that he doesn't mention Captain Jope by name. Perhaps he thinks it would be too painful for her.

John whips the stick in his hand back and forth. "Thomas Goodman has agreed to support me, and I have written to William Ewens as well. Sheppard is more interested in you than Mihill. He says he'll let him go for a reasonable payment. We could make it part of the divorce settlement."

They walk on in silence past gnarled oak trunks as Margaret tries to understand. "Let's say things go as you wish. What would happen then?" she asks. "You can't raise him by yourself."

"You're right," John admits and hesitates before going on. "The way to assure his freedom is to indenture him to another plantation owner. Sheppard mentioned Captain Christopher Stafford in Charles City as a good choice. He knows him quite well, as they've been fighting Indians together for some time. Having a contract will give Mihill legal standing and guarantee his freedom at the age written in the document."

Margaret is so shocked that she doesn't register his growing excitement. The idea of giving up Mihill and have him become a servant on a plantation far away from her is inconceivable. She looks at John, nonplussed.

"I have discussed this with Emmanuel, and he agrees that it is the best way," John responds. "Perhaps the only way."

To stall for time, she says, "Let me discuss it with Robert."

John's face darkens and he squeezes the stick hard. "This is between you and me," he insists. "I know Robert is a good man, but Mihill is not his child."

"You've sprung this on me with no warning," she reproves him. "You must give me time to think about it, what it means."

Seeing the anguish in her face, John realizes that he has been too hasty. "I understand," he says. "By all means, talk it over with Robert. Then let us speak again. If you agree, I will talk further with Sheppard." He adds, "A good word from you will help persuade him."

He tosses the stick carelessly into the woods. It is time to head back, but he doesn't move. Margaret gazes at him uncertainly and perceives his discomfort. Knowing him better than anyone else, she realizes that there is something else.

"What are you not telling me?"

Refusing to meet her eyes, John says quietly, "We will have to make it look like the separation is your fault, or the court won't grant me custody of Mihill."

Margaret rubs her forehead, confused. "But isn't that already the case? You and I broke up because of what I did."

John gives her a sidelong glance. "Wyatt is a fanatic. We will have to make the argument on religious grounds."

Still perplexed, she says, "Why not just remind him that I committed a sin? I know he thinks I'm a hussy already."

"Yes, but we will have to go further, much further," John says with regret in his voice.

* * *

The gavel banging on the judge's bench marks the conclusion of the hearing in late March before the Governor's Council in James City. "We will now confer to reach a verdict," Governor Wyatt says, looking ominously at the two men standing before him.

While he and his six fellow justices gather, muttering among each other, John and Goodman, the manager of Ewens's plantation, look at one another. They are dressed in their Sunday's best, brown doublets and pants. The church that houses the court is only partially filled with petitioners and their friends, and Margaret is not present. John is glad that she heeded him when he asked her not to attend the proceedings. It made it easier to paint her in the most unfavorable terms, calling her not only a depraved woman, but a sinful, unchristian heathen. John is certain that she could not have brought herself to go along with that aspect of the deception in person. She may not be a devout believer anymore, but she has been a Christian since her time with the Portuguese nuns in Africa. At first reluctant, she agreed to it only when he told her what he would be sacrificing.

John knows that he did everything in his power to state his case in his favor. After denouncing Margaret, he explained that he has amassed money in the hog trade with the support of William Ewens, by returning half of his profits to the plantation owner. Goodman backed him up and presented a deposition from Ewens attesting to his agreement to the proposal regarding Mihill. John also submitted Lieutenant Sheppard's written and notarized statement that the financial terms of giving up the rights to Mihill were agreeable to him. John hopes it will be enough to sway the court.

It doesn't take the justices long to reach a verdict. As they return to their seats, John feels his gut tense. He takes a deep breath to face the court with a calm expression.

Looking at him with his remorseless, black eyes, Wyatt raps the bench once again. Then he says, "Having heard the testimony and acquainted ourselves with the words of two upstanding citizens of the colony to our satisfaction, we order the following:

"That the marriage between John Gower, a negro servant of William Ewens, and Margaret Cornish, a negro servant of Lieutenant Robert Sheppard, is hereby dissolved.

"That the request by John Gower to take the young child of said negro woman in order to raise him as a Christian is hereby granted.

"John Gower may purchase the child's freedom from Lieutenant Sheppard with the consent of Thomas Goodman, overseer, as well as by the deposition of William Ewens, plantation owner. The court hereby orders that the child shall be free from any obligation and remain at the disposing and education of John Gowen, who will undertake to see it brought up in the Church of England."

He strikes the gavel three times, and calls out, "Next case!"

John heaves a sigh of relief and smiles at Goodman for the first time since he stepped inside the court.

* * *

Two days later, Margaret and Robert bring Mihill to the tree bridge. The deciduous trees are showing the first light green leaves, and the ground has the musty smell of early spring, but the air is still chilly.

By then, Margaret has talked at length with Lieutenant Sheppard, who has assured her that Captain Stafford is a fair man. Together with William Gibbs, he owns a sizeable plantation about ten miles upriver from where she attended Abraham Piersey's wedding in Floridew when she was still working for John Chew and his family.

When they get to the fallen oak tree, John is waiting. Swett steps back to give him and Margaret privacy. It has been a trying time. Explaining what is about to happen to Mihill has been as difficult as coming up with a reason for why she and John are no longer together. Margaret didn't have an answer that made sense to Mihill then, and she has faltered here as well.

Although Margaret has done her best, telling Mihill he will be going on a great adventure, he doesn't really believe her. For most of the walk, he has been on the verge of tears. When he sees John standing on this side of the creek, he asks in a small, forlorn voice, "Do I have to go?"

Margaret kneels and says, "Yes, you must."

"But I don't want to leave you," he cries out and throws his arms around her, clinging to her with all his strength.

Margaret feels helpless. She looks to John for support, but he stands stock-still as if struck by lightning. When she finally manages to pry Mihill's hands away, she holds them in hers and says, "It will be all right, but you must be strong now." Her voice fills with urgency and she continues, "Always know that I love you with all my heart and that you are special."

When Mihill sighs, giving in, she gives him a final hug and encouraging smile. Then she gets up and leads him by the hand to John.

He nods to her once and says to his son, "Believe me, Mihill. It is for your own good."

Then he helps him up on the branch that spans the creek and guides him across. On the other side, Mihill turns and waves to Margaret. She waves back and throws him a kiss. As they walk away, Mihill looks back from time to time to make sure she is still there, and it nearly breaks her heart.

She continues to wave until they disappear among the budding trees. Then she sinks to the ground, sobbing, and rakes the dark earth, her hands like claws. Robert rushes to her to take her into his arms, but it takes a long time before she quiets down.

As promised, a few days later John indentures Mihill to Robert Stafford until his eighteenth birthday. Although it pains him deeply, he is confident that the boy will be well cared for and that his servitude will come to an end. As they travel upriver by boat to Charles City, Mihill asks again why he can't stay with him, and John has no good answer. The boy wouldn't understand if he told him the real reason—that John gave up his own freedom as a part of the arrangement. William Ewens, appreciating what an asset John is to the plantation, exacted a big price for giving his support. John had to agree to indenture himself again, this time for a period of five years. Keeping Mihill at his side under those circumstances would be impossible. His son would have become the property of the plantation owner.

* * *

With Mihill gone, Margaret and Robert begin building a house on land at the southern edge of Sheppard's plantation. Margaret didn't want them to start while her son was still with them and, unable to share in their new future, feel even more rejected.

Lieutenant Sheppard has been crafty as well as generous. The fifty acres he deeded to Margaret include a good deal of swampland, but there is enough high ground for a comfortable home, a garden, and fields to grow vegetables, corn, and tobacco, if they want to.

MONHEGAN
7/95

PART IV

CHILDREN OF
THE FUTURE

R.C.Moore

42

CHANGES ON BOTH SIDES OF THE OCEAN

England and Virginia—1641–1642

In the summer of 1641, the Earl of Warwick receives news so upsetting that he goes on a rampage through his house in Holborn, London, upending furniture and tearing tapestries from the walls. After two earlier, unsuccessful attempts, a Spanish fleet has attacked Providence Island and destroyed the English settlement there, putting an end to Rich's imperialist ambitions in the Caribbean. This is not just a setback but a catastrophe, and it couldn't have come at a worse time. Three years earlier, with no end in sight to the impasse between King Charles and Parliament, Rich and his fellow Puritan investors had considered immigrating to New Providence to escape the intensifying struggles. Now, just as political strife in England is coming to a head, that option is no longer available.

When King Charles finally recalls Parliament to obtain funds for his military campaign against Scotland and the Irish Rebellion, the elections give his enemies an overwhelming majority in the House of Commons. Led by the irascible John Pym, things become so contentious that in January 1642, King Charles enters the House of Commons with his guards to personally arrest Pym and four members of his faction. Forewarned, they escape, and the gambit misfires. Outraged by the monarch's invasion of one of its chambers, Parliament seizes London, and King Charles, fearing for his safety, flees the city with his family and retinue.

Over the next months, both sides start to raise armies in preparation for war. The Earl of Warwick assumes command of the English navy at the behest of Parliament. The dogs of war are baying loudly to be unleashed.

* * *

The impending civil war sends adverse ripples across the Atlantic Ocean as well. Many of Virginia's wealthy planters who have extended families and land holdings in England worry about what will happen to them. At the same time, as rumors of the approaching conflict flourish in Virginia, the economic uncertainty depresses tobacco prices and reduces the profits of the plantation owners.

The foreboding climate affects John and his fellow Africans, too, but another event in a rival colony to the north has more immediate implications.

On December 10, 1641, Massachusetts's General Court publishes the *Body of Liberties*, a list of a hundred laws enumerating the rights of individual landowners and freemen. News of the first legal code in the New World travels quickly to the other colonies. By January 1642, the news reaches Virginia, where it generates considerable interest, in large part because Sir Francis Wyatt's brief time as governor has come to an end. His successor, Sir William Berkeley, is a young, ambitious man who spent considerable time at the court of King Charles.

At first, rumor had it that the appointment was the result of Sir John Harvey and his crony, Richard Kemp, succeeding in their relentless pursuit of revenge against the man who ousted them. But then a more mundane explanation emerged: money and greed. Wealthy friends and relatives of Berkeley paved the way for him to buy the office from Wyatt. The appeal to King Charles involved a financial incentive as well, and the monarch, desperate for funds, was happy to sign the commission making Sir William the new governor of Virginia.

Anticipating his arrival in the late spring, members of the colony's landed gentry and other burgesses worry about what the change in administration will bring. Although word from England has it that Berkeley is a moderate royalist, those who suffered through Harvey's and Wyatt's tenures are wary of anyone who takes the monarch's side in any colonial disputes.

So, when a copy of the *Body of Liberties* finds its way to the courthouse in James City, a number of burgesses who have some legal background pore over the document to determine if it can help them gain power. For several weeks, the code becomes the main topic of conversation at church gatherings and other social functions. Although few people have any personal knowledge of what it actually says, they voice their opinions with conviction and fervor. English Protestants like Richard Bennett laud its expansion of individual liberties. Anglican loyalists, including Lieutenant Sheppard, William Spencer, and John Upton, dismiss it as so much "Puritan hogwash." They see it as an expression of the resentment New England settlers have always had toward the Stuart kings, who prosecuted them for their faith. Not only do the heated exchanges lay bare religious differences in Virginia, but they also reflect the growing concern about the drums of war beating in England and how the colony will respond when the fighting starts.

John travels to James City to look over the copy of the *Body of Liberties* on behalf of Thomas Goodman and William Ewens. He spends the better part of a morning at the archives of Virginia's court documents. The room housing the scroll is not as large as the library at the plantation, but because there are fewer books and more bins and shelves for legal documents, there is still plenty of space.

Reading the parchment scroll, John is amazed at the wide range of individual rights specified in the code of laws, both for property owners and ordinary Massachusetts freemen. But toward the end of the document, he comes upon a section that takes his breath away. It states, "There shall never be any bond slavery, villeinage, or captivity amongst us unless it be lawful captives taken in just wars, and such strangers as willingly sell themselves or are sold to us."

Stunned, John reads the sentence several times to be sure he doesn't misconstrue its meaning. Although he doesn't know what "villeinage" means, he understands the last part of the statement all too well. "Sold to us" refers to the trade in slaves and, by implication, grants it legitimacy. The realization that the *Body of Liberties* has legalized slavery in Massachusetts burns like fire in his brain.

After returning to Ewens's plantation, John spends several sleepless nights mulling over the implications. Is this a harbinger of things to come in Virginia? How soon before the General Council adopts similar laws? The more he thinks about it, the more troubled he becomes.

That Sunday, John shares his foreboding with Anthony and other members of the small African community at Lawne's Creek Church. He speaks quietly so as not to alarm anyone, but the urgency in his voice gets everyone's attention. Anthony grasps right away what is at stake. Having lived in England on the Earl of Warwick's estate, he knows from personal experience how quickly a wealthy, powerful Englishman will break his promises to an African servant. If the Virginia Governor's Council and General Assembly adopted a similar law enshrining slavery, it could apply not only to black slaves brought to the colony but to servants and field-workers who live here already but have no legal standing. Michael, Katherine, and Mathew are not convinced that John's warnings have merit. They continue to trust Thomas Goodman to do right by them. John does not contradict them in public.

He considers whether to inform Margaret and Robert Swett. Since they keep to themselves at church, John rarely talks to them anymore. In the end, he decides that this matter is important enough. After the service, as they head toward the boats to go back to Sheppard's plantation, he approaches them and says, "I'd like to speak with you about an urgent matter."

Startled and worried by his serious demeanor, Margaret exclaims, "Is anything the matter with Mihill?"

"No, not at all," John assures her. "If anything happened to him, you'd probably hear it from Lieutenant Sheppard before me. I'm sure you'll get a report as soon as he and Captain Stafford meet during the spring training of the militia."

"What is it then?" Swett asks.

"I don't want to discuss it here," John says, keeping his voice low. "May I come visit you at your home this afternoon?"

After a quick glance at Margaret, Swett nods.

John returns to Ewens's plantation only long enough to eat the midday meal with Katherine, Michael, and Mathew. Then he heads for the forest. Although it is a chilly day, the first signs of spring are everywhere. Buds and sprouts of light green leaves have emerged on the trees, and with most of the underbrush still bare, John could move through it swiftly but chooses to walk with deliberation. While he has not been to Margaret and Robert's homestead before, John knows its location on the southern edge of the side of Sheppard's property close to Ewens's plantation. He considers trying a shortcut through the woods, but unsure of finding a convenient spot to ford the creek, he takes the familiar path that leads across the natural tree bridge.

It is mid-afternoon by the time he reaches the thatch-roofed cottage. While not as expansive as Ewens's mansion or Lieutenant Sheppard's main house, it looks comfortable and roomy. No doubt, Swett has plans for a large brood of children.

As he gets closer, John notices a patch of dry weeds and flower stalks by the side of the house. The ground is dug up in places.

Margaret has been busy already. As long as she has lived in Virginia, she has cultivated her special gardens. John smiles pensively. What would she be without her flowers and herbs?

When he calls out to the house, Margaret appears on the porch and waves to him. Her belly doesn't show yet that she is pregnant again, but she has that special radiance about her that John has learned at Ewens's plantation to recognize in women who are with child.

Swett emerges behind her, carrying their six-month-old son. Resting his head against his father's shoulder, Robert Jr. yawns. "Hello, John," Swett says in greeting. "Won't you come inside?"

John hesitates. "I don't wish to intrude."

Margaret smiles at him. "You're always welcome here, John."

Feeling uncomfortable, John makes a show of removing a large ham from his travel bag and holds it out to Margaret. "I know you have your share of hog meat from this year's harvest already, but I brought you another smoked loin." He points to her belly. "You'll need it when you have one more mouth to feed."

"It's kind of you to notice and much appreciated," she says, acknowledging John's observant remark. Taking the ham from him, she adds, "Can I get you something to eat? We have leftovers from dinner."

"No, thank you. I've had my fill," he says. "But I'll take a draft of cider if you can spare it."

When they go inside, Margaret heads to the kitchen and Swett takes the boy into a bedroom for a nap, leaving John to look around. The furnishings are simple—a sturdy table and a few wooden chairs with pillows for comfort—but there is a large, stone fireplace with burning logs. The afternoon sunlight streaming through the window brightens the room. John admires how the cottage is positioned just right to keep things cool in the middle of the day, yet take advantage of maximum light later.

When Swett returns, he indicates one of the chairs. "Please, sit." He adds, "No need to speak softly here. Not even a thunderbolt would wake the boy."

Margaret brings in a tray with three cups of cider and puts it on the table. As she hands a cup each to John and Robert, keeping the third for herself, the smell of cinnamon pervades the room.

John takes a sip of the warm liquid and says, "It's good."

It is the first time all three have been together alone for any length of time, and they observe each other covertly as they drink. John notes the beginnings of crow's feet around Swett's eyes. Margaret's face has matured as well, but her ordeal has left no visible marks or worry lines. If anything, she is more beautiful than ever.

Margaret searches for the familiar boy in John but finds only a stern, serious-minded man. It pains her to see him look older than his years.

Finally, Swett breaks the silence. "Why don't you tell us why you are here, John? What is this about?"

John takes another sip. Then he starts to explain what he found in the *Body of Liberties* document in James City and what it would mean if a similar law legalizing slavery were enacted in Virginia.

When he finishes, Swett frowns and says, "I understand your concern, John, but what does that have to do with us? Margaret already has her freedom."

John also frowns. "Such a law would affect anyone without official legal standing. That is why I persuaded Margaret to let me indenture Mihill. I am thinking of your children and what you might want to do for them." He continues carefully, "Things are changing in Virginia. There are not that many of us Africans, and the white planters and merchants who wield power are beginning to treat us differently. It started with the law prohibiting us from carrying weapons in public. In court cases, black defendants receive harsher punishments than whites, as you well know." When he sees

Swett's face harden, he realizes that his comment cut too close to the bone and adds quickly, "John Punch was made a slave for the same offense as the white servants who escaped with him. They had only a few years added to their contracts, but he was indentured for life!" His stare is hard and penetrating. "Your children will be considered Negroes and treated accordingly once they leave the safety of your home and Sheppard's plantation."

Margaret glances at Swett with a flicker of fear in her eyes. He reaches for her hand and squeezes it. When she faces John again, her look is composed and detached as if she no longer worries, and he feels that he has lost her.

Meanwhile, Swett says stiffly, "I thank you for bringing this matter to our attention, John. Rest assured, we are perfectly capable of taking care of our children and will make sure their future is secure."

John wants to argue but holds his tongue. It is not his business to interfere in their lives. He downs the last of his cider and forces himself to smile. "Then I have accomplished my purpose," he says formally and rises. "Thank you for your hospitality, but you'll have to excuse me. I must get back before it gets dark. I wish you both well."

Swett nods and gets up as well to accompany him to the door.

Margaret knows John too well not to realize that he feels rejected. She wishes there were something she could do to soften the blow. "I'll let you know as soon as I hear anything about Mihill," she calls after him.

He waves to her, shakes hands with Swett, and walks outside, stepping quickly down from the porch. Back on solid ground, he can't get away fast enough. Hurrying toward the trees he feels a lump in his throat. When he enters the safety of the forest, he slows down but keeps walking and doesn't stop until he is a good distance from the cottage. Suddenly, a sharp pain in his stomach doubles him over. It is just about a year since he first found out that Margaret was pregnant and having an affair with Swett. In all that time, he has kept his emotions under control, and now they explode with a vengeance. To escape the searing anguish, he starts to run like a wild beast pursued by merciless hounds. Unmindful of his surroundings, he trips over exposed roots and doesn't notice the twigs whipping him across the face. Ignoring the stabbing pain in his side, he keeps racing on like a man possessed until, utterly spent, he crashes to the ground.

Sobbing in great gasps, he grieves for everything he has lost. Margaret has been his anchor ever since they were chained together on the slave caravan in Africa and she kept up his spirits, and now she has become a stranger. He can't imagine ever having someone like her in his life again.

Finally he gets up and brushes the leaves and burrs from his coat. As he lumbers on with sagging shoulders, he views his situation almost dispassionately. He thinks about the conversation with Swett and Margaret and how comfortable and content they were together in their small cottage. He realizes that he never had that kind of relationship with Margaret. Even when they were married, he saw more of Katherine during the week at Ewens's plantation.

With a clarity he has not felt before, he grasps that a quiet, domestic life would not work for him. He prefers the bustle of James City. He remembers his brief time with Captain Jope in London and Vlissingen in Holland. They were exhilarating experiences, even if they were sad occasions of leave-taking. John doesn't have the character for running a plantation or pursuing a trade. He just can't imagine what the alternatives might be. He has another four years of indenture ahead of him at Ewens's plantation and knows for certain now that he doesn't want to stay there after that. But where else to go? What else to do?

He hopes Emmanuel will travel upriver and come to James City soon. It is spring and there are provisions to be bought. As far as John knows, Emmanuel and Frances are close to fulfilling their indenture contracts, too. Surely Emmanuel has thought about what comes next for them. Perhaps he has ideas about possibilities John hasn't considered. From the *Body of Liberties* to their respective futures, they will have a lot to discuss.

43

THREE WEDDINGS

Virginia—1642–1643

For Margaret, John's visit marks a turning point as well. It confirms that she made the right decision for Mihill. She has been missing him and thinks of him every day, often blaming herself for agreeing to let him go. Being with Robert makes her feel loved and secure, and she doesn't really want to believe John's warning that legalized slavery could reach Virginia soon. But she has to admit the possibility. John has been right about many things affecting the Africans she knows—John Punch, Anthony and Mary Johnson, and above all, Mihill. Without John's foresight, their son would not be on a path to freedom.

Seeing John at close quarters for the first time after many months apart also made clear that she still cares deeply for him. Margaret hates to watch him struggle between his desire to act as her friend and his desire for her as a woman, a quandary that she cannot resolve for him. Yes, she loved him once—still loves him—but not that way anymore. If he could only accept that he is now on his own, she thought, separate from her, and move on.

Margaret has done so and without any regrets. Her relationship with John never reached the joy and passion she experiences daily with Robert. She loves the way his eyes light up when they happen to see each other at the plantation during the day, and how he bows to her courteously like a gallant suitor when he arrives at their cottage after work, only to lust after her once she invites him inside.

He dotes on her in amorous and humorous ways, and never seems to tire of whispering sweet nothings in her ear or touching and kissing her. At night after supper, when their baby son has fallen asleep, they sit on the porch holding hands and watch the fireflies dance, turning the meadow into a carpet of sparkling gems. Or they count the shooting stars that streak across the sky. Margaret always makes the same wish—that her destiny will soon reveal itself.

Above all, she adores Robert for loving children. He enjoys playing with his son, even though Robert Jr. is still tiny and utters only a few words. Since Margaret became pregnant again, before they go to sleep at night, Robert always puts his hands on her belly and whispers endearments to the baby growing inside her.

Confident of their future together, he doesn't seem bothered that Sheppard will extend his contract of indenture an additional three years after the child is born. In his presence, Margaret feels that all the pain and humiliation they endured to be with each other was worth it.

In the meantime, a number of developments occur at Sheppard's plantation that improve her situation there as well.

After getting over her anger of feeling jilted by Swett, Agnes regains her arrogant pride and decides to cast her eyes elsewhere. Being a cousin of Lieutenant Sheppard, a man of excellent repute, with a handsome dowry to boot, she knows she is a good catch.

Still, everyone at the plantation is surprised when Agnes meets George Alderman, a recently widowed planter, at the welcoming reception for Governor Berkeley. As a burgess and member of the General Council, he ranks high enough in social circles for her ambitions, and she sends him appropriate signals letting him know that she is interested and available. Within a fortnight, he calls on Lieutenant Sheppard to ask for her hand. The three come to a mutually agreeable arrangement and publish the bans in James City and at Lawne's Creek Church.

Although Agnes would like a lavish wedding, her future husband is a miser and insists that the ceremony take place on his plantation on the York River near King's Creek. Margaret, along with others, is delighted that the bride will move there permanently. The only hitch is that Agnes insists Jane accompany her to her new home. She and Dorothy nearly come to blows over it. Margaret is gutting a pheasant in the kitchen when the shouts, screams, and insults the two sisters hurl at each other echo through the house. At some point, Lieutenant Sheppard wades into the fray and restores calm.

But then Jane burst into the kitchen, sobbing, and throws herself into Margaret's arms.

"I don't want to go with her," she blubbers. "I don't know what to do."

Gently stroking her hair, Margaret asks, "How many years do you have to stay in her service?"

Sniveling, Jane says, "I don't know."

Margaret takes her by the shoulders. "Then you must speak with Lieutenant Sheppard and find out. Have him put it in writing for you if he hasn't done so already. Talk to Dorothy first. She'll support you, if only to spite Agnes. Tell her you would like to work for her when you are free of your indenture."

Jane's eyes flit around the kitchen like a frightened rabbit's.

Grabbing hold of her chin and forcing Jane to pay attention, Margaret says, "Do you understand?"

Lowering her head, Jane sighs and nods earnestly.

It turns out that she has three years left on her contract. Margaret, remembering how Mrs. Chew abused her personal maid both verbally and physically, imagines it will feel like a lifetime.

Agnes does not leave Sheppard's plantation graciously. She finds as many occasions as she can to criticize Margaret, but her venomous comments miss their mark. By then, the child growing inside Margaret occupies much of her attention—the baby has started to kick—and anticipating its birth makes her impervious to petty insults. They make for amusing supper conversation at the cottage for her and Robert.

When Agnes leaves for good on the day before the wedding, everybody on the plantation assembles at the dock to see her off. Margaret hugs Jane, who is doing her best to put on a brave face. After the boat carrying the wedding party of Agnes, Dorothy, Sheppard, Jane, and Lucy casts off and disappears around the bend of the creek, some of the field hands start to express how they really feel about the departure of Sheppard's cousin. Jason quickly puts an end to their mocking, but the ridiculing continues out of his earshot.

When Lucy returns from the wedding, all the plantation workers gather around to hear what happened. Apparently, it was a small, hurried affair, with only immediate members of the families and a few neighbors and their families in attendance. Alderman was pleased. Agnes felt slighted. Lucy, a spirited young woman who likes to have fun, sums it up by saying, "The food was decent, but there was no dancing."

* * *

Dorothy, not to be outdone, deepens her relationship with Henry Meddows, a young worker who arrived on the same ship as Robert Swett. Now that Agnes is gone, she spends more time with him after supper and on weekends. Henry is a pleasant enough fellow, hardworking and levelheaded, and no one is surprised when they announce their plans to get married. Sheppard gives them a sizeable parcel of land as a wedding present, and they make plans to build a house there for themselves.

With her nagging sister gone, Dorothy no longer carries a grudge toward Margaret, and they develop a cordial relationship. The young couple asks her and Swett for advice on many matters, including the building of their new home. Robert is happy to help. With everyone on the plantation assisting, the cottage is finished in plenty of time before the wedding.

Dorothy, in turn, joins Lucy to help when Margaret goes into labor. The delivery takes fourteen hours, and Swett nearly goes mad listening to Margaret's erratic screams. By the time Margaret has the baby, she is utterly worn out.

Swett is spent, too, but elated that her ordeal is over and that they have another boy. They will christen him "William." When he goes into her bedroom and kisses her forehead, he says, "Let's have a girl next time." Margaret barely registers his presence and soon passes out from exhaustion.

Yet she recovers in plenty of time to participate fully in the preparations for the wedding of Dorothy and Henry Meddows.

The ceremony takes place at Lawne's Creek Church, and everyone in the surrounding area who can comes to celebrate. To everyone's surprise, Agnes and George Alderman make the two-day trip to attend. Visiting her sister's cottage, Agnes comments how small it feels compared to her own home, but nothing can dim the joyful atmosphere of the wedding or happiness of the young couple. Margaret and Lucy prepare a sumptuous feast, and the musicians play long into the night until everyone is too tired to dance another reel or jig.

Life soon returns to normal. What no one expected after Agnes and George depart, least of all Lieutenant Sheppard, is how empty the main house feels. In the past, before his cousins arrived and he expanded the plantation, everyone—Jason and the rest of the workers—took their meals together in the sitting room. Now, Sheppard's only companions are Margaret, Jeremiah, and Lucy, who has become the full-time caretaker for the children. In the evenings, Margaret goes home after preparing supper, leaving Lucy to serve it by herself.

The emptiness in the house becomes oppressive as Sheppard feels increasingly isolated and lonely. In the late afternoon, Margaret often comes upon him sitting in the living room, looking wistfully out the window. She would like to encourage him to look for another wife, but because of their history regarding Priscilla's death, she doesn't feel it is her place to talk to him about it.

The only relief comes when his military duties take him away from home. Sheppard spends more time in James City, too, on behalf of the government and returns with news of William Berkeley's latest plan for the colony, which he shares with Jason, Swett, and anyone else interested.

It turns out that the new governor, despite his relative youth—he is in his early thirties—has more skill as a politician than his predecessors. While he can be as impatient and irascible as Harvey and Wyatt, his genuine interest in Virginia's future and boundless enthusiasm draw people to him. Although he officially represents King Charles, he shrewdly realizes that he must walk a tightrope between Virginia's rival factions.

Berkeley quietly withdraws his support from the Reverend Faulkner, who agitates for the colony to be governed by a single faith: the Anglican religion. Instead, Berkeley courts the wealthiest and most powerful planters, even if they have Puritan leanings and openly challenge some of his ideas. By appointing them to prestigious offices and giving them access to new land, he cultivates their allegiance.

Early on in his tenure, Berkeley opposes the efforts to revive the Virginia Company. Although his parents were members before it folded in 1624, he speaks out vigorously against its resurgence. Many of the planters who remember how the company exploited them, putting profits above the colony's well-being, are grateful that the governor supports them.

Berkeley also takes steps to join the circle of elite planters. Unlike Wyatt and Harvey, his aristocratic background provides him with plenty of money of his own. He does not have to abuse the power of his office to earn his keep. Shortly after his arrival, he leases a large tract of land in James City County and takes advantage of readily available labor to raise his first crop of tobacco. Among the properties, he purchases a large piece of land three miles to the northwest of James City called Green Spring. Berkeley announces that he will build a country retreat there. In the meantime, he starts to experiment with crops other than tobacco—rice, flax, silk, grapes, and other fruit.

While many locals consider it a harebrained scheme, having seen governors from Yeardley on failing in their efforts to replace tobacco as a crop, they respect Berkeley's passion for bringing prosperity to Virginia. When he announces that he will share power with the General Assembly, he actually increases support for his own programs and ideas—furthering trade with the Indian tribes, bringing more people to the colony, exploring land outside Virginia's frontiers, and expanding markets beyond England to other colonies, the Netherlands, and the West Indies.

Lieutenant Sheppard always returns from his visits to James City with optimism and a sense of renewed purpose. When his military exploits take him upriver, he usually brings back news of Mihill, who seems to be doing well as a servant in Captain Stafford's household. Margaret, grateful for any tidbit of information about her son, always shares what she learns with John when she sees him at church.

Unfortunately, Sheppard's cheerful mood never lasts long. Within a week of his return, the atmosphere in the house plunges back into darkness and depression. Finally, Margaret has enough and resolves to do something about it. When she tells Robert of her plan, he counsels against it, but she ignores him. At Dorothy's wedding, she noticed Elizabeth Spencer glance at Sheppard with yearning. The girl has continued to do so at church services, despite the lieutenant being oblivious. Margaret decides to play matchmaker.

The next time Sheppard is away, she invites Elizabeth to come to the plantation. When she arrives, Margaret lets her play with the children, knowing how much she likes them. Then she asks Elizabeth to help her, Lucy, and Jeremiah do a second spring cleaning—washing the floors, curtains, and bed linens; polishing the candle holders on the mantle; beating the dust from carpets and blankets; wiping the cobwebs from the windows. Elizabeth has a good idea what Margaret is up to and agrees cheerfully. By the time she leaves, the interior of the house almost glows.

Even Sheppard can't help but notice the change upon his return. "What brought this on?" he asks gruffly when he first sets foot inside the living room. Seeing Margaret narrow her eyes, he adds quickly, "It looks very nice."

"I'm glad you like it," she says pleasantly, helping Lucy set the table for the midday meal. "Elizabeth Spencer happened to come by yesterday for a visit. She took one look and said the place needed a good cleaning." Registering Sheppard's shocked expression, she continues blithely, "I didn't think she would be so forward, but she just pulled up her sleeves and got to work."

"You mean you let her do all this by herself?" the lieutenant gasps, incredulous. "How could you! I'll never be able to face her father again!"

"Of course, Lucy, Jeremiah, and I pitched in," Margaret assures him. "But Elizabeth organized everything. She is really quite good at it."

Sheppard gives her a hard look, which Margaret returns sweetly on her way to the kitchen. Jeremiah strings along. But Lucy blushes and refuses to meet his eyes. At the first opportunity, she bolts after Margaret. Sheppard looks around the room again and decides not to pursue it further.

On Sunday, he finds Elizabeth before church and thanks her. Observing their awkward encounter from a distance amuses Margaret, and she and Swett share a quiet chuckle.

"See, it worked," she says triumphantly.

"Just don't overstep your bounds," he warns her, and she playfully slaps his arm.

Soon, Sheppard and Elizabeth start spending more time with each other, pursuing a casual courtship. After church, they go on walks together to the bluff overlooking the James River, enjoying each other's company. On Mondays, Margaret assesses how things went by how happy Sheppard looks. Before long, he travels to Spencer's plantation to ask for Elizabeth's hand. Having known for some time how she feels about the lieutenant, William Spencer gives his blessing right away. He can't imagine a better husband for his daughter.

By the time the marriage ceremony takes place in late summer, Margaret is pregnant again and starting to show. The wedding is a big affair, held at the church in James City. Guests include not only Agnes and Dorothy and their spouses, and planters from the southern shore of the river, but burgesses from all over Virginia and Sheppard's military friends. Governor Berkeley himself attends and makes his mansion available for the reception afterward, an indication of the high esteem with which everyone regards the lieutenant.

It is a warm September day when Sheppard and Elizabeth emerge from the church to cheers from the eager crowd. As they start walking through the aisle formed by a military honor guard, Margaret tosses corn seeds at the newlyweds, happy for them and pleased that she had something to do with the blissful expressions on their faces.

Suddenly, John appears at her side and points to a man Sheppard's age in the line of uniformed militiamen. "That is Captain Christopher Stafford, Mihill's master—for now," he says.

Margaret feels a small jolt in her breast as she takes a closer look. Stafford has a weathered face, thin lips, and a beaklike nose. He is not a handsome man, but the twinkle in his eyes suggests that he has a sense of humor.

When she looks back, John has disappeared. Instead, she sees Emmanuel and Frances coming toward her through the thinning crowd. A squeal of delight escapes her. "What are you two doing here?"

"Francis Pott insisted on coming to the wedding, and we couldn't very well let him go alone," Emmanuel says drily.

As Frances embraces her, she whispers to Margaret, "I see you are having another baby. I am so proud of you."

Joining the crowd heading toward the governor's mansion, they walk at a leisurely pace. Knowing they have all afternoon, they don't feel they have to rush to catch up on everything that has transpired since the last time they saw each other. Emmanuel and Swett renew their acquaintanceship from their brief encounter after Robert was released from the pillory. Margaret keeps looking at Frances as if she can't quite believe she is real.

But the biggest surprise occurs when Margaret and Swett join the receiving line at the mansion to congratulate the newlyweds. After they have offered their good wishes, Lieutenant Sheppard looks at Margaret and, with a sidelong glance at Elizabeth, says, "Thank you." Then he smiles and points past tables and benches filled with wedding guests. "There is someone waiting to see you."

When Margaret turns, she sees John standing at the fence and Mihill by his side. Forgetting all decorum, she hikes up her skirt and runs toward them. Mihill rushes into her arms, and she covers his face with kisses. Near tears, she holds him at arm's length to get a good look at him. "How you have grown," she marvels.

Mihill gazes at her belly and says, "You have too, Mother."

It takes her a moment to realize that he has made a joke.

Swett comes up behind her and greets Mihill warmly. Then Emmanuel and Frances join them, and they find a quiet corner. Emmanuel and John move aside to engage in serious conversation. Frances and Robert get to know each other better, giving Margaret more time with Mihill.

At some point, Margaret looks up at them talking and listening to one another. These are the people she cares about most in her life. She can't imagine a better way to spend an afternoon.

44
LIFE AND DEATH
Virginia—1643–1644

Elizabeth's arrival at Sheppard's plantation at the main house is like a breath of spring air driving out the stale, musty smell of winter. She has much of the youthful exuberance Priscilla developed, but with the benefit of years of experience of life in Virginia. She also brings another maid with her. Eunice is a fifteen-year-old, plain-faced girl with thin lips and flaxen hair. Her eagerness to work both as Elizabeth's personal servant and kitchen helper pleases everyone and allows her to fit in quickly. Before long, a welcome sense of domesticity envelops the household.

But Elizabeth wants to mix socially with others, too. To begin with, she invites Dorothy and her new husband, and Margaret and Robert, as well as Jason to join her and the lieutenant for midday meals and supper, restoring a sense of family on the plantation. Later, she expands the circle to neighbors willing to give up part of their Sunday afternoon, and a surprising number accept her invitations, curious to hear more of Sheppard's firsthand knowledge of James City politics. With Elizabeth's enthusiasm and guidance, the lieutenant loses some of his reserve and, becoming downright voluble at times, recovers his natural sense of humor.

The changes make Margaret's day-to-day life easier and more enjoyable. As her pregnancy reaches its late stage, she gets winded carrying things and can't move about as quickly. When she and Robert accept Elizabeth's invitations, she listens with only half an ear to Sheppard's accounts of Governor Berkeley's latest plans and the increasingly dire news of the civil war in England, preferring to save her limited energy and attention for Robert and her children.

Then the General Assembly passes a law requiring all Negro females in the colony to submit to annual tithing. Since there are not many African women in Virginia—fewer than a hundred—it affects only a small number and brings in very little tax money for the government. But the law creates a distinction between Negro and English women since it does not obligate white females to pay.

Although Sheppard tries to mitigate the impact of the law on Margaret, promising to pay the tithe himself, the unfairness of it rankles. At church, it becomes clear that the other African women and their husbands are just as upset, especially Mary and Anthony Johnson, who have two daughters as well. Even Katherine and Michael join the group of discontented. They congregate around John, asking what they can do, but he has no immediate answers other than to reiterate that gaining their freedom is of utmost importance. Once they achieve that, they can consider where and how they wish to live, even it means leaving Virginia for other, more welcoming territory. At some point, a long look passes between him and Margaret across the church grounds, and she nods to him, acknowledging that he has been right all along.

Swett shares her anger, and the law's enactment does not cloud their relationship. They continue to enjoy each other's company and eagerly anticipate the birth of their next child.

"I really do hope it is a girl," Robert says repeatedly, endearing him further to Margaret.

The time comes in early January, just before the annual hog killing. When Margaret goes into labor while preparing dinner at the main house, Elizabeth helps her into one of the empty bedrooms. She and Eunice remain by her side while Lucy takes care of the other children.

The baby comes surprisingly quickly. Robert arrives at the house out of breath, having hurried from an outer part of the plantation, just in time to hear the first cries of his daughter. When he is allowed into the room, Margaret is wide awake and flushed with pride, the baby at her breast. Overjoyed, he rushes to them and looks at them with such love and affection that Margaret almost bursts into tears.

They decide to name the newborn Jane, and two weeks later, the christening takes place at Lawne's Creek Church, with Lieutenant Sheppard doing the honors.

* * *

Spring comes late in 1644, and one afternoon toward the end of March, Margaret looks with satisfaction at the neat rows of furrows in her garden. Some have small green shoots of spring flowers and herbs peeking through the mulching leaves. Others are still bare ruts of dark-brown earth. It won't be long before she will have a riot of colors on her hands—yellow and white crocus, forget-me-not, blue knight's spur, white bloodroot, white and lilac hellebore, phlox, bluebells, and trillium.

She watches Robert Jr. poke the ground with a stick as William toddles toward her holding a leaf in the air to show her. Jane is sleeping in her wooden crib on the porch.

Swett arrives from his day's labors. He has been hard at work with a group of young men, moving and mending the snake fences along the southern border of the plantation. The new field of tobacco, ready for planting, needs protection. He looks tired but happy to see her. Bowing low, he says, "'Tis good to see, my lady"—his formal, humorous greeting for her when they are alone.

"Supper's ready," Margaret says. "I hope you're hungry. I've cooked smoked pork ribs."

After the children are asleep, they bring blankets and two chairs out on the porch to watch the stars and listen to the mating calls of frogs coming from the pond. They put on quite a performance, sounding like a large flock of nattering ducks.

At some point, Margaret hears Jane fussing and goes inside to feed her. Robert follows her and puts his arms around them from behind, watching over Margaret's shoulder as his daughter sucks eagerly at her breast.

When Jane is satisfied, Margaret burps her and puts her back in her crib. After she drifts off to sleep, Robert and Margaret go to bed and make love.

* * *

The next morning after breakfast, Margaret is alone in the kitchen at the main house preparing a venison stew for dinner. The men, including Robert and Lieutenant Sheppard, have all gone to work at different places on the plantation. Margaret checks the winter storage. Carrot and corn supplies are getting low. Soon it will be time to collect mushrooms and dig up tubers in the forest to supplement their meals, until cabbage and other early crops ripen.

Suddenly there are gunshots in the distance followed by the clanging of a bell from the field-workers' quarters. It isn't the triple ringing that announces mealtimes, but a desperate alarm. It startles Margaret as memories crash in on her of the moments before the Imbangala assaulted her village in Pongo and the Indian uprising more than twenty years ago.

She pulls Jane from the crib by the hearth, ignoring her startled protests, and rushes into the house. In the living room, Elizabeth, Lucy, and Eunice have gathered the other children, unsure of what to do.

Suddenly, the front door flies open, banging against the wall, and Jason rushes in. Breathing hard, he holds on to the jamb and stammers, "Indian . . . attack! The lieutenant is rallying everyone in defense . . . needs weapons!"

Elizabeth rushes to action. "Come with me."

She dashes into the bedroom that has been used for storage since Agnes left. Margaret starts to herd the children to another bedroom when she sees Eunice cowering in the corner, rocking back and forth in terror.

Margaret hurries to her, pulls away the hands covering her ears, and yells close to her face, "Take Priscilla and Susannah into the bedroom and help Lucy barricade the window! Now!"

Eunice shivers, her face ghostly white. As more men arrive, she recovers enough to follow Margaret's command.

By then, Elizabeth, Jeremiah, and Jason return carrying an armful of muskets and bags of bullets and gunpowder. They start to load the weapons as quickly as they can. While Lucy and Eunice usher and carry the children into the most protected bedroom, Margaret races to the kitchen, douses the fire, and gathers all the carving and cutting knives. She doesn't want to leave any potential weapons for the attackers, should they succeed and enter the house. She wishes she had Robert's hammer with the iron head to defend herself.

That thought throws her into a momentary panic. Robert has been working at the outer edge of the plantation. If the Indians struck there first, he and his crew would have borne the brunt of the onslaught. And what about Mihill? John? If this is not an isolated attack, but a coordinated offensive like the one in 1622, will they be safe?

She shakes her head violently to clear her thoughts. Now is not the time for any of that.

When she returns to the living room, Jason and some of the men have left already with the muskets and Sheppard's sword. Those remaining have taken up their guard posts outside. They will come into the house only as a last resort. Margaret is glad that they are there. Even though Indians in their part of the colony have been quiet for some years, the lieutenant has been vigilant preparing for just such an attack, and she can trust everyone to do their part.

Elizabeth comes from the bedroom where she has checked on Lucy, Eunice, and the children. "They're all right for now," she says calmly, although her frown and hard-set eyes indicate how tense she is.

Jeremiah helps them gather sheets of bed linens to tear into strips and hangs a large pot filled with water over the burning logs in the living room fireplace to get ready to dress wounds. From time to time, they hear high-pitched yells in the distance. Margaret recognizes them as Indian battle cries, intended to intimidate the enemy. But every outburst is followed by the popping sound of musket shots. Soon the yells become less determined, and finally silence descends on the plantation.

In the hushed stillness, Thomas comes inside. "It sounds like we have beaten them off, but we'll remain on our guard here," he says. "I'm sending Virgil to see what's happening."

Everyone at the house waits anxiously until the young man returns. He looks grim as he reports to Elizabeth, "The Indians are gone for now. We managed to kill a bunch of them, but we've got some dead and injured, too. Lieutenant Sheppard is checking on missing people. He also sent several men to Ewens's plantation and your father's farm to check on people there."

Elizabeth says, "Thank you. Now, bring the wounded here. We will take care of them."

Margaret wants to ask about Robert, but there isn't time. She checks on the children. They are wide-eyed and terrified, knowing that something is wrong, but not comprehending what. Margaret hugs Robert Jr., William, Priscilla, and Susannah to give them reassurance. Jane, to Margaret's amazement, seems to have slept through everything.

Leaving them in Lucy's capable hands, Margaret heads to the kitchen to gather herbs and prepare ointments. By the time she returns to the living room, the first of the wounded men have arrived. They have suffered cuts and gashes from the Indian's tomahawks. Two have broken-off arrows lodged in their chests. Most of the injuries are more painful than life-threatening. The muskets made all the difference, preventing the Indians from engaging in close hand-to-hand combat.

Still, a number of the men are in agony and groan and cry out as Margaret and Elizabeth clean the wounds and, with the help of Thomas, Jeremiah, and Eunice, bandage them. When they cut out arrowheads from the wounded, even with leather straps to bite down on, two men scream at the top of their voices, upsetting everyone in the house. Several of the victims need slings to support their limp arms. One who was slashed just above the knee isn't likely to walk without a crutch for some time.

Animated conversation on the porch from the men waiting to be treated spills into the living room. Sharing what happened to each of them—where they were when the attack first came and how they received their wounds—makes it easier to deal with the inevitable letdown after battle.

All of a sudden, everyone hushes. Margaret hears the sound of boots tramping up the porch steps and looks up just as Lieutenant Sheppard enters the living room. His clothes are dirty and blood-spattered, and his face is distorted in an angry grimace.

When Elizabeth cries out, he holds up his hand and says, "I am all right." His eyes lock on Margaret's. "It's Robert and the others."

Margaret bites her lips. "Is he . . . ?"

Sheppard shakes his head. "He's alive, but he's in a bad way. The others are all slain. The Indians left him for dead. I'm sorry, Margaret."

When she starts up, ready to bolt outside, he holds her back. "They're bringing him here. Get ready to take care of him. He has lost a lot of blood. We'll do everything we can."

Margaret straightens her blood-covered apron to let him know she has herself under control. "Make sure the children don't see him," she calls to Eunice. Then she walks out onto the front porch.

Six men led by Jason are carrying Robert on a makeshift stretcher across the clearing up to the house, straining under the weight. As they set it down, the two who have been pressing bandages against Robert's chest and head remain by his side. Margaret grits her teeth and goes over to look at him. Seeing him lying lifeless on the wooden boards, his face the color of ash, she does not gasp or cry out, but her heart feels as if clamped in a vise.

"Bring him inside," she says bravely and leads the men to the far-off bedroom where Dorothy used to sleep.

When they have laid him on the bed, Margaret and Elizabeth go to work. Sheppard watches as they strip off the crimson shirt. There is a deep gash in his side where a tomahawk struck him. Blood seeps from the wound. When Margaret examines it, she can tell two of his ribs are broken. The other injury came from a blow that glanced off his temple and severed his ear.

"That kind of wound gushes a lot of blood and is probably the reason they left him for dead," says Sheppard.

After Margaret rubs herbal ointment into the gash in Robert's side and applies a poultice, the lieutenant and Elizabeth help her sit him up. They bandage his ear and wrap linen strips around his chest.

Suddenly, Swett's eyes open and he calls out, "Margaret, Margaret, where are you?"

"I'm here, Robert, right here," she says, continuing to wrap linen strips around him. "You hush now. We'll get you well."

Her voice seems to soothe him and he relaxes. As they lower him into the pillow, he passes out.

* * *

For two days and three nights, Swett battles death. Margaret leaves his side only to brew him tea and to feed Jane. Sometimes she keeps

418

the baby with her so that Robert can see her when he regains his senses. Most of the time, he is delirious, racked with fever. But there are moments when he is conscious and lucid, and when he recognizes Margaret and the children, he smiles weakly.

When he whispers to Margaret that he loves her, she kisses his pale lips, then shushes him. "Save your strength. We will have all the time in the world to speak when you are well again."

Even when Robert is asleep, she keeps holding his hand and talks to him, telling him how much she loves him, how much the children need him, how everything will be all right. She changes his dressings, alarmed that the big gash in the side of his chest is beginning to fester, yet clinging to the hope that the herbal remedies and ointments will overcome the infection.

Although Robert never stops fighting, it becomes apparent to others that he is dying. His shining sapphire eyes have turned a dull blue. Sometimes, when Margaret begs him, "Robert, don't leave me. Please don't go," a wisp of regret crosses his face before he heeds her and rallies with what determination he has left.

In the end, his body gives out. After lying restlessly in the bed, he rears up. His entire figure tenses in a prolonged shudder. Then he falls back, motionless in the sweat-stained sheets.

Margaret stares at him in shocked disbelief. Suddenly, she cries out, "*No, no, no, no, noooh!*" She clutches at his chest in a frenzy, trying to lift him up and shake life into him. The howls that issue from her are so primitive and unhuman that they send shivers down the spine of the people in the room with her. It frightens the children next door, too, and they start to weep. Even Jane awakens and cries inconsolably until Margaret collapses in a faint over Robert's prostrate body.

45
SWETT'S LEGACY
Virginia—Summer 1644

In the days following Robert Swett's death, Margaret walks around in a daze. She barely manages to feed Jane and refuses all nourishment herself. Having lost any interest in her surroundings, she walks away from people talking to her in mid-sentence and responds to their questions in a dull monotone. The only time she emerges from her stupor is to answer the question of where to bury Swett. While he was still clinging to life, his five companions who were slaughtered by the Indians were laid to rest in the cemetery by the copse behind the main house. But when Sheppard suggests doing the same with him, Margaret balks.

"I want Robert buried on the plot of land that belongs to me," she says. "I want to be near him!" The fierceness of her response brooks no argument.

So, on a warm April morning, everyone on the plantation gathers by the pond near Margaret's cottage to witness Robert Swett's funeral. Margaret stands at the open gravesite with Robert Jr. and William by her side, holding on to their small hands. Lucy is next to her carrying Jane in her arms. A surprising number of the men speak up, saying what a good, upstanding man Swett was, eager to lend a helping hand at all times. Lucy mentions how he always had a kind word for her. Margaret keeps quiet.

Then they sing a simple hymn, and Lieutenant Sheppard reads from the Book of Common Prayer:

> I am the resurrection and the life, saith the Lord: he that believeth in me, though he were dead, yet shall he live: and whosoever liveth and believeth in me, shall never die.

The sentiment gives Margaret little comfort, but the other section Sheppard reads speaks to her:

> We brought nothing into this world, and it is certain we can carry nothing out. The Lord gave, and the Lord hath taken away; blessed be the name of the Lord.

At the end of the ceremony, Sheppard, Jason, and Thomas fire muskets into the air saluting their fallen comrade.

Then Margaret takes a handful of black earth from the mound next to the grave and tosses it into the open hole. It makes a hollow thud on the simple pine coffin. One by one, the other attendees do the same and express their condolences to her. She receives them, erect and unmoving like a tree trunk, her face a stoic mask.

Afterward, Sheppard suggests that Margaret come with them and use one of the empty bedrooms in the main house to recover, but she declines. Elizabeth insists that Lucy stay with Margaret and take care of the children until she regains her strength. Jason quietly assigns two men to remain nearby as guards.

When Margaret finally closes her eyes, she sleeps for the rest of the day and night. Waking, she feels no better, but she returns to the main house and starts to do her chores again. Staying active helps her cope. She ignores the bustle around her, everyone remaining on special alert, and pays little attention to news from other plantations trickling in—who was killed and who survived. She perks up a little when she hears that John is fine. Sheppard confirming that Mihill is safe, after one of his meetings with the colony's militia leaders, brings a rare flicker of gladness to her face, but it passes quickly.

Sheppard is away more often, participating in emergency sessions with Governor Berkeley and his advisers to assess the damage and devastation the Indians caused and make plans for defending the survivors.

It turns out that the massacre was a coordinated attack involving all of the Powhatans and their allies. Led by Opechancanough, the ninety-year-old chief and head of the tribal confederacy, who also planned the 1622 uprising, the Indians did not threaten James City and other fortified villages. Instead, they concentrated on the outlying farms and plantations, doing their best to ravage the south side of the James River, the western reaches of the colony, and the peninsula between the York and Rappahannock Rivers. The carnage is horrific. The Indians slaughtered more than five hundred settlers, including women and children—more than during the 1622 uprising—and burned homes and fledgling crops. As the extent of the bloodshed becomes clear, the government leaders can take heart only in the realization that the overall impact is not as devastating as during the earlier catastrophe. Then, more than a third of the people in the colony were killed, threatening its very survival. This time, because Virginia's population is so much larger, there are plenty of people to carry forward.

What surprises everyone is that there are no follow-up attacks. All the scouts come back reporting that the Indians seem to have vanished from the immediate vicinity of the plantations. Consulting leaders from peaceful tribes provides some insight into what happened. Apparently, Opechancanough had become increasingly frustrated by settlers invading his people's hunting grounds and converting ever more forestland to fields for tobacco cultivation. Feeling he had no recourse and knowing he is near the end of his life, he decided to show the colonists what their relentless expansion would cost them. Having made his bloody statement, he has withdrawn his forces, waiting to see how they will react.

The settlers appreciate the respite but refuse to be lulled into a false sense of safety and shore up defenses everywhere. At the same time, they call for retaliation and revenge. The problem is that the militia lacks the weapons and manpower to conduct an extensive military campaign and settle accounts with the Indian tribes once and for all.

In the midst of heated discussions about how best to proceed, Governor Berkeley announces that he will travel to England to purchase armaments—pistols, muskets, and cannons—and recruit men with soldiering experience to wage a decisive war against the "heathens." The decision makes sense: Berkeley has the contacts at King Charles's court and the prestige of his aristocratic family to raise the necessary support. He receives a hopeful send-off, but many of the burgesses believe he is abandoning the colony, using the opportunity to get away to the relative safety of England.

Not that he is returning to a peaceful, prosperous nation. The civil war has been raging in England for the past two years, spilling into Scotland and Ireland as well, with more than twenty battles fought between the parliamentary and royalist armies. Overall, King Charles's forces seem to have had the upper hand, but there are signs that the tide is turning. London, like James City, has been spared the ravages of war, but uncertainty reigns about who will ultimately win.

In the meantime, Sheppard and the militia continue to build up fortifications and buttress existing defenses. They also make forays into Indian territory, following the same tactics as during the aftermath of the 1622 massacre—attacking Indian villages, looting and burning food supplies, and destroying fields of corn and vegetable crops, hoping to starve the Natives during the next winter. But these incursions are haphazard, and efforts to locate the leaders of the uprising—Opechancanough in particular—meet with failure.

When Sheppard is away, he leaves Jason in charge to oversee both the protective measures and ongoing agricultural work. Armed patrols make regular rounds at the perimeter of the plantation, and some workers carry weapons to protect the laboring field hands. On Sundays, when most people are away at church, a small armed contingent stays behind.

For the sake of her safety, Sheppard insists that Margaret and her children live at the main house again, and she willingly accepts his offer of shelter. But she continues to keep to herself, as if living in a world apart, and refuses to join the Sunday services at Lawne's Creek Church. Instead, she heads to her cottage and spends time tending to Robert's grave.

When Lieutenant Sheppard finds out about it, he confronts her angrily. "You must stop endangering yourself. I order you to stay away from there for the sake of public safety!"

Margaret calmly replies, "I am doing no one harm."

Seeing her pain-etched face, he continues less vehemently, "Please understand, Margaret. I am responsible for everyone on the plantation and can't let you put yourself in danger."

"You'll have to lock me up then," Margaret says.

There is no challenge in her voice, and Sheppard realizes he can't persuade her. When Margaret visits her cottage again the following Sunday, he sends Elizabeth to reason with her, but the result is the same. Accepting the inevitable, he asks Jason to post two of the workers nearby, armed with muskets, to quietly watch out for her from a distance. Margaret accepts the compromise without complaint.

Sometimes, she takes Robert Jr. and William along, but mostly she goes by herself, carrying Jane in a sling at her hip. After checking on the cottage, she brings a wooden stool to the gravesite, puts Jane next to her on a blanket, and sits there communing with Robert.

That is the place where John finds her one afternoon in June.

As Thomas Goodman's second-in-command, he has been responsible for organizing the defensive measures for Ewens's plantation. He has spent considerable time meeting with Sheppard to develop a plan. Now, in the summer, with corn and tobacco requiring daily care and the Indians likely occupied doing the same, he can take some time for himself without feeling that he is shirking his responsibilities.

"Hello, Margaret," he says softly as he comes up by her side, hoping not to startle her.

"Hello, John," she says, as if she expected him. "Has Sheppard asked you to persuade me to come to my senses?"

John chuckles without mirth. "No. I'm here of my own accord. I would have come sooner, but I have been busy making sure everyone at Ewens's plantation is safe. We lost only ten men and a young woman. After the initial attack, the Indians must have figured there were too many of us and went elsewhere first. I am very sorry about what happened to you."

Margaret looks at him for the first time. He seems well, although his face shows signs of chronic exhaustion. There is sweat on his forehead. He must have walked briskly through the humid forest. She notices his pistol in his belt.

In response to her questioning glance, he smiles and says, "No one has said anything about it. Of course, I don't parade down the street with it when I visit James City."

Margaret does not return his smile and makes no effort to continue with the conversation. John goes over Swett's grave and stands there in silence, paying his respects. Finally, he turns to her. "Robert was a good man," he says softly. "He did right by you. It's not fair what happened to him." When Margaret doesn't respond, he continues, "Katherine, Michael, and Mathew send their love and condolences, as do Anthony and Mary. We all miss you at church."

Margaret shifts her weight. "I don't wish to pray to a god that has abandoned us," she says as if speaking to herself. "I would rather spend my time here with Robert. It comforts me."

Her voice sounds mild, yet assured. But when John looks at her careworn face, her dull brown eyes and lips locked tight, he feels the depth of her grief. He has never seen her in such despair. To spare her embarrassment, John bends over the sleeping child, lying on the blanket. She is well swaddled, so all he can see of Jane is her closed eyes, purplish lips, and curly black hair. She has Margaret's nose.

"Why are you here, John?" Margaret asks, catching him by surprise. "It's not that I don't appreciate you coming here, but please don't dither with me. Say what you have to say."

He feels a pinprick of irritation. Others have suffered, too. He has seen it on his plantation and has heard many horror tales of what happened elsewhere. Regardless of how devastated Margaret may feel, she is not the only one who has lost a loved one.

But he lets it go and says, "I saw Emmanuel Driggers in James City. He and Frances were at Point Comfort and remained unharmed since the Indians steered clear of the town. Frances has had her baby without mishap—a boy. They named him Thomas."

For the first time, he detects a spark of interest on Margaret's part and decides to press his advantage. "I've also heard from Lieutenant Sheppard that Mihill is all right. Captain Stafford was quite impressed at the courage our son showed at his young age. That's what I came to tell you."

Margaret looks up at him, her weary eyes apologetic and pleading. "I'm sorry, John. I'm not myself, haven't been for some time. Please forgive me."

"I understand. But our children need us, Margaret. Now more than ever."

"I know that, John. But this is all I can do right now."

John considers her response. On impulse, he sits down by her side. He takes her hand and holds it in his, gently, like a wounded bird. She does not resist. They sit in silence for some time, watching the breeze rustle the leaves of the birch trees by the pond, letting the warm sunrays play over their faces.

As the sun sinks close to the crowns of the trees on the far side of the pond, he disengages and gets up. "Time to go," he says, brushing himself off.

"Thank you for coming, John," Margaret says.

"I'll be back," he replies.

He leaves, reluctantly, not sure he managed to reach her. Margaret does not look after him. A tremendous sense of weariness overcomes her.

On his way to the forest, John acknowledges the young man standing as sentry by the oak trees marking the edge of the woods. As he walks under the darkening canopy, he feels wistful. After all that has happened to her, Margaret is still the most beautiful woman he has ever laid eyes on, and his heart aches for her in more ways than one.

Margaret hears the baby stirring next to her. As she picks her up to feed her, Jane opens her eyes and smiles at her in recognition. Margaret feels a moment of joy, but it is not enough to pull her out of her deep melancholy.

Then, a week later, something happens that does. After recurring bouts of sickness in the morning, Margaret realizes she is pregnant. It is the last thing she expected to happen since she has been nursing Jane since she was born. She feels a rush of euphoria, knowing that a physical part of Robert is still alive inside her.

Over the next days, her spirits lift. At times, she feels almost giddy with delight. In her exhilaration, she senses deep in her heart that this development has to do with her destiny. She comprehends that she must relish it, honor it, and approach it with joy and her hard-earned wisdom. She has a greater responsibility now more than ever. She remembers her conversations with John about freedom and decides that she must find a way to talk to Emmanuel and Frances.

46
EMMANUEL
Virginia—Summer–Late Fall 1644

At Sheppard's house, everyone notices the change in Margaret, although they don't understand how it happened. She not only regains her composure but she also engages others again, smiling, laughing at their jokes, and expressing interest in the latest news from James City and other parts of the colony. Above all, she spends as much time as she can with her children, Robert Jr. and William, to make up for their father having disappeared from their lives. They respond well to the attention and become more outgoing as well.

The first Sunday back at Lawne's Creek Church, many attendees from the other plantations seek her out. Margaret deflects with equanimity their awkward attempts to offer condolences for her loss, asking about what has happened to them in the meantime and allowing them to change the subject gracefully.

That doesn't, however, prevent the group of Africans from welcoming her like a long-lost traveler. Katherine, Michael, Anthony, and Mary all embrace her and congratulate her on her pregnancy.

"It is good to see you smile, Margaret," Anthony says.

Margaret feels comforted in their circle. With Robert gone, she spends her most of her time at church with them. John makes it easy for her, acting like there is nothing unresolved between them. She appreciates it, knowing that doing so is more difficult for him than he lets on.

One morning after the service, though, she takes him aside and asks, "I would like to speak with Emmanuel Driggers. Will you let me know when he comes to town? If Frances is with him, so much the better."

John gives her an evaluating look. He would like to know why but decides not to press her. "I will," he says.

As her belly grows, Margaret keeps waiting, hiding her impatience. After several months, she almost gives up hope that she will see Emmanuel before the year is out and her and Robert's child is born.

* * *

Late that fall, Governor Berkeley returns from England. Surprising the many settlers in the colony, who thought they never would see him again, he arrives at Point Comfort in a frigate at the head of a small fleet. By the time the ships reach James City, a large, lively crowd has gathered at the docks to welcome him, and the governor steps off his boat like a conqueror, bathing in the adulation of his constituents. Berkeley's return impresses even his enemies and swells the ranks of his supporters throughout Virginia.

They soon have more to cheer about. Berkeley not only purchased a considerable arsenal of weapons but recruited a sizeable contingent of military men, persuading them to make their fame and fortune in the colony. The newcomers include several sons of England's landed gentry that supports King Charles in his war against the parliamentarians. They call themselves "Cavaliers" and worry that they will end up on the losing side, and in that case, forfeiting their rights and privileges, at best. More likely they will end up with their heads on the executioner's block. Berkeley has promised them safety and a better future, painting Virginia as a paradise of natural riches, wonders, and opportunities for men with vision, ability, and money. Their arrival marks the beginning of an exodus that swells, and soon more young, wealthy adventurers follow.

Unlike the Puritan founders of the New England colonies, the Cavaliers are not looking to escape religious persecution but seek asylum from social and political disfavor. They want a place where they can assert what they believe to be their natural superiority over everyone else not born to privilege. With considerable money at their disposal, they amass land and create successful plantations in no time. Unlike the thousands of menials, workers, and trades- men and -women servants who also immigrate to the colony, the Cavaliers quickly join Virginia's elite. Berkeley's decision to share decision-making with the General Assembly aids their cause by mov- ing power away from James City and spreading political influence throughout the colony. As a result, the Cavaliers become part of a dominant class that determines the course of economic, political, and legal development. In time, the latter includes the gradual yet relentless march toward slavery that will affect the descendants of Margaret and John and other Africans in Virginia and the surround- ing colonies for centuries to come.

For now, the arrival of men with considerable military skills and experience swells the ranks of the local militia and allows Berkeley and the Governor's Council to forge plans for launching an assault on several fronts against the Indians responsible for the uprising. Soon after his return, Berkeley calls for a large meeting to map out a spring offensive. Central to the mission will be the capture of Chief Opechancanough. Like many of his advisers, Berkeley believes that cutting off the head of the snake decisively would guarantee Virginia's safety for the future.

The weeklong planning session takes Lieutenant Sheppard to James City, along with military leaders from all over Virginia. As harbormaster of Point Comfort, Francis Pott participates and brings Emmanuel Driggers with him to James City.

John has spent substantial time in discussions with Sheppard about military matters, impressing him with his grasps of offensive and defensive. When the lieutenant mentions all the people expected to attend the assembly, John realizes that he will have the opportunity to get together with his best friend. He gets excited because he has a great deal on his mind, and Emmanuel is the only one with whom he can share it.

* * *

Since the weather is quite brisk, Emmanuel and John forgo their usual walk along the river and meet in Francis Pott's house instead. It feels much more substantial than what John is used to at Ewens's plantation. Even the big house containing the library seems cobbled together by comparison. He admires it and experiences a moment of envy, knowing that he will never have a place like this.

They sit together in the living room in front of the blazing fire. It takes little time to feel comfortable in each other's presence again, and they make small talk catching up with each other's lives. John had hoped that Frances might make the journey, but with baby Thomas barely four months old, it made more sense for her to stay home.

"She sends her warmest greetings to you and to Margaret," Emmanuel says.

"Margaret will be so pleased," John says. He hesitates before bringing up the big news. "She is pregnant with Swett's child."

At first, Emmanuel is astonished, then he starts to smile. "Frances will be delighted," he says. "But it will be hard on Margaret, a single woman with four children, two of them infants."

"For the time being, it has given her something to live for, which is a good thing," John says. "She wants to speak with you and Frances."

"What about?" Emmanuel asks, intrigued.

John shrugs. Margaret didn't tell him the reason.

"Why don't we go to see her tomorrow afternoon?" Emmanuel proposes. "I'm sure Francis Pott won't mind. He'll be consumed with the governor and council meetings, and I can do the purchasing of supplies we need in the morning." When John seems reluctant, he says, "You don't have to go if you don't want to."

John gets up and moves to the fireplace, watching the blue flames lick at one of the logs. "It's not that," he finally says. "My indenture will be finished next fall. I don't want to stay at Ewens's plantation and raise hogs forever, but I'm not sure what to do." He turns back and holds up his hands as if to ward off any unwelcome suggestions. "And, before you say it, I'm not interested in buying land and becoming a tobacco planter or farmer raising livestock."

The combination of tension and urgency tells Emmanuel that there are complex emotions and thoughts at war in his friend. "It is a big step to take, and I am glad you are thinking about it well ahead of time," he says carefully. "Let me ask Francis Pott when he is not so preoccupied. He may have some suggestions. With the colony continuing to expand, there is need of men with your skills, John. Most of the people who'll come can't read or write, and they don't have your abilities to organize and manage things."

John looks as if a heavy weight has lifted from his shoulders. He has been carrying this burden with him for some time and beginning to articulate what is on his mind with someone who cares for him helps.

"You are right," he says. "Perhaps when the time is right, I will confer with Lieutenant Sheppard as well."

"An excellent idea—this is something that people in positions of authority know more about than you and me." Emmanuel hesitates, not sure if to go ahead, then decides to test the water. "Are there any other concerns on your mind?"

"What do you mean?"

Emmanuel scratches his head. He knows he must tread gingerly. "I would certainly understand that you might want to put some distance between yourself and Margaret," he ventures.

An involuntary shudder wracks his body. Emmanuel has voiced something he has not yet fully admitted to himself.

"I will always love her," he says in a voice laced with sadness.

* * *

After the midday meal at Sheppard's house, Margaret keeps looking out the window toward the dock on the creek. John has notified her of Emmanuel's desire to visit her so that he would not arrive unexpectedly. With Lieutenant Sheppard gone, Jason has joined Elizabeth, Lucy, and Eunice so that they don't feel unprotected in the presence of a stranger.

When Margaret finally sees the rowboat bringing Emmanuel, she dashes out onto the porch and down the meadow toward the dock. By the time Emmanuel has set foot ashore, bundled in an overcoat, she rushes into his arms, nearly knocking him over.

"It has been much too long," he says, whispering into her ear. "Frances so wanted to come, but she has to take care of Thomas. She knew you'd understand."

Nodding, Margaret buries her head farther against his chest. When they part, they take a good look at one another. Seeing how Margaret has matured, without losing any of her attractiveness, he understands why John continues to have conflicting feelings. Her dark eyes are lively and curious, taking him in all at once. Her skin has no blemish. She is not only beautiful but radiates a quiet sensuality.

For her part, Margaret sees a mature, muscular man with a kind expression and deeper crow's feet and furrows in his forehead than she remembers from before. As always, he carries himself with a natural dignity. Only the glint in his eyes signals his mischievous sense of humor.

Hooking her arm into his and leading him up to the house, she says, "Come and meet Elizabeth Sheppard and the others."

Inside, the women are waiting in a line, curious about Margaret's visitor. Jason seems amused by their eagerness.

Emmanuel greets their stares with no signs of awkwardness. He bows smartly to Elizabeth and says, "Thank you for inviting me into your house."

Taken by his courteousness, Elizabeth curtseys and says, "Any friend of Margaret's is always welcome here."

"When are you expecting?" he asks.

Surprised, she blushes and inadvertently smoothes the fabric of her dress over her flat belly. "In the spring of next year. How did you know?" She turns to Margaret. "Did you tell him?"

As Margaret shakes her head, Driggers smiles and says, "My wife, Frances, had a flush just like you early on when she was pregnant with our son, Thomas."

Elizabeth blushes all over again, obviously pleased.

Following introductions all around and an offer of cider, which Emmanuel declines, Lucy and Eunice bring out the children. The oldest, Priscilla and Susannah, wearing simple dresses with lace collars, gaze at Emmanuel with big eyes, as do Robert Jr. and William, wearing children's gowns. Lucy shows off Jane, and Emmanuel looks at the small face, light brown in color. He tickles her under the chin, eliciting a pleased gurgle from her.

Seeing that things are going well, Jason excuses himself. Margaret takes the opportunity to allow Emmanuel to escape also. Putting on a woolen coat, she says, "I want to show you my place." She nods to Elizabeth and Lucy. "We will be back anon. Thank you for taking care of Robert, William, and Jane."

Soon, Margaret leads Emmanuel through the forest. The sky is light gray overhead. Many of the trees are bare already, and as they walk along, the fallen, wrinkled leaves crackle under their feet. When she asks about Frances and their baby, Emmanuel's eyes glisten.

"What can I say? Of course, I'm pleased, and Frances is jubilant." Then he smiles impishly. "But at this early age, children are not really all that interesting, are they?"

"Spoken like a man," Margaret teases him.

When they reach the edge of the clearing to her home, Margaret stops and points, "There." As Emmanuel looks from the cottage to the pond, she says, "I have decided to call it 'Swett's Swamp' in Robert's memory."

They walk down to the pond and stop at Swett's grave. As they look at the meager mound of earth, tamped solid by rain and summer heat, Margaret starts to tear up. Emmanuel puts his arm around her shoulders and pulls her close to him.

After a few moments, she takes him to the cottage. When she opens the door and they step inside, it is no warmer than outside, but the light from the windows illuminates the interior, allowing Emmanuel to admire the craftsmanship.

"It is well built, a good house to raise a family," he says regretfully.

As they step onto the porch again, Margaret says, "I wish we had a fire going. This is not the warmest place to have a conversation, but I wanted us to be away from the others. I know you and John have been talking for some time how important it is for us to make sure our children will attain their freedom, and I agree."

Emmanuel remains silent, listening carefully.

"Robert indentured our first two children to Lieutenant Sheppard. He negotiated reasonable terms by agreeing to add time to his own contract," she continues. "Since we were married, the lieutenant was assured that I would stay for the duration. But now that Robert is gone, the situation has changed. Since I am a free woman, the child I am carrying will be born free."

"But Jane is another matter," Emmanuel says softly.

Margaret nods. Shivering, she draws the coat tighter around her. "I have considered indenturing Jane to Sheppard, but taking care of her and this baby, as well as my two older children, and working for him is more than I can handle. I would not have enough time for it all."

To keep herself from trembling uncontrollably she grips the wooden railing tightly. "I want her to have a real family, Emmanuel." She takes a deep breath to regain control and says, "I would like you and Frances to adopt Jane and indenture her, just as John did with Mihill. It would ensure her freedom at some point." Her voice is close to breaking. "I'd be certain that she would be with two people who'd love her as much as I do. Would you be willing to do that?"

Her question is such a heartfelt plea it touches Emmanuel deeply. To give himself time to recover, he looks searchingly at her and says, "I see you have given this a lot of thought."

Margaret stares ahead and nods seriously.

He looks at the sky, which has cleared and is now permeated with wisps of gold-colored clouds. "Your reasoning is sound, Margaret," he says slowly. "Let me talk about it with Frances. You understand I can't make such a momentous decision without her. You should keep considering it, too. Giving up your only daughter won't be easy."

Tears well up in her eyes and she wipes them away without embarrassment. "Of course. You're right," she says. "But I have made up my mind."

Emmanuel glances at her in admiration. "You know, you'll have to work something out with Sheppard. Jane was born when Robert was still alive, so she belongs to him."

Margaret's lips tighten with determination. Then she says, "She is my daughter now. I will do whatever I must."

47

JANE

Virginia—Spring 1645

In late March of the following year, Margaret heads down the creek in a skiff. It is a warm day, and she is wearing only a woolen shawl over her simple gray dress. Feeling both happy and heavyhearted, she is traveling with her daughter to James City. Emmanuel and Frances Driggers have agreed to adopt Jane, and Francis Pott will indenture her. Margaret will make the transfer at his house. Sitting next to Jane, she hugs her close to steady her against the rocking motion of the boat. At her request, John has come along to make sure the documents are in order. He sits on the wooden bench behind them with a stone-faced expression.

Margaret adjusts the sling around her waist to shift her new baby to a more comfortable position. Just two months old, Anthony has been a healthy, energetic child from the get-go. When Elizabeth gave him two slaps on his bottom after he was born to get him breathing, he displayed surprising lung power, crying out so forcefully that Lucy covered her ears. Margaret decided to name him after one of Robert Swett's uncles, as well as her longtime friend on John Upton's plantation, whose optimism and resolve she has always admired. When Anthony Johnson found out, he and his wife, Mary, agreed to be the baby's godparents and stood proudly at his side during the christening. Once again, the Anglican minister in James City refused to make the trip across the river—he didn't say whether it was because he didn't consider an African child worth his while or because he still thought of Margaret as an unchristian heathen—so William Spencer presided over the baptism.

As Margaret, Jane, and little Anthony reach the mouth of the creek, signs of spring are everywhere. Trees and bushes on both banks display young leaves and shoots in a tapestry of light greens. Migratory birds—pipits, warblers, kinglets, and thrushes—have made their appearance, some nesting, others resting on branches and feeding before continuing on their journey north. Jane, delighted, points a tiny finger at a swarm of birds flying across the water, dipping toward the waves before rising as one into the blue sky.

Observing her daughter smiling and unafraid—it is Jane's first time away from the plantation—Margaret feels a little better about what will transpire and manages to look forward to spending time with Frances, Emmanuel, and their new baby.

When Margaret first approached Sheppard and Elizabeth about having Jane adopted, the lieutenant was taken aback that she would give up her daughter to strangers rather than raise her on the plantation in familiar surroundings. After Margaret explained her reasons and reminded him that it was no different than what John had done with Mihill, he gave her a calculating glance. Figuring that Margaret wanted to limit her time serving in his household, he named an impossibly large amount of money to let Jane go and raised the possibility of Margaret re-indenturing herself again as an alternative. Only when Elizabeth, who had been quite taken with Emmanuel, gave her husband a quiet scolding in their bedroom did he change his mind. She explained how much Margaret was still hurting after losing Swett, how hard it was to let go of a daughter, and that she would stay on the plantation anyway to be with her other children. Sheppard relented and accepted Margaret's assurances that she would remain in his household until her younger indentured son was twelve years old and gave his consent for Jane to be adopted.

Ever since, Margaret has been losing sleep, wondering if she has made the right decision for her daughter.

When they get to Francis Pott's house, Frances greets her with open arms. For a moment it feels as if they have never been apart, and the shadow of impending leave-taking lifts from their joyous reunion. They hug and fuss over each other's children. Thomas is only a few months older than Anthony and looks like a little Emmanuel. Margaret is happy that Jane and Frances take to each other right away, as she had hoped. Before long, the women sit on the sofa together and catch up.

Meanwhile, Emmanuel and John go to a cherrywood desk in the corner of the room. They look over the adoption contracts—two identical documents—and quietly discuss the matter John raised during their previous talk.

"I mentioned your legal interests and skills to Francis Pott, and he promised to tell me when he hears of a suitable position," Emmanuel says. "Every day brings new immigrants to Point Comfort who settle inland and create new communities. Something is sure to turn up."

"I appreciate your looking out for me," John says. He glances toward Margaret and Frances and is satisfied that the two women are too preoccupied to have noticed.

Finally, there is a lull in the conversations, and a look passes between Frances and Emmanuel. He clears his throat to get Margaret's attention and says, "Before you decide to sign the papers, there is something you should know. Francis Pott is giving up his post as harbormaster at Point Comfort and will move his household to his plantation on the Eastern Shore."

Mystified, Margaret asks, "What do you mean?"

"We will all be living much farther away, on the other side of the Chesapeake Bay. We won't come to James City as often, if at all," Emmanuel says.

Frances puts her hand on Margaret's arm. "If this means you want to reconsider our arrangement, Emmanuel and I will certainly understand."

"When will this happen?"

"In May. We've already started packing up some of his belongings for the move."

Margaret gets up from the sofa and starts to pace, her mind in turmoil. She glances at Jane sitting on the carpet, tracing the pattern of the weave with her fingers. Suddenly, Margaret has a vision of herself sitting next to her. They are both older and have their arms around each other. Jane's head rests comfortably on her shoulder. The image is so vivid that Margaret squeezes her eyes shut to make sure she isn't dreaming. When she opens them, a feeling of serenity sweeps over her. She is certain that she is doing the right thing and that she will see Jane again.

Margaret walks over to the desk where John is standing. She looks at the two pieces of parchment, covered with writing, and asks, "Is everything in order?" When John nods, she continues, "Where do I need to sign?"

"Are you sure this is what you want?" he asks.

In a firm voice, she answers, "Yes."

John takes a sharpened feather and dips the point in an inkwell. He hands the quill to her and points to a spot near the bottom of both documents. Margaret writes her full name twice, slowly and deliberately—she has been practicing in her garden using a stick to trace "Margaret Cornish" in the smooth, black earth. Her signature is angular but legible. When she finishes, Emmanuel adds his first name below hers, and Frances makes an X next to it.

After John signs as a witness, he sprinkles drying powder on the ink, rolls up the documents, and ties each with string. He hands one to Emmanuel and says, "For Francis Pott when you draw up the terms of indenture. I will file the other one here in the James City court archive."

They stand around in an awkward circle. Eventually, Margaret breaks the silence and says, "Let's be done with it quickly."

She goes over to Jane and picks her up. Hugging her close, she whispers in her ear, "I love you like a ray of sunshine, and you will always be my darling girl. But now you must go with Frances and Emmanuel."

When Margaret kisses her, Jane holds on tightly as if sensing what is about to happen. But when Margaret disentangles her arms and hands her to Frances, she reaches out to her new mother without protest.

As Margaret embraces Emmanuel, he says, "Don't worry. We'll take good care of her," and kisses her on the forehead.

Margaret kisses him back. "I know that, Emmanuel, and I am so grateful to both of you."

Grasping Frances by the hand, she gives Jane a parting caress, stroking her cheek with all the affection she can marshal. Then she turns away and walks out of the room.

Outside, the air is still balmy. On the way to the harbor, people walking up and down the street greet her and John, but Margaret does not notice them. At the dock, the boat and rowing crew are waiting for them. Getting in, she almost slips, and one of the oarsmen steadies her. She thanks him and takes a seat on the wooden bench facing the other side of the river. John sits next to her and takes her hand. When the boat pulls away from the dock, Margaret doesn't look back.

It isn't until they are far out on the water that Margaret starts to cry.

* * *

In early April, Lieutenant Sheppard gets ready to muster his troops and march against the Appomattox, Weyanoke, Warraskoyak, and Nansemond, the Indian tribes on the south side of the James River that participated in the recent uprising that cost so many settlers their lives. His company is part of a larger campaign of retaliation throughout Virginia with the goal of destroying the Powhatan Confederacy once and for all. Although eager to do battle, Sheppard is reluctant to leave Elizabeth, who is due to give birth any day now, until he feels she will receive the best care he can provide. He arranges for her to move back to her father's plantation because he wants Dr. Woodson, who lives close by, to be there when she goes into labor. Sheppard does not inform Margaret about his decision. He simply announces it two days before his departure, giving the servants in the household barely enough time to adjust to the changes.

With Elizabeth gone, everyone has more work to do. Jason, as overseer of the plantation, sends a few young men to help out, but they seem to be all thumbs when it comes to domestic activities. Lucy, Eunice, and Jeremiah grumble more than once in frustration. Margaret finds it all quite amusing. Not being called to act as a midwife actually pleases her. After Priscilla's death in childbirth, the last thing she wants is to be responsible for the delivery of Elizabeth's baby. Having no involvement whatsoever is even better. Margaret doesn't know whether it was Sheppard's or Elizabeth's idea to exclude her, but she utters a quiet "thank you" when she goes to bed at night and hopes for an easy birthing.

Her prayers are answered when, a week later, Elizabeth goes into labor and delivers a baby girl after just eight hours. Although the lieutenant is not by her side to welcome his new daughter, Anne, he rushes to Spencer's plantation as soon as he receives the news. The Indian campaign has barely started, and he can take the time to celebrate with his wife and make all the arrangements for her and the baby to return to the plantation.

When Elizabeth arrives in a wagon pulled by oxen, carrying Anne in her arms, everyone surrounds them with well wishes and shouts of acclamation. Margaret and Lucy have prepared the bedroom, but Elizabeth waves them off. She is more tired of all the to-do than the journey home. Eventually she yields to their suggestion to rest, but the next morning she gets up early to take up the reins as mistress of the house again, earning Margaret's admiration and respect.

Two weeks later, Sheppard manages to participate in Anne's christening at Lawne's Creek Church as well. This time, the Reverend Faulkner has himself rowed across the river to officiate at the baptism. Anthony catches Margaret's eye with a knowing, ironic glance when he first makes his appearance. Later, the African attendees gather in a small group, and Katherine makes snide comments on the preferential treatment accorded the lieutenant and his family.

Margaret doesn't care. She is happy for Sheppard, glad that he is pleased with having another daughter. But when she goes up to him at the reception afterward, with Anthony in her arms and Robert Jr. and William at her side, and congratulates him and Elizabeth, she gets another impression. The lieutenant's eyes narrow and a resentful look crosses his face before he recovers and smiles graciously.

Walking away, Margaret realizes that he envies her for having three sons while he is still waiting for a male heir.

48
LEAVE-TAKING
Virginia—1645–1648

For the next two years, the Virginia militias wage a brutal war against the Indian tribes. Killing en masse, burning fields, and devastating villages, they do everything they can to subdue the Powhatan Confederacy forever. Settlers on the outlying plantations live in continual vigilance and anxiety, afraid that the Indians will retaliate. It makes for a tense, worrisome existence, but the expected counterattacks never come. The relentless pursuit by the militias drives the Indians and their families ever deeper into the forests. To consolidate their gains, the colonists construct four new forts inland on the main rivers, keeping the Natives further at bay.

Early in 1646, word reaches James City of Opechancanough's whereabouts. Led by Governor Berkeley, militia forces and friendly Indians storm his stronghold between the Appomattox and James Rivers and capture the Powhatan chief. The victorious troops transport all males over the age of eleven in the village to a prison stockade on Tangier Island, a small, isolated outpost in the middle of the Chesapeake Bay. Many of them and other captured Indians get sold into slavery to Cuba, Barbados, and other Caribbean islands. The soldiers taking Opechancanough to James City exhibit him as a curiosity to the civilian population along the way. The venerable tribal leader can no longer walk on his own but comports himself with remarkable dignity against the onslaught of ridicule and hostility as many settlers—men, women, and children—spit at him.

When he arrives in the colony's capital, he complains to Governor Berkeley, who puts a stop to the abuse. Berkeley is displeased at the mistreatment of the Werowance—the leader—of the Powhatans because, not understanding the culture of the Indians, he thinks of Opechancanough as a king. He also can't decide whether to send him to England and King Charles as a royal prisoner or put him on trial in James City to make an example of him. While he dithers, a prison guard shoots Opechancanough in the back with his musket, claiming he tried to escape. No legal action is taken against the assassin.

The death of their great leader and the sustained attacks by the militia throw the Indian tribes into disarray. Facing another lean winter with insufficient provisions to feed their families, they need everyone to help with the corn harvest. At the end of August, they sue for peace.

Lieutenant Sheppard, who has been away from home for much of the conflict, looks forward to spending more time with his family. To his surprise, the governor first promotes him for his service to the colony. Captain Sheppard makes a triumphant return to his plantation and, like many war heroes in Virginia, enters the political arena. The people on the south side of the river choose him their burgess for the General Assembly in the next election, adding to his honors as a trusted military adviser to the governor.

Showing considerable foresight, he and others counsel to be magnanimous in victory. Trade with the Indian tribes is essential to the colony's economy and long-term survival. The voices calling for revenge and banishment of the Natives to other territories have their supporters, but their emotional appeals fail to carry the day. In October, Berkeley signs a peace treaty with Necotowance, the new Werowance of the Powhatans. All tribes in the confederacy agree to become tributaries to the King of England. At the same time, the colonists gain vast tracts of undeveloped land, much of it to the south and west of the James River and on the eastern shore of the Chesapeake Bay. The Indians will keep to the north side of the York River. For now, that territory is declared off limits for further colonial development, although existing white settlements will remain. Trafficking between Natives and settlers is forbidden, except through traders authorized by the colonial administration. Necotowance signs as "King of the Indians," and the agreement ushers in thirty years of peace between the tribes and Virginia's colonists.

* * *

Like everyone else on Sheppard's plantation, Margaret is happy that the war is over. She can return to her cottage without worry and constant guard. She spends many a Sunday afternoon cleaning the interior of cobwebs, fixing it up to her liking, and readying the rooms for her children. She puts in the kind of garden she prefers, in which eye-pleasing, colorful flowers surround the more useful herbs and medicinal plants. After a busy week, she wants nothing more than to sit on her porch in the afternoon sun, smell the fragrant aroma of rosemary, thyme, and mint, and watch her children play. She wishes Robert Jr. and William didn't enact battles between settlers and Indians so often, using tree branches as muskets and bows and arrow. It reminds her too vividly of their father's death.

She often thinks of Jane growing up on the Eastern Shore. Apparently, the lands on the other side of the Chesapeake Bay were spared much of the fighting, but Margaret has received only one communication from Frances and Emmanuel since she gave Jane up. When Francis Pott visited his property in James City, he conveyed the message to John who passed it on to Margaret that Jane is thriving.

Word reaching England that the Indian war is settled coincides with the end of the civil war there when, after a series of defeats for the royalists, King Charles surrenders. Soon after his capture and imprisonment in January 1647, a flood of Cavaliers and soldiers who fought for him reach Virginia's shores, emigrating to escape the wrath of Oliver Cromwell and his Puritan armies. The economic turmoil after a ruinous war makes Virginia attractive to many workers, servants, and adventurers as well. Some of them end up south of the James River, where the tobacco planters are all expanding. Now that the Indian tribes have withdrawn as far away as the Carolina colony, all the tribes are growing. Margaret watches with amusement as the new arrivals, many of them half her age, show up for the first time at church. She wonders if she looked as flustered and frightened as they do when she first came to Virginia.

Ironically, as immigrants swell the ranks of the colony, Margaret faces the departure of people she cares for most.

The first are Anthony, Mary, and their four children. Having finished their indenture at John Upton's plantation, they are now officially "free Negroes" and want to establish a place of their own as soon as possible. With John's advice, they claim the 50-acre parcel due to each of them but apply it to procure land on the Eastern Shore. From what John has learned from Emmanuel, the area has enough settlers to create a sense of community, yet the land is not as forested as the inland frontier of Virginia, which would require backbreaking work to clear for grazing fields. With the purchase of two additional headrights and their oldest son, the Johnsons can obtain 250 acres. With what Anthony has saved breeding horses and cattle, and earning money on the side like John in the hog trade, they will have enough to buy a small herd to get started. Perhaps they can even acquire an indentured worker or two.

When John finds a suitable property through intermediaries and registers the deed in James City, the Johnsons get ready to move. They want to leave in the late spring, in time to build a house for themselves and get settled before the summer rains. The week before their ship departs, the African community in the area gives them a farewell feast at Lawne's Creek Church. After the service, several of the white workers who have known Anthony and Mary for years say their good-byes and wish them good luck. Then the small group of *malungu* gathers for the last time to eat and tell stories.

As Margaret watches Anthony talking to Katherine and Michael, she thinks about the time when she first met him at Warrosquoake Plantation and he took her under his wing. He was so much younger then. They both were. Nearly twenty years of servitude have left their mark on him. Although Anthony is still rugged and energetic, his beard has patches of gray, and the downward curl of his lip conveys years of frustration working unwillingly for someone else. Yet his seriousness conveys a sense of indomitable strength. He may not say much, but when he does, others listen. Mary, in contrast, seems more delicate, her sensitive demeanor disguising an unbendable tenaciousness. Their children, especially the two older boys, take after their father. Hard-working and spirited, they will be a great help to their parents on their new farm. Margaret reckons that, besides Emmanuel Driggers and Frances, if any black family can succeed on its own in Virginia, it is the Johnsons.

She hasn't been close to them in recent years, but their affection for each other is as strong as ever, and she knows the feeling is mutual.

"I'm happy for you, all of you," she told them right after they announced their decision. "But part of me wishes you wouldn't go."

"Why don't you come along with us?" Anthony offered. He didn't mention that she would be living closer to Jane, not wanting to open old wounds.

Margaret appreciated his discretion but brought it up herself. "I would love to be near Jane," she admitted. "But I must take care of my children here."

"Of course, you must," Mary said with understanding. She has always been fiercely protective of her own children.

Having said their good-byes earlier, and knowing that Anthony is anything but sentimental, Margaret doesn't linger when the dinner breaks up. She gives them all a quick hug, including the children, and leaves with her own three boys. Sheppard has been kind enough to keep a boat behind for them. The two young oarsmen are chatty and take her mind off the sadness she feels. On the way home, Margaret wonders if she will ever see any of the Johnsons again.

* * *

In early fall while attending church, Margaret notices Sheppard talking with John. The captain claps him on the shoulder and they shake hands. Then Katherine and Michael give her an odd look, but John acts as if nothing significant happened. Margaret is curious but doesn't think anything of it.

Later that day, after the main meal has been cleared away, she returns from the kitchen unexpectedly. Before she enters the living room, she hears Sheppard mention her name to Elizabeth. Ducking behind the doorway, she listens.

"Becoming bailiff at the court in York County is a great opportunity for John," Sheppard says while getting his clay pipe from the mantle above the fireplace. "York Town is a distance away, though, and he will have little opportunity to return to James City."

"It is high time for him to make a new life for himself, but his leaving will be hard on Margaret," Elizabeth replies.

"That's why I'm telling you," Sheppard says, "in case she acts strangely in the coming days."

The news hits Margaret like a tidal wave and she has to steady herself against the doorway. When she has recovered, she finds Lucy and asks her to watch her children for the afternoon. Lucy agrees without asking why. The intensity of Margaret's stare frightens her.

Thanking her hastily, Margaret sets off, sweeping toward the woods like a gathering storm. After spring, early autumn is Margaret's favorite time of year, but today she has no eyes or ears for her surroundings. She fails to see the leaves on the elm, hickory, and maple trees beginning to turn, nor does she hear the squirrels rousing the migratory birds from their resting places. She pushes through bushes in her way, brushing stems aside as if they didn't exist.

Thoughts tumble through her mind. John leaving the area is terrible enough, but not telling her? Some things that occurred over the past few weeks make sense now. The time Sheppard sought John out after church, and they remained deep in conversation. John seemed more alert, even buoyed, but also preoccupied afterward. When she asked him what it was about, he claimed it concerned an indenture matter with a new arrival. At the time, she believed him and didn't give a second thought, but now she knows better. The way Katherine and Michael looked at her earlier makes sense, too. Does everybody except her know already?

By the time she gets to Ewens's plantation, there are twigs in her hair and burrs cling to her skirt. Having worked herself into a frenzy, she heads to the main house. John likes to spend his free time in the library, his nose buried in a book or scroll. As expected, she finds him sitting at a table by the window poring over a map. He is so absorbed that he doesn't notice her stepping into the room.

"When were you going to tell me?"

The accusatory tone in her voice strikes him like an arrow and he shivers involuntarily. When he turns to her, he looks stricken.

Margaret marches up to him. Her pupils are pinpoints. "All these years and you don't have the courage to tell me yourself? I have to find out from others?"

John slumps in his chair. "Sheppard told you," he says. "I asked him to wait."

"What did you expect? He told Elizabeth."

When he rises and starts to protest, she cuts him off. "You are a coward! A bastard! How long have you been scheming behind my back to leave me?" When he says nothing, she continues to attack. "It must make you feel so proud! Slinking away like an opossum hiding in the bushes."

Although his eyes blaze in anger, he remains silent.

"Well, aren't you going to say anything?"

Suddenly he shouts, "You left me first! Don't you ever forget that!"

His intensity shocks her.

Before she can respond, he continues with anguished passion. "You broke my heart, Margaret, but I have done nothing but support you. I've been there for you whenever you needed me, and now you spit in my face. I am not a monster. I've been cudgeling my brain to figure out how to tell you because it tears me apart to have to go. I'll never make anything of myself here, but I'll never stop loving you."

His tortured outcry takes all the fight out of Margaret.

Uncertain what to do next, they face each other in silence for a long time.

Finally, she says, "I am sorry, John. Everybody I care about is leaving me. I don't know if I can bear it."

"I am sorry, too."

He looks down, giving her the opportunity to compose herself. When he raises his eyes, Margaret has a wistful smile on her face.

"Come and see me before you go."

He nods. "I will. I promise."

* * *

Two weeks later, John visits Margaret at her cottage for the last time. She has been expecting him and left her children at Sheppard's in the care of Lucy. He waves to her from afar and walks to the pond to spend time at Swett's grave. Then he goes up to the house where Margaret is waiting on the front porch. There are two wooden chairs, and they sit down next to each other and start to talk. As they reminisce about their many years together and apart, one memory leads to another, and they share familiar stories and things they haven't told each other before, reacting with laughter, sadness, amusement, and seriousness. They chat about their children and what hopes they have for them. They acknowledge how pleased they are that they are all free or on a path to freedom.

"We have done good by them," John says.

"So far," Margaret replies with a melancholy smile.

When their fingers touch as if by accident, they grab hold and sit together hand in hand, like an old couple resting in the sunshine. Although they continue to talk, there is too much to say, and much remains unspoken between them.

At some point, John asks, "Do you think we will ever know our destinies? Before we die?"

Margaret thinks for a moment, then says, "I don't know."

When the sun starts to dip toward the birch trees at the pond, John opens a pouch at his belt. He pulls out a small pearl and offers it to Margaret. It gleams in the sunlight. "I found this among the pieces of silver I've been hiding in the library. I want you to have it."

"Oh, John. It is beautiful," Margaret says. "I wish I had something to give you to remember me by."

She looks at him, his familiar face boyish and sad. Impulsively, she takes his head in her hands and kisses him passionately. He responds to her soft lips, then draws back. They look into each other's eyes. Getting up, they embrace, seeking to hold on as long as they can to the familiar feeling of their bodies fitting well together, as if they belonged to each other.

When they finally pull apart, John puts the pearl in Margaret's hand and closes her fingers over it. "You lost your first two through no fault of your own. Keep this one safe."

Then he kisses her again and says, "Good luck to you, Margaret."

She answers, "Good luck to you, John."

As he walks down the porch steps, his boots make a hollow, clomping sound. Heading toward the forest, his gait is unhurried yet purposeful. He does not look back.

Margaret gazes after him long after he disappears among the pine and cedar trees. Her eyes brim with tears. There are parts of her she has shared with no one else. Robert has touched her perhaps more fully, but John has affected her just as profoundly. She knows with a deep, sad sense of certainty that she will never see him again.

49

MARGARET
Virginia—1648-1671

Communications from Emmanuel Driggers have become rare, so Margaret hears little about Jane while she continues to live and work at Sheppard's plantation. She looks after her three sons, happy to watch them grow and flourish. Robert Jr. seems to be taking after his father, showing an interest in working with tools and fixing things. William befriends Samuel, the caretaker of horses and cattle on the plantation, who soon treats him like an apprentice. Anthony stays close to Margaret in the kitchen and helps with serving food and other household chores.

As the population of Hogg Island and environs continues to grow, Lawne's Creek Church becomes too small to accommodate all those wishing to attend. Under Captain Sheppard's leadership, the plantation owners get together and decide to replace the wooden building with a larger structure made of bricks. Because no one can spare any workers during the harvest season, they start on the project in the spring of 1650. While construction is going on, Sunday services take place outside before a makeshift altar. The wealthy planters and their families sit on wooden benches. The rest stand in back of them. It is not as primitive as the worship at Warrosquoake Margaret remembers, but more than once, unexpected rains drench the congregation. When the new building is finished at the beginning of summer, there is a big celebration.

All attendees agree that the "second church," as everyone calls it, is a vast improvement, although there are a few older members who claim to miss the old building and all the memories it held. Margaret agrees with them about two instances from her own experience—she recalls with bittersweet pleasure the times she and Robert had their first two sons baptized there.

Now that Anthony, Mary, and John are gone, Margaret, Katherine, Michael, and Mathew grow closer during their Sunday encounters. Although their little black community has shrunk, there are more of their children now after Margaret helped Katherine give birth to Amos and Frances. Before John left for good, he advised Katherine and Michael to take a surname as it would make things easier when they finish their contracts and need to indenture their children, even if they decide to remain as hired workers at Ewens's plantation. Following his advice, they have chosen "Blizzard," after a severe snowstorm a few winters back that covered the land with several feet of snow for weeks, making it all but impossible to get from one place to the next.

After services, they all share the latest news and rumors. Michael has cultivated a line of communication with Africans up and down the James River, and when his hog trade takes him to James City, he always comes back with the most recent reports and gossip. At first he feels uncomfortable relating any news about John in Margaret's presence, but after Katherine mentions it to her, Margaret assures him that she wants to know everything. She already receives information about Mihill and John from Captain Sheppard whenever he returns from General Council sessions where he meets up with military friends like Colonel Christopher Stafford and Colonel Richard Lee.

So, Margaret learns that John is well regarded as bailiff in York Town. As the county seat, it is a lively community. Although not as large as James City, its favorable location as a harbor town close to the mouth of the Chesapeake Bay attracts considerable maritime traffic. Sailors and other workers commit theft, drunkenness, and blasphemy frequently, and as keeper of the jail and an officer of the court, John is responsible for meting out punishment to offenders. Every week, he puts lawbreakers in the pillory and stocks, and trashes offenders at the whipping post, men and women, white and African alike. The first time Margaret hears of it, she feels nauseated. Taken back to her own time under the lash, she feels chagrined and hopes that John has become inured enough so that having to dole out punishment doesn't gnaw at him but he is able to treat it as a necessary evil. Being John, she imagines he would lay on the stripes fairly, with vigor and dispassion.

Another, more welcome surprise is learning that York County has a larger black population than Margaret knew. When Captain Guy and his ship *Fortune* brought Africans rescued from a Spanish galleon to Virginia in 1628, many ended up on plantations there. Margaret remembers comforting them after they arrived in James City, a miserable, frightened group of men and women. They were sold at auction like slaves and none received a contract of indenture. Still, she imagines that now, more than twenty years later, John is probably helping them remedy the situation in whatever way he can, if not for them, then perhaps for their children.

When Katherine tells Margaret, reluctantly, that John has gotten married to a black woman named Cicely and that they have a son, Philip, she is genuinely pleased.

"I am glad that John is making another life for himself," she says.

It surprises Katherine that Margaret seems to feel no sadness, no sense of loss at the news. "What about you?" she asks. "Are you going to get married again?"

Margaret shakes her head. "Who would want to marry a woman my age with three children and no money?"

Looking at her askance, Katherine says, "You're still young and you have your hundred acres at Swett's Swamp."

When Margaret smiles regretfully, Katherine realizes that it is time to change the subject.

Yet her question gives Margaret pause. She knows how much she misses being physically close to someone. There are many nights when she lies awake aching with loneliness. It is easier for her during the days when she can concentrate her energy on her children and working for Sheppard and Elizabeth. Her place in the household is secure, especially after Elizabeth gives birth to three successive sons, John, Robert, and William, and Sheppard no longer feels jealous of her. Priscilla and Susannah, the captain's children by his first wife, adore Margaret. Elizabeth's daughter, Anne, and Anthony are close in age and like playing with each other. It does not surprise Margaret that the captain dotes on his daughters with as much affection as can be expected of a military man, yet clearly he prefers his male heirs.

For the most part, though, the main house has a distinctly female atmosphere because Sheppard is away so often in his capacities as a burgess in the General Council and as military adviser to the governor. Ever since the Puritans took over in England and executed King Charles early in 1649, the settlers have been on alert, expecting trouble because Virginia, unlike the other colonies in the New World, continues to champion the royal cause, supporting Charles II, who lives in exile in the Netherlands. With so many Cavaliers and Governor Berkeley loyal to the crown, the Cromwell government is none too pleased and threatens to send the English Navy to coerce the administration to come to its senses.

In dinner-table conversations, Margaret hears the name "Robert Rich" for the first time in many years when Sheppard shares news about the brewing conflict. Apparently, the Earl of Warwick, though no longer commander of the British fleet, still has the ear of Oliver Cromwell. As an unrepentant colonizer promoting Puritan enterprises despite his failures with the Virginia Company and Providence Island, Warwick advised sending an overwhelming force to bring the colony to heel.

Cromwell listens to his counsel. At first, Berkeley puts on a brave face, vowing to fight, but when the size of the English armada becomes apparent, wiser heads prevail. No one wants another bloody war that would tear the colony apart and benefit no one. Richard Bennett, by now a wealthy planter whose reputation as a loyal Puritan reassures the English fleet commander, helps negotiate a settlement that keeps the Virginia social and political fabric intact. Berkeley signs the treaty of surrender in the spring of 1652 and retires to his house at Green Spring to continue his experiments with crops that might replace tobacco. Richard Bennett takes over as governor. He puts Anglicans and royalist supporters in the colony at ease by continuing to involve them in decision making and retaining military leaders like Captain Sheppard as advisers while pursuing a policy of religious tolerance.

Later that summer, in the early afternoon when Margaret is chopping vegetables to add to the supper stew, Lucy bustles into the kitchen and says, "Captain Sheppard is back from James City and wants to see you."

Flustered to be summoned—it is unusual for him to ask for her so soon after his return—she wipes her hands on her apron and tells Eunice, "Keep stirring the pot. I'll be back anon."

She finds the captain in the living room, sitting in his favorite chair, smoking a pipe of tobacco. His relaxed demeanor gives Margaret some assurance, but she remains standing in the doorway, rubbing her fingers nervously.

"You wanted to see me, Robert?" she says.

Sheppard looks up and beckons her to come in. "Yes. I have news for you from Francis Pott."

Catching her breath, Margaret advances into the room. "Is it about Jane? Is she all right?"

Sheppard nods, smiling indulgently. "Yes, she is fine." He takes a puff on his pipe and expels the smoke, glancing at Margaret as if enjoying her discomfort. Finally, he says, "Emmanuel Driggers and his wife have completed their terms of indenture with him and are leaving his plantation to start a cattle farm of their own."

Margaret's heart starts to beat faster. "What will happen to Jane? They must not give her up!" she cries out.

Sheppard grins. "They won't. She will go with them. Emmanuel bought out her contract. He paid Francis with some of his live-stock—a heifer and young mare."

It takes Margaret a moment to realize what he's saying. Jane is only seven years old. She was indentured to Francis Pott until age thirty-one. "Does that mean she is free?" she gasps.

As Sheppard nods, Elizabeth comes up behind him, seemingly out of nowhere, and says, "Yes, isn't it wonderful?"

Margaret looks around in confusion. Then she whispers, "Thank you for telling me," and bolts out the front door.

She makes it down the porch steps and halfway to the creek before she sinks to her knees. A wave of delirious joy sweeps over her, and she starts to roll on the ground, back and forth, laughing and crying. When she finally stops, she looks up at the sky. It is a bright blue, the color of Captain Jope's and Robert Swett's eyes. Margaret sits up and lets the warm sunlight caress her face.

When she opens her eyes, she sees Elizabeth standing on the front porch, looking worried.

"Are you all right, Margaret?" she asks.

"Yes, yes, I am," Margaret shouts at the top of her voice. "I couldn't be happier!"

* * *

In August 1654, Captain Sheppard takes to his bed, makes his will, and dies after a brief illness. Margaret's ministrations with herbal poultices, teas, and compresses have no effect, and Elizabeth buries him in the cemetery near the house. Always practical, she does not stay in mourning for long and soon after marries Thomas Warren, a local planter from her social circle at Lawne's Creek Church. After the wedding, a small ceremony at the church, she takes her children—hers and Priscilla's—to live with him at her new husband's land east of Ewens's plantation. Lucy and Jeremiah go with her while Jason continues as manager of Sheppard's thousand-acre property. Dorothy and Henry Meddows move back into the main house. The captain has remembered her kindly in his will.

Margaret, unwilling to go with Elizabeth or work for Dorothy again, decides it is time for her to leave. As a free woman, she can choose to work wherever she pleases. Although her line of communication with Mihill through Sheppard no longer exists, she has made sure to stay in touch with her son through Colonel Stafford. He recommends her to Colonel Rawleigh Travers, a retired militia man in Lancaster County, north of the Rappahannock River, who is looking for someone to keep his household. Margret hires on with him even though, as a condition of employment, Travers insists she stay on his plantation at all times. Her two older sons, now twelve and fourteen and still indentured, remain at Sheppard's. Confident that they are mature enough to be on their own, she trusts Jason to watch out for them. She takes young Anthony with her.

Travers's plantation is located far away from Virginia's populated areas along the James and York Rivers. To Margaret it feels like the wilderness frontier she experienced when she first arrived in the colony. She likes roaming the lush, dense forests rife with mushrooms, berries, and medicinal plants, and encounters Indians again, who come to trade furs and game they hunted. The colonel, a lifelong bachelor, suffers from an old injury incurred during the last Indian uprising, and Margaret's herbal ministrations ease his frequent pain and rheumatism. News from other parts of Virginia reaches her, weeks and months later, via Travers's contacts throughout the colony.

That is how Margaret hears the following year that Frances has died on the Eastern Shore. Grief-stricken, she goes about her work as if in a daze. The pain in her heart doesn't go away for a long time.

Her best friend, the only woman she trusted with her innermost thoughts and feelings, is gone, and Margaret never got to thank her for taking care of Jane. She can only imagine how deeply hurt Emmanuel must feel. The fact that he married again within months doesn't change what Margaret knows very well: how much he loved Frances. But Emmanuel was always pragmatic, and even in his grief, he thought of others. He knew he could not take care of his young children on his own. Margaret admires him for it and thanks him in her heart that she can count on him to take care of Jane. She wishes she could be with them.

In 1657, Anne Barnhouse, the sister of Captain Christopher Stafford, agrees to finally honor her brother's will and set Mihill free. By then, Mihill has worked at her place, Martin's Hundred, a plantation east of James City, for three years. From what Margaret hears about the terms of his release, she is confident that John had a hand in it, bringing his legal knowledge to bear. Mihill has a child with a young African woman named Prossa. He and his son, William, gain their freedom, but Prossa remains with Anne Barnhouse. Mihill continues to live near James City and soon after marries a free white woman, also named Anne. They have four more children.

John, living in York Town, visits his son and grandchildren occasionally. Margaret is happy that he has the opportunity to enjoy the company of his offspring.

After gaining his freedom, Robert Jr. moves to Norfolk, closer to the Atlantic Ocean, and works as a carpenter. With the continued arrival of immigrants, he does not lack work and marries an Englishwoman.

William takes care of horses for Thomas Binn, who, coincidentally, married Agnes's servant Jane after she finished her indenture and moved as far away from her former mistress as she could.

Upon Colonel Travers's death, Margaret finds employment in the household of Charles Barham, also a former militiaman. Barham lives in Southwark Parrish on the south bank of the James River upstream from Ewens's plantation. Closer to home, it becomes easier for Margaret to communicate with all her children except Jane.

* * *

When Margaret turns sixty-one in 1671, she returns to her land at Swett's Swamp for good. Anthony hires on at Sheppard's plantation to be close to her. Although she has visited over the years, the cottage has fallen into disrepair and needs fixing up. Robert's grave has become overgrown with grasses and plants. It takes some time for her to clear away the cobwebs and weeds and restore everything to its proper order. Anthony helps her, and she soon lives contentedly back in her home.

Word of her return spreads quickly throughout the Hogg Island area. Because of her reputation as a midwife and healer, people start to visit her, asking for her help. Margaret is pleased to offer aid to others and apply her knowledge wherever she can, traveling to plantations in the vicinity as needed. Her patients usually pay her with food.

Although Margaret has earned enough money by then to stay in her cottage in comfort for as long as she wishes, she petitions the colonial administration in James City to relieve her of having to pay annual tithes on the grounds that she is destitute. By then, she is angry with what has been happening in Virginia, and she no longer wants to support the colonial government with her taxes.

Over the past decades, the gradual disenfranchisement of black people has continued unabated, just as John and Emmanuel Driggers foresaw. In 1662, the General Assembly passed a law that any child born to a woman indentured for life will also be indentured for life, effectively making them both slaves. Only Negro women are affected; white female servants always receive contracts with a limited time of service. Five years later, the burgesses decided to no longer allow blacks to claim Christian baptism as a justification to attain freedom.

At the same time, in a show of hypocrisy, the lawmakers encourage plantation owners to bring all their workers into the Christian fold. In 1669, the legislators enacted a law that permits owners to kill their black workers with impunity. If a Negro dies while resisting a master, it will not be construed as an act of premeditated malice.

Margaret no longer doubts John and Emmanuel's prescience that slavery will become legal in Virginia. She just hopes that she won't live long enough to witness it.

She tends her garden and takes care of Robert's grave. She spends time there every day and talks to him about their children and other matters on her mind. Occasionally she visits Anthony at Sheppard's plantation and gets news from Jason about what is happening in the world. She attends church regularly, not for the service, but for seeing her few remaining friends.

One Sunday afternoon, Anthony tells her that Mihill has contacted him. "He wants to visit you but is unsure how you feel about it," he explains. "He doesn't want to show up unexpectedly."

Margaret has not seen her oldest son in more than thirty years, and her heart suddenly beats as loud as a drum. "Of course I want to see him," she exclaims.

Mihill arrives at her cottage two weeks later. For a moment, Margaret can't breathe. The handsome, forty-year-old man standing before her looks just like John the day he came to say good-bye. He has the same features—small ears, flared nostrils, and penetrating eyes—and the same uncertain, almost shy demeanor.

Then Margaret opens her arms and Mihill comes to her.

Spending the day together, they get to know each other again, both as adults and as mother and child. They discover that, not only do they get along well, more importantly, they like each other.

There is no lingering anger on Mihill's part that Margaret sent him away as a boy. Taking her hand, he says, "I have talked with my father about what happened and know you both were in an impossible situation. I have always remembered what you said to me that day."

As they part Margaret kisses him on the cheek and says, "I love you with all my heart, and you are special. Come back soon."

On his next visit, Mihill brings his entire family. For Margaret, seeing her four grandchildren for the first time, recognizing herself in them, is a profound moment. They are lighter skinned than her and have some of John's features, too; and she has an intimation of the future—how their line will carry on. Anne, a bit shy at first, warms up to her quickly. The day passes too fast, and Margaret is pleased when Mihill promises to visit every few months.

Margaret always prepares plenty of food for their arrival because her grandchildren come with big appetites. Afterward, she plays hopscotch, tag, and hide-and-seek with them outside, giving their parents time to relax with each other.

Mihill always brings news of his father. John, now retired from his work as a constable, continues to be well regarded in York Town. He takes care of his family. Except for Philip, he and his wife have no other children. Neither Margaret nor Katherine can figure out why, and Mihill, if he knows, won't say.

One time, when Margaret asks if John is happy, Mihill hesitates slightly and says, "When he sees his grandchildren."

It bothers Margaret that John, while he may be living a productive life, has had few moments of genuine joy since he left Ewens's plantation.

One morning in July while pulling up weeds in her garden, Margaret experiences an odd ringing in her ears. Suddenly she feels a stabbing pain deep in her belly. She cries out and doubles over. Then her knees give out and she sinks to the ground. Sitting on her haunches, she knows that John has died. Just as when Captain Jope perished in her dream, the intimate connection she has had with John for most of her life is broken. A wave of grief sweeps over her.

For the next few days, she is inconsolable, walking around in a daze, bursting into tears at unexpected moments.

The people at church worry that she is going mad when she insists that John has died and try to reason with her. But two weeks later, both Mihill and Michael's communication network confirm that it is true. By then Margaret has recovered enough to accept their condolences with grace.

Many people start to look at her with wonderment. They've known her as a midwife and healer. Now they believe she is clairvoyant as well, a woman with secret knowledge and mysterious power, and they treat her with greater respect and some apprehension.

The news of John's death strikes Katherine like a terrible blow. When Margaret first announced it to everyone, Katherine was one of the most vocal dissenters, denying it fiercely, and now her world has collapsed. Realizing how shaken Katherine is by John's death, Margaret comforts her as best she can. When Katherine slowly recovers, they take walks together, reminiscing. It brings them closer than they ever were in the past.

50

THE EASTERN SHORE
Virginia—1676

Oone spring morning, a year after John died, Margaret is sitting on her front porch when Anthony hails her from the forest. His familiar voice puts her at ease, and she waits for him to approach. As she squints in his direction and recognizes the familiar figure of her strapping thirty-year-old son, she sees that he has another visitor with him. The older black man next to him walks with a steady, deliberate gait. He is wearing a travel cap, but white hair spills out from under it. Margaret gets up, her heart beating more quickly. It is Emmanuel Driggers!

She steps off the porch and rushes to meet him in the meadow, halfway between the house and the pond. Although they haven't seen each other in more than two decades, they embrace without hesitation.

"You are as beautiful as ever, Margaret," he says gallantly when they separate.

"And you look as distinguished as always," she teases in reply, although she notes the deep wrinkles etched in his face and his sober expression. "What brings you to this side of the river?"

"It's Jane. Her husband, William Harman, died two months ago. We have done everything we know to lift her spirits, but to no avail. I'm hoping you'll come with me to the Eastern Shore to help."

Margaret, who has grown ashen-faced, doesn't think twice. "When do we leave?"

When Anthony looks surprised, Driggers chuckles knowingly and says, "Told you."

Anthony shakes his head in amazement. "I guess you know my mother better than I do."

Margaret goes inside the cottage only long enough to change into her best dress and fill a basket with bread, smoked meat, and cheese. She puts on her woolen overcoat, and they set off through the greening forest.

At Sheppard's dock on the creek, Anthony sees them off. In James City, she and Emmanuel board a pinnace and head down the James River. In an effort to distract herself, Margaret looks at the forested banks on both sides. Though unfamiliar, they bring back a fleeting memory of when she first arrived from England. It is the first time in a long time she has traveled this far east.

They stop at Point Comfort and spend the night. The next morning, they board a larger ship carrying barrels, wooden boxes and crates, and a greater number of passengers. As they reach the mouth of the Chesapeake Bay, the air grows brisk and salty. Margaret is amazed at the vast expanse of open water. Emmanuel points to the east so that she can catch a glimpse of the Atlantic Ocean. Instantly, memories flood her mind of her time with Captain Jope, dinners in his candle-lit cabin, going to sleep on his bed, sitting with John at the rear windows of the *White Lion* and watching the churning waves of its wake.

The weather remains sunny, and Margaret spends most of the crossing at the bow, looking ahead, feeling the cool breeze on her face. In the early afternoon, they catch sight of the Eastern Shore and soon arrive at a small village, where a smattering of wooden houses and storage barns surrounds a large dock. A small crowd has gathered to welcome them.

In front of a horse-drawn wagon, Margaret notices a young black man who waves excitedly to the ship.

Emmanuel waves back and says to Margaret, "My son, Edward. He was born five years after Jane came to us."

"I'm glad he stayed with you, Emmanuel," she says.

When they step ashore, Edward hurries over. Emmanuel embraces him. Then he says, "This is Margaret, Jane's mother."

"She looks like you," Edward says.

"How is she?"

Thomas looks at Emmanuel and displays a regretful expression.

On the way to the Driggerses' cattle farm, they make small talk about how the trip was. Soon they reach a dirt path. To either side are pastures where cattle graze.

When they get to the house, Margaret meets Emmanuel's wife and likes her right away. Elizabeth came from England as a servant to the farm next door. Emmanuel bought out the last year of her contract of indenture. They have an affectionate relationship. Their children, Deverick and Mary, are lighter-skinned than Edward and his younger brother, William, both Frances's children. Their older offspring and other adopted children have left home to get married and work elsewhere.

There are four other youngsters of different ages who eye Margaret uncertainly. "These are Jane's children—Frances, Margaret, William, and John," Emmanuel says. "Say hello to your grandmother."

They greet her shyly. Margaret recognizes their distress, remembering her own children after Robert died.

Hearing the names brings tears to Margaret's eyes. It tells her a great deal about her daughter. She looks at Frances, the younger of the two girls, and notes the resemblance to Robert in her mouth. Putting her hand on her cheek, she says, "You look just like your grandfather. While I'm here, I'm going to tell you all about him."

A small smile creeps across the girl's face.

"I'll tell you all stories anon," Margaret tells the others. Although she feels tired from the journey, she turns to Emmanuel. "I want to see Jane now. Where is she?" she asks.

"I'll take you to her," Emmanuel says.

A look passes between him and Elizabeth, and his wife takes the young children into the kitchen.

Emmanuel and Margaret walk down the hallway. At the last door, he knocks and goes into the room. In the dim light, Margaret sees the shape of a woman in the bed. She is lying on her side under the linen sheet with her back to them. She seems asleep.

But when Emmanuel says softly, "Jane, your mother is here to see you. She has come all the way from James City," a small shiver runs across Jane's back.

Margaret walks around the bed until she can see her daughter's face. It is haggard and drawn. Her dull eyes stare straight ahead, showing no interest in her visitor. Her dark black skin looks unhealthy.

When Margaret says, "Hello, Jane," there is no reaction either.

After looking at the unresponsive young woman for a long moment, she says, "I will take care of you. I promise. You will be all right."

She leaves with Emmanuel and spends time with Elizabeth, asking what herbs are available.

Then she returns to Jane's room with a wash basin to bathe her and discovers the scars on her back. Margaret goes back to the living room and asks Emmanuel about them. He tells her that, when Jane was nineteen, she had a child out of wedlock with a young Irishman and was whipped for it by the court. Margaret doesn't berate him for not telling her. She simply goes back to Jane's room and strips off her own dress. Then she lies next to Jane and guides her hand to her own scarred back. She lies still, sensing her daughter's shocked, frozen hand and tentative exploration. When Jane stops, Margaret says, "You can overcome anything."

Then she puts her dress on and lies back down next to Jane, holding her until she falls asleep.

Over the next week, she leaves Jane's side only long enough to take meals and relieve herself. Even though the weather is getting warmer, she wraps her in blankets and binds compresses and warm towels dunked in water heated over the fire to her sides.

For much of the day and through the night, she lies next to Jane with her arms wrapped tightly about her. She talks to her, telling her stories about her father, Robert, and how happy he was when she was born. Then she tells her how she herself came to Virginia and all that has happened to her.

At meals, she finds time to share stories with her grandchildren going all the way back to how Frances and Margaret first met after the Indian uprising. The two boys listen with rapt attention and surprise her by asking about her time in Pongo, her mother and father, and her time on the slave ship. "You are the offspring of a king and queen," she tells them.

One morning, Jane wakes after sleeping for nearly sixteen hours, looks at Margaret, and says, "Tell me what happened to you."

Margaret smiles kindly and replies, "I will, but you must do the same."

Jane nods.

Over the next week, Jane gradually comes back to life. She starts to take food and drinks the herbal teas. Soon she sits up and starts to smile. She welcomes visits from Emmanuel, Elizabeth, her brothers and sisters, and her children. Before long, she rejoins the family at meals.

She and Margaret start to take long walks. As they stroll along the fences of the farm, sometimes holding hands, sometimes arm in arm, Margaret answers all of Jane's questions. In turn, she learns what has happened to Jane since she was adopted, what she remembers of her life on Francis Pott's plantation, of the years with Frances and Emmanuel, and of her two marriages. Margaret realizes that

Frances and Emmanuel have been the devoted parents they promised to be and raised her to be a fine, young woman who, after an early mistake, met and lost someone who loved her and she loved in return.

Margaret also learns about the fate of Anthony and Mary, including the court case Anthony won against a white man in a dispute over the ownership of a servant. She is happy to hear about their successful horse and cattle farm but sad that they sold it and moved to Maryland. She would have liked to see them.

At some point, Jane takes Margaret behind the house to a small gathering of trees. There are three mounds of earth with crosses on them, one of them recent.

"This is my first husband, John Gossall, who died a decade ago," she says, indicating the second grave. Then she starts to choke up. "This is William."

Margaret puts an arm around her and lets her cry.

When Jane recovers, she points to the first mound. "This one is Frances," she says quietly. "It was a canker that killed her, a growth in her side. She often talked about you and how much she loved you."

Tears come to Margaret's eyes as she looks down on the ground where her friend is buried.

"Except for our time together at Warrosquoake, we didn't see each other more than a handful of times," she explains. "But she was the best friend I ever had."

Jane nods and smiles. "I have been blessed to have two good mothers."

Margaret kneels by the grave and says, "I wish I could have told you this when you were still alive, Frances. Thank you for taking care of Jane and making sure she was freed long before her time."

An odd expression crosses Jane's face, but she remains silent.

But as they return to the house, Jane says, "You know that it wasn't Frances and Emmanuel."

Margaret says, "What do you mean?"

"Freeing me early."

When Margaret looks baffled, Jane says, "You didn't know?"

"Didn't know what?"

"It was John. He gave them the money."

Margaret stops walking.

Jane continues, "Emmanuel and Frances didn't have the where-withal to do it themselves then. They needed every penny to start the farm."

Stunned by the enormity of the revelation, Margaret stands still and her lips start to quiver. John looked out for her and her family even after he left.

Jane takes her hand and quickly goes on: "John and Emmanuel helped a number of indentured Africans, here and in York County, paying for them to be free. Neither of them ever wanted any credit for it."

Margaret squeezes her hand to tell her that it's all right.

The following afternoon, Margaret and Jane take a walk to the sandy shore of the Chesapeake Bay. The water seems to go on forever. With the land on the other side far beyond the horizon, it feels like they're on the ocean. They find a small log of bleached driftwood and sit together, watching the sun light up the wispy clouds.

Margaret suddenly has the vision again of herself on top of the large mountain in Pongo with her schoolmates, looking at the shimmering horizon. Far beyond lies *Kalungu*, the Atlantic Ocean, and beyond that, according to her father, the land of ghosts where everything is upside-down—where she has lived most of her life. Margaret muses that the Indians think that the dark-skinned Africans are ghosts, but her father was right. It is the white men and women who want to enslave them. They are the real ghosts.

Lately, she has been thinking about her destiny again. So many people early on in her life told her she was special, but she has been feeling ordinary and a little sorry for herself. Looking out across the water, she realizes that she and John—and Anthony, Mary, Frances, and Emmanuel—have accomplished something remarkable. They all became free in a land where the ghosts wanted to enslave them. Not only did they leave the long trail of captivity behind, but they managed to lead their children to freedom as well. She imagines Mihill, Philip, Robert Jr., William, Anthony, and Jane, and their children, and their children's children, traveling to new places, just as she and John did. Perhaps they will have even greater adventures and settle in more hospitable places. But whatever happens to them, in Virginia and beyond, regardless of what the ghosts conspire to do to them, they will continue on the road to freedom.

She feels the rays of the setting sun on her face and puts an arm around her daughter.

Jane rests her head on Margaret's shoulder and says, "I have talked it over with Emmanuel, and they agree. My children and I will come back with you and take care of you. I want to meet Anthony and visit my other brothers, all of them, and their children, too."

Margaret feels the warmth penetrate deep inside her. "I'd like that."

They continue to sit together in silence, enjoying the early spring. The breeze gently ruffles the water and turns the bay into an iridescent expanse of dancing waves.

* * *

Margaret lives for another fifteen years. During that time, she continues to cultivate her land and helps others who have need of her skills. At night and in her waking dreams, she communes with the three men who have mattered most in her life—Captain Jope, John, and Robert Swett—who keep her company until the end.

Until then, she enjoys visits from her children and grandchildren and, occasionally, lets Jane indulge her.

EPILOGUE

Robert Rich, the second Earl of Warwick, dies on April 19, 1658. His impact on the New World, direct and indirect, is commemorated in the names of towns in Virginia, Massachusetts, and Rhode Island.

The location of the grave of Captain John Jocelyn Jope remains unknown. Because of the mystery of his disappearance, his reputation as "The Flying Dutchman" lives on, having become part of maritime lore.

Sometime in 1670, on a cargo voyage from Holland, the *White Lion* has an accident in the Indian Ocean and is scuttled and turned into firewood.

In 1691, Virginia's General Assembly restricts interracial marriage. An Englishwoman giving birth to a mulatto child is fined fifteen pounds and the child indentured for thirty years. Partners in an interracial marriage cannot stay in the colony and have to leave within three months of their union.

The same act requires a master who emancipates a slave to transport him or her out of the colony within six months of manumission.

In 1705, in "An Act Concerning Servants and Slaves," the Virginia General Assembly legalizes slavery:

All servants imported and brought into the Country . . . who were not Christians in their native Country . . . shall be accounted and be slaves. All Negro, mulatto and Indian slaves within this dominion . . . shall be held to be real estate. If any slave resist his master . . . and shall happen to be killed . . . the master shall be free of all punishment . . . as if such accident never happened.

The act also imposes harsh physical punishments. Slaves found guilty of murder or rape are to be hanged. Slaves convicted for robbery would receive sixty lashes and be placed in stocks, where their ears would be cut off. For minor offenses, such as associating with whites, slaves would be whipped, branded, or maimed.

By that time, most of the offspring of Margaret and John have left the colony.

Today, their many descendants live in freedom throughout the United States, although the work for them to attain their ultimate freedom—equality and an end to racial discrimination—goes on.

CPSIA information can be obtained
at www.ICGtesting.com
Printed in the USA
FSHW021522060819
60772FS